AT EMPIRE'S EDGE

AT EMPIRE'S EDGE

WILLIAM C. DIETZ

ACE BOOKS, NEW YORK

THE BERKLEY PUBLISHING GROUP
Published by the Penguin Group
Penguin Group (USA) Inc.
375 Hudson Street, New York, New York 10014, USA
Penguin Group (Canada), 90 Eglinton Avenue East, Suite 700, Toronto, Ontario M4P 2Y3, Canada
(a division of Pearson Penguin Canada Inc.)
Penguin Books Ltd., 80 Strand, London WC2R 0RL, England
Penguin Group Ireland, 25 St. Stephen's Green, Dublin 2, Ireland (a division of Penguin Books Ltd.)
Penguin Group (Australia), 250 Camberwell Road, Camberwell, Victoria 3124, Australia
(a division of Pearson Australia Group Pty. Ltd.)
Penguin Books India Pvt. Ltd., 11 Community Centre, Panchsheel Park, New Delhi—110 017, India
Penguin Group (NZ), 67 Apollo Drive, Rosedale, North Shore 0632, New Zealand
(a division of Pearson New Zealand Ltd.)
Penguin Books (South Africa) (Pty.) Ltd., 24 Sturdee Avenue, Rosebank, Johannesburg 2196,
South Africa

Penguin Books Ltd., Registered Offices: 80 Strand, London WC2R 0RL, England

This is an original publication of The Berkley Publishing Group.

This is a work of fiction. Names, characters, places, and incidents either are the product of the author's imagination or are used fictitiously, and any resemblance to actual persons, living or dead, business establishments, events, or locales is entirely coincidental. The publisher does not have any control over and does not assume any responsibility for author or third-party websites or their content.

FIRST EDITION: October 2009

Library of Congress Cataloging-in-Publication Data

Dietz, William C.
   At empire's edge / William C. Dietz.—1st ed.
      p. cm.
   ISBN 978-0-441-01759-1
   I. Title.
   PS3554.I388A84 2009
   813'.54—dc22
                              2009026786

PRINTED IN THE UNITED STATES OF AMERICA

10 9 8 7 6 5 4 3 2 1

For Marjorie,
with all my love

AT EMPIRE'S EDGE

ONE

Aboard the Imperial prison ship
Pax Umana, in hyperspace

IN ORDER FOR SECTION LEADER JAK CATO TO REACH
the cabin assigned to Xeno Corps Centurion Ben Sivio, it
was necessary to walk half the length of the prison ship's
quarter-mile-long hull. The air was cool, verging on cold,
because that was the way the *Pax Umana*'s computer system
liked it. The overhead lighting fixtures were exactly twelve
feet apart, the decals that identified first-aid kits, weapons
lockers, and fire extinguishers appeared with monotonous
regularity, and Cato's boots clanged as they hit the metal
gratings that kept him up out of the sheet of half-inch-deep
water that glistened below. For unlike most ships, which
had solid decks, the *Umana* had metal gratings so the crew
could hose down the cells when necessary. The wastewater was continually pumped out of the sluiceways, purified
by onboard systems, and used for everything other than
drinking.

That didn't represent much of a problem at the moment,
however, since the ship was carrying only *one* prisoner, and
he had ways to get back at his jailers other than pissing on

the deck. Cato was the person he hated the most, especially after an incident eight hours earlier, during which Cato's shock baton sent a hundred thousand volts of electricity coursing through the Sagathan shape shifter's body. So, as Cato approached his cell, Verafti put on a display for him.

The Sagathi were a race of sentient shape-shifting empaths who had the ability to assume the form of any living creature having roughly the same mass as they did. This not only explained why they were so dangerous, but why the Uman Empire had been forced to create the Xeno Corps, a police force made up of bioengineered variants bred to hunt, capture, and imprison aliens of every description, the Sagathies being the most dangerous of the bunch.

As Cato drew level with Verafti's barred cell, he was treated to a first-class display of what the Sagathi could do as the naked alien morphed into a startling likeness of Officer Kath Larsy. She was arguably the most beautiful woman on the ship, and as the fake Larsy brought both hands up to cup a pair of large, pink-nippled breasts, she smiled suggestively. "Come on, Cato," Larsy said huskily. "Feel them! You know you want to."

And Cato *did* want to, but knew that all of the men who had succumbed to such invitations in the past were dead and buried in the Xeno Corps graveyard adjacent to the high-security prison compound on Sagatha. "Go fuck yourself," Cato replied contemptuously, as he stalked by. "Which you are uniquely qualified to do!"

Verafti responded by morphing into a replica of Cato, which he immediately turned inside out, but Cato was gone by then. "You're scared, Cato. I can *feel* it," the shape shifter yelled through what looked like raw hamburger. "Sivio's going to break you down to F-1. When we get to Sagatha, you'll be shoveling shit out of my cell!"

Cato made no reply, but as he cleared the cellblock and entered officer country, he knew the claim was probably true. Cato had served under Sivio long enough to know that the Centurion wasn't one to waste time on idle chatter. So having used what many would consider to be excessive force on Verafti, Cato was about to get his ass reamed, a process both he and it had been through many times before.

The Xeno Corps was not only organized along military lines, it was part of the Army, which generally wanted nothing to do with it. In fact, most Imperial legionnaires looked down on the variants, were afraid of the police officers, and jealous of their elite status all at the same time. Now, as Cato approached Sivio's cabin, he paused to check his uniform. It consisted of a helmet, held in the crook of his left arm, sculpted body armor, a kilt with a subtle plaid intended to remind people that the Xeno Corps was technically part of the 3rd Legion, and a pair of black, high-gloss combat boots.

The *real* Kath Larsy walked past at that point, winked at Cato, and said, "Good luck!" The Xeno Corps was a small organization, the detachment on the *Umana* was even smaller, and everyone knew what everyone else was doing. And that included the fact that Sivio was about to take Cato's head off.

Cato forced a smile, wasted a full second wondering if Larsy's nipples really were pink, and rapped on the knock block mounted beside the durasteel hatch. Sivio had a parade-ground voice that could be heard through three inches of solid metal, and there was no mistaking the gruff, one-word invitation: "Come!"

Cato palmed the access plate, waited for the hatch to slide out of the way, and took the standard three steps forward. Then, with a degree of panache befitting a member of the Emperor's Praetorian Guard, he crashed to attention. "Section Leader Jak Cato reporting as ordered, *sir*!"

At that point, had the purpose of the meeting been something other than what it was, Sivio would have said,

"At ease." And depending on circumstances, as well as the Centurion's mood that day, might have invited his second-in-command to sit down. But Sivio was angry, and forcing Cato to stand at attention was a good way to communicate that fact. If that bothered Cato, the hard, angular planes of his face gave no sign of it, although Sivio was an empath and could "feel" at least some of his subordinate's emotions. And that was indicative of Cato's major flaw, because in spite of the fact that he had been created to deal with Sagathi empaths, he couldn't shield his emotions the way most of his peers could. A dead, with the emphasis on the word "dead," giveaway for a creature like Verafti.

And Cato had other faults as well, including his rebelliousness, contempt for authority, and occasional drunkenness. Were such shortcomings the result of a DNA-related glitch that had left him unable to shield his emotions? Or would he have been a pain in the ass regardless of his disability? There was no way to know. One thing was certain, however, and that was the fact that Cato was a born leader and, as such, could have a detrimental effect on morale. Especially where the younger members of the team were concerned. Which was why Sivio planned to land on Cato with both feet. "At ease."

Cato, his eyes on a spot exactly six inches over Sivio's head, slid his right foot away from his left, and moved his right fist to the small of his back. Even though he wasn't looking straight at the Centurion, he could still *see* the bastard, and he wasn't encouraged by what he saw. Sivio had black hair, the same olive skin that *all* the members of the Xeno Corps had, and a pair of beady brown eyes. They glowed with latent hostility, and were set too close to the officer's nose, which was undeniably crooked. A none-too-subtle reminder that Sivio had been a champion kickboxer in his younger days. His lips were so thin they looked more like a well-healed incision rather than a mouth—and his massive jaw had a pugnacious quality. "So," Sivio began ominously. "Prisoner Verafti claims that you zapped him. And for no apparent reason. Is that true?"

"It's partly true, sir," Cato temporized, his eyes still focused on a spot over Sivio's head. "I shocked him all right—but I was provoked."

Sivio worked his jaw as if preparing it for action. "You were provoked. In what way?"

"The prisoner called the Emperor a bad name," Cato answered self-righteously. "Which left me with no choice but to respond."

Sivio shook his head sadly. "That has to be the most pathetic lie anyone has ever had the balls to tell me! The truth is that you were playing cards with Verafti through the bars, when for reasons unknown, you drew your shock baton and hit him with a hundred thousand volts of electricity! The security camera mounted in front of Verafti's cell captured the whole thing. So don't bother to deny it."

"The bastard was cheating!" Cato responded defensively. "So what was I supposed to do? Let him get away with it?"

The conversation was interrupted by a tone—followed by the flat, emotion-free sound of the NAVCOMP's synthesized voice. "Be advised that the ship will exit hyperspace in ninety seconds. Primary, secondary, and tertiary weapons systems have been activated, and all members of the *Umana*'s crew will remain at battle stations until ordered to stand down."

It was a routine announcement, and since neither one of the variants qualified as a member of the ship's crew, their conversation continued. "Shooting the shit with prisoners, playing games with prisoners, and all other interactions not specifically authorized by a superior officer are specifically prohibited," Sivio said sternly. "And you know that. Even worse is the fact that having flouted regulations, you chose to administer corporal punishment to a prisoner, who is presumed to be innocent until proven otherwise."

That was too much for Cato. For first time since the session had begun, he allowed his eyes to come down and make direct contact with Sivio's. "Innocent? You must be joking, sir. When the Beta Team arrested Verafti, he was crouched next to his most recent victim, gnawing on the poor bastard's arm!"

There was a stomach-flipping lurch as the *Umana* exited hyperspace 2,070 miles sunward from Nav Beacon INS4721-8402, and began to prepare for the next jump. "That makes no difference," Sivio said pedantically. "As you are well aware! Which is why I'm going to . . ."

But Cato never learned what Sivio intended to do, because that was the moment when the ship lurched violently, and he was thrown into a bulkhead. A host of Klaxons, buzzers, and other alarms went off as the PA system came back on. "The ship is under attack," the NAVCOMP announced calmly. "All weapons systems are under centralized control, nonessential personnel will report to their emergency duty stations, and Centurion Sivio will report to the bridge."

"God damn it to hell!" Sivio said vehemently, as he rose from his chair. "Get down to the cellblock and make sure Verafti is secure. What we don't need is to have that murderous bastard running around loose while we fight the Vords."

Cato was tempted to remind Sivio that Verafti was innocent until proven guilty, but thought better of it, and said, "Yes, sir," as he came to attention. He brought his right fist up over his heart, received a similar salute in return, and did a picture-perfect about-face. The meeting was over.

Most of the light in the *Umana*'s control room originated from the hundreds of multicolored LEDs that surrounded Captain Simy Hong and her bridge crew as they struggled to understand what was taking place and react to it. "It looks like there's only one of them," Flight Officer Peter Umbaya said, from his position to Hong's right.

"Thank God for that," Hong said evenly. She was thirty-six years old, wore her hair pageboy style, and was pretty in a no-nonsense sort of way. "What kind of ship are we up against?"

Umbaya eyed the data that was scrolling down the screens in front of him. The combined glow lit his dark features from below and gave the officer's face a spectral appearance. "It looks like a Vord M-Class Destroyer, Captain."

Like everyone else aboard the *Umana*, Hong knew that the tall, long-faced Vords, and the sluglike parasites they were hosts to, controlled an empire of their own. Some said it was equal in size to the 1,817 worlds that constituted the Uman Empire, but others claimed it was even bigger. Regardless of which group was correct, everyone knew that the aliens were nibbling at the edges of the Uman Empire. There hadn't been any full-scale battles as yet, but hit-and-run raids on the Imperial rim worlds were becoming increasingly common, as were individual encounters with the M-Class Destroyers, which were widely believed to function as long-distance reconnaissance vessels. Was the ship that had launched a flight of missiles at them on such a mission? Yes, Hong thought it was, because Vord recon vessels had demonstrated a persistent interest in Nav Beacons like the one orbiting the local sun a couple of thousand miles off the port bow. Not that the reason made much difference as three torpedoes struck the *Umana*'s protective screens, blew up, and sent a shudder through the ship.

The *Umana* was a prison ship, and as such she didn't carry very many offensive weapons, but Hong felt the command chair lurch as the screens went down long enough for a pair of Mark IV missiles to race away, before coming back up again. It was a reasonably potent response to the unprovoked attack, the problem being that the ship carried only six of the ship-to-ship weapons, and would soon be entirely reliant on four batteries of medium-duty energy cannons for its defense. Only two of them could be brought to bear on a single target at any given time.

The most obvious strategy was to make an emergency hyperspace jump because almost anywhere would be a better place to be than their present location. But, since they had exited hyperspace only minutes earlier, it would be a quarter of an hour before the *Umana*'s accumulators could launch the ship into the never-never land of FTL travel once again. And that was an eternity in a space battle, especially when faced with a larger and better-armed foe.

"Captain? You sent for me?" The voice came from Hong's right, and the naval officer turned to find that Centurion Sivio was standing on the other side of the railing that circled the command tub, holding on to the metal tubing as the ship took another hit.

"Yes," Hong replied grimly. "A Vord raider has us outgunned. But, if we can get in close enough, they won't be able to fire their missile batteries without being caught in the back blast."

"So?" Sivio wanted to know. "What can I do to help?"

Hong took comfort from Sivio's calm, unflinching manner. If her extremely unorthodox plan was to succeed, it would depend on Sivio and the men and women under his command. "Once we close with the Vords, the battle will turn into an exchange of broadsides, and given the fact that they mount more guns than we do, the outcome is nearly certain. *Unless* we can come alongside, blow their lock, and board! The only trouble is that we don't carry any combat troops—and my crew will be *very* busy."

The *Umana* shook violently, and Sivio was forced to hang on to the railing as something hit the screens, and they flared brightly. "Meaning that you want my team to fight its way onto the Vord ship?"

"That's right," Hong confirmed. "Will you do it?"

"We'll try," Sivio said grimly. "Assuming you've got someone who can blow that lock."

"I do," Hong replied. "Get your people into space armor and take them to the main lock. A weapons tech named Raybley will be there to meet you."

Then, turning to Umbaya, the naval officer gave an order. "Turn the ship *into* the enemy, and accelerate. Even if we die, we're going to take some of those ugly bastards with us!"

Having no reason to look like anyone other than himself, Verafti had reverted to what the Sagathi thought of as his *true* form. Like all his kind, the shape shifter had a vaguely triangular skull that narrowed to an abbreviated snout and a mouth filled with razor-sharp teeth. His green lizardlike body was humanoid, and covered with iridescent scales, which offered good camouflage within the thick foliage of Sagatha's equatorial jungles, an extremely dangerous environment where his race's ability to morph from form to form enabled them to survive and eventually rise to sentience.

Now, as Sivio, Cato, and two sections of heavily armed Xeno Corps variants marched past on their way to the main lock, Verafti rattled the bars on his cell in an effort to get their attention. Though he was not privy to Hong's plan, the fact that his jailers were dressed in space armor told Verafti everything he needed to know. "Take me with you!" Verafti demanded loudly. "You know what I'm capable of. I'll rip their guts out!" The words had a sibilant sound, reminiscent of the so-called hiss speech that the Sagathies spoke to each other.

Sivio knew that much was true, but he was also aware that once free, the carnivore would kill *everyone* if he could, which was why two of his most reliable officers had been detailed to guard the prisoner.

For his part, Cato was thinking about the job ahead. It was a task that none of them were trained for but which he likened to entering an urban structure occupied by well-armed criminals. They faced a very dangerous room-by-room clearing process in which the defenders would have a distinct advantage. This was an unsettling thought and one he was determined to ignore.

Technician Raybley was waiting for the police detachment when it arrived at the lock. His voice was clearly male, but his face was invisible behind a visor, and, like the rest of the Umans', his body was sealed in a suit of space armor. The police officers could "sense" his personality, however, and all of them took comfort from Raybley's calm persona. Cato felt a sudden jolt and struggled to keep his feet as the *Umana*'s NAVCOMP spoke. "Hull-to-hull contact has been made. . . . The boarding party has entered the lock. . . . All crew members will don their helmets and lock them down in case of a partial or full decompression."

Cato felt a sudden emptiness at the pit of his stomach as he and his companions were sealed into what could turn into a communal coffin, and the air was systematically pumped out of the *Umana*'s lock. Then it was time to question everything that could be questioned, including Cato's decision to remain in the Xeno Corps despite his so-called disability, his choice of two energy pistols rather than a more powerful rifle, and the time spent preparing his subordinates for battle rather than taking a much-needed pee.

The time for self doubts was over as the outer door cycled open to provide the would-be boarders a clear view of the enemy ship's gray, nearly black, hull. It was pitted from the wear imposed on it by hundreds of planetary landings and had been scorched by at least one hit from the *Umana*'s energy cannons. The two locks were slightly mismatched, but not by much, which constituted a miracle given the hellish conditions under which the two ships had been brought together. Light flared from both sides as the ships fired into each other at point-blank range. A battle the Vord warship was bound to win unless Sivio and his subordinates could board quickly and seize control of the destroyer.

Raybley knew that too, and was quick to step forward and slap a self-adhesive preshaped charge against the other vessel's lock, before backing out of the blast zone. The silent explosion came three seconds later, followed by a flash of light, and a miraculous transformation as what had been solid metal morphed into a large man-sized hole. The jagged edges were bent inwards as if pointing which way to go.

A squad of six suit-clad Vords had been waiting inside the lock, but the superhot jet of plasma created by Raybley's demolitions charge had cut through the aliens like a hot knife through butter and scorched the hatch beyond.

Sivio started to advance, but Raybley motioned for the Centurion to stay back as he stepped over a half-cooked body to place a second charge against the inner hatch. Then, having backed away, the technician triggered another explosion almost identical to the first. That was when Sivio shouted, "Now!" and led his eight-person section into the swirling smoke.

Cato saw one of the dead bodies start to sit up, shot the Vord through his faceplate, and saw the surrounding vacuum pull a column of viscous goo out through the newly created hole. At that point Cato had to step over the bodies as he followed Sivio into the ship's interior, where they came under fire. Such were the close conditions, however, that only a few of the defenders could fire at any given time. Of course the reverse was true as well, which was why Cato tossed an energy grenade down the corridor to his right, and waited for the telltale flash before advancing farther.

Two dead bodies lay where the grenade had gone off, but a third Vord had survived the explosion. A thin stream of vapor shot away from his left knee as the air inside his suit continued to escape through a pin-sized hole. Because each Vord had a sluglike Ya wrapped around his neck, their space suits incorporated large, collarlike extensions that stuck up behind their helmets, and were intended to protect the parasites. That made the aliens *look* clumsy, but such was not the case, as the defender lurched out of a side passageway and knocked one of Cato's pistols away. Then, having created an opening, the Vord made a grab for Cato's space armor.

Cato didn't recognize the significance of the act at first, and was in the process of bringing the other handgun to bear, when he remembered that the release lever for his suit was located in a recess on the front surface of his armor! The Vord was trying to open his suit!

So Cato made use of his free hand to push the alien away, fired the pistol at point-blank range, and swore as the bright blue beam of energy was momentarily dissipated. Strong though it was, however, the Vord armor couldn't take the punishment for long, and as the alien fumbled for the double-edged battle-axe slung across his back, the space suit gave way, allowing an energy bolt to punch its way through his heart. The Vord's Ya was still alive, of course, but the parasite couldn't exert enough control to keep its host upright, so both of them went down. The whole experience scared the hell out of Cato, so he shot the Vord *again*, just to make sure.

Then it was time to rally his section and lead them deeper into the belly of the alien ship. A quick glance at the data projected on the inside surface of Cato's visor showed that while Ritori was down, Honis, Batia, Tonver, Moshath, and Kelkaw were still on their feet and immediately behind him. Sivio's section was headed toward the ship's bow. "All right," Cato said into his lip mike, "let's keep moving. Remember, stay close to your partner, and eyeball *everything*. These assholes play for keeps."

There was a series of double *click*s as the rest of the section acknowledged his instructions. Then it was time to split up into pairs, put their backs to both sides of the corridor, and edge along. There was no resistance at first, which caused Cato to wonder if the aliens had given up, but any hopes of a relatively easy victory were shattered when the passageway opened into an area dedicated to the ship's life-support systems. From his position at the entry hatch Cato could see the tanks that were required to recycle water, the big rack-shaped air scrubbers, and a sealed climate-controlled hydroponics section in which fresh vegetables were grown. It all made for a maze of machinery and pipes.

Cato was forced to retreat into the corridor as four or five Vords opened fire and ruby red energy beams sleeted his way. Cato removed a "roller" from a pouch at his waist, pinched the device "on," and tossed the little camera into the area beyond. Video appeared in front of him, turned topsy-turvy, and finally came to a rest. The panoramic shot was somewhat distorted, but crystal clear, and therefore useful, especially when the defenders were stupid enough to fire at the roller, thereby signaling their various positions.

"Okay," Cato said evenly, as he turned to address his team. "I'll toss a flash-bang in there. Once it goes off, we enter. Honis, Batia, you take the targets on the right. Tonver and Moshath will go after the slimeballs on the left. Kelkaw and I will go straight up the middle. Questions? No? Let's do this thing."

Like the other members of Cato's section, Brice Kelkaw had a generally low opinion of the Section Leader (SL) because of his tendency to duck work, break rules, and drink too much. But there was one category of activity in which Cato excelled, and that was the area of tactical operations, where he was second to none. For some unfathomable reason, Cato's freewheeling ways were frequently successful when the chips were down, a fact that accounted for both the stripes on his arms and the handful of badly tarnished medals buried at the bottom of his footlocker.

So Kelkaw was secretly glad of the fact that he had been assigned to Cato's section rather than Sivio's, as he followed the noncom out into a sleet of incoming fire. Some of which left scorch marks on Kelkaw's light gray armor but failed to hole it. Projectile weapons would have been much more deadly, but could have caused serious damage to the ship, which neither side wanted to do. But even though the so-called blasters weren't immediately lethal, they could drill holes in armor if given the three or four seconds required to do so. And that made it important to keep moving.

As Cato fired on a Vord who was hiding between a recycling tank and the air scrubbers, Kelkaw heard someone shout, "Above you!" and raised his energy weapon just in time to fire at the alien on the catwalk above.

The Vord got off a series of energy bolts as well, some of which came within inches of Cato's helmet, but that took time. Enough time for Kelkaw's energy rifle to stitch a line of black divots across the alien's chest plate. The last bolt found the seam between shoulder and arm, burned its way through, and opened the suit to the vacuum. The results were not very pretty.

Having nailed his target, Cato took a quick look around. The incoming fire had stopped, Honis and Batia were busy securing a group of Vord prisoners, and the other two were going from body to body checking to make sure that the beings inside were truly dead. "Hey, Cato," Tonver said, as he knelt next to a badly scorched Vord. "The big sonofabitch is history—but it looks like the slug might be alive. It's sealed in a pressurized pouch."

Cato went over to inspect the body and saw that Tonver was correct. Even though the Vord was dead, a pressurized sack had been deployed to protect the parasite wrapped around his neck. Tonver winced as Cato put an energy bolt through the taut semitransparent plastic film. Green goo erupted from the newly created hole as all of the pent-up air gushed out of the container. "That's for Ritori," Cato said grimly. "Rot in hell."

Tonver wasn't sure that aliens went to hell, but it was a moot point, so he let it go. The battle was over.

The better part of one standard day passed while both of the badly damaged ships floated side by side off Nav Beacon INS4721-8402. There was a lot to do, including treating the wounded, in-processing the Vord prisoners, and conducting a bow-to-stern survey of the *Pax Umana* to determine how spaceworthy the vessel was.

Finally, having completed their inspection, Captain Hong and her engineering officer concluded that while one of the ship's in-system drives was still functional, her hyperdrive was going to require a complete overhaul before the *Umana* would be able to complete the journey to Sagatha.

That was the beginning of an effort to identify a planet with a Class III or better shipyard that was within the range of a vessel traveling at sublight speeds from Navpoint INS4721-8402. The answer, because there was only *one* possibility, was a former prison planet named Dantha. None of those on the *Umana* had ever been there; but, according to the NAVCOMP's files, Dantha was a mostly preindustrial Corin-Class planet, having large deposits of iridium located due west of a Level Eight settlement named Solace. And Solace, in turn, based on a two-year-old database, was home to a Class III shipyard.

So with nowhere else to go, Hong had her crew place explosive charges aboard the Vord raider, cut the destroyer loose, then put a lot of distance between the two ships before sending the necessary signal. Most of the crew were watching the video feed when the explosion took place, but the momentary flash of light was strangely anticlimactic, and left most of them feeling sad rather than jubilant. All except for Cato, that is, who was taking a nap when the charges went off, and was snoring loudly.

It took almost two standard weeks to reach Dantha. Long, increasingly difficult days, during which one of the four air scrubbers went down, the water-purification system failed, and everyone went on short rations. Including the Vord prisoners, who suffered in silence, unlike Verafti, who complained nonstop.

The Xeno cops were used to that, however, and proceeded to ignore the shape shifter, who was forced to entertain himself by showing the neighboring Vords what they would look like if turned inside out! It was a pastime Cato rather enjoyed—and did nothing to discourage.

So it was with a communal sigh of relief that the *Pax Umana* entered Dantha's atmosphere, bumped her way down through layers of air, and leveled out over a vast water-filled crater created some fifty million years earlier when a sizeable meteorite had roared out of the sky to slam into Dantha's surface.

The lake glittered with reflected sunlight as the spaceship flew over both it and the vast plain beyond, on its way to the Imperial settlement of Solace. And it was then, as the ship circled the city prior to landing, that Captain Hong felt the first stirrings of concern. Because rather than the neat, carefully laid out city typical of Uman-controlled planets, Solace was a sprawling undisciplined maze of structures that been allowed to evolve according to the whims of those who lived there. People who, according to information supplied by the NAVCOMP, were the descendants of prisoners brought in 242 years earlier to work the now-abandoned iridium mines.

Still, the way the local population chose to live was unimportant so long as Hong could get repairs to her ship, and return it to service. That thought gave the naval officer a renewed sense of confidence as the third, and final, clearance was given by the spaceport's Traffic Control computer, and the NAVCOMP brought the badly damaged *Pax Umana* in for a landing. Both Hong and her pilot were on standby in case the NAVCOMP failed, so there was very little opportunity to eyeball the spaceport as the ship's powerful repellers sent clouds of reddish dust billowing up into the air.

Minutes later, once the ship's massive skids were safely on the ground, the air began to clear. That was when the main cargo hatch whirred open, a ramp was deployed, and Hong made her way down onto Imperial soil. Sivio was by her side, and the ship's hull made loud pinging noises as it began to cool.

Both Imperials expected a reception of some sort. No brass bands, or anything like that, but a Port Captain and some of his or her subordinates at a minimum. What they *weren't* ready for was a portly civilian in stained overalls, a work-worn robot with mismatched arms, and a black-and-white mongrel, who immediately took a possessive pee on one of the *Umana*'s landing skids. "Hello!" the man in the ragged overalls said cheerfully. "Welcome to Dantha! My name is Kinkel. Homer Kinkel. I'm the Port Administrator, Port Captain, and Maintenance Chief."

Nearly all of the dust had settled by then, and as Hong eyed the blast-scarred area around her, she saw three dilapidated in-system freighters, an old liner that had been cannibalized for parts, six Imperial fighters that constituted the planet's entire air defense capability, a low-slung prefab building that was at least fifty years old, and a row of multicolored atmospheric craft of various designs that presumably belonged to wealthy citizens. Assuming there were any. "It's a pleasure to meet you," Hong lied as she offered Kinkel her hand. "No offense, but we need a Class III yard, and your spaceport looks like it might be a Class V at best."

"Yup," Kinkel responded unapologetically. "We were decertified about a year and a half ago. There isn't enough money to keep things up. Or that's what Procurator Nalomy tells me—and she oughtta know." At that point his tiny eyes went up to the ship that loomed above them. There was plenty of visible damage, including blackened craters, metal-bright scars, and a collection of scorch marks. "What hit you anyway? A swarm of meteorites?"

Hong shook her head. "No, we were attacked by a Vord raider. The ship needs a whole lot of things—but a reconditioned hyperdrive tops the list. If we had that, we could make it to a Class III yard."

Kinkel shook his head sympathetically. "I'm sorry to hear that. . . . The Vords are starting to get out of hand. The Emperor needs to teach the ugly bastards a lesson! As for the hyperdrive—well that's gonna take some time. Say a month to get the request in, another month for the bureaucrats to approve it, and a third month to ship it here. Then it'll be up to me to install it, and I'm shorthanded at the moment."

A dust devil appeared out in the middle of Landing Zone Two, the dog gave chase, and the robot's head began to twitch uncontrollably. The journey was over.

TWO

Imperial City, on the planet Corin

LEGATE ISULU USURLUS WAS SEATED AT HIS SCRUPU-lously clean glass desk, reviewing the items he hoped to discuss with Emperor Emor, when he heard the familiar swish of expensive fabric as Satha entered the sun-splashed room. She was tall, willowy, and as beautiful as a slave costing ten thousand Imperials should be. Satha had luxuriant shoulder-length brown hair, a shapely body that was only partially concealed by a diaphanous gown, and perfectly formed bare feet. She brought her hands together in front of her chest and lowered her forehead until it came into contact with them. "The cars are here."

Usurlus said, "Thank you," rose, and took a thin leather briefcase with him as he crossed the study to the point where an oval mirror was set into the wall. Appearances were important within the upper reaches of Uman society, especially on the home world of Corin, so good looks were something of a necessity. Usurlus knew he was vain—and why not? The man who stared back at him had artfully tousled blond hair, gray eyes, and an aquiline nose. Women liked him, as did men, which made his sex life wonderfully complicated.

It was important to be careful, however. The key to success was to look good, but not *too* good, lest one unintentionally overshadow the Emperor. Because even though Emor was in good shape, he wasn't especially beautiful to look upon, even after plastic surgery! So, by wearing a plain red-edged toga, a pleated kilt, and open-toed sandals, Usurlus hoped to fall well below the level of sartorial elegance Emor was known for. "You are very handsome," Satha said, as their eyes met in the mirror.

Usurlus smiled. He was genuinely fond of Satha—and she knew it. "And you are very beautiful!" the Legate said sincerely. "Wish me luck."

"I do," Satha replied seriously. "Be careful. . . . You have enemies."

"Most of whom are wildly incompetent," Usurlus said dismissively. "I plan to be home for dinner. Will you join me?"

The question was a formality, of course, since a slave could hardly say no, but Satha was genuinely pleased. Her hands came together, and her forehead made contact with them. "Yes, master. It would be my pleasure to do so."

Usurlus gave Satha a peck on the cheek, left the study, and entered the hallway that led out to the public areas beyond. The elegantly furnished great room was large enough to hold a hundred people, which it frequently did whenever Usurlus had to throw a party. A robot that looked exactly like Usurlus was waiting and fell into step next to him as sliding glass doors parted company to let the "twins" pass.

The doors closed with a discreet whisper as the two seemingly identical men stepped out onto the carefully landscaped veranda and made their way around the rooftop swimming pool to the landing pad, where two air cars sat waiting. One was for Usurlus, the other for his body double, making it that much more difficult for potential assassins to score a kill.

Four of the Legate's bodyguards were present, including

Vedius Albus, the ex-legionnaire who was in charge of over-all security. He was a hard-eyed man in his midforties who, having served the 33rd Legion with distinction for twenty-five years, had left Imperial military service to spend the rest of his life with his family on Corin. A decision Usurlus was grateful for since Albus had saved his life on two occasions. "Good morning, sire," the ex-legionnaire said soberly, as the contingent of bodyguards came to attention.

"Good morning, Vedius," the real Usurlus replied cheer-fully. "How's Olivia? Well, I hope."

Olivia was Albus's wife, and even though the bodyguard knew that Usurlus was being polite, he also knew that most men of his employer's rank wouldn't know her name, much less inquire as to her health. "She's doing well, sire," Albus said, as the doors for both air cars swished open. "Thank you."

Two bodyguards followed the body double into the first car, while Usurlus, Albus, and an ex-legionnaire named Livius took seats in the second vehicle and strapped themselves in. Both Albus and Livius wore plain togas, secured by metal pins in the shape of the Usurlus family crest, each of which included a secure two-way com device that could be used in an emergency. The men were equipped with ID implants, body armor, and one pistol each, the maximum amount of armament that the Emperor's security detail would allow outsiders to bring into the Imperial Tower. More men were on call, of course, and could reach the Tower in a matter of minutes, should an emergency extraction become necessary.

Not that there was any reason to expect trouble—since the race-day party would be smothered in security. Of the sixty-two people who had ruled the Uman Empire over the last five-hundred-plus years, eighteen had been murdered while in power. Usually by rivals or psychopaths, though two of them had been murdered by lovers, and one had blown her brains out in the Senate rotunda.

But assassinations were a fact of life, which was why many officials wore pseudoflesh faces while in transit to public functions, or made use of custom-made robotic body doubles like the one Usurlus sometimes referred to as "my brother." The android's car departed first, banked to the east, and soon disappeared.

Usurlus was forced back into the plush upholstery as the air car took off, banked to the west, and turned toward the 1,600-foot-tall Imperial Tower, which rose above the city's jagged skyline. The cylindrical building was thicker at the bottom than the top, was home to the government's senior officials, and was said to be impregnable to anything less than a direct hit by a nuclear device. That scenario was theoretically impossible given the fleet of warships in orbit around Corin, the fighters that circled above the Imperial City, and other precautions, all of which were secret.

Below, and visible for as far as the eye could see in every direction, was a city that occupied roughly five hundred square miles of land, and boasted a population of more than fifteen million people. Most of them were forced to live in high-rise buildings. So, in spite of a well-run subway system, air travel was important to the Empire's movers and shakers, who preferred to be flown from building to building rather than compete with plebs for the dubious privilege of traveling on extremely crowded surface streets or aboard underground trains.

Of course that meant airborne traffic jams were a fact of life, too, even though a host of computers were dedicated to trying to prevent such problems. There was very little air traffic over the city on that particular day, however, because of the race scheduled for early afternoon, so the pilot was able to deliver Usurlus to the twenty-second floor of the Imperial Tower with a minimum of delay. The entire floor was dedicated to the task of launching and retrieving official vehicles; but the facility was crowded in spite of all the space dedicated to it, so the atmosphere was one of eternally impending chaos as a steady stream of air cars arrived and departed.

Thanks to his passenger's rank, the pilot was allowed to land in one of the VIP slots, where one of the Emperor's army of administrative androids was waiting to receive Usurlus and escort the official and his bodyguards off the noisome flight deck and into a spacious elevator lobby. During the short journey the visitors were examined by a variety of hidden scanners, and had any unauthorized weapons been identified, sections of the seemingly solid black granite walls would have opened to allow remotely operated weapons to kill specific individuals or everyone present. Then, once the bodies had been removed and the floors hosed down, the entryway would be opened for business once again. Estimated turnaround time: thirteen minutes and twenty seconds. Because, as Emperor Emor liked to say, "A good government is an *efficient* government."

As the foursome entered the lobby, the acrid odor of ozone, mixed with throat-clogging exhaust fumes, came in with them but was quickly removed by the building's extremely efficient air-conditioning system. "Greetings on behalf of Emperor Emor," the machine said smoothly, as he led the Umans toward a bank of gleaming elevators. "My name is Olious. Please let me know if there is anything I can do to make your visit to the Imperial Tower more pleasant. Assuming that you and your staff are ready to join the other guests, I will escort you up to the eighty-eighth floor, where the party is presently under way."

"Thank you," Usurlus replied politely. "Please lead the way."

So, with bodyguards in tow, Usurlus was led onto a high-speed elevator already loaded with a richly robed Senator, and her all-female security detail. Her name was Claudia Sulla, and the Legate knew that he had met her before, and might want to meet her again. Especially given the size and shape of the breast she had chosen to expose, as well as the come-hither look in her eye, and the Sulla clan's political connections.

A mild and rather brief flirtation ensued, as the platform lifted all of them up to the eighty-eighth floor in less than a minute. Then it was time to exchange unlisted numbers, before stepping out into what could only be described as a very dangerous party, since every single one of the three-hundred-plus invited guests harbored not just one private agenda but, in most cases, at least a dozen. Some of which they were willing to pursue regardless of cost.

But, having been reared within a patrician family, Usurlus was used to that and ready for verbal combat. It began almost immediately as Usurlus followed Olious out of the elevator lobby and into the swirling crowd. Dozens of competing essences vied with each other for dominance, togas of every possible hue swirled around him, and the rumble of conversation was so loud that when the businessman from Regus managed to take possession of the small space in front of Usurlus, he was forced to shout in order to make himself heard. "Legate Usurlus! I was hoping you would be here! My name is Burlus, Femo Burlus, and my family owns the Dark Sun Line." Burlus was of average height, with eyes that were too green to be real, and a softly rounded face.

Usurlus accepted the quick man-hug appropriate to such encounters, checked an almost encyclopedic memory, and immediately knew what Burlus was after. The Dark Sun Line owned a fleet of small easy-to-land ships that were perfect for running freight out to the sector of the rim that he was responsible for. The problem was that an increasing number of Vord raiders were preying on little cargo vessels like the ones that Dark Sun owned.

So what Burlus and his family were after was a promise that Imperial warships would escort their freighters into the Nigor Sector and, thereby, protect them. However, if Emperor Emor acceded to that request, he would soon be swamped by a thousand others, and there weren't enough warships to protect the core worlds effectively, never mind the sparsely settled planets out along the frontier.

But solving such conundrums was the sort of thing that Imperial Legates were paid one hundred Imperials a year to do, plus expenses of course, which typically ran into the millions. So Usurlus began by letting the businessman know that he was not only familiar with the family's shipping line and its difficulties but stood ready to help. Not by providing each freighter with a military escort, but by asking the Imperial Commerce Department to organize regularly scheduled convoys, each of which would include a contingent of warships. That would still put added pressure on the Navy, but less than individual escorts would have, thereby serving the greater good.

The conversation took fifteen minutes, and by the time it was over, another constituent was waiting to speak with Usurlus. And so it went for the next hour until the Emperor's Majordomo strolled through the crowd repeating the same announcement over and over again. "Citizens of the Empire! The Emperor is pleased to inform you that the 108th running of the Imperial Air Race will begin in thirty minutes. Please make your way to the outside walkway, where chairs have been set up for your convenience. Citizens of the . . ."

But Usurlus didn't get to hear the spiel all over again, or go out onto the circular walkway to watch the race, because that was the moment when Olious reappeared. "Excuse me, Legate Usurlus," the android said from inches away. "The Emperor will see you now. Your staff will have to remain here consistent with Imperial security procedures. Please follow me."

Usurlus turned to inform Albus, who nodded his understanding. "Call us when you're ready, sire. We'll be ready."

As Olious and Usurlus made their way toward the elevators, most of the other guests were headed in the opposite direction. So it was difficult to make headway at first, but three minutes later the Legate was aboard Emor's private elevator and headed for the top floor. Once the short ride was over, Usurlus was ushered into a large reception area. Like the rest of the Imperial residence, the ceilings were sixteen feet high. The walls were covered with idealized murals depicting life on the Imperial core worlds, and the floors were paved with slabs of gleaming black marble. In marked contrast to all of the noise on the eighty-eighth floor, the only sound was the muted *clack, clack, clack* that the official's sandals made as he followed Olious through a spectacular living area, and out to the circular veranda beyond.

As a sliding door opened to provide access to the deck, the eternal roar of the city could be heard once more, because no one could stop that, not even the Emperor. And the sound was about to grow even louder as the air races began and six jet-powered planes threaded their way through a course marked out by the city's tallest buildings. For the purposes of the race, the Imperial Tower had been designated as Pylon Five.

The whole thing was a bit crazy, since the high-powered aircraft could crash into both buildings *and* each other, which they frequently did. The death toll from the previous year had been thirty-seven people, almost half of whom had been killed by falling debris after a plane slammed into the twentieth floor of the Osawa Building.

Yet people still loved the races and still crowded rooftops in order to see them, even though there was a chance they would be killed. This was why Emperor Emor continued to authorize the event. It would have been political suicide not to.

As Usurlus followed Olious around the curve of the building, he wondered which Emperor he was about to meet with. The brash, occasionally inebriated man who had been known to make whimsical policy decisions? Or the thoughtful, often creative individual, who seemed to genuinely care about the citizens who depended on him?

Though ready for anything, Usurlus was pleased to see that Emor appeared to be not only sober, but in business mode as he said good-bye to a woman in a bright yellow sari, and turned to greet his next visitor. "Isulu!" the Emperor said warmly, as the two came together for a brief embrace. "It's good to see you."

"And you, Highness," Usurlus said, as he went to one knee.

"Stop it!" the Emperor demanded, as he offered a hand. "There's no need to kneel—we're family!"

That was true in a very remote sense since the two men were distant cousins. In fact, just about all of the people who held key government appointments were members of the extended clan that Emor represented, a hard-driving family that had finally succeeded in putting one of their own on the throne after working on the project for generations. Like many of his male relatives, the Emperor had thick black hair, a beard so heavy it was necessary to shave twice a day, and a short, stocky body. But he was strong, *very* strong, which was apparent from the grip that nearly crushed the Legate's hand. "Come," Emor said, as he pulled Usurlus up into a standing position. "We'll sit over there," the Emperor said, as he gestured toward a well-shaded table. "The race will start soon, but we can talk in the meantime."

Usurlus felt a surge of resentment and sought to suppress it. How much time would he have? Ten minutes? Fifteen at most? Why couldn't Emor meet subordinates in his office? Instead of between various events? *Because he has very little time,* Usurlus told himself, *and by packing people in between things, he forces them to be concise. So be concise.*

Cold drinks appeared as if by magic as the two men took

their seats and Usurlus began his report. "Vord raiders continue to be a problem in the Nigor Sector, Highness, especially where commerce is concerned. So I plan to petition the Commerce Department to create regular convoys which will have armed escorts. Doing so will put increased pressure on the Navy, but require fewer ships than individual escorts would, thereby conserving Imperial resources."

Emor liked Usurlus for a number of reasons, not the least of which was the way his cousin always kept the big picture in mind even as he sought to obtain additional resources for his sector. An approach that was all too rare where other Legates were concerned. He took a sip of his drink and nodded. "That's a good idea, Isulu. I'll support it."

It was a win! But Usurlus knew that the clock was ticking, and once the air race began, the session would end. "Thank you, Excellency. I will inform your constituents. There's another problem, however—one we have spoken of in the past, and which continues to fester."

Emor raised a knowing eyebrow. "Procurator Nalomy?"

"Yes, Excellency," the Legate replied simply.

"You understand the politics involved?" the Emperor inquired. "I need the Nalomy family's support for a number of my more controversial initiatives. Universal health care is an excellent example."

"Yes," Usurlus answered, "I *do* understand. But, with all due respect, Procurator Nalomy is governing Dantha for her own benefit. If the situation continues uncorrected, I fear there will be civil unrest, you will be forced to send an entire Legion to put the rebellion down, and Senators opposed to your policies will take advantage of the situation by claiming you are either ignorant of what's taking place or simply don't care."

Emor sighed. What Usurlus said was true. But accusations were one thing. Facts were another. "You have proof to support your claims?"

"Yes, Excellency," Usurlus answered, and removed the printout from his briefcase. "I have an agent on Dantha. He wrote this report, which arrived last week. An electronic copy of this document will be sent to your office later this afternoon."

Emor accepted the packet and skimmed the front page. It was a long list of items received from the Imperial government, condemned before they could be used, and sold at discounted prices. Assuming it was accurate, the inventory included everything from medical supplies to a wide range of machinery, and most disturbingly a large quantity of weapons. "You'll notice that *one* company purchased almost all of those goods," Usurlus said meaningfully. "An importer-exporter called Star Crossed Enterprises, which is a wholly owned subsidiary of Imperial Industries, belonging to the Nalomy clan."

The Emperor swore and brought a hard fist down onto the surface of the table. The glasses jumped, and his bodyguards took notice. "The bastards! Senator Nalomy hopes to succeed me. . . . You'd think that he and his clan could wait until then to rape the Empire! But mark my words, Isulu. . . . Good as it is, the evidence you have isn't good enough. The Nalomys will claim that the Procurator's subordinates were to blame, or that we're out to get her for political reasons, or who knows what else. So you're going to need a lot more than what you have to nail Senator Nalomy's only daughter. But I agree that something has to be done. So go to Dantha, see what you can dig up, and take the bitch into custody if you come up with solid evidence that ties her to a crime. And I mean *solid* evidence. Of the sort that will hold up no matter what."

"Yes, Highness," Usurlus agreed soberly. "How large a force are you willing to authorize?"

Emor looked away then back again. "I'm sorry, Isulu. . . . I know it isn't fair. . . . But I can't spare *any* troops right now. Not with the Vord situation the way it is. So watch your step. . . . I'd hate to lose such a valuable cousin!"

The last part was meant to be a joke, but it wasn't very funny, not to Usurlus. Since the only force at his disposal was a personal bodyguard consisting of about sixty ex-legionnaires, while Nalomy had a regiment of militia, all of whom were bound to be loyal to her. But there was only one response Usurlus could give and he gave it. "Yes, Highness, it shall be as you say."

The race began five minutes later, and Usurlus was standing next to the Emperor as a sleek bullet-shaped racer flashed past only a hundred feet below the railing, entered a tight turn two miles north of the Imperial Tower, and crashed into the twenty-third floor of the Hamadi Bank Building. It was very early in the race, so the plane still had a lot of fuel on board, which meant the explosion was very loud. It echoed through the canyons of the Imperial City like thunder. Those rooting for other planes cheered—and those who had money on the dead pilot groaned. The cost of living was high—but life was cheap.

Near the city of Solace, on the planet Dantha

The city of Solace was situated between the towering Saw-tooth Mountains to the west, and Lake Imperium to the east, on a relatively narrow strip of land. So after the heavily burdened transport took off from the spaceport, it was necessary for the aircraft to wind its way through an S-shaped mountain pass before passing out over rolling foothills, to skim the desert beyond.

From his position behind the pilots, Centurion Sivio could see what early settlers had named the Plain of Pain, which stretched toward the Great Crater more than fifty miles straight ahead. A long, hard march, that thousands of convict-settlers had been forced to endure on their way to the iridium mines.

It had taken the better part of three nerve-wracking days for Sivio to overcome the local bureaucracy, obtain all of the permissions that were required, and load his extremely dangerous prisoner onto the militia transport. The transport, in striking contrast to so much of the public infrastructure in and around the city of Solace, was in tiptop shape. For while Procurator Nalomy had been unable to find the funds to maintain what had once been a Class III shipyard, her militia was very well equipped. So well equipped that it put every other militia regiment Sivio had seen to shame. And that was saying something because the law officer had been to dozens of Imperial planets.

Still, curious as the situation might be, it really didn't matter to Sivio so long as he was given the resources necessary to carry out his mission, which was to hold Verafti until such time as the *Pax Umana* could be repaired and put back into service.

But there were regulations, a lot of them, which pertained to how shape shifters could and could not be held. One of them specified that ". . . Should it be necessary to hold a Sagathi in something less than a Class A prison, then such prisoners will be incarcerated in the most secure structure available, providing that it is at least twenty-five miles from any settlement, town, or city with a population of more than ten people, and providing that said structure would be vulnerable to an air strike should such an attack become necessary."

This was a fancy way of saying that if a Sagathi were to take control of an interim holding facility, the Imperial government was prepared to bomb it regardless of the consequences for any Xeno Corps personnel who might be inside, rather than run the risk of having someone like Verafti running loose. A sobering thought indeed, but not one Sivio cared to dwell on, as the transport began to bank. "There it is," the pilot said laconically, as he pointed toward the ground. "Station 3."

Back when Dantha had been used as a prison planet, and the people who were sent there had been forced to work in the mines, a series of fortified way stations had been set up. And for good reason too, because as the convicts were forced to trudge across the aptly named Plain of Pain toward the iridium-rich crater beyond, they had been easy prey for a variety of carnivores, as well as escaped convicts, who would gladly kill a "newbie" for his or her rations.

Eventually, after other less expensive ways of obtaining iridium came online and Dantha was opened to settlement by people other than convicts, the way stations had fallen into disuse. Which meant that before the Xeno Corps personnel could make use of Station 3, it would be necessary to repair it.

And, from what Sivio could see as he looked down on it, there was plenty of work to do. One section of the protective wall that surrounded the fortlike building was down, there was a large hole in one side of the roof, and the western defenses were nearly submerged under windblown sand. "It looks lovely," Sivio said dryly. "I can hardly wait to move in."

The pilot laughed politely as he brought the boxy transport in for a landing. But the truth was that he was looking forward to off-loading Sivio, his bioengineered freaks, *and* the Sagathi shape shifter, who had assumed the pilot's identity a few minutes earlier and was pretending to masturbate. It was a rather disturbing sight, which the pilot could watch via one of the cameras in the main hold but sought to ignore as a cloud of dust rose to envelop the ship.

*   *   *

Jak Cato was asleep as the transport's landing skids made contact with the ground, but opened his eyes when Sivio's knuckles made contact with the top of his helmet. "Hello," Sivio said experimentally. "Is anyone home?"

The line produced a chorus of chuckles from the rest of the team, and a grunt of acknowledgment from the SL himself, as the peace officers hit their harness releases and went to work. A sweaty business, since it was hot outside, and the transport's air-conditioning system was no match for the superheated air that invaded the hold.

The first task was to off-load Verafti, cage and all. Not only did the pilot want to leave as soon as possible; he claimed that conditions were right for a sandstorm. Sivio had no way to gauge whether that was true, or if the pilot was simply in a hurry to leave, but there was no reason to tarry. So Sivio ordered his officers to roll the cage down the metal ramp, onto the hardpan, and into the walled compound beyond.

Having grown tired of impersonating the pilot, Verafti had reverted to his true form by then, and was uncharacteristically silent as Cato and four members of his section pushed the rolling cage under a stone archway and into the courtyard. Except for some chunks of fallen rock, and a cluster of sand-drifted campfires, the area was empty. Beyond it stood a structure made of tightly fitted stone. The front steps were visible, as were an open door, and the relatively cool darkness beyond. "Welcome home," Cato said, as the cage rattled across the courtyard. "It's better than you deserve!"

But Verafti was busy taking it all in, memorizing every detail, as the variants were forced to stop in front of the stairs. "It looks like we're going to have to build a ramp," Cato announced sourly. "Kelkaw, take Tonver, and return to the transport. See what you can find. We'll wait here."

Once the variants had left, Cato posted guards, and set off to reconnoiter. After activating his helmet light the noncom entered the dark, gloomy building. The white blob led him past an office, and what might have been a guard-room, into a large space that was partially illuminated by the sunlight that streamed down through the hole in the roof. Cato paused there to look around. And that was when he saw the rows of ring bolts that were anchored to the stone floor and the sand-drifted channels that ran between them. Open sewers most likely, which the prisoners had been forced to use, so the guards wouldn't have to unchain them.

The place was a mess, a *big* mess, but Cato knew Sivio well enough to know that the prospect of some hard work wouldn't be enough to deter him. And it wasn't long before the prediction was proven true as a ramp was constructed, Verafti was wheeled inside, and a variety of construction materials were removed from the transport. The aircraft departed shortly after the last crate came off, leaving the police officers to clean out decades' worth of accumulated filth and establish rudimentary living quarters within the fortresslike station.

But before the variants could make much progress, the formerly blue skies took on a grayish hue—and a vast cloud of billowing dust bore down on them from the southwest. Sivio ordered the team to bring the remaining supplies inside the compound as quickly as possible. It wasn't long before Cato felt a stinging sensation as the wind fired tiny grains of silica into his exposed skin. Ten minutes later a blinding sandstorm drove the entire team inside and attacked every-thing they had left behind. There was nothing the police officers could do at that point except try to make themselves comfortable and wait for conditions to improve.

Finally, having cleaned out the largest room, those not assigned to guard duty attempted to get some sleep. It was quiet except for the persistent roar of the wind, until Verafti's slightly sibilant voice was heard. "You know," the shape shifter observed philosophically, "it's hard to say who is going to suffer more out here . . . me or *you*."

Cato told Verafti to "Shut the hell up," but Sivio was pretty sure that he knew the answer, and didn't like the idea one bit.

It was a long night, and when morning came, the skies were clear once more. So after a cold breakfast, Cato and his section were put to work digging supplies out from under the drifts of sand that had covered them and hauling the crates inside where they were unloaded. Once that chore was accomplished, it was time to begin work on some much-needed repairs.

The hole in the roof came first. By using materials salvaged from an outbuilding, the police officers were able to recover enough wood to sister the existing rafters. With the support structure secure, large pieces of resin-infused fabric were nailed in place. Then, once the catalyst contained in the regularly spaced blister packs was released, the formerly pliable covering hardened into something comparable to sheets of plastic.

Meanwhile, as Cato and his people completed repairs to the roof, Sivio put the other section to work revitalizing the well by repairing the old pump and bringing a steady flow of water up to the surface. It was lunchtime by then, so those variants who weren't on guard duty sought shady spots in which to eat, complain about the heat, and trade well-polished lies.

Everyone except Cato, that is, who went looking for Sivio and found him sitting on an empty crate. Cato started to come to attention, but Sivio shook his head. "Save it for when I'm mad at you," he said. "Which, knowing you, will be later in the day. Nice job on the roof by the way—the patch looks like it will hold for quite a while."

"Thank you, sir," Cato replied. "I'll pass that along to my team."

"Please do," Sivio said as he squinted up at the noncom. "So, what's on your mind?"

"I heard that you plan to put up solar panels this afternoon," Cato said. "Is that true?"

Sivio removed an unlikely-looking piece of dried fruit from the dessert pack, took an experimental bite, and came to the conclusion that it would be necessary to soak the morsel before chewing it. "Yeah," Sivio replied casually, "that's correct. It would be nice to have some power in this dump. Especially at night. Wouldn't you agree?"

"Sir, yes, sir," Cato answered respectfully. "But what about the external defenses? Maybe we should tackle those first."

Sivio looked surprised. "'External defenses'? What for? We're on an Imperial planet, out in the middle of a frigging desert. Who would attack us here?"

"I don't know, sir," Cato replied lamely. "It's a feeling, that's all. Kelkaw saw a glint of reflected light off to the east, as if someone was watching us, and Honis happened across some weird com traffic. It was in another language, sir, and that got me to thinking. We'd make a pretty good target out here. Our weapons alone are worth a lot of money."

"Point taken," Sivio said thoughtfully. "And I'm glad you spoke up. That's the kind of thing I wish you did more often. But I think the solar panels are a priority. Especially if you're correct! I'd sleep better at night if we could place a few spotlights around the perimeter. But the day after tomorrow, or maybe the day after that, we'll get to work on that outer wall. How does that sound?"

Cato was disappointed, and Sivio could "feel" it, as his subordinate came to attention. "Sir, thank you, sir."

Sivio nodded. "Anytime, Section Leader. Go get some lunch."

Cato did a smart about-face, and marched away as Sivio dunked the piece of fruit into a mug filled with water, and distant eyes continued to watch the fortress.

The second day at Station 3 was as long and hard as the first—but once some technical glitches were solved, the solar panels came online. That was good, but not as good as it might have been, since it was going to take two additional batteries in order to take full advantage of the power the solar arrays were able to produce. And the law officers needed more construction materials, food, and personal items. That was why Sivio went looking for Cato.

What the Centurion found were *two* Catos, one of whom was standing inside of Fiss Verafti's cage, while the other sat at a makeshift table fifteen feet away. The second Cato was seated in front of a disassembled service pistol, the pieces of which were laid out in orderly rows, waiting to be cleaned. The desert environment was hard on weapons because the sand seemed to find its way into every nook and cranny. Cato was scrubbing the trigger assembly with an oily toothbrush as Sivio entered, and Verafti shouted, "Atten-hut!" Only in Kelkaw's voice.

The light produced by a newly installed glow rod threw harsh shadows down onto the stone floor as both Catos came to attention. Sivio said, "At ease," as Verafti morphed into a likeness of him. "I've got a job for you," the Centurion said, sitting down on the opposite side of the table from Cato. "One I think you're going to like."

Cato's eyebrows rose incrementally. "You want someone to shoot the prisoner, sir? If so, then I'm your man."

Sivio grinned sympathetically. "No, the assignment isn't *that* pleasurable I'm afraid. We need supplies, a lot of them, and I'm sending you into Solace to buy them. A transport will arrive here in about forty-five minutes to pick you up."

Cato was surprised, and Sivio could not only see it on his face but "feel" it as well. Sivio nodded understandingly. "Yeah, I chose *you*. Partly because of the way you handled yourself when we took the Vord ship, but also because of the way you've done your job since, which if not perfect is still a lot better than before. This isn't to say that I don't have some concerns," he added ominously. "Especially when it comes to booze. But, if you can go into town, buy what we need, and return sober, I'll leave your stripes where they are. But if you fail me," Sivio said in a voice so low only Cato could hear, "I'll bust you to patrolman and put you on the shit list until the day you retire. Do you read me?"

Cato felt a profound sense of gratitude, because even though he liked to pretend that his stripes were unimportant to him, the truth was they were all he had to show for his years in the Corps. But going to Solace would be tough. . . . There would be plenty of temptations, and Cato wasn't sure he could ignore them. He wasn't about to admit that, however, so he said, "Yes, sir. I read you loud and clear."

Verafti, who had witnessed the entire interchange, laughed uproariously. "You'll be sorry!" he predicted. "Cato is more like *me* than you!"

There was a series of lightning-fast *click*s as the pieces of the pistol flew together as if by magic, and the weapon swung around until the ruby red targeting laser was centered on Verafti's narrow chest. The Sagathi flinched as the hammer fell on an empty chamber. Then it was Cato's turn to laugh, and Sivio thought about what the shape shifter had said, wondering if the alien was correct.

The transport put down forty-five minutes later, and Cato, with a heavily laden money belt secured under his tunic, went out to meet it. There were all of the predictable insults, catcalls, and requests for things the other law officers weren't going to get as the Section Leader paused to wave before proceeding up the ramp.

A cloud of sand and dust rose to obscure the transport as its repellers jabbed at the ground and pushed the aircraft up into the air. Then, once it had sufficient altitude, the transport pivoted toward the east and took off.

Sivio stood and watched until the aircraft was little more than a dot before he turned and walked away. It was hot, and what looked like a lake shimmered in the distance. But that, like so many things on Dantha, was a lie.

THREE

The city of Solace, on the planet Dantha

THE DAZZLINGLY WHITE PALACE HAD BEEN BUILT ON A rise where those who occupied it could look out over the city of Solace and the azure waters of Lake Imperium to the east. The fifty-six-room structure truly was fit for a king or an emperor because it, like all of the Imperial residences scattered around the Empire, was based on a common template established 252 years earlier during the reign of Emperor Deronious. A systematic sort of man, he wanted to make sure that both he and his extensive entourage would be comfortable regardless of where duty took him. This was a plan that Uma Nalomy benefited from since she, like Procurators on all the Imperial planets, was entitled to live in the sprawling complex so long as Emperor Emor wasn't there on a visit. That possibility was so remote as to be laughable.

At the moment, Nalomy was floating in the small swimming pool that was part of the Imperial suite. Bells tinkled merrily as Majordomo Imood Hingo entered the huge room. He was tall, well built, and dressed in the male version of the uniform that Nalomy required all members of her household staff to wear regardless of rank. The outfit consisted of a short, waist-length blue jacket left open in the front, a white sash through which the baton that symbolized his office was thrust, and a carefully pleated white kilt that fell to midthigh. A pair of open-toed, lace-up boots completed the outfit. Hingo's shaved head gleamed with reflected light, his prominent cheekbones gave his face a skeletal appearance, and his lips made a hard, thin line. "Yes?" Nalomy demanded, as her servant came to a stop at the other end of the pool. "What do you want?"

Nalomy was twenty-six years old, pretty in a hard sort of way, and quite shapely, a fact that she liked to emphasize by wearing skimpy outfits, and when the mood struck her, nothing at all. As was the case in the pool. And rather than conceal her body, as some women would have, the Procurator chose to leave her charms on display, a strategy intended to torment Hingo, who could look but wasn't allowed to touch.

For his part Hingo knew what his mistress was up to, but he was powerless to stop her, or keep his eyes off Nalomy's partially submerged breasts. "The meeting will be held fifteen minutes from now, Your Highness. The guards have been warned, the East Room is ready, and the refreshments are on the way." Hingo knew that a Procurator wasn't entitled to be called "Highness," but Nalomy insisted on the honorific, and, with no one of higher rank around to object, Nalomy's staff was forced to obey.

Nalomy stood. Water cascaded off her slender body as she turned to climb a couple of steps before entering the warm embrace of the towel that one of her nearly identical maids was holding. That gave Hingo an opportunity to enjoy Nalomy's narrow waist, flared hips, and nicely tapered legs. But the interlude was all too brief, as Nalomy's pet Fulu dog yapped for attention, and she turned to confront him. "Thank you, Hingo. . . . That will be all."

The Majordomo bowed, took three steps back, and turned to go. He couldn't have Nalomy, but there were plenty of slave girls in the palace, and one of them was going to have a very active evening.

The East Room was a large space intended for private parties and receptions. Windows, plus big double doors, looked out onto a sprawling terrace, and the dark waters of the lake beyond. All of them had been left open to let the warm evening air in—and for the convenience of Nalomy's guests.

It was nighttime, so the guards stationed on the terrace couldn't see the Lir bandits as they came in for a landing, but they could hear the gentle *whuf, whuf, whuf* of leathery wings and a few words of a language that no Uman would ever be able to speak. Then the first birdlike sentient was down, his head jerking from side to side as he looked for potential threats. Centurion Rax Pasayo was there to greet the Lir by name and escort him in through the double doors. He was a small but fastidious man whose skin was tanned and wrinkled from years spent patrolling the desert wastes. "This is Hybor Iddyn, Highness," Pasayo announced, as Nalomy waited to receive her visitor.

Iddyn was about five feet tall and extremely slender, a trait that was emphasized by the long, narrow wings folded along his back. Strong muscles were required to lift a seventy-pound body off the ground, and the source of that power was evident in a wedge-shaped torso and strong legs. A white crest began just above the Lir's hooklike beak and ran back along the top surface of his rounded skull to the point where it merged with the feathery collar that surrounded his neck.

Iddyn's yellow eyes were huge, being at least twice the size of a Uman's, and were packed with three times as many cones. That meant his vision was greatly superior to Nalomy's as their eyes made contact. "It's a pleasure to meet you," Nalomy said sincerely, as she stepped forward to greet her visitor. The young woman was dressed by that time, and rather conservatively, too, both because the Lir were prudes and Nalomy knew her body held no interest for Iddyn. No, Iddyn was after better weapons, or the money required to buy them. Never mind the fact that he would happily use the guns on Nalomy's citizens if given the chance. That was the price the people of Dantha would have to pay.

"Good meet you," Iddyn said solemnly, as he unfurled both wings and brought them forward to touch the floor.

The gesture was the equivalent of an extravagant bow, which pleased Nalomy, who smiled engagingly. "Welcome to my home."

Two additional Lir had entered the East Room by that time—and Pasayo hurried to introduce both. "This is Pak Nassali, Highness, and Etir Lood. Both of them are accomplished warriors."

Nalomy could well believe that, given the way they looked. Both Lir wore leather harnesses, to which a variety of weapons were attached. Energy pistols for the most part, because of how light they were, and razor-sharp ceramic knives. But could they take on and defeat a detachment of Xeno Corps variants? That remained to be seen. "Welcome," Nalomy said politely, as more yellow eyes darted around the room. "I know you flew a long way to get here. You must be hungry. Please help yourselves to some refreshments."

A buffet table had been set up along one wall, and it was loaded with delicacies, including big half-pound rock bugs, which continued to squirm in spite of the skewers that held their segmented bodies in place, mounds of lightly toasted Nenor seeds, and a Vevor carcass that had been left to bake in the sun for three days before being stuffed with sweet Susu berries and served at room temperature.

The banquet was disgusting by most people's standards,

but Nalomy wasn't most people, and she watched in fascination as the ravenous Lir ripped chunks of half-rotted meat off the dead Vevor, swallowing the gobbets whole. And, much to Centurion Pasayo's amazement, the Procurator even went so far as to sample the Susu-berry stuffing, which she pronounced to be quite delicious.

Eventually, having eaten their fill, the bandits were invited to sit on tall stools that allowed their wings to extend down behind them. Rather than use a Uman chair, Nalomy chose to perch on a Lir-style stool, thereby further ingratiating herself with Iddyn who, having a generally low opinion of Umans, found this one to his liking. "Thank you," he said sincerely. "Food good."

"I'm glad you enjoyed it," the Procurator said graciously, as she popped a final Susu berry into her mouth. "Now, if you have no objections, let's get down to business. An Imperial prison ship was forced to land on Dantha earlier this week, and because repairs are going to take a while, I gave permission for the Xeno Corps officers to move their prisoner to Station 3 in the Plain of Pain. Where, if what Centurion Pasayo tells me is correct, you have them under observation."

"That right," Iddyn said feelingly. "Hate Xeno freaks."

That was true, and Nalomy knew why. Unlike the specimens seated in front of her, most Lir were not only loyal Citizens of the Empire, but highly respected residents of a variety of planets. But Iddyn and his "flock" were descendants of Nest Cult fanatics, who had been tried by Imperial courts more than two hundred years previously and sent to Dantha as punishment for a long list of violent crimes. That bit of history explained both their hatred of the Empire, *and* of the Xeno Corps, which they saw as the modern-day equivalent of the sadistic prison guards who had been in charge of their ancestors. The Procurator planned to use that fact to her advantage. "Of course you do," Nalomy said sympathetically. "So, how would you like to attack them without fear of a reprisal from Centurion Pasayo's troops? And get paid five thousand Imperials for doing so?"

"*Ten* thousand," Iddyn said thickly. "We kill them good!"

Nalomy would have been willing to pay twice that amount but did her best to hide that fact. "Okay," she said reluctantly, "ten thousand it is, but only if you do exactly what you're told. . . . Centurion Pasayo will give you half the money up front—and half when the mission is completed."

That was a problem for Iddyn, since he wasn't sure he could fly five thousand Imperials back to High Hold Meor, even if they were divided three ways. He wasn't about to say that, however, so it was a good time to change the subject. "Why?" Iddyn demanded. "Why you want Xenos dead?"

"It isn't about the Xenos," Nalomy responded noncommittally. "I want their prisoner. And I want him alive. That's all you need to know."

Iddyn already knew more than that because, under the cover of darkness, his number two son had landed on top of Station 3's roof and peered down through a hole. This was when he saw the cage, the not-Uman inside of it, and what the creature could do. Clearly such a being could be useful if properly harnessed. Especially if the person who controlled the not-Uman wanted to kill someone. So whom did the Procurator want to eliminate? And why? There was no way to find out without revealing how much he already knew. Iddyn nodded. "You pay. We go."

Pasayo produced three identical money belts, laid them out on a table, and ritualistically loaded each one of them with coins. Though considered archaic, not to mention annoying, on the core worlds, the metal disks remained popular on rim worlds like Dantha, where electronic commerce wasn't fully implemented.

Then, once the Lir were ready, they left the same way they had come. Nalomy and Pasayo watched as they took off. "They won't get far," Nalomy predicted, as the steady beat of powerful wings was heard. "Not with all that extra weight strapped to them."

"No," Pasayo agreed. "I suspect they will land outside the city, bury half of it, and come back later."

"So, can they do it?" Nalomy wanted to know. "*Can* they kill the variants and free the shape shifter?"

"It won't be easy," Pasayo replied gravely. "But I believe they can."

Having arrived at the spaceport the day before, Cato was surprised to find that there wasn't any regularly scheduled transportation into Solace. That meant he was forced to make the ten-mile trip riding in the back of a smelly farm wagon. The four-wheeled conveyance had no suspension to speak of, and the old tractor pulling it rattled noisily as it belched sooty smoke out of a four-foot-tall exhaust pipe. There wasn't anything to sit on other than the cages occupied by raucous stee-stee birds, so Cato's butt was sore, and he was glad to pay the boy, getting off the wagon as soon as the tractor arrived at the south end of Market Street.

It was evening by then, and all of the businesses that Cato was supposed to visit were closed, which meant the variant couldn't accomplish much of anything until the next morning. So, being eager to find a place to stay and get something to eat, he set off to explore Solace. And with the surety of a man who had been forced to plumb the depths of many an exotic city, it wasn't long before Cato entered The Warrens. This section of Solace was not only the oldest part of the settlement, but home to the public market, the slave pens, and the sorts of dives Cato had promised to steer clear of.

With Sivio's admonitions still ringing in his ears, and a money belt buckled around his waist, Cato forced himself to ignore the bars that lined Market Street and zeroed in on the Spaceman's Hotel. It was a respectable-looking establishment that was three stories tall, boasted a stone façade, and appeared to be supporting the less prosperous structures located to either side of it.

Being well aware of the hostility that was often shown to police officers, especially on rim worlds, Cato was dressed in the sort of plain everyday tunic and kilt that any male citizen might wear. Of course that meant he couldn't *command* the hotel's owner to provide him with a room, as was a policeman's right, but would have to hope for a vacancy.

Cato followed a couple into what turned out to be a reasonably well furnished lobby and made his way to the front desk. The woman who stood behind the counter had short blond hair worn in a stiff flattop. Half her face was covered with tattoos so well executed that they had to be the work of a Noma II needle artisan. A spacer perhaps? Who had jumped ship in Dantha? And made a life for herself in Solace? Yes, quite possibly, not that it made any difference as the clerk produced a smile. "Good evening, Citizen. How can I help you?"

After paying for two nights in advance, Cato was shown to a room so small there was barely space for a bed. But it was clean, and located at the back of the building, where it was well insulated from the street noise out front. And that suited Cato just fine.

Having secured a place to stay, Cato went looking for something to eat. There were plenty of pubs along the city's winding streets, and while most of them served food, Cato was careful to avoid such establishments knowing that once inside it would be tempting to have a drink. Or two . . . Or three.

That was why Cato chose to eat dinner in a small hole-in-the-wall restaurant called The Five Tables. Cato had one of the tables, and the other four were occupied by regulars, judging from their interactions with the eatery's only waitress.

It was an excellent if somewhat lonely meal, which Cato polished off rather quickly, being hungry and having no one to talk to. Having left a generous tip, he made his way out onto the street. There weren't very many streetlights, the number of pedestrians had decreased by at least 50 percent over the previous hour, and pockets of deep shadow occupied both sides of the street. A made-to-order environment for muggers, thieves, and rapists.

So Cato placed one hand on the pistol hidden beneath his cloak and made his way up the very center of the street. There, assailants, if any, would be forced to charge out of the shadows, providing him with an opportunity to draw his weapon and fire.

That strategy entailed a degree of risk, however, because on two different occasions it was necessary to sprint for the side of the road or risk being hit. Once by a private limo so quiet he wouldn't have known the vehicle was coming had it not been for the car's bright headlights, and once by a team of clattering angens pulling a wagonload of garbage. They were large animals, bred for strength, and made snorting noises as they passed.

Ten minutes later, Cato was back at the hotel, in his room, preparing for bed. It was comfortable, especially when compared to a bivouac bag on Station 3's cold floor, and sleep came quickly.

Cato awoke early, took a shower in the shared bathroom down the hall, and was soon out on the street. Breakfast consisted of a pastry stuffed with scrambled egg, cheese, and spicy meat. It was everyday food, for everyday people, and immensely satisfying. He drank two mugs of hot caf to wash it down.

Then, having solicited directions from the street vendor, Cato was ready to begin what promised to be a long, hard day traipsing from one merchant to the next in an attempt to buy the supplies without being cheated.

A rainstorm had passed through the area during the early hours of the morning, so the streets were still damp and the air relatively clean. But it wasn't going to remain that way for long because, as Cato made his way deeper into The Warrens, the smoke produced by thousands of charcoal braziers was already trickling up into the atmosphere to form a gray haze.

Meanwhile, down on the ground, the open drainage channels that paralleled each street were filled to overflowing with polluted water, which would start to smell when the sun rose higher in the sky.

Most of the dwellings to either side of Market Street were only one or two stories high. The more prosperous homes were made of stone, quarried in the mountains to the west, and brought down by train. Citizens with more modest incomes lived in houses made of blown concrete, some of which had been treated with pigments to produce blocky structures of various colors. Tile roofs were popular, as were sheets of scrap metal and ratty tarps. Many homes had miniature temples in front of them, where daily offerings could be made to dozens of highly specialized gods.

But *most* of the structures that people lived in were little more than hovels made from shipping containers, junked vehicles, and scraps of this and that salvaged from who knew where. All of which were inhabited by an army of filthy children, many of whom ran up to Cato and demanded money, until he left their territory and entered the *next* block, where another mob of street urchins waited to attack him.

Meanwhile, as the sun inched higher in the eastern sky, and the city's rancid smell reasserted itself, all manner of traffic began to appear. It wasn't long before the confusing maze of mostly unmarked streets was packed. There were angen-drawn wagons, two-wheeled carts pulled by half-naked slaves, and unicycles that whined as gyros battled to keep them upright. Caravans of work-worn androids lumbered along, each burdened by an enormous backpack. Specially trained dogs, serving as mounts for diminutive Kelfs, competed for space with the occasional palanquin, each with a screened enclosure and a mystery therein.

And, as if to celebrate the chaos in the streets, it wasn't long before the clotheslines that crisscrossed the open areas above were thick with laundry. The clothes flapped like multicolored flags each time a breeze found its way down out of the mountains to caress Solace and ruffle the surface of the lake beyond.

The whole thing made for a scene so filled with sensory input it was a relief to spot the provisioner Cato was looking for and open the hammered-metal door, entering the relative silence beyond. That was the first stop in a long and often frustrating day spent trudging from place to place, dodging aggressive street vendors, and haggling with avaricious merchants.

Finally, as the sun fell behind the mountains, Cato came to agreement with a furniture maker named Hason Ovidius. A burly character with black, slicked-back hair, intelligent eyes, and a ready smile. "So, my friend," Ovidius said genially. "Twelve Imperials per bed. . . . Including haulage. Are we agreed?"

The original price had been fifteen Imperials, *plus* transportation, and having spoken with the owners of two other shops earlier in the afternoon Cato knew the quote was fair. Especially given that the bed frames would be custom-made according to military specs. "Yes," the police officer replied. "It's a deal."

"Good!" Ovidius said enthusiastically. "Come . . . The day is nearly over. Let's have a drink."

Cato's mouth felt dry. He knew he shouldn't have a drink, but genuinely liked Ovidius, and didn't want to offend him.

Besides, Cato reasoned, *one drink will be okay. It's when I have more than one that I get into trouble.*

So, having signed the necessary papers, the two men left the furniture shop, and walked two blocks to a pub called The Black Stocking. The sign that hung over the front door consisted of a piece of wood that had been carved into the shape of a nicely proportioned female leg complete with a painted stocking. It hung low enough to touch, which nearly everyone did, as they pushed the door open.

Ovidius was a regular, and was greeted with considerable warmth, as the two men were shown to a large table not far from the open fire. An amenity that wasn't necessary yet, but soon would be, as the outside air began to cool. Appetizers in the form of hearty pot stickers arrived moments later along with the large leg-shaped steins of beer for which the establishment was famous. "A pox upon the Procurator!" Ovidius said cheerfully, thereby echoing a toast offered hundreds, if not thousands of times per day.

Though not the sort of sentiment that an Imperial law officer should endorse, Cato was in plain clothes, and saw no reason to make an issue of the matter. So their beer steins came into contact, and foam slopped onto the tabletop, as Cato let the delightfully cold liquid slide down his throat. It felt good to know that his duty was done, the worst of the mission was behind him, and he could finally relax.

And relax he did, as an hour slipped by, Ovidius went home to his wife, and the beer continued to flow. Of course Cato had *new* friends by then, all of whom seemed to be as personable as the furniture maker had been, until a man with coarse bristly hair, gimlet eyes, and a pug nose took a seat on the other side of the table. His name was Lorkin. Unlike most of those around him, Lorkin wasn't drunk, even though the stranger had purchased four rounds by then, thereby establishing a new record for The Black Stocking. And as the regulars celebrated their good fortune, Lorkin was evaluating what might be an opportunity to enrich himself. How deep were the stranger's pockets anyway? Was he nearly tapped out? Or did the man have a fat money belt hidden under his tunic? If so, that would account for his ability to buy four rounds of beer for two dozen people.

It was Lorkin's desire to find out, and never having been one to carry out his own dirty work if that could be avoided, the con man, gambler, and part-time thief waited for an opening and dropped a word bomb into the midst of the often chaotic conversation. "So," the con man said calmly. "Why would a stranger buy drinks for everyone—unless he's one of the Procurator's spies? Trolling for names he can sell to the militia?"

There were such people; all of the tavern's customers knew that, so a sudden silence fell on the formerly happy crowd as Cato's alcohol-befuddled brain struggled to come up with an appropriate response. "I'm not a spy," Cato said stupidly. "I'm here to buy supplies. For the Xeno Corps."

There was a unanimous growl of anger as the people seated around the table heard what they interpreted as an admission of guilt to an offense that was even *more* egregious than spying for Nalomy. Because if the Procurator was bad, the government responsible for putting the rotten bitch in office was even worse, and that included members of the Xeno Corps.

Lorkin waited for someone else to land the first blow and, as Cato rose to defend himself, plunged into the fray. That meant taking a blow to the face, but the con man had his arms around Cato by then, and could feel the money belt as bony fists struck from every direction. The spring-loaded hook blade produced a gentle *click* as it shot forward into the palm of Lorkin's hand. With the weapon in position it was a simple matter to slice through clothing and leather alike. One of Cato's pouches was cut in two, which sent four Imperials clattering to the floor. That triggered a mad scramble as practically everyone fought to recover them.

Meanwhile, having jerked the belt free, Lorkin made it disappear as Cato went down under a flurry of additional punches. "Stop him!" Cato shouted, as Lorkin backed away. "He stole my money!"

But it was too late by then, as the floor came up to strike the back of his head, and the lights went out. The battle was over.

Another long, hard day had come to a close, and dinner was over, as Centurion Ben Sivio took a mug of hot caf and left Station 3's warm, fuggy interior for the cold, crisp air outside. Even though the Plain of Pain was hot during the day, it was cold at night. And as Sivio paused to sip his drink and look up at the night sky, it occurred to him that the multitude of stars looked like crystals of ice.

Still, cold as the night air was, it felt good to be by himself for a moment. Because the pressures associated with always being in charge, always being responsible, were starting to weigh on Sivio. Especially since there was no way to know how long the team would have to remain camped in the middle of the desert, and his second-in-command was still a question mark, even if he was showing signs of improvement.

Of course, conditions would get better once Cato secured the supplies needed to make Station 3 more comfortable and brought them back from Solace. That was reassuring, but Sivio's train of thought was interrupted by a shadow that slid across the stars, and disappeared half a second later.

Sivio frowned and did a 360 while staring up into the sky. Were his eyes playing tricks on him? Had a cloud drifted past? No, clouds don't have emotions, and Sivio had "felt" something. A presence of some sort. So what was it? A bird perhaps? Hunting for a meal?

More curious than concerned, Sivio made his way across

the courtyard to the spot where a flight of stone stairs led to the top of the defensive wall and Moshath was on sentry duty. Perhaps he had witnessed the same phenomenon and could explain it.

But, as Sivio arrived on the walkway that ran along the top of the four-foot-thick wall, there was no sign of Moshath. And that made Sivio angry because if Moshath was sick, or needed to take a dump, then all he had to do was get on the com and let someone know.

That was when Sivio heard a gentle *whuff*ing, wondered what Moshath was up to, and put the mug down on top of the waist-high wall. Having retrieved his flashlight from his belt, the officer followed the blob of yellow light eastward. He hadn't gone more than ten feet when he saw Moshath's boots, his legs, and the black blood that was pooled beneath the officer's torso. As for Moshath's head, well that was missing, along with his assault rifle!

Sivio felt ice water squirt into his veins, and was fumbling for the switch that would turn his com set on, when he ran out of time. The police officer "sensed" the assailant before he actually saw him, knew the feeling of hate was coming from a non-Uman, and was in the process of reaching for his sidearm when Hybor Iddyn landed in front of him.

The Lir Chieftain's chest was still wet with Moshath's blood and he held an energy pistol in each clawlike hand. Sivio's service pistol had cleared leather by then but wasn't going to come up in time. Sivio remembered Cato's warning, wished he had taken it seriously, and tried to shout.

But Iddyn had anticipated such a possibility, and when the Lir fired, both of the bright blue energy bolts pulped the Uman's vulnerable throat. There was no pain to speak of, just a momentary sense of warmth, as Sivio's hands came up to touch the wound. At point Sivio's eyes rolled back in his head, the flashlight and the handgun clattered to the walkway, and he toppled over backward. There was a muted *thump* as Sivio's body landed on the stone walkway.

Iddyn couldn't smile, not given the nature of his physiology, but the way the feathers around his neck rose and fell signaled his pleasure. Two Umans were dead, which meant that eleven of the Imperials were still alive, not counting the individual who had been flown out the day before yesterday. A significant number to be sure, but vulnerable nevertheless, thanks to the element of surprise.

Iddyn made a high-pitched keening sound that Umans couldn't hear, listened for the soft *whuf*, *whuf*, *whuf* of leathery wings, and was soon rewarded as more than a dozen heavily armed warriors swept in out of the surrounding darkness. A war was under way, the first battle had been won, and the enemy was blissfully unaware that the next one was about to begin.

Though very primitive, the strange half-lit scene inside Station 3 had a homey quality because of the odor of warmed rations, the items of clothing that had been hung up to dry, and the gentle murmur of conversation. Some of the officers were trying to sleep, but Honis, Batia, and Tonver were playing cards. Not for money, which they didn't have, but for the stim strips that were included in their rations. Three or four of the strips chewed all at once would produce a buzz equivalent to a shot of liquor. And that was worth something out in the middle of the Plain of Pain.

Meanwhile, as the threesome sat in a circle, each guarding his or her cards, Verafti was quietly alert. There were strangers in the area. The shape shifter could "feel" their presence—and the rich amalgam of hatred and fear that surrounded them.

Were the Xeno cops aware of the intruders? No, it was

clear that they weren't. And that presented a problem. Or was it an opportunity? Because if the beings that were closing in on Station 3 meant to kill the Umans, that would be good. And it would behoove him to remain silent. But if it was their intention to kill *everyone* inside the building, then that would be bad, and a warning was in order.

Of course that was the problem with reading emotions rather than thoughts; it was virtually impossible to make such fine discriminations, and that could result in a fatal error. Still, given the prospect of remaining cooped up in his cage for many months to come, Verafti was willing to take a chance. So, rather than give the alarm, Verafti moved to the corner of his cage, sat down as a way to make himself less visible, and focused his eyes on the front door.

While some of his peers slept, and others played cards, Officer Brice Kelkaw was sitting cross-legged on his sleeping bag deep in meditation, a process that was not only relaxing but served to hone his DNA-given talent as an empath. Most of his peers took the talent for granted. But it was Kelkaw's belief that, like muscles, empathy grew stronger when exercised and, given how important it was to his job, was worth putting some effort into. And that was why Kelkaw was in a receptive state as the Lir bandits landed in the courtyard outside, checked their weapons, and approached the entrance to the building. Their combined emotions were like a powerful fist that buried itself in the officer's gut and caused his eyes to fly open. "Outside!" Kelkaw shouted. "Grab your weapons!"

Unfortunately, it was too late by then. The unlocked door slammed open as Iddyn entered and half a dozen armed warriors followed him inside. Kelkaw was diving for his assault rifle as the Lir bandits opened fire. Where was Sivio? he wondered. Dead most likely, somewhere outside the station, and Moshath as well.

Then the policeman was there, scooping up the rifle, and releasing the safety, as he brought the weapon up. Half the team were already dead as the crisscrossing energy beams cut Tonver, Batia, and Honis down before they knew an attack was under way. Half a dozen more were killed while still struggling to exit their sleeping bags. So by the time Kelkaw pulled the trigger, the battle was already lost.

But that didn't stop Kelkaw from shooting both a Lir named Ibb Shyod, and the warrior standing behind him, as one bullet did the job of two.

That gave the Xeno cop a half second of satisfaction before he, too, was cut down by a dozen bolts of blue energy. The Lir warriors were angry by that time and would have continued to fire, had it not been for Iddyn's order to stop. There was a moment of silence as the acrid smell of ozone melded with the pungent odor of burned flesh to create a throat-clogging stench. And that was when Verafti spoke from his cell. "Watch out! Behind you!"

Nearly all of the Lir turned to see a lone Uman standing framed in the doorway. When the battle began, Kath Larsy had been outside, in the temporary outhouse the team had established while they waited for Cato to bring plumbing supplies back from Solace.

And, in keeping with regulations, Larsy was armed. The pistol was held in both hands, and had she been aiming at the Lir, at least three or four of them would have died. But Larsy's attention was focused elsewhere, and Verafti knew it. He went facedown on the bottom of his cell as Larsy fired, and felt a bullet cut a painful furrow across his unprotected back.

Unfortunately Larsy's act of self-sacrifice was in vain as the Lir fired at her; the police officer staggered under the impact of a dozen energy bolts and backpedaled out the door, before falling to the ground. Wisps of smoke curled up out of the blackened craters that made a random pattern across the front of her body.

"Good work!" Verafti said brightly, as he came to his feet. The shallow bullet wound was painful, but the shape shifter had survived worse. "Now, if you would be so kind as to open the cage, I could use some fresh air."

Iddyn and his warriors stared in amazement at the creature who looked like one of them. Pak Nassali to be exact—only without clothes or weapons. The real Nassali made a hissing noise, and was in the process of bringing his weapon up into firing position, when Iddyn reached over to push it back down. "So they right," the bandit leader observed thoughtfully. "Creature *can* change shape."

"Yes," a Uman voice said grimly, as Centurion Pasayo entered the great room. "He certainly can. And leave him right where he is for the moment. The next task is to move the cage outside. My transport is waiting."

It took the better part of a half hour to move the cage into the transport and strap it down. Once that task was accomplished, it was time for Pasayo to pay Iddyn and give the bandit chieftain some advice. They were standing under one of the transport's stubby wings where they were lit from above. "Go ahead and take whatever you want, but leave the bodies where they are, so that the scene will look like what it was: a bandit attack. Understood?"

"Yes," the Lir replied expressionlessly. "Understood."

"I'm glad to hear it," the Imperial replied. "And remember this: If you use the money to buy weapons, and use the weapons to fire on *my* troops, I will pay a visit to High Hold Meor and reduce it to a pile of slag."

It was a potent threat, and one that Iddyn took seriously, which was why he made a mental note to have Pasayo killed as soon as possible. "You no worry," Iddyn said reassuringly. "We friends."

Pasayo wasn't so sure about that, but ordered a soldier to hand over the money belts containing the second half of

Iddyn's fee and made his way up the cargo ramp and onto the ship.

There was a loud roar as repellers flared, and the ship rose out of a cloud of dust before swiveling toward the east. Iddyn saw a momentary glow as the pilot fired both engines, and the ship was gone, leaving the stars to glitter above. They had been witness to horrific crimes before—and they were as silent as the grains of sand under the Lir's three-toed feet. There were secrets in the desert, lots of them, and they were buried deep.

FOUR

The city of Solace, on the planet Dantha

IT WAS EARLY MORNING WHEN THE MILITIAMEN CAME, their boots pounding out a rhythm as old as the history of warfare as they marched down the center of the nearly empty street, weapons at port arms. It was raining, and had been for hours, which was why the troops wore water-slicked ponchos that hung down skirtlike around their knobby knees.

There wasn't much foot traffic at that time of day, and what little bit there was seemed to fade away as the Procurator's soldiers entered The Warrens and went straight to the pub called The Black Stocking. It wasn't open yet. But when a burly Section Leader hammered on the door and ordered those within to, "Open up, or be shut down," the saloon's proprietor hurried to comply. He had shaggy gray hair, a bulbous nose, and a potbelly that strained the fabric of his long nightshirt. "Yes?" he said suspiciously, as he eyed the militiamen arrayed in front of him. "What can I do for you?"

"You can get the hell out of the way," Centurion Pasayo answered arrogantly, as he pushed past and entered the great room beyond. It was about 6:00 AM, which meant the pub had been closed for three hours, and wasn't scheduled to re-open until midafternoon. So, The Black Stocking's interior was exactly as customers had left it, which was to say filthy. An army of empty beer steins occupied the tables, plates of half-eaten food sat here and there, and the combined odors of beer and vomit filled Pasayo's nostrils as he made his way toward the back.

"What are you looking for?" the saloon's owner inquired as he hurried to catch up. "Perhaps I can help."

"Not 'what,'" Pasayo replied, as he paused to look around. "But *who*. We have information that a man named Cato was drinking here last night."

"Yes!" the saloon keeper responded eagerly. "There was such a man! He started a fight, got the beating he deserved, and passed out."

"That's interesting," Pasayo replied ominously. "*Very* interesting. Were you aware that the man in question is a police officer?"

"No!" the proprietor replied emphatically, his mind reeling. Nobody liked the Xeno Corps, and that included Nalomy's militia, so why would they come to the variant's aid? And how much trouble was he in? "I had no idea that he was a police officer," the businessman maintained. "He was seated over there, next to the fire, where all of the broken furniture is."

Shards of glass crunched under Pasayo's boots as he made his way over to the area in question. The fire had burned down by then, leaving little more than a pile of glowing embers, and a few tendrils of smoke. As Pasayo eyed the wreckage, he spotted what might be an outflung foot, and immediately went to work removing pieces of debris. The Section Leader was there to help—and it wasn't long before a body was unearthed.

The saloon owner looked on in horror. What if the policeman was dead? And the militia blamed *him*? Procurator Nalomy would pronounce him guilty, sentence him to be hanged, and order his family to hoist his still-kicking body up into the air. Then, as spectators watched his corpse twist slowly in the wind, they would eat the deep-fried meat pies that the city's food vendors always hawked at such events, and bet on when the first stink bird would arrive to peck at his eyes.

"It's him all right," Pasayo said grimly. "Check his pulse. Let's see if he's alive."

Five of the longest seconds in the saloon owner's life ticked by as the Section Leader placed two thick fingers on Cato's neck and frowned. Finally, after what seemed like an eternity, the soldier delivered his report. "He's alive, sir."

Pasayo nodded. "All right then, haul the worthless bastard outside, and drop him into the angen trough. Maybe that will bring him around."

The pub's proprietor heaved a silent sigh of relief as Cato's limp body was carried out toward the street, and Pasayo turned to confront him. "You were lucky, old man. Pay attention to who you serve in the future. And one more thing . . . I hear that in spite of her unceasing work on behalf of the citizens of Dantha, your regulars have unpleasant things to say about Procurator Nalomy. That could be bad for business. Which is to say, bad for *you*. I suggest that you give that some thought before you open for business in the afternoon."

Having said his piece, Pasayo turned and made his way out through the front door—leaving the portly businessman to wonder which one of his seemingly loyal customers was spying for the government.

Cato was floating in a sea of darkness. A peaceful place where Centurion Sivio couldn't find him, where there were no problems and life was good. Then came the sound of distant voices, the feel of steely fingers at his wrists and ankles, and a sudden jab of pain as he was jerked up off the floor.

Cato tried to object, but discovered that the words wouldn't come, as he was carried out into the cold morning air and felt what might have been raindrops hit his face. Then as Cato's mind began to clear, he heard a male voice say, "Let him go," and experienced a brief moment of free fall before hitting the water and sinking below the surface. The cold liquid triggered Cato's involuntary reflexes; he began to thrash about, and his hands found the trough's algae-slicked sides.

There was a sudden explosion of brownish water as Cato sat up, spat some of the foul brew out of his mouth, and began to cough. Pasayo placed one boot on the edge of the trough and watched with amusement. "Take a good look," the Centurion said to the soldiers who were gathered around. "That's what a member of the much-vaunted Xeno Corps looks like! Don't you feel safer? I know I do!"

The jest produced a round of hearty guffaws as the militiamen enjoyed their moment of artfully induced superiority. Cato had cleared his airway by then and was taking inventory of his various aches and pains. The alcohol-induced headache was worst, closely followed by an extremely tender black eye and some very sore ribs. As his right hand went down to touch his side, Cato was reminded of the money belt and the man who had stolen it.

The loss stimulated a groan, and Pasayo grinned unsympathetically. "So Section Leader Cato, now that I have your full and undivided attention, here's some news. At about 0400 this morning we received a com call from Station 3. It was from a group of prospectors who paused to refill their canteens—and walked into the aftermath of a massacre. It seems that all of your freak friends were killed. Lir bandits are the best bet, not that it matters, since dead is dead.

"Anyway," Pasayo continued heartlessly, "given that you're the only member of the group who's still alive, it's up to you to go out there and take care of the bodies. It gets pretty hot in the desert—so I'd get a move on if I were you."

It was a lot to take in, and Cato was still trying to do so, when Pasayo turned away. The water made splashing sounds as Cato struggled to his feet. Pasayo turned to look. "*All* of them?" Cato demanded.

"That's what the prospectors said," Pasayo answered clinically.

"And the prisoner?"

The Centurion shrugged. "There wasn't any mention of him. Maybe he was killed—or maybe he escaped."

Cato felt a chill run down his spine, and knew it had nothing to do with his water-soaked clothing, or the rain that continued to fall from above. Because if Verafti had survived the attack and was on the loose, then no one was safe. "I need help," Cato said. "To reach Station 3, bury my friends, and find the prisoner if he's alive."

"Please feel free to submit a written request to Procurator Nalomy's Civil Administrator," Pasayo replied. "Then, assuming that he feels your petition has merit, he will forward a copy to me for comment. Once that part of the process is complete, I will pass the request on to Procurator Nalomy for a final decision."

Cato gritted his teeth. He was cold, *very* cold, and they started to chatter. "H-h-how long will that process take?"

"We're pretty busy right now," Pasayo replied callously, "what with the Legate's impending visit and all. So I'd allow seven or eight months." Cato caught a glimpse of the other man's smug smile before the officer turned away and gave a series of curt orders. The militiamen fell in, came to attention, and were subsequently marched away.

So no one other than a single mongrel was present to stare

as Cato stood knee deep in the dirty water, chest heaving as a series of sobs racked his body and tears ran down his cheeks. Tears for those who were dead—and ultimately for himself.

Hason Ovidius's furniture shop consisted of a long, rectangular room in which most of the illumination originated from a large skylight, identical workbenches stood in orderly rows, and his employees were at work by 7:00 AM. So when Cato entered through the back door and began to make his way toward the front office, no one took notice of him at first. Then a slave named Fidius spotted the disreputable-looking intruder and moved to intercept him. "Good morning, sir," the slave said politely. "Can I help you?"

"I'm here to see Citizen Ovidius," Cato answered. "He's building a dozen bed frames for me."

Like everyone else in the shop, Fidius was well aware of the Xeno Corps order because of its size and the short turnaround involved. So Fidius led Cato through a doorway and into the front office. It was a comfortable room, with windows that looked out onto the rain-slicked street, and a glowing potbellied stove. Ovidius was seated at a large, beautifully crafted desk, and when he turned, Cato saw the look of shock on the businessman's face. "It's that bad, is it?" he inquired. "I can't wait to see myself in the mirror."

Ovidius stood, offered Cato a chair, and sent for the local midwife. And while she worked to treat Cato's cuts, and reduce the swelling around his eye, a hot breakfast was summoned from the restaurant located two doors down the street. And much to Cato's surprise, he was hungry. Ovidius interpreted that as a good sign.

Some dry clothes summoned from a shop owned by one of Ovidius's cousins completed the rehabilitation effort, so that finally, when the dishes were cleared away, Cato was ready to tell Ovidius about the manner in which the man named Lorkin had not only been able to turn the bar patrons against him but steal his money as well.

"I know of the man," Ovidius admitted grimly. "He's a con artist, a gambler, and a thief. I blame myself for leaving you alone."

"Don't be silly," Cato replied wryly. "I not only *could* have left when you did, I *should* have left, but chose to stay. Worse yet, while I was buying beer for a roomfull of strangers, my team was being murdered in the desert! And, insofar as I can tell, the local authorities don't plan to investigate."

Ovidius wanted to know more. So Cato gave the businessman all of the information he had, and finished by saying, "I need to bury them—*and* find the bastards who are responsible. But the first step is to find Lorkin. He has my money, and I need it. Can you help?"

Ovidius was silent for a moment. Lorkin was a dangerous man. And it didn't make sense to offend dangerous men. Not without a very good reason. And, having lost the Xeno Corps order, Ovidius had no reason to help Cato. Other than to do what was right, which nearly always led to trouble! Ovidius sighed fatalistically. "I don't know where Lorkin is. . . . But I know people who can find out. Will you need anything else?"

"Yes," Cato replied thoughtfully. "I'm going to need a chair leg. A very *special* chair leg. Can you help me?"

Ovidius nodded soberly. "If you can describe it—we can make it."

"Good," Cato said, as he took a sip of caf. "Let's get to work."

The rain had stopped, the clouds had been blown off to the east by a persistent wind from the west, and the afternoon sun was beating down on The Warrens as if to make up for its recent absence. As the additional warmth teased moisture up out of the ground a shoulder-high blanket of mist appeared, so that as Bif Kregor stood guard in front of the boat shed a procession of seemingly disembodied heads floated past him. It was a sight that might have been of interest to an artist, but was completely lost on Kregor, who was mainly interested in money, sex, and power. Though not necessarily in that order.

Kregor was attentive, however, so when the cowled man appeared, the street tough took notice. Not that some old geezer in a ragged robe was of any concern to *him*. The bully frowned as the mist-clad man stopped a few feet away. "Keep moving, old man," Kregor said gruffly, "or I'll kick your ass down the street."

Cato reached up to push the hood back. That was when Kregor realized that the old man wasn't so old after all. Not that it made any difference because the amateur pugilist had won twenty-seven cage fights and lost only two. So there were very few men young or old who scared him—and that was visible in his eyes. They looked like chips of coal that someone had transplanted into caverns of fist-scarred flesh. A piece of tape was fastened across Kregor's nose, two days' worth of stubble covered a sizeable jaw, and if he had a neck, it was nowhere to be seen. The rest of the man was not only *big*, but exuded a male magnetism that scared men, and was generally attractive to women. Until he began to beat them, that is. "Good morning," Cato said lightly. "I'm a police officer. Would you be so kind as to step away from the door? I want to enter the building."

Kregor was so stunned by the other man's effrontery that when he worked his jaw no words came out. So, having been rendered speechless, the bully expressed himself the way he normally did, by launching an attack on the source of his frustration. That was the plan anyway, but Cato was already in motion by then, as was the twenty-four-inch-long "chair leg." It looked quite similar to a standard police baton, but the steel rod that had been inserted into the wooden shaft made the weapon heavier and, therefore, more dangerous. So as Kregor cocked a fist, preliminary to throwing a punch, Cato brought the nightstick up between Kregor's legs.

An expression of wonderment appeared on Kregor's face, quickly followed by a look of agony, as both hands went down to clutch at his genitals. That opened the bully to a head tap that not only took care of the pain he was experiencing but dropped Kregor onto the street. "Some people say I have a tendency to use excessive force," Cato said lightly, as he stepped over Kregor's unconscious body. "So don't forget to file a complaint. *If* you know how to write—which seems unlikely."

The door that Kregor had been hired to guard opened and swung closed. At that point Cato was inside the building where the man named Lorkin was said to be staying. The lower area consisted of a large room in which boats were repaired, or had been in the past, since there were no signs of recent activity. Cato could hear the gentle slapping sounds that the waves made as they broke against the pilings below, plus distant laughter, as he made his way over to a flight of stairs and began to climb. Would Lorkin be armed? Probably. With Cato's gun if nothing else. So his nerves were on edge, and he kept a tight grip on the baton as he made his way upward.

If Trev Lorkin had a virtue, it was his ability to live in the moment, without regard for whatever the future might bring. So having scored a significant hit the night before, the con man, gambler, and thief was busy enjoying his new-found wealth in the company of two rather shapely prostitutes. And the fact they were a mother-daughter team made the experience that much more enjoyable.

The ménage-à-trois was taking place on a mattress,

which, lacking a frame, had been placed on the floor. What light there was emanated from the cracks between the closely pulled blinds, more than a dozen candles that had been placed around the room, and three luminescent glow strips that dangled from the water-stained ceiling.

There was a steady slapping sound as flesh met flesh, which was accompanied by various oaths from Lorkin, and grunts of what might have been pleasure from the woman who was kneeling in front of him. The second female, who was naked except for a pair of red shoes, was busy trying to pleasure both of the principals while offering commentary from the sidelines.

So when Cato arrived at the top of the stairs, it soon became apparent that his target was fully engaged, and likely to remain so for the next few minutes. That gave Cato an opportunity to approach the table where two pistols lay, before the younger prostitute brought her head up, and took notice of the intruder. "Who the hell are *you*?" the whore wanted to know, as Lorkin turned to look as well.

"I'm a policeman," Cato replied honestly, as he traded the baton for the pistol that Lorkin had stolen from him. "And you are a very naughty girl. Fortunately for you, it's Citizen Lorkin that I'm interested in today. So grab your clothes, take your friend, and get out. *Now*."

The prostitute didn't believe that the man wearing the tattered robe was a policeman, but she knew he had a gun. And, judging from the businesslike manner in which the intruder had ejected the pistol's magazine and checked to ensure it was full, he knew how to use it. So she removed Lorkin's wallet from his pants as her mother rolled off the other side of the bed, and both women hurried to gather their clothes.

Lorkin's formerly erect penis had shriveled by then, but if the thief was embarrassed by that fact, there was no sign of it on his face as he eyed Cato. "So you survived," Lorkin said matter-of-factly, as he turned to let a pile of pillows accept his weight. "Congratulations."

"Thanks," Cato said dryly, as the prostitutes clattered down the stairs. "I came for my money. Where is it?"

"Gone," Lorkin replied calmly. "Once I left The Black Stocking, I went directly to an all-night card game, and having lost most of the money there, decided to party with the rest. Which is what I was doing when you arrived. Where's Kregor by the way? He was supposed to keep people like you out."

"Now that's an interesting point," Cato said thoughtfully. "Why would a person who doesn't have any money hire a guard? Tell me where the money is, and tell me now, or I'm going to shoot you in the right knee. A rather painful wound which, given the level of medical care available around here, could leave you crippled."

"That's bullshit," Lorkin replied contemptuously. "You're a cop. You said as much in The Black Stocking. So take me in. . . . I've been there before."

There was a loud *bang* as the gun went off—and the ten-millimeter bullet shattered Lorkin's kneecap. "I operate a little differently than most cops do," Cato explained patiently. "So listen up. Where is the money?"

A blood-splattered Lorkin hugged his badly pulped knee and moaned softly as he rocked back and forth. "It's over there," he said through tightly clenched teeth, "behind the mirror. I need a doctor!"

"You sure as hell do," Cato agreed unsympathetically. "And who knows? I might even send one to see you if the money is where you say it is." The pistol was still pointed at Lorkin, but in order to move the mirror, Cato had to turn his back for a moment. That was when Lorkin slid a hand under a pile of pillows, found what he was looking for, and pulled a sawed-off shotgun out into the open.

Cato wouldn't have been aware of the move if it hadn't

been for the mirror. But having seen Lorkin's reflection go for a weapon Cato had time to turn and squeeze off two shots as the shotgun blew a hole through the ceiling. There was a look of pained astonishment on Lorkin's face as two blue-edged holes appeared in the middle of his chest, and plaster rained down on him from above.

"That was a stupid thing to do," Cato said conversationally, as the body toppled over sideways. "But who said you were smart?"

Fortunately, the money belt *was* concealed in a nook behind the mirror, along with the rest of Lorkin's loot, which meant that Cato was able to recover the Corps's money with some interest thrown in.

When he had secured the money belt around his waist, and filled his pockets with coins, it was time to recover the spent casings and leave through the front door. The street tough was gone, as was the mist, leaving The Warrens to bake in the sun. One of the city's predators had been killed; but just a block away, another one was about to be born.

The sandal factory consisted of a long, low, one-story building tucked in between a noisy junkyard and an odiferous tallow plant. Small cubicles lined the interior walls, each with its own window, so that the sandal makers could see what they were doing. Not that veterans like seventeen-year-old CeCe Alamy needed to see what they were working on because after a year and a half in the factory, the young woman could have assembled sandals blindfolded had she been asked to.

The process of pulling straps through small holes, and hand stitching soles that incorporated three layers of material was hard on Alamy's hands, which were callused and covered with tiny cuts. The fumes from the glue that the sandal makers were required to use were toxic as well, which was why so many of them were sick, and had a tendency to die young.

But there weren't very many jobs in The Warrens, not for young, poorly educated girls like Alamy, so the youngster had been forced to take the only work she could find when her father took sick two years earlier. One decim for each pair of finished sandals wasn't much, but the steady flow of square coins had been helpful during the final months of Roj Alamy's life, as the formerly robust blacksmith lay dying on his bed. And now that he was gone, having left his second wife and daughter behind, Alamy continued to help support the household. Something she was proud to do.

But the days were long, frequently hot, and consistently tedious. So when the bell rang, Alamy was happy to put a half-stitched sandal aside and carry the basket of finished footwear to the front desk, where the owner's sharp-eyed wife inspected each pair of sandals prior to paying for them. And, because Alamy's work was consistently good, all ten pairs of sandals were approved. The accomplishment earned the teenager an approving smile plus one Imperial, which Alamy hurried to tuck away.

Then, when she had exited the building, it was time to make her way home, where all of the usual chores were waiting. At least half of them had originally been her stepmother's responsibility but had gradually been delegated to Alamy after her father's death. That was part of a larger pattern, because the moment Domna Alamy had legal ownership of her dead husband's possessions, she'd been quick to sell his tools and bring in a male "boarder" who never paid rent.

The arrangement was far from fair, Alamy knew that; but she had plans to leave on her eighteenth birthday, when she would become an adult and a Citizen of the Empire. Then, with the money earned as a sandal maker, it was Alamy's hope to buy an apprenticeship as part of a plan to become a dressmaker.

Such were Alamy's dreams as she turned off Market Street onto a narrow passageway that led into the metalsmith's quarter, where the clatter of hammers, the screech of power wrenches, and the rattle of rivet guns combined to create a familiar din. The Alamy home was five blocks back. It consisted of a ground-level shop, presently being leased by a coppersmith, second-floor living quarters, and a rooftop garden that had once been Roj Alamy's pride and joy, but was presently turning brown as a result of Domna's systematic neglect.

Still, the whitewashed structure was home, and Alamy was happy to see it as she waved to the coppersmith and ran up a long flight of stairs to the second-floor entrance. It was cooler inside, thanks to the solar-powered ceiling fan that Roj Alamy had cobbled together for the living room, and that was where Domna and her guest were seated.

Domna had been pretty once, but that was many years in the past. Now her hair was dyed an unlikely shade of brown, dark lines were drawn in where her overplucked eyebrows had once been, and an excessive amount of red lipstick had been applied to her mouth in a vain attempt to make her lips appear fuller. But Domna could be charming when she chose to be—and was quick to introduce her visitor. "This is Citizen Mortha, CeCe. He's been looking forward to meeting you! But, before we get into that, how many sandals did you make today?"

"Ten," Alamy answered proudly, and produced the Imperial to prove it.

"You see?" Domna said, as her plump fingers reached out to pluck the coin from the girl's hand. "It's just as I told you. . . . CeCe's a hard worker—and that should be worth something."

"It is," Mortha allowed indulgently. "It certainly is. But, if you don't mind my saying so, I suspect she'll spend quite a bit of time lying down on the job!"

It was a wonderful joke, or that's what Domna thought anyway, and she laughed uproariously as Alamy felt liquid lead trickle into the pit of her stomach. Mortha had shoulder-length white hair, a long, heavily lined face, and a sturdy body that was clothed in what the girl knew to be expensive fabric. Mortha's calves were visible, however, as were his scrupulously clean feet, both of which were shod in the same type of sandals Alamy had been manufacturing earlier that day. "What do you mean?" the girl inquired anxiously, as she looked from face to face.

Domna had been laughing so hard mascara-blackened tears had carved twin pathways down along her heavily rouged cheeks. She dabbed at the tears with a handkerchief before answering. "Citizen Mortha and I have finalized an agreement," the older woman replied importantly. "He's going to put you up for sale the day after tomorrow. And, if all goes well, I should receive around a thousand Imperials. Minus Citizen Mortha's commission, of course, but a significant sum nevertheless. And a good deal better than one Imperial a day!"

"But you *can't* sell me!" Alamy objected desperately. "My father was free, and I'll be free on my eighteenth birthday!"

"Which is still more than a month away," Domna reminded her sternly. "And until that time, you are my property. . . . To do with as I see fit. And it's my intention to sell you! So skip the tears, spare me the drama you're so fond of, and concentrate on pleasing your new owner. Who knows? Maybe you'll *enjoy* your new line of work!"

That produced another gale of laughter, which Alamy saw as her opportunity to escape, so she ran for the door. Domna couldn't sell something she didn't have, so if the girl could hide in The Warrens until her birthday rolled around, she could claim Imperial citizenship thereafter! Would the local magistrate support that claim? Or side with her stepmother? Alamy didn't know, but figured that some chance was better than none, as she ran down the front steps toward the street.

But Citizen Mortha had anticipated such a possibility, and two burly slave handlers were waiting to grab Alamy and secure her hands behind her. Then, once an iron collar had been secured around Alamy's neck, a single pull on the six-foot-long chain was sufficient to jerk her off her feet. A demonstration *all* slaves were subjected to as a way to communicate how helpless they were.

So there was nothing Alamy could do but lie there and sob, until Citizen Mortha emerged from the house five minutes later. Then, with his newest consignment in tow, the trader led Alamy through the neighborhood she'd grown up in toward Market Street and the slave pens located north of the slaughterhouse.

Alamy looked back over her shoulder at one point, in hopes that Domna might change her mind, but the older woman was nowhere to be seen. The coppersmith was visible though—and he was the only person to wave.

FIVE

The Plain of Pain, on the planet Dantha

THE SKIMMER HAD A CRACKED WINDSHIELD, HANDLE-
bars rather than a steering wheel, and was capable of carrying
two people with one seated in front of the other. Hot desert
air pressed against Cato's face as the vehicle's cranky engine
propelled it across the desert toward Station 3. Like the rest
of the vehicles on Dantha, the EX-9 had been manufactured
off-planet and shipped in. That made the beat-up skimmer
valuable, even after fifteen years of hard service, which was
why Cato had been forced to spend 556 Imperials on it. It
wasn't the way Cato had wanted to spend a large chunk of
his remaining cash, but that was the way he'd had to spend
it, since the planetary government was unwilling to provide
him with any support.

Was the lack of cooperation on the part of Nalomy's government the result of the hostility that many rim worlders
felt toward the Xeno Corps? Or did Centurion Pasayo and
the people around him know more about the massacre than
they cared to admit? There wasn't any evidence of governmental involvement yet, but Cato was determined to remain

alert to that possibility, as a dark smudge appeared on the shimmery horizon.

Of course there had been other smudges over the last hour, all of which eventually morphed into rock formations, but thanks to the amount of distance Cato had traveled, he knew this one could be Station 3. The prospect opened up a chasm at the pit of his stomach because of what awaited him there. Especially after days in the hot desert sun.

Fifteen minutes later it became clear that Cato's journey was nearly over as the last smudge resolved itself into the now-familiar outlines of Station 3 and the defensive wall that surrounded it. A wall which, though not entirely intact, should have been sufficient to keep attackers out. Yet it hadn't been. *Why?*

With that question foremost in his mind, Cato reduced power and put the skimmer into a wide turn, so he could examine the surrounding area for telltale tracks. But as Cato circled the station, no footprints or vehicle tracks were visible. That wasn't too surprising, however, given both the scouring action of the wind and the amount of time that had elapsed since the murders.

Confident that he hadn't missed anything, and reluctant to ride the skimmer into the middle of a murder scene, Cato brought the vehicle to a stop. The machine wallowed from side to side as it settled onto the sand, and the hot metal began to make pinging noises as it cooled. Cato was wearing his sidearm in a cross-draw holster, but because the empath could "feel" a second presence in the area, it seemed prudent to carry a weapon with more clout. So Cato removed the secondhand combat-style pump gun from its scabbard and carried the weapon one-handed as he made his way across the sand-drifted hardpan toward the fortresslike structure beyond. A hot breeze slid in from the west and brought the formerly limp Xeno Corps flag back to momentary life as two dozen stink birds exploded up out of the enclosure and circled above.

The freshly repaired gate was wide open, but that didn't mean much, since it had probably been left that way by the prospectors who called the murders in. As Cato passed through the opening, he was greeted by the throat-clogging stench of rotting flesh. He had encountered the odor in the past, but never as strong, and never in connection with people he had known.

The first body Cato came across was that of Officer Kath Larsy. She was lying just outside the main entrance to the building, and it didn't take a medical degree to figure out that she'd been killed by multiple energy bolts to the chest. Larsy's once-shapely body was swollen by internal gases, and because her face had been made unrecognizable by scavengers, Cato would have been unable to positively identify the body had it not been for the name tag sewn to her uniform.

The way Larsy looked, combined with the way she smelled, brought Cato's breakfast up. He turned, walked a few feet away, and threw up. Then, having rinsed his mouth with water from his canteen, he made a conscious effort to enter the neutral-observer mode, and went back to work.

After removing the camcorder from a cargo pocket, and clipping a wireless mike to his body armor, Cato began to narrate the video as he shot it. "Judging from the stains visible around Officer Larsy's corpse, it looks as though the body is where it was at the moment of death, lying faceup in front of the main entrance to the building. That, plus the entry wounds on the front of her body, suggest that the fatal blaster bolts originated from *inside* Station 3. If true, it would indicate that the prisoner got loose somehow, or that a person or persons unknown were allowed to enter the building. A third, but less likely scenario, would be some sort of disagreement that resulted in a firefight between members of the team."

Having examined Larsy's body, Cato pushed the door open, and was nearly overwhelmed by the stench that awaited him within. It was so bad that he was forced to back away and wait for the smell to dissipate before trying again.

Based on the strength of the input from his sixth sense, Cato knew that while the "other" presence was still in the area, he, she, or it was a long ways off. So rather than take the shotgun with him, he left the weapon propped just inside the door as he reentered the building.

Once inside, the first thing Cato noticed was the blaster burns on the inside surface of the front door. He brought the camcorder up to document the scorch marks while resuming the narration. "The burns visible on the inside surface of the door seem to support the thesis that the person or persons who shot Officer Larsy were already inside the building when they opened fire," Cato said grimly.

Then, having noticed the bloodstains near his feet, Cato tilted the camera down. "Here, just inside the front door, is what appears to be a large quantity of dried blood. And, given the absence of a body or bodies at this particular location, there is a distinct possibility that one or more of the intruders were wounded or killed and removed from the crime scene subsequent to a firefight. That theory will be confirmed," Cato continued, "if I can account for the rest of the team members."

The next thing that caught Cato's attention was the glaring absence of both Fiss Verafti *and* his containment. "The prisoner's cage was located right *here*," Cato commented grimly, as the camcorder's light panned a section of empty floor. "And it's missing, which would seem to suggest that rather than escaping on his own, Verafti was *freed*. Or if not freed, then removed to another location, cell and all! If that is true, it raises the question of *why*, given how dangerous the prisoner is, not to mention *how* since the cage is large and heavy."

But Cato knew that, fascinating as such questions might be, they would have to wait while he examined the rest of the crime scene. The nauseating task required him to cut fluid-soaked sleeping bags open in order to identify the bloated bodies cocooned within, then poke and prod at three rotting corpses to determine which ones were which.

Finally, having positively identified Tonver, Batia, and Honis, Cato allowed himself to go back outside, both to get some fresh air—and to find more bodies. For, assuming his preliminary identifications were correct, both Sivio and Moshath were missing.

It was midafternoon by that time, the sky was clear, and Cato could feel the heat that came off the stone stairs through the soles of his boots as he climbed onto the wall and paused to look around. It was quiet, almost eerily so, with nothing more than an occasional rumble of wind to break the near-perfect silence. But even though Cato couldn't hear anything, he could "feel" the same presence that had been evident earlier in the day, and knew he was under surveillance.

So Cato opened a pouch, removed a small but powerful pair of binos, and began a painstaking sweep of the horizon. At first there was nothing to see other than the shimmer of a distant mirage, but the moment Cato tilted the glasses upward, he spotted what looked like a black cross circling high above. Except that the object wasn't a cross but a living being, and far too large to be a bird.

Having seen them on other planets, Cato was fairly sure that the airborne creature was a Lir. This was sufficient to remind Cato of what Pasayo had volunteered back in Solace, that the massacre might have been carried out by Lir bandits. The theory made quite a bit of sense since the team had been largely unprepared for an attack from above.

But what about Verafti and his cage? Both were far too heavy for the Lir to fly away with, unless they had some sort of transport, and where would a group of bandits obtain something like that? And who would put them up to such a thing since it was hard to imagine how the Lir would profit from such an abduction?

Still, the presence of a Lir scout seemed to suggest that the mountain dwellers had some sort of interest in Station 3, otherwise, why keep it under observation? So Cato put the binos away and continued along the walkway until he came to what he immediately recognized as Sivio's red caf mug. It was sitting on top of the outside wall.

The sight of the common everyday object brought a lump to Cato's throat, and he wasn't surprised to see the body lying about ten feet beyond, right next to a service-issue flashlight. Unlike the corpses Cato had inspected earlier, Sivio's body had been subjected to direct sunlight and nearly nonstop feeding by stink birds for the better part of four days. As a result, very little remained except for an eyeless skull to which a few tufts of hair still adhered—and a skeleton that was largely lost inside a puddle of beak-ripped clothes. But the mug, plus the silver comets on Sivio's body armor, left little doubt as to who the dead man was.

Farther on, Cato found the remains of Moshath's body as well as his severed head. It had been picked clean by the birds and seemed to grin at Cato from where it lay on the walkway. "It appears that Moshath was on sentry duty," Cato said for the camcorder's benefit, "when he was taken by surprise. Quite possibly from above.

"Judging from the presence of Sivio's caf mug," Cato added, "it's my guess that he was out making the rounds when the intruders killed him as well. All of the team's weapons are missing, so there's no way to know if Sivio and Moshath were able to fight back, but it seems unlikely since the sound of gunshots would have brought the rest of the team out of the main building on the double." It was a sad commentary, and one that Cato was happy to conclude, as he made his way down off the wall.

The sun had started to set by then, and the air was beginning to cool, so Cato went out to bring the skimmer into the compound. With that accomplished, it was time to light a fuel tab and cook a simple meal as stars began to appear in the lavender sky. Cato couldn't see the Lir spy anymore, but he could "feel" an alien presence, although the emanations had a different quality by then. As if another Lir had arrived to relieve the bandit spotted earlier that day. Not that it made much difference since Cato had a lot of work to do and lacked the means to blow the winged sentient out of the sky. Something he would have enjoyed had it been possible.

Cato was tired by that time, *very* tired, but couldn't bear the thought of leaving his friends unburied during another long, hot day. So that, plus the knowledge that it would be easier to dig graves at night, combined to send him out to the rise where he planned to bury his teammates. It was the beginning of a long, often frustrating, night. Because it wasn't long before Cato discovered that while the surrounding hardpan was impossibly resistant to his shovel, the occasional pockets of windblown sand were *too* loose, thereby causing every hole he dug to cave in.

Finally, in a fit of what amounted to an act of desperation, Cato returned to Station 3 and went looking for lumber. Then, when he had stacked a quantity of it near the front gate, it was time to carry the boards out to the lee side of the small hillock.

Once the necessary materials were on-site, the blob of light produced by Cato's headlamp wandered left and right as he went about the lonely task of constructing an enclosure large enough to contain nearly a dozen bodies laid side by side. Though time-consuming, that effort went well, so that by the time a long horizontal smear of pink light lit the eastern horizon, Cato was towing the last body out to the burial site on what had been Station 3's front door. Silence closed around the Xeno cop as he shut the engine down, removed

Sivio's remains from the makeshift sled, and gently placed them to the left of the other team members in the location where the Centurion would normally stand had he and the other team members been in formation.

With the first rays of the morning sun spiking up over the Sawtooth Mountains, Section Leader Jak Cato came to rigid attention. "I don't know if you're out there, God," Cato said frankly, as the Lir spy circled in the distance. "Or if you would be willing to listen to a person like me . . . But these men and women are members of the Xeno Corps—and they were killed trying to protect other people from harm. So if there *is* a heaven, then assign them to guard the gates, knowing you won't find any who are better. Meanwhile," Cato added grimly, "you might want to notify the devil, because I plan to send whoever killed my team straight to hell."

The salute was parade-ground perfect, and as Cato held it, tears began to trickle down his stubble-covered cheeks. "I'm sorry, sir," Cato said as he looked down at what remained of Sivio. "I wasn't here when you needed me, I failed to carry out your orders successfully, and I broke my word. But I swear I'll make it up to you—no matter what that requires."

There was no reply, and there *couldn't* be any reply, as Cato dropped his arm and turned to grab a shovel. Thanks to the enclosure, which served to hold the sand in place, Cato was able to fill the newly constructed box fairly quickly, so that by the time the sun rose above distant mountain peaks, he was running the team's flag up an improvised pole. An early-morning breeze found the piece of fabric, caused it to pop open, and held the flag straight out.

Having completed his task, Cato drove the skimmer back into Station 3's enclosure, went looking for a spot that would remain in the shade for the balance of the morning, and threw his bedroll onto the ground. He was asleep three minutes later, something the Lir spy soon took notice of as his shadow caressed the fortress, and he prepared to land.

The city of Solace, on the planet Dantha

Having just returned from a trip to the city of Comfort, which was located on the opposite side of the planet, Nalomy was still clad in her travel clothes as she stepped into the palace elevator. Imood Hingo pressed the button for the third subbasement, and both felt a slight jerk as the platform began to descend. Though originally intended as a bomb shelter, to which the Emperor could retreat should Dantha be attacked while he was in residence, the underground facility was the perfect place to keep a prisoner like Fiss Verafti. For had he been allowed to escape, he would have cut through Nalomy's troops like a hot knife through butter.

The platform coasted to a stop, the stainless-steel doors hissed open and Nalomy felt warm, humid air embrace her body as she stepped out into a small, utilitarian lobby. From there it was a short walk to Storage Room 3B13, where Verafti was being held. Four heavily armed guards were posted outside—each of whom was wearing a tamperproof ID bracelet. All came to attention as Nalomy approached, and extended their right arms, so Hingo could pass a reader over their bracelets. Then, having confirmed their identities, Hingo bowed. "Everything is as it should be, Highness," he intoned. "It's safe to enter."

Nalomy wasn't entirely sure of that, but she knew the being she was about to interact with could sense what she felt, and sought to push her fears aside. "Excellent. . . . Is the technician present? Good. . . . Open the door."

Hingo went over to the control kiosk and took a careful look at the monitor that was set into the pedestal's surface. A ceiling-mounted camera showed the cage, the reptilian prisoner housed inside of it, and the uniformed technician, who was busy cutting through one of the sturdy bars. He was wearing protective goggles, and as the plasma torch cut through durasteel, a six-inch length of metal hit the floor. It made a ringing noise, and the hot end continued to glow as Hingo pressed the OPEN button.

Servos whined as the blastproof doors parted company, and a wave of slightly rank air washed over Nalomy. Was that the way the Sagathi actually smelled? Or was it the odor of the meat he insisted on—some of which had started to rot? Not that it mattered so long as Verafti did what she wanted him to do. . . . Which was to assassinate Legate Isulu Usurlus.

Confident that she had the upper hand, Nalomy entered the room, but stopped well short of the cage. "Good evening," she said politely. "My name is Nalomy. *Procurator* Nalomy . . . And I'm here to talk about freedom. *Your* freedom if you agree to my proposal."

There was a long moment of silence as their eyes met. Verafti's orbs were yellow, with space-black pupils, and they stared at the Uman as if able to see right through her. Finally, with the slight sibilance typical of his kind, Verafti spoke. His voice was deep and commanding. "I can feel your hunger," the Sagathi said. "It burns like a flame. . . . You want to control *everything*. . . . But the more power you have, the more you want, which means your hunger can never be sated."

Nalomy felt her stomach lurch. Not because she was afraid of Verafti, but because of the ease with which the empath had been able to penetrate the very core of her being. Nalomy's mouth was dry, her heart beating faster, and she was intensely aware of the fact that Hingo and the technician were present. "We aren't here to discuss me," the Procurator said coolly, "we're here to discuss *you*. And the possibility of freedom."

"Though not an empath, you have an excellent appreciation of what I want most," Verafti admitted gravely. "What must I do to earn my freedom?"

There was a metallic *clang* as the last length of durasteel hit the concrete floor and began to cool. "You can leave," Nalomy said, as the technician removed his goggles. "And that goes for you as well," Nalomy said, as she turned to direct a glance at Hingo.

Hingo didn't want to leave, not because of a concern for Nalomy's personal safety, but because the conversation between the Procurator and the prisoner had been quite interesting up until that point. Especially the part about the young woman's motivations. But an order was an order, which left Hingo with no choice except to bow and back toward the door.

Once the others had left, Nalomy turned back toward the cage. Hingo, who was standing in front of the control kiosk by that time, pulled a wireless headset on over his bare scalp. Not because it was his duty to do so but because knowledge equals power, and if there was one thing that the Major-domo and his mistress had in common, it was a desire to control those around him.

Having cleared the room, Nalomy eyed her prisoner. And, as if to demonstrate what he was capable of, Verafti morphed into an exact likeness of Centurion Sivio. Sans clothes, that is, which might have caused another woman to look away, but brought a wry smile to Nalomy's lips. "That's very impressive," she said, leaving it unclear as to whether she was referring to the Uman's physique, or Verafti's ability to imitate it.

"Thank you," the Sagathi replied politely. "Now, whom do you want me to kill?"

The tone was such that it felt as though Verafti was taking charge of the situation and Nalomy didn't care for that. "Don't be presumptuous," she said sternly.

"I'm not," Verafti countered loftily. "I'm being *logical*. Killing people is what I do best. . . . So it seems safe to assume that's why you brought me here."

"There is that I suppose," Nalomy allowed reluctantly. "Here's the situation. . . . Legate Isulu Usurlus will arrive on Dantha a few days from now, and I want him dead."

"Done," the Sagathi said agreeably. "Now, if you'd be so kind as to unlock my cage, I'd like to stretch my legs."

"Aren't you going to ask *why* I want him dead?" Nalomy inquired curiously.

"No," Verafti responded. "I'm sure you have your reasons—and that's good enough for me. So, let me out, and we can discuss the details of how the assassination will be carried out while we take a stroll."

"I will," Nalomy assured him, "after I fasten this metal band around your wrist." So saying, the official went over to a waist-high pedestal, removed a mutable durasteel bracelet from its box, and turned to face Verafti.

"What is it?" Verafti demanded suspiciously.

"It's a remotely controlled explosive device," Nalomy answered sweetly. "Surely you didn't expect me to release you without putting some safeguards in place? I will carry a remote control, as will my Majordomo, and a third individual who will remain anonymous. Should you violate our agreement, or kill someone other than Usurlus, any one of us will have the ability to blow your right hand off."

"I don't like it," Verafti objected, as he morphed into his true form.

"Then remain in your cage," Nalomy suggested. "And

I'll ship you to Sagatha, where the Xeno Corps will put you on trial."

"I could tell them what you wanted me to do," Verafti said ominously.

"It would be your word against mine," Nalomy countered coolly. "And I think you know who they would believe! Or, you might be shot while trying to escape, which would be unfortunate to say the least. Those are your options. . . . So what's it going to be?"

There was a long moment of silence, followed by a sudden transformation as the shape shifter morphed into a likeness of Nalomy who, like his impersonation of Sivio, was naked.

"My breasts are larger than that," Nalomy observed clinically.

Verafti made the necessary adjustment and Nalomy smiled. "That's better! Now, go over and stick your left arm through the hole."

Verafti did as he was told, which allowed Nalomy to place the explosive bracelet on what looked like her own wrist, before backing away. He felt the metal band contract and heard a series of *click*s as the device locked itself in place, followed by a sustained *beep* when the built-in transmitter came online.

The pendant hanging around Nalomy's neck beeped in sympathy, indicating that the remote was working. "Hingo, I know you're watching," Nalomy said tartly, as she looked up into a camera. "So come in and open the cage."

Hingo swore softly, pressed the button that controlled the storeroom door, and went inside. Five minutes later, Nalomy, Hingo, and a man who looked exactly like Centurion Ben Sivio entered the elevator together. An assassin was on the loose.

*   *   *

The Plain of Pain, on the planet Dantha

It was early afternoon by the time Cato awoke, feeling hot, sore, and somewhat groggy. But the pump was still operational, as was the outdoor shower, so he was able to cool down and clean up at the same time.

Finally, after a shamefully long shower, Cato patted himself dry before getting dressed again. The plan was to pack his gear, return to the city of Solace, and look for a way off Dantha. Then, with two or three hundred legionnaires for backup, Cato planned to come back and scour the surface of the planet until he found Verafti. Because if anyone could tell him who was responsible for the massacre, it was Verafti. He represented a threat to everyone on Dantha and would have to be retaken regardless of cost.

That was the plan anyway, but when Cato went to the skimmer in order to place some of his belongings in the vehicle's saddlebags, everything changed. The venerable EX-9 looked normal enough from a distance, but once Cato came close, the damage was obvious. Someone, the Lir spy being the most likely candidate, had fired an energy bolt into the engine compartment! *And* the com set.

Cato swore, fumbled for the binos, and brought them up to his eyes. It took about thirty seconds to locate the slowly circling spy. In retrospect the decision to leave the skimmer out in the open where the Lir could fire at it was unforgivably stupid. Although fatigue had certainly been a factor, as had the fact that the Lir had kept their distance up until then.

But why not me? Cato wondered. *Why disable the skimmer yet leave me alive?*

Because the bastards want to see you suffer, came the answer. If so, their plan stood a good chance of success; his com set had been transformed into a piece of junk, and the nearest settlement was a long ways off. So far away that he might not survive the trek. But *why*? Who would want him dead? The same people who killed Sivio, Larsy, and the rest of the team. That was who.

And difficult though it was obviously going to be, Cato was left with no choice but to cross the desert on foot. Because, while there was a pretty good chance that another party of prospectors would eventually stop at Station 3, it might be weeks or even months before they did so.

The logical thing to do was travel at night, when it was cooler, so Cato spent the balance of the day gathering items he would need and strapping them to an improvised pack frame. The main problem was water and the fact that each gallon of the precious liquid weighed more than eight pounds. This effectively limited what water he could reasonably carry to about four gallons, or thirty-two pounds, because it was going to be necessary to carry food as well. Not to mention weapons and ammo, both of which were heavy as sin.

But there was no getting around it, so once darkness fell, it was time to shoulder the pack and pay one last visit to his teammates, before beginning what promised to be a long, hard walk. Cato had a headlamp, but rather than use it and thereby reveal his position to the Lir spies, he chose to proceed with nothing more than starlight to illuminate the desert. That strategy worked fairly well since most of the terrain was flat.

There were dry riverbeds to cross, not to mention wind-cut rock formations that rose to block the way, and plenty of treacherous dunes. All of them caused accidents; some were quite painful, not to mention frightening. Because Cato knew that if he broke a leg, or suffered some other form of catastrophic injury, it would only be a matter of days before he died of exposure.

After every fall, Cato forced himself to get back up and march on until the gradually rising sun began to backlight the mountain peaks to the east, and he knew it was time to seek shelter. Only there wasn't anywhere to hide at that particular moment, so he was forced to continue for another hour and a half, before finally arriving in front of an island of upthrust rock.

The sun had cleared the mountaintops by that time, and it was already quite warm, as Cato paused to take a swig of lukewarm water. Then, when his thirst had been quenched, he set off to circumnavigate the huge chunk of rock in hopes of finding a cave, or failing that, a shady recess that would offer at least some protection from the sun *and* the Lir spy who circled above.

There were two false alarms, each of which required Cato to expend precious ergs of energy, only to discover that neither crevice was big enough to accommodate both him and his gear. A *third* opening, however, led to a cavern large enough for three people. Cato subjected it to a bombardment of fist-sized rocks calculated to drive current residents out. But if the recess had been home to hostile life-forms there was no sign of them as he pushed his pack through a narrow opening and crawled inside.

It was definitely cooler inside the cave, but the air grew steadily warmer as the sun continued to rise, forcing Cato to consume more water. The heat made it difficult to sleep; but after eating some cold rations, Cato was eventually able to doze off. However, the knowledge that the Lir were watching him fostered bad dreams, and when the heat caused a rock to explode, Cato awoke with gun in hand, his heart racing out of control.

So Cato was tired by the time he set off that evening, and even though his pack was lighter because of the water he'd been forced to consume, it felt just as heavy. But there was nothing he could do except put one foot in front of the other, concentrate on his goal, and check his luminescent compass from time to time. It would have been easy to lose his way as a bank of clouds swept in to obscure the stars, and the night grew even darker.

It was cold. *Very* cold. Cato stopped for a quick brew-up at 0200. The hot caf felt good as it trickled into his stomach and that, plus a chewy ration bar, kept Cato going until the eastern sky began to brighten a bit. Then it was time to look for a hole to crawl into, except there weren't any rock formations in the area, making it necessary to seek some other form of shelter. As Cato skidded down into a dry riverbed, he knew that seasonal floods could have carved one or more caves into the bank. Sleeping in such a recess was dangerous because a serious rainstorm in the mountains could send a wall of water rushing down the formerly bone-dry channel to sweep him away. That was a chance he'd have to take if he wanted shelter from the sun.

It took the better part of twenty minutes to find a spot where the river had undercut the bank—but not so severely as to suggest an imminent collapse. By stacking loose rocks to form a three-foot-high wall opposite the bank, Cato was able to create a well-shaded recess that would provide shelter from the sun until early afternoon. It wasn't perfect, since he'd be driven out of his hidey-hole during the worst heat of the day, but a lot better than nothing.

So Cato ate cold rations, washed them down with a mug of precious water, and lay down to sleep. It was still cold, and the ground was hard, but sleep came quickly.

Having lost more than three hundred feet of altitude, Nor Issit had little choice but to flap his wings and begin another sweeping turn. There was no way to know exactly where the next thermal would be, so all the Lir could do was hope for the best, knowing that without the columns of rising air, he wouldn't have the strength to remain aloft until a warrior was sent to relieve him. And being forced to the ground could be disastrous, because, although Issit was graceful in the air, the Uman could outmaneuver him on the planet's surface.

So Issit continued to fight his way upward, giving thanks to the Air God when he felt warm air push up against his widespread wings, and he was suddenly borne upward, as if by an invisible hand. Then with wings spread wide, all Issit had to do was stay inside the column of rising air and eye the wasteland below.

Issit knew that the Uman had taken refuge in a riverbed some six hours earlier. But now, as the sun began to drop into the western sky, the temperature inside the alien's hidey-hole was steadily rising. So Issit was anything but surprised when the Uman appeared ten minutes later, scrambled up out of the dry riverbed, and began to walk.

Issit's cross-shaped shadow seemed to slide across the surface of the rocky desert as the warrior followed behind. It was boring work, so the bandit invented a game to amuse himself. The objective was to position the Uman directly under his shadow, so that the X-shaped pattern looked like a set of crosshairs, floating on top of the target below.

That was what Issit was doing when the Uman stumbled and fell. This was a first so far as Issit knew, and raised the possibility that the alien had begun to weaken. But no sooner had that thought crossed Issit's mind than the Uman was back on his feet, swaying from side to side. He had a piece of fabric wound around his head to protect him from the sun, and could be seen taking a long drink of water, before tossing a presumably empty canteen away.

As the Uman resumed his march, Issit saw the shotgun and a bandolier of ammunition hit the ground. The meaning was obvious. The Xeno freak was growing tired, *too* tired to carry any extra weight, and would soon succumb. The thought produced a sense of fierce exultation in the bandit as he continued to circle above. Because although there were those who wanted the Uman dead, they wanted him to die what would look like a natural death if possible. This was why he'd been deprived of transportation and forced into the desert.

The day wore on. During the following hour, Issit saw the Uman fall on two occasions. He got up each time, but with increasing difficulty, as the heat took its inevitable toll. And, after the second fall, the alien set off in the wrong direction! Walking *toward* the sun rather than away from it. Eventually, having tumbled down a steep slope onto a section of reddish orange hardpan, the variant lay motionless on the ground.

Five minutes passed. Then ten minutes, as Issit spiraled slowly downward, coming ever closer to the hostile ground. Finally, certain that his quarry was dead, or incapacitated, Issit came in for a landing. Having drawn his energy pistol from a shoulder holster, he approached the body. Partly because it was his duty to confirm the Uman's painful death, but also to rifle through his pockets, just in case the alien was carrying some loose change. Because anything that Issit could steal, and subsequently hide away, wouldn't have to be shared with the rest of the flock.

So with his pistol at the ready, and his heart beating just a little bit faster, Issit knelt next to the Uman's left shoulder. Then, with the fingers of his free hand, he began to explore the alien corpse.

Cato felt light-headed; even though the fall had been staged, the symptoms of heat prostration were quite real. He was not entirely out of water, but because he wanted the Lir to *believe* that he was, he couldn't take a drink as long as the bandit was circling above. So, with the birdlike sentient only inches away, it was time to execute the final step of his plan, assuming he had the strength to do so.

*   *   *

Issit's clawlike fingers found the money belt, and having correctly deduced what the object was, the Lir was overcome by greed. In order to remove the belt Issit knew he would need both hands, so he put the pistol down on the ground next to him, and went to work on the recalcitrant buckle. That was why both of Issit's hands were busy when Cato opened his eyes and made a two-handed grab for the Lir's neck!

Head swimming, Cato rolled to the right and took Issit with him. The warrior fought back, but rather than going for his knife as he should have, Issit made a futile attempt to break the grip around his throat. However, thanks to the fact that Cato was more than twice as heavy, he soon took control.

Having pinned both of the Lir's skinny arms under his knees, Cato was able to release the bandit's windpipe, take possession of the energy pistol, and press it against the warrior's skull. Cato's right leg was beginning to cramp by then, but he forced himself to ignore the pain, as he spoke through clenched teeth. "Do you want to live? If so, do exactly as I say."

The Lir's eyes were huge, and Cato could not only see the hatred in them, but "feel" the animosity that seethed around him. But Issit had a strong desire to live, so he had little choice but to nod, and wait to find out what the fates had in store for him.

"Good," Cato said wearily. Now listen carefully. Because I won't tell you twice."

It took the better part of fifteen minutes to secure both of Issit's wings and his arms, prior to marching the Lir back toward the riverbank cave where Cato had slept the night before. During the hour-long walk, Cato worked to rehydrate himself with tiny sips of warm water—while pausing occasionally to collect the gear he had discarded along the way. Then, having forced Issit down into the dry riverbed, he led him to the cave. Not surprisingly, the gear he had left behind was still there, including a full gallon of water, which wouldn't go as far with two bodies to hydrate.

Still, there were advantages to having a prisoner, not the least of which was the opportunity to rest while Issit stacked some additional rocks on the outside wall. Because within the next hour or so Cato knew that another Lir would arrive and discover that the warrior he was supposed to relieve was missing.

That would trigger a search that could last for days. Although he was hoping for something less. Meanwhile, as the Uman and the Lir spent some quality time together, Cato was going to interrogate Issit. Who, if he was smart, would reveal everything he knew regarding the massacre at Station 3. And if he *wasn't* smart? That prospect brought a grin to Cato's sunburned face. Cato had questions, and one way or another, Issit was going to provide some much-needed answers.

SIX

The city of Solace, on the planet Dantha

IT WAS JUST AFTER NOON, THE SUN COULD BE SEEN through occasional breaks in the clouds, and a crowd had begun to form in front of the wooden platform commonly referred to as "the block." At the moment there was nothing for people to look at other than what amounted to an empty stage and the wooden backdrop that stood behind it which was covered by a surprisingly well-executed mural. The painting depicted a group of well-dressed slaves living in apparent luxury on an imaginary estate.

But that was of little interest to the townsfolk gathered in front of the platform, most of whom couldn't afford to buy a slave, but were looking forward to enjoying some free entertainment. Because miserable though their own lives might be, most of the onlookers were *free*—which meant they were better off than those about to be sold. And it felt good to be better off than someone else even if the difference was more conceptual than real.

And there were other reasons to attend the slave auction as well, especially for those who enjoyed seeing people without any clothes on. That explained why so many teenaged boys were lurking about. Men armed with thin whips were paid to drive gawkers away, but the boys saw that as part of the fun, and took a perverse pride in how many welts they could accumulate during a single auction. Each red mark was counted as a badge of honor.

Naturally, the presence of so many people drew food vendors, pickpockets, drug dealers, religious fanatics, and beggars, all of whom hoped to profit from the event. Some of them were driven away by the monitors, but most contrived to stay, and were part of the constantly roiling mix as the crowd continued to swell.

Less visible, because most of them preferred it that way, were the buyers—people from all walks of life who for one reason or another wanted to buy a slave. A few of them were flamboyant, and eager to demonstrate how wealthy they were, but most wore such low-key clothing they were impossible to distinguish from shopkeepers. One such individual wore a hooded robe that hung nearly to his feet and stood with his hands hidden inside voluminous sleeves. It was nearly impossible to see his face, and that was by design, since had his identity been known prices would have gone up.

Meanwhile, beyond the painted backdrop and below ground level, was what had originally been a gravel pit back during the city's early days, but had been subdivided into a multiplicity of slave pens since then. The cubicles were protected from the elements by sheets of pressboard, rusting metal, and old sails. And it was there, in female pen four, that CeCe Alamy and two other young women were being held.

Like the roof over their heads, the walls were made from pieces of scrap and were intended to limit communication between groups of slaves rather than provide them with privacy. The space was six-feet wide, eight feet long, and equipped with two crudely made bunk beds. The bedding was filthy, the toilet consisted of a shared bucket that sat in a corner, and the floor was made of gray lumber salvaged from an old warehouse.

One of the three, a girl named Gertha, was barely capable of holding a conversation. But she was comely in an empty-eyed sort of way and would probably be put to use in someone's bedroom. Presently, being blissfully unaware of what was about to happen to her, Gertha sat cross-legged on a top bunk talking to a handmade doll. "Are you going to school today? Me too! We'll have lots of fun."

Alamy was sitting on one of the lower bunks and turned to look at the young woman who was seated next to her. Her name was Nita Persus, and, while not especially pretty, she was sturdy, a quality that was much sought after where slaves were concerned. Persus had brown hair, unplucked brows, and tattoos that began on her shoulders and flowed down over her arms, torso, and legs. All of which had been forced on her by an owner who liked to decorate his slaves with what he called "skin art," so that each one became a walking, talking example of what he could do.

Persus had been born into slavery and, while she had no education to speak of, was unfailingly optimistic. That was one of the reasons Alamy liked her. "Maybe a nice person will buy her," Persus said hopefully, as she eyed Gertha.

"Maybe," Alamy replied doubtfully, "but what are the chances?"

Persus shrugged. "Not very good I suppose—but there's always hope. I was reasonably happy until my owner's business failed."

The conversation was interrupted as both women heard a distant cheer. The auction was under way, and as the first group of slaves went forth to meet their various fates, Alamy's chin began to tremble. Persus put an arm around the younger woman's shoulders. "Don't cry," she said kindly. "I've been through this twice—and crying won't help. Life isn't fair, but what is *is*, and we must make the best of it. Remember, steal what you can, and save *all* of it. That way you'll be able to buy yourself someday. That's what I plan to do."

It was a distant hope, but some sort of hope was better than none, so Alamy sought to wipe the tears away. There were scuffling sounds as a slave handler arrived, turned a key in the padlock, and opened the door. The slaves called him Skanker, after his body odor, and he had a thing for Gertha. "Come on, sweetie," Skanker said seductively, as he crooked a finger. "And leave your friend behind. You can come back for her later."

That was a lie, of course, but neither Alamy nor Persus saw any reason to say so, as the other woman propped her doll up against the wall before sliding down off the top bunk. Then, as Gertha exited the cell, Skanker took the opportunity to pinch her bottom. That sort of thing was common in the slave pens, and a perk that most of the handlers were not only glad of, but considered to be an important part of their compensation.

Thanks to Skanker's interest in Gertha, Alamy and Persus were able to pass through the gate unmolested and join a group of three other women who were waiting outside. With a handler named Honker leading the way, and Skanker to bring up the rear, all six of the slaves were led through a maze of passageways to a series of switchback ramps that led up to the holding area located directly behind the mural. Once in place, they were required to wait. Alamy couldn't see what was happening on the other side of the mural, but the young woman could imagine it, as she listened to Mortha address the crowd.

"They're twins," the slave master said, "and while too young to perform heavy labor now, they'll be ready in three short years! Two, if you feed them some decent food, and see to their medical needs. Bidding will start at eighteen hundred for the pair. But remember, if the boys are sold separately, they'll fetch at least a thousand each. . . . And that makes the package price very attractive. So, what do you say? Do I hear eighteen hundred? Excellent! We have eighteen hundred, do I hear nineteen hundred? Yes, thank you, ma'am, how about two thousand?"

And so it went until the preteen boys were sold for twenty-three hundred Imperials. Alamy felt sorry for the youngsters, Persus wore a stoic expression, and Gertha was singing to herself as an order was given, and the slaves shuffled up the last ramp. The journey ended at the side of the platform, and when the young women appeared, a cheer went up from the men in the crowd. Many of them stood down front, where they would be able to see that much better when the group took its place at the center of the stage. Persus saw Alamy's look of dismay and had to shout in order to make herself heard. "Send yourself somewhere else! Go to a pretty place. . . . And stay there until it's over."

It was good advice, and Alamy knew that, so she pictured the island her father had taken her to three years earlier. It was a beautiful locale, with soaring bristle trees, and rocky cliffs where birds made their nests. But the sight of so many leering faces was impossible to ignore, as were the lecherous comments directed to individual women, including herself. So Alamy's head fell, as liquid lead trickled into her stomach, and Mortha began his time-tested spiel. "Here are six young women, any of whom could clean your house, help out in the kitchen, or warm your bed! Assuming your wife will move over, that is!"

The risqué joke got a big laugh from the crowd, and Mortha waited for the noise to die down, before giving the order that at least half the crowd had been waiting for. "Remove your clothes, slaves—and show the citizens what a few Imperials can buy."

Alamy had been both expecting the command and dread-ing it. Her face turned bright red as she fumbled with the cheap pin that held her soiled toga in place and let the fabric fall. That left her wearing nothing more than a pair of panties—which one of the handlers ordered her to remove. There was an enthusiastic burst of applause as she did so, quickly followed by the sharp *crack* of a whip, and a cry of pain as Gertha staggered under the force of the blow. Because rather than remove her clothing as she'd been ordered to, the young woman had been talking to herself, while swaying from side to side. "Cut her clothes off," Mortha said coldly, and there were *more* cheers as one of his employees hurried to comply.

Alamy wanted to cover her breasts *and* her pubic area, but knew any attempt to do so would earn her a whipping, so she forced both hands down to her sides. And, because Alamy was very shapely, hundreds of eyes bored into her.

Alamy directed a sidelong glance at Persus, and saw that while naked, the other woman was clearly disengaged. In fact, judging from the beatific expression she wore, Persus was looking at something beautiful rather than a crowd of brutish plebeians.

"So," Mortha continued smoothly, "let the bidding begin! The first slave up for sale is on the far-left-hand side of the block. Her name is Tara. She's twenty-two years old and can read and write. Bidding will start at eight hundred Imperials. Do I have eight? Yes, I do. How 'bout eight fifty?" And so it went as a bidding war quickly developed between the man in the hooded robe and a wealthy landowner who was seated on a sedan chair. It had fold-down legs and was designed to resemble a throne. In spite of the fact that the seat was extra wide—the matron's synsilk-swathed body filled it from side to side. Rings glittered on each pudgy finger, and a bodyguard comprised of six well-armed men formed a semicircle behind her. A well-groomed slave stood upwind of the woman, so that the scented smoke produced by the brazier he was holding would waft past his mistress, and thereby protect her sensitive nostrils from offensive odors. Of which there were many.

Though a lot less flamboyant, the hooded man won the bidding for Tara, but lost the next round to the woman in the sedan chair. A shopkeeper bought the third woman, which made it Gertha's turn, and she sold quickly thanks to her beauty. Though for a relatively low price since everyone could see that her potential usefulness was limited.

Neither the hooded man nor the woman in the sedan chair put in a bid for Gertha, but when Persus came up for auction, both became active again. If Alamy's friend was aware of what was taking place she gave no sign of it as the man bid sixteen hundred Imperials, and the matron signaled her surrender with a disapproving frown.

Then it was Alamy's turn, and as all eyes turned to her, the young woman felt a profound sense of humiliation. A sense of stubborn pride brought her head up, but the teenager felt dizzy, and feared that she might faint. "The last slave is not only a fine-looking specimen," Mortha said approvingly, "but a skilled sandal maker as well! Not to mention her ability to clean the house, cook simple meals, and do sums. Though not born into slavery, there's little doubt that obedience can be learned, although it may require a strong hand! Bidding will begin at a thousand Imperials."

There were six potential buyers at first, but four dropped out, as the hooded man and the society matron battled for dominance. Finally, having made a dismissive gesture with one bejeweled hand, the woman surrendered when the bidding topped eighteen hundred Imperials. If the man was jubilant, the expression was hidden in the shadow cast by his hood, and Mortha finalized the sale.

Then, much to Alamy's relief, she was allowed to pick up her toga and wrap it around her body as she followed Persus off the platform and down a short flight of stairs to a holding pen, where a group of male slaves stood waiting. The older ones eyed the young women hungrily, but the youngest were little more than boys, and were clearly frightened. Persus took the situation in stride. "I don't know who our new owner is," she commented, "but he's well-heeled! That's a good sign since there should be plenty of food and a warm place to sleep."

Although Alamy's father hadn't been wealthy, far from it, she had never gone without food or a warm place to sleep and was shocked to hear that such things were possible. Once a substantial amount of money changed hands, the newly purchased slaves were ordered out of the holding pen and onto the plaza, where half a dozen militiamen were waiting to receive them. A Section Leader ordered them to form a column of twos, swore voluminously when they failed to do so quickly enough, and made use of some well-placed kicks to put things right.

Then, once the formation was to his liking, the noncom fell in at the head of the column three paces back from the man in the long, flowing robe. The crowd parted to let the formation pass, and as it did so, Alamy recognized her stepmother.

Domna was in the process of consuming a meat pie as Alamy walked past, and when the big gob of spit hit her cheek, those around Domna laughed. Including the militiamen, who had no reason to favor the heavily made-up woman, or anyone else in the crowd for that matter. It wasn't much of a victory, but one that gave Alamy a small measure of satisfaction, as she followed the men in front of her up the busy street. The question foremost on her mind, and others' as well, was where were they being taken?

But there was no way to know as they were led up Market Street, and from there onto Imperial Boulevard, which was a double-wide thoroughfare designed to inspire a sense of awe as people approached the palace. Of course it was also intended to facilitate a quick and expeditious movement of troops should that become necessary.

Persus, who was walking beside Alamy, was the first to voice what all of them were thinking. And, as was her habit, the comment was hopeful. "Well, I'll be damned!" the slave exclaimed cheerfully. "We belong to Procurator Nalomy! Life is looking up."

But as Hingo threw his hood back, and the group passed a gibbet from which three half-rotted bodies hung, Alamy wasn't so sure. Because Nalomy's reputation was anything but positive, there were worse things than going without a meal, and the blocky palace looked a lot like a prison. A gate swung open, the column marched through, and there was a loud *clang* as the barrier closed behind them. Alamy was home.

The Plain of Pain, on the planet Dantha

The foothills were closer now, or that was the way it looked as the Lir named Issit put one weary foot in front of the other, and Cato followed behind. Of course distances could be, and often were, deceiving on the Plain of Pain, as Cato had already learned. Based on how close the foothills appeared Cato had assumed that he and his prisoner would reach them by nightfall of the day before. But they hadn't. So there they were, trudging across a large expanse of white saltpan, with the dark shadowy hills shimmering in the distance.

It had been a long, torturous three days since Cato had taken Issit by surprise, and the two of them had been forced into hiding while a dozen members of the Lir's extended family patrolled the skies above, searching for both the warrior and the Uman he had been assigned to monitor.

But while Cato was hot, thirsty, and uncomfortable, the time spent with Issit had been productive since Cato had been able to learn more about the massacre at Station 3. Not the bloody details because Issit hadn't taken part in the attack, but the identities of the clan leaders who were in charge, the name of the High Hold where they lived, and the fact that they had been acting on behalf of unnamed individuals in Solace. People who, for reasons unknown, wanted to seize control of Fiss Verafti. All of that was quite consistent with what Cato had discovered during his investigation.

Was Issit telling the truth? There was no way to be absolutely sure; but, like all members of the Xeno Corps, Cato had something "normal" policemen didn't, and that was a built-in lie detector. When a suspect lied to Cato, the empath could "feel" the increased anxiety associated with telling a falsehood—regardless of what species the person might belong to.

That, at least, was good, but as an entire day and a half passed, and Issit's relatives continued to search for the missing warrior, Cato's water supply was quickly exhausted. So by the time the searchers finally gave up, and the unlikely twosome finally set off, both of them were extremely thirsty.

But once Cato explained it was going to be necessary to shoot Issit before heat prostration overwhelmed him, the formerly taciturn Lir became suddenly voluble. Like the other members of his flock, Issit knew the Plain of Pain extremely well, including the location of half a dozen widely dispersed water holes.

The claim "felt" truthful, so Cato allowed the footsore Lir to lead him to a large jumble of weather-sculpted rocks, where deep inside a hidden recess a pool of crystal-clear water was waiting. A small population of nearly transparent fish lived in the pool, and had for more than a million years, ever since the lake that once covered the Plain of Pain disappeared. They flitted this way and that as both sentients drank their fill.

Once all of Cato's canteens were full, it was time for the twosome to crawl back out of the recess, and resume their journey. Issit's wings had been freed by then, but having been forced to carry more than half of Cato's gear, the warrior was too heavy to take off. Not to mention the fact that Cato was armed and would shoot Issit if he tried.

Having been fooled before, Cato was understandably cynical about how close the hills really were when something new appeared up ahead. Light reflected off one of them, and it had a hard, angular quality. And when Cato paused to examine them through his binos, he saw rows of computer-controlled solar panels that were set up to track the sun throughout the day and produce electricity for the city of Solace.

That meant that Cato was very close to the freewheeling community of Donk's Well, which had grown up around a good source of water, and the solar array, which employed more than a hundred technicians.

When Cato stopped, Issit had been forced to do likewise, due to the eight-foot-long leash that was connected to his throat. So he was only a few feet away when Cato turned to address him. "I've got some good news for you," Cato said cheerfully, as he restored the glasses to their pouch. "We'll be in Donk's Well by dinnertime. . . . So I'll carry the pack for a while. You deserve a rest."

Issit was both surprised and pleased, because if the desert journey had been difficult for Cato, it had been doubly so for him given that his species wasn't equipped to travel long distances on the ground. Not to mention the fact that Issit was alert to any chance of escape, and once freed from the weight of the pack, could easily take to the air. Assuming the Lir could sever the leash that is—which had *always* been within his power.

So, having rid himself of the pack, Issit was ready when the Uman turned his back as if to take a pee, and immediately bit through the cord, something Issit's razor-sharp beak could accomplish with ease. Then, having sprung up into the air, Issit began to beat his wings. Cato was going to shoot him, he knew that, but Issit preferred death to being led into Donk's Well on a leash for all of the drifters, prospectors, and townspeople to stare at.

Cato heard the steady *whuf, whuf, whuf* of the Lir's wings and had a smile on his face when he turned back. There was a soft whisper as the handgun cleared leather, followed by a loud *bang* as the lawman fired.

Issit was amazed to discover that he was still alive, and redoubled his efforts to gain more altitude, knowing full well that he was still within range. But Cato had returned the pistol to his holster by then—and shaded his eyes as he watched the Lir spiral ever upward. The warrior's emotions were starting to fade but there was no mistaking the sense of jubilation and the fierce sense of pride that Issit felt.

Would Issit tell his clan leaders how much information had been divulged to the Uman? No, Cato didn't think so, and since he had no way to secure and house a prisoner, it served him to let the Lir go. Especially given the nature of the task ahead.

So when Issit was little more than a high-flying speck, Cato took up the pack and pushed his arms through the straps. There was still a lot of ground to cover, but knowing that a cold beer was waiting for him in Donk's Well, he was eager to get started. Cato began to walk, and as he did, his long, dark shadow pointed the way.

The town of Donk's Well, on the planet Dantha

For those who lived in the community of Donk's Well there were only two places to go after the sun set, Ril's Bar, or the Universalist Church. And, given the fact that the local pastor spent most of *his* evenings in the saloon, it was clearly the more popular of the two.

The long, rectangular room included a much-abused bar that ran the length of the left side of the room, a scattering of mismatched tables, and a small stage where a local band played every six days. But on that particular night there was other entertainment to be had in the form of a work-worn android who went by the name of Phelonious. The A-7276 utility droid was seated at a table around which half a dozen of the bar's patrons were gathered, all of whom watched intently as the robot's skeletal hands manipulated a set of matched measuring cups. They knew that a pea-sized rubber ball was concealed under one of the containers, but which one?

When the cups eventually came to a stop, they formed a straight line. Phelonious eyed the faces around him. His plastiflesh face couldn't register all the nuances that a real flesh-and-blood countenance could, but his stiff number two smile was serviceable enough. "So, my friends," the android said genially. "Where's the ball?"

"That's easy," a bearded prospector replied confidently. "The ball is under the middle cup."

Phelonious lifted the middle cup, and sure enough, there was the ball! The robot frowned. "Everybody gets lucky once in a while," he grumbled. "Let's try it again."

The second go-round played out exactly like the first, except that a half-drunk solar tech made the call, which the rest of the onlookers took note of. Phelonious was visibly agitated by that time. "Okay," the android said irritably, "it looks like *everybody* is lucky tonight! But it can't continue— and I'm willing to bet on it."

The prospector raised two bushy eyebrows. White circles marked the hollows where sun goggles had protected his eyes out in the desert. "How much?"

"If you choose a cup, and you turn out to be wrong, then I get to keep your money," the robot replied. "But, if you get it right, then I'll *double* your money! So a one-Imperial investment would pay off with two!"

"I'll take some of that action," a high-pitched voice said, and all eyes went to the Kelf who was standing on top of the wooden table. His name was Belok, and, like all of his kind, the furry sentient was about three feet tall. His grandparents had been brought to Dantha to work in the high-altitude silver mines, where their small size and capacity to deal with wintry conditions were a real advantage, but Belok wasn't interested in that sort of employment.

Belok had a rounded head, beady eyes, and a short muzzle. He was dressed in a hand-tooled leather vest and matching shorts. Having climbed up onto the table so he could see what was going on, the Kelf waddled forward. The shiny Imperial rattled as it hit the table, then settled into place. Some of the others were interested in placing bets, too, especially on what looked like a sure thing, but were happy to let someone else risk their money first.

Phelonious nodded gravely, raised the right-hand cup to remind everyone where the so-called pea was hidden, and put all three of the aluminum cups into motion. They circled, swooped, and finally came to rest. "Well?" Phelonious demanded, as he eyed Belok. "Where is it?"

"Under the cup on your left," the diminutive said unhesitatingly. And, when Phelonious lifted the shell, the ball was right where Belok said it would be!

The android looked disappointed, and was forced to pay out two Imperials, as bets flooded in from all sides. The next bettor lost, as did the one who followed him, but the next gambler *won*. That served to stimulate the betting once again, and thanks to the fact that most of the participants had been drinking, none of the people gathered around the table noticed that the overall ratio of wins to losses had shifted subtly so that Phelonious was taking in more money than he was paying out. A result that was a foregone conclusion given the android's ability to shift the rubber ball from one cup to another without being detected.

So everything was going very well indeed until an off-duty lineman entered the saloon and went straight to the bar to get a beer before wandering over to join the crowd. That was when a look of anger appeared on his weathered face. "What the hell is going on here?" he demanded loudly. "The robot is cheating you! And so is the Kelf! They work together. . . . I saw them run the same scam over in Tolly's Crossing."

That announcement produced a brief moment of silence, followed by a roar of outrage, as the crowd turned on both coconspirators. But the larcenous duo had been in such situations before and knew what to do. There was a soft *pop* as Phelonious triggered a smoke grenade and rolled it under the table. Then, as a cloud of thick gray smoke billowed upward, people collided as they sought to grab onto the con beings.

Meanwhile, the patter of small feet could be heard as Belok crossed the table, made the leap onto his friend's back, and was careful to hold on tight as Phelonious ran for the front door. The android could see the exit quite clearly thanks to his alternative infrared vision.

But the lineman had seen all of it before, and knowing what to expect, sought to rally the bar's patrons. "Don't let them get away!" he bellowed, and successfully led half the group out through the door and into the street beyond.

Phelonious could run, but not fast enough, as one of the more fleet-footed members of the crowd tackled the android from behind and threw both con artists to the ground. "I've got them!" a townsman trumpeted triumphantly as he managed to grab Belok by the scruff of the neck and hang on to Phelonious at the same time. The rest of the mob arrived seconds later.

At that point, the twosome was subjected to some very rough treatment as members of the crowd battled not only to recover *their* money but even more if that was possible.

Once the rough-and-tumble process was over, it was time to mete out some vigilante justice. "Let's take them to the pit," the prospector with the beard proposed. "But remember. . . . Only one rock per person."

"What about the droid?" somebody wanted to know. "He ain't no person!"

"Wait!" Belok insisted, as he was hoisted over the solar technician's head, and borne toward the town's garbage pit. "This isn't fair! We deserve a trial! Put me down!"

But the crowd was in no mood for trials, so when the mob arrived at the edge of the man-made pit, they threw both of the miscreants down into the stinking hole. There were squeals of outrage, and rustling sounds, as more than a hundred red-eyed rot rats scurried away. There were no streetlights in Donk's Well, so many of those present routinely carried flashlights, and a dozen blobs of light converged on the filth-covered twosome as they struggled to find firm footing on top of the latest layer of garbage. "Okay," the prospector said. "One rock apiece! Let 'em have it!"

There was a *clang* as one of the missiles hit Phelonious, followed by the unmistakable double-*clack* of a pump-style shotgun, as Jak Cato emerged from the surrounding gloom. The red dot projected by the weapon's targeting laser slipped from chest to chest and that was sufficient to bring the stoning to a halt. Cato had just entered town and was still carrying his pack. "Hold it right there," he ordered, as people turned to look at him.

"Why the hell should we?" a grizzled drifter demanded defiantly.

"Because I'm an Imperial law officer," Cato replied calmly, and raised his left hand to prove it. Like all his kind, Cato had a phosphor badge that had been chemically "printed" onto the palm of his hand shortly after graduating from the Xeno Corps Academy on Regulus IV. He could trigger it simply by thinking about it, and, while visible in daylight, the device was especially effective at night. And the bright green glow left no doubt as to the extent of his authority.

The solar tech swore bitterly. "Well, I'll be damned. . . . A Xeno Corps freak in Donk's Well! What's this planet coming to?"

"Not much," Cato commented matter-of-factly, as he swung the shotgun from left to right. "But let's see if we can't maintain at least the appearance of civilization. Now drop the rocks, and crawl back into your various holes, or I'll arrest the whole lot of you and let Procurator Nalomy sort you out."

That wasn't entirely true, of course, since there was very little chance that Nalomy would back him, but the residents of Donk's Well didn't know that.

There was grumbling, but the crowd melted away, as most returned to the bar. Cato waited until all of the townspeople were gone before stepping over to the edge of the pit. The light from his torch wandered a bit before spotlighting Phelonious and Belok. They were halfway up the other slope and clearly headed for the desert. "That's the wrong direction," the policeman said mildly. "Keep those hands where I can see them. . . . That's right. Now turn around and come this way. I don't know what you two did to make everyone so unhappy with you, but we're going to have a nice chat." Though long absent—the rule of law had returned to Donk's Well.

SEVEN

The city of Solace, on the planet Dantha

THOUGH LOCATED ONE STORY UNDERGROUND, Imood Hingo's office was large and well-appointed. An abundance of sunlight had been piped in via solar tubes to provide the room with a sense of warmth. Well-chosen pieces of art conveyed a sense of restrained elegance, the huge granite-slab desk testified to Hingo's authority, and the fact that it sat on a raised platform ensured Hingo's dominance over those who came before him. However, comfortable though his surroundings were, there was plenty to worry about.

Legate Isulu Usurlus was going to arrive on Dantha in two days, and there was a tremendous amount of work to get done prior to the dignitary's arrival, which was why Nalomy had instructed Hingo to buy more slaves. The investment would probably pay dividends in the future but was something of a liability at the moment since the newly acquired slaves were untrained and had a tendency to make mistakes.

But there was nothing Hingo could do about the situation other than make some carefully considered assignments and hope for the best. With that in mind, he was interviewing the new slaves to identify those who could be assigned to the more-visible tasks, while the rest would be put to work in the kitchen, or out on the grounds where they would be less likely to cause trouble. And that was where the awkward-looking boy who stood in front of him clearly belonged. "That will be all," Hingo said sternly. "Remember what I told you. . . . Follow orders, work hard, and don't steal. Because I'll have the hide off your back if you do! Dismissed."

The sixteen-year-old mumbled, "Yes, sir," bowed awkwardly, and shuffled away.

Hingo sighed, put a check mark next to the boy's name, and said, "Next!"

All of the slaves who hadn't been interviewed yet were lined up in the sterile corridor outside of the Majordomo's office. Alamy heard Hingo's voice, saw the boy leave, and knew it was her turn to enter. She wasn't looking forward to the visit. Life in the palace was a shock after a youth spent in The Warrens, and the young woman had been in trouble twice. Once for failing to curtsy to a visitor, and once for dropping a vaseful of freshly cut flowers, which exploded into a hundred pieces as it hit the marble floor.

So knowing that there were already two strikes against her, the young woman was understandably anxious as she passed through the door and went to stand on the large "X" that had been set into the stone floor directly opposite Hingo's raised desk. It was made out of white marble and seemed to glow as she placed both feet on it. Alamy curtsied and the Majordomo nodded approvingly. "A slave who learns from her mistakes. I like that.

"Now," Hingo continued, as his fingers formed a steeple, "let's talk about the future. You were born free, unlike many of your fellow slaves, and that could present a problem. Some of the people who find themselves in your position waste a lot of time and energy trying to fight the system. Others, those who are more adaptable, learn to accept their circumstances and try to better themselves."

Alamy was surprised to hear that a slave could better him- or herself, and that must have been visible on her face, because Hingo smiled bleakly. "That's right," Hingo assured her. "There are slaves—and then there are slaves. Because those lucky enough to join an establishment such as this one can rise to high office if they work hard and keep their wits about them.

"By now you may have realized that a hierarchy exists within the palace walls," Hingo added clinically, "with groundskeepers on the bottom, kitchen help in the middle ranks, and housekeeping at the top. You were placed in housekeeping, largely because Procurator Nalomy likes to surround herself with beauty. It will be a while before you can return to that assignment given the vase incident.

"However," Hingo said, as he rose from behind the desk, and came around to stand in front of Alamy, "a kitchen assignment can be useful as well. Especially if you have the opportunity to become a server, because once the Procurator sees how pretty your face is, she might decide to promote you over the head housekeeper's objections. Especially if I concur."

By that time Hingo was standing only inches away, so close that Alamy could smell the garlic on his breath, and feel the male energy that surrounded him. Their eyes were locked as Hingo brought the knuckles of his left hand up to caress her right cheek. "CeCe," Hingo said experimentally. "I like that name. And people that I like have a tendency to do well."

Alamy shivered and bit her lower lip, as the hand followed her cheek down to her neck and from there to the curve of her breast. "So follow orders, work hard, and don't steal," Hingo advised. "Do we understand each other?"

Alamy nodded, because there was nothing else she *could* do, other than feel slightly sick to her stomach. "Yes, sir."

"Good," Hingo said, as he turned away. "You are dismissed." The interview was over, but as Alamy left the room, she knew something far worse had begun.

The town of Donk's Well, on the planet Dantha

More than a full day had passed since Cato's arrival in Donk's Well, and he was asleep in his hotel room, when a persistent tapping noise woke him up. It took a moment to realize that the sound was coming from the window rather than the door and to roll out of bed. That sent a spike of pain deep into his brain and triggered the usual regrets. One beer had led to another, and he was suffering from a full-fledged hangover.

It was second nature to grab the pistol off the nightstand and take it with him as Cato padded across the floor. The sun hadn't cleared the mountain peaks yet, but there was enough light to see by, even if he couldn't believe his eyes. Because there, peering through the dirty glass, was a Kelf! And not just *any* Kelf but one of the con beings he had rescued two days earlier. The window rattled as he pushed it up. "What the hell do you want?" Cato demanded irritably, as cold morning air flooded into his room. "And why couldn't you simply knock on the door?"

"We need protection," Belok said grimly, as he jumped down into the room. "And the desk clerk wouldn't let us come up to see you."

Cato frowned. "Protection? From what?"

"From the yokels who run this town," the Kelf answered indignantly. "First they stole our money, then they threw us into the garbage pit, and now they refuse to let us leave!"

Cato closed the window, crossed the room, and put the gun on the nightstand. The bed creaked as he sat down. "They won't let you leave? What's stopping you?"

"We need transportation," Belok explained, "or, failing that, enough supplies to reach the next town on foot. But the locals won't return the money they stole from us or provide us with supplies."

"That's because they know you and Phelonious are crooks," Cato replied mildly, as he stifled a yawn.

"We aren't crooks, we're entrepreneurs," Belok countered defensively. "But even if we were crooks, they shouldn't be allowed to kill us."

Cato's head throbbed painfully. He held it with both hands. "*Kill you?* What makes you think they plan to kill you?"

"'Once the freak leaves, you're going down.' That's what a prospector told Phelonious," Belok said. "And there have been other threats as well. And that's why we're coming with you."

"Oh no you aren't," Cato replied, as he opened his shaving kit and began to rummage through the contents looking for a pain tab.

"Yes, we are," Belok insisted doggedly. "You took us into custody—and that means you are responsible for us!"

Cato found a pain tab, popped it into his foul-tasting mouth, and chased it with a gulp of water from the glass next to his bed. Then, having put the glass down, he eyed the Kelf. "Phelonious is an android," Cato observed gravely, "so it doesn't matter what the locals do to him, unless his owner shows up to file a complaint."

Belok started to object, but Cato raised a hand. "Save the 'robots are self-aware' speech for someone who gives a shit. The point is that you are the only one who qualifies as a person. As such you are entitled to my protection. However, before you request it, consider this. While the townspeople *might* kill you, the people I'm going after *will* kill you if given half a chance, so think about that.

"And one more thing," Cato added sternly. "If you're stupid enough to tag along, then I'll expect you to work for a living, and there will be no turning back. That goes for the robot, too. Now get the hell out of my room. I have things to do."

The Kelf started to reply, apparently thought better of it, and exited via the door.

Cato stood and went over to examine himself in the cracked mirror that hung over the rust-stained sink. The man who looked back at him had red eyes, two days' worth of stubble on his face, and didn't look like someone he should trust. Sivio would have been disappointed—and so was Cato.

The city of Solace, on the planet Dantha

In spite of all the progress the Uman race had made over thousands of years, some things never seemed to change, and large kitchens were among them. Because no matter how modern the appliances might be, kitchens were hot, steamy places in which timing was everything, and tempers were eternally short. And the huge facility located one level below the palace was no exception. Especially around meal-times since Chef Undara and his staff were not only expected to prepare meals for Procurator Nalomy and her guests, but for the facility's staff as well, which included a total of 356 citizen employees, slaves, and militia. Not just once, but *three* times a day, year-round.

So being sent down into the first basement was a little bit like being sent to hell, especially since Alamy had a lot to learn, and people had a tendency to yell at her. Partly because just about everything constituted an emergency—and partly because the environment was so noisy that the staff was forced to yell in order to make themselves heard.

Like most of the unskilled slaves who were sent to the kitchen, Alamy was immediately put to work loading and unloading dishes from the huge dishwashers. The task required considerable care, especially since the penalty for each broken plate, bowl, or cup was a blow from Undara's long, flexible cane.

Eventually, having worked a number of twelve-hour shifts without breaking a single item, Alamy was promoted to hand-washing Nalomy's personal china, which bore the official's family crest, and was custom-made. The penalty for breaking one of the Procurator's dishes was *five* lashes. So Alamy was extremely careful as she hand-dried each item before checking it off an inventory list and returning it to a special cabinet.

And that was what the slave was doing when the chef appeared at her side. He had a round, moonlike face, ears that reminded her of handles on a jug, and a very unusual torso. Because instead of two arms, Undara was equipped with *four*, two of which were so-called bod mods. These were surgically installed enhancements that enabled people to perform particular tasks better, or, in the case of body cultists, were intended to make them physically attractive. A relatively common phenomenon on the inner worlds, but rare out on the rim, where very few people could afford extra limbs, eyes set into the back of their skulls, or six-inch-long tongues.

In fact, Undara was the only such individual that Alamy had ever seen. So it had been hard not to stare at first. But having worked in the kitchen for a while, the slave was used to the fact that the chef could gesture with *four* pudgy hands. "Ooly was supposed to assist Santha, but she's ill," the chef announced. "You will replace her. Santha will be in charge. Follow her example, and everything will be fine."

Santha was one of the elite individuals who were assigned to serve Nalomy's meals, and Alamy didn't like her much, mainly because of how snotty she was. So the need to work with Santha, *and* run the extra risks attendant upon serving food to the Procurator, filled Alamy with dread. The normally gruff Undara must have sensed her hesitation because a rare smile appeared on his face. "There's no need to worry, child. You'll do well. Remember, the key is to be present, but unseen."

With that somewhat enigmatic advice still ringing in her ears, Alamy was sent off to collect one of the crisp white togas that female housekeepers routinely wore, before returning to the kitchen, where Santha was waiting. The other slave was about five-five. Her carefully maintained brown hair hung down to her shoulders, one of which was bare, and there was no hiding the curves underneath her loose-fitting toga. Curves which, if the rumors were true, Hingo had explored on more than one occasion.

Santha saw all of those who served food to Nalomy as members of a team, *her* team, and was constantly on the lookout for potential competitors. So, since looks were considered to be an important qualification for the job, the fact that Alamy was pretty made her both useful and a threat at the same time. Santha frowned, glanced at the clock on the wall, and said, "You're late."

The comment was entirely unfair, since Alamy had been given the assignment at the very last minute and had dressed as fast as she could. And tempting as it was to talk back, especially to another slave, Alamy had learned a lot during the last few days. She knew that if she were to object, Santha could use her words against her by characterizing the newest team member as "combative."

So Alamy said, "I'm sorry," even though she wasn't, and saw what might have been a look of disappointment flit through the other woman's big brown eyes. Then the moment was over as two stainless-steel warming carts were wheeled into the alcove. "The first two courses have been served," Santha explained, "and it's important to keep the main course hot, so we'll have to hurry. Once we arrive in the pantry adjacent to the Procurator's private dining room, your job will be to remove trays from the carts, and carry them into the dining room. Place them on the side table that runs along one wall. Trista and I will serve the food. Do not speak unless spoken to, and limit your responses to 'yes, ma'am,' or 'yes, sir.' Understood?"

Alamy nodded. "Yes, ma'am."

Santha smiled in spite of herself. "Good. Let's go."

The décor within Procurator Nalomy's private dining room was modeled on the one in her father's villa on Corin. Everything was smaller, of course, but both rooms were dominated by long, oval tables, each of which was served by chairs so substantial they might have done duty in a living room. The walls were decorated with six of the bright, impressionistic paintings for which Nalomy's mother had been known prior to her death.

Rather than dine alone, Nalomy liked to invite members of Dantha's upper class to eat with her. The tradition enabled her to keep an eye out for potential troublemakers, foster useful relationships, and hear the latest gossip.

None of that held any interest for Fiss Verafti, who looked exactly like Centurion Sivio, but had been introduced to his fellow guests as Inhor Rypool. According to Nalomy, Rypool was an up-and-coming businessman on his way to Corin.

So, while some of those present found the interaction to be stimulating, Verafti was bored—not only by the content of the dreary conversation, but by the murky emotions that swirled around him. The most notable of these was the fear that the businessman seated to his left felt every time Nalomy looked his way, the self-centered greed that the Magistrate from the city of Comfort exuded, and the pathetic desire for approval that the woman on his right leaked into the ether.

Perhaps, had the businessman's fear been a good deal stronger, Verafti could have fed off it. But the only emotions of any consequence emanated from Nalomy, who continued to revel in the knowledge that she, and only she, knew Inhor Rypool's *true* identity. And, more than that, she took considerable pleasure in the power she had over him, even going so far as to toy with the pendant hanging between her breasts—knowing that doing so would bother him. So when the main course arrived, it was a welcome diversion even if the entrées weren't to Verafti's liking.

Strangely, from Verafti's perspective at least, the slaves responsible for serving the food were a good deal more interesting than their social betters. Perhaps that was because their circumstances, and therefore their emotions, were very similar to his own. Like him, they were prisoners and had very little to hope for.

Would Nalomy grant his freedom once Usurlus was dead? Or break her word and choose to retain a very valuable weapon? The answer was anything but certain.

And, even if he were to break free somehow, what then? The Umans were in control of his home planet, the one person he cared about more than life itself was lost to him, and the chances of finding her were vanishingly small.

So the emotions the slaves felt seemed to echo and amplify Verafti's own feelings, thereby stimulating something that had been sadly missing of late, which was the deep and abiding hunger natural to all Sagathies. The shape shifter watched the slave named Alamy bring trays into the room, wondered what her fear would taste like, and allowed himself a smile.

*   *   *

East of the town of Donk's Well,
on the planet Dantha

The first part of the journey verged on pleasant, as the trail left the town of Donk's Well, and took the travelers up into gently rising foothills. The hills were barren at first, but grew progressively green as Cato, Belok, and Phelonious continued to gain altitude. The vegetation was sparse, and low to the ground, as if conscious of the fact that the snow level could suddenly fall and cover everything with a thick white shroud. Cato dreaded the possibility but was prepared for it, having purchased cold-weather gear in Donk's Well.

Phelonious led the way, with Belok perched on his shoulders, which left Cato to follow along behind. The arrangement was anything but accidental, since the variant had no reason to trust the pair, and wanted to keep the devious duo where he could see them. And, if the con artists happened to trigger an ambush, then so much the better. . . . Because that would give Cato more time to react.

The other concern, and the one that worried Cato the most, was the possibility that Lir bandits would spot the party from the air and attack them. Fortunately there was a good deal of cloud cover, and the higher they went, the lower the ceiling was. So even though Cato spent a lot of his time scanning the sky—there were no high-flying warriors to be seen.

The cloud cover meant no sunset as such, just a slow fade to black, as if the light was being absorbed into the planet itself. So, having marched as far as Cato thought they reasonably could, the threesome took shelter under a rocky overhang, which had clearly been used for that purpose many times before. And judging from the angen dung that lay scattered on *top* of the snow, and the live coals deep within the remains of a campfire, a pack train had passed through recently. But who were they? Miners, making their

way back to a lonely shaft in the hills, or a party of Lir hauling supplies up to one of the castlelike high holds in the
mountains?

Cato hoped for the first but thought the second possibility was more likely because, even though they could fly, the
Lir had to bring most of their supplies up into the mountains on angens like everyone else. Supplies which, ironically
enough, they had probably purchased from the same merchants Cato had done business with over the last couple of
days. In spite of its location inside bandit territory, the town
of Donk's Well had never been attacked by Lir raiders, and
there was an obvious reason for that.

There wasn't much to do while sitting around the campfire other than talk, so it was an opportunity for Cato to
learn more about his traveling companions. It turned out
that Phelonious had been the property of a retired roboticist,
who having acquired three A-7276 carcasses, combined the
parts to create a *fourth* machine, albeit without many of the
built-in software restrictions that Imperial law insisted on.
That explained why Phelonious was free to make his own
decisions, cheat people out of their money, and generally be-
have the way Umans did.

Life was good at first, but all things must come to an end,
as was the case when a financial setback forced the roboticist
to sell Phelonious, who immediately ran away from his new
owner. And it wasn't long thereafter when the android fell
in with bad company, which was to say Perat Belok, a Kelf
who fled his clan rather than accede to an arranged marriage.
"You should have seen her," Belok said, his eyes glittering
with reflected firelight. "She was uglier than Phelonious, too
damned tall, and dumb as a rock! No wonder the bride price
was so low! If the deal had gone through, my parents would
have been able to save a lot of money. Damn them to hell."

The temperature fell to well below freezing during the
night, but that didn't matter to Phelonious, who could in-

crease his temperature by simply "thinking" about it, or the Kelf, who was equipped with a thick layer of fur *and* a miniature sleeping bag.

Phelonious didn't need to sleep, so he volunteered to stay up all night, just in case someone tried to sneak up on the campsite. That was comforting, but Cato found it difficult to get much rest even with a sentry, and felt grateful when the sun finally rose.

The policeman had seen the con artists as little more than deadweight until then, but thanks to the fire Phelonious had built, and the breakfast that Belok produced, Cato was feeling better about the strange twosome by the time the three of them hit the trail.

With the heavily laden robot walking ahead, Cato shouldered Belok, and carried the new rifle at port arms as he followed the path upward. And the strange thing was that the skeletal sniper's rifle wasn't just new to him, it was *brand-new*, meaning just out of the box. Judging from the way the weapon was set up, it had originally been intended for use by one of the Emperor's Legions or a planetary militia. Perhaps Dantha's militia. Which raised the question as to why such a weapon would be available in Donk's Well. It was a question that would have been worth investigating had there been more time.

In any case, the rifle was light, powerful, and capable of hitting targets up to a thousand yards away, all of which made it a lot more useful in mountainous terrain than the shotgun would have been. Unless they were ambushed—when a good close-quarters weapon would be ideal. But there was only so much weight Cato could carry, and having no desire to arm his companions, he was limited to one long gun.

The morning wore on, and the trail grew steeper as they left the last of the foothills behind and found themselves on a raw trail that switched back and forth along the west flank of an enormous mountain. The people down in Donk's Well referred to it as The Tooth because of its triangular shape. The Lir called it something that Cato was unable to pronounce.

And that was good, because according to the information Issit had given him, the lofty aerie called High Hold Meor was located about halfway to the top. That was the home of clan leader Hybor Iddyn, as well as senior warriors Pak Nassali, and Etir Lood. All were Lir bandits who not only took part in the attack on Station 3, but had engineered it on behalf of someone in Solace, a person or persons Cato was determined to bring to justice. Or, failing that, to execute on his own. Because one way or another, someone was going to pay.

The threesome paused around noontime so that Cato and Belok could eat a cold lunch before pressing on. The people who had been ahead of them the day before were *still* ahead of them, as evidenced by fresh angen dung and tracks in the snow. Phelonious claimed that the party included three Lir, leading six angens, but Cato had no way to know if that analysis was correct.

Cato was worried, though, because it would be easy to unknowingly overtake the caravan, and wind up on the losing end of a firefight. So he suggested that Phelonious scout ahead in hopes that the robot would be able to detect trouble before he walked into it.

The android agreed, and that left Cato to carry the supplies, while Belok scampered along behind. Climbing the steep trail was hard work, made even harder by a biting wind, and snow that grew ever deeper the higher they went. So it was something of a relief when Cato rounded a bend to find Phelonious waiting for him. It was late afternoon by that time—and the light had begun to fade. "They're camped up ahead," Phelonious announced, "and I was correct. There are three of them."

"Lir warriors?"

Phelonious nodded. "They're armed with assault rifles."

Cato swore. "Damn! We can't get past them. Not without being seen."

Belok had arrived by then and looked from face to face. "Why don't I go up and have a little chat with them? Then, while they're talking to me, you can get into position. Once you're ready, you can call on them to surrender. I'll collect their weapons, and you can take them into custody, it's as simple as that."

Cato didn't *want* the Lir to surrender but couldn't say that, so he nodded, even though the prospect of being forced to cope with three Lir prisoners was extremely daunting. "That sounds like a good idea," Cato allowed cautiously, "unless they start shooting. What then?"

"I'm pretty good at making myself scarce," the Kelf replied confidently. "But if it comes to that, don't miss. The metal man and I would be in a lot of trouble."

"The fur ball is correct," Phelonious agreed soberly. "The Lir would kill us—and it would be *your* fault!"

"I'll keep that in mind," Cato said dryly. "All right, let's stash the pack, and get up there before the light disappears."

Having hidden the pack in a jumble of snowcapped boulders, Cato followed Phelonious up the slippery slope that bordered the trail in an attempt to flank the Lir and gain a height advantage at the same time. In the meantime, Belok had instructions to wait a full ten minutes before starting up the trail, since, even though his legs were short, the Kelf was likely to make much better time than Cato and Phelonious would. And, were Belok to arrive too early, there was the distinct possibility that the Lir might kill him before help could arrive.

So Cato felt a sense of urgency as icy scree slid away from his boots and clattered toward the trail below. Though he was not designed for the task at hand, it quickly became apparent that Phelonious was quite agile. The android's servos whined loudly as he battled his way upward, using sturdy shrubs for handholds. The climb took time, and as they worked their way up the slope, Cato realized that a fifteen-minute head start would have been better. But it was too late for that now, so all he could do was concentrate on his footing, and use such handholds as there were.

Finally, having attained a ledge that would allow them to proceed in parallel to the trail below, the twosome was able to make better time. It was necessary to thread their way between shoulder-high evergreens that opened up like inverted umbrellas when the sun rose and closed into vertical shrubs when the temperature fell. The transformation had already begun by that time.

The ledge nearly petered out at the point where the mountain bulged outward. But by slinging his rifle over one shoulder, and choosing his handholds with care, Cato managed to follow Phelonious out and around the obstruction. If the android was experiencing something akin to fear, there were no signs of it, but since the empath couldn't "read" machines there was no way to know what was going on inside Phelonious.

Cato's right boot slipped while he was edging his way around the bulge. That forced him to shift his weight to the other foot as a dozen pebbles rattled away. What could have been a fatal fall was averted as Cato clung to the cliff face and focused all of his attention on selecting good handholds.

After they skirted the bulge, the ledge reappeared, and that allowed the twosome to make better time as a column of telltale smoke rose to merge with the sky ahead. By looking down, Cato could see a section of the trail, but there was no sign of Belok, which suggested that the Kelf had passed them by. That theory was confirmed moments later, when Cato and Phelonious arrived above the Lir campsite.

The shaggy pack angens had been unloaded by then and herded into a rustic corral, where they would spend the night. The fire, which was centered inside a ring of already-blackened rocks, was crackling cheerfully, and as Cato peered over the edge, he could see Belok standing about three feet away from it, talking to a contingent of three Lir warriors. It was impossible to hear any of the conversation, but Cato knew Belok was never at a loss for words, and could be counted upon to keep the bandits entertained for at least five minutes. But how long had Belok been there? And how much of that time remained?

There was no way to know as Cato brought the rifle around, worked a cartridge into the chamber, and was just about to call down to the group when Belok attempted to bolt. In spite of the claim made earlier, the Kelf wasn't quick enough. A Lir warrior pounced on Belok by the scruff of the neck and hoisted him off the ground, as a second bandit drew a ceramic knife. "They're going to kill him!" Phelonious exclaimed unnecessarily. "Do something!"

Cato already had the rifle in position by then and was staring into the telescopic sight as Belok's feet kicked uselessly two feet off the ground. Then, as the crosshairs came to rest on the Lir's temple, the trigger gave, and a sharp cracking sound was heard.

The bullet blew half of the warrior's head away, Belok was drenched in gore as he hit the ground, and the echoes from the first shot were still being heard as Cato fired *again*. The Lir who had the knife staggered as a slug punched its way through his torso. He took two hesitant steps, and went beak down in the snow, as Phelonious shouted a warning. "Watch out! The third warrior is getting away!"

Cato looked up and saw that the android was correct. Having seen both of his companions gunned down, the third Lir had jettisoned his heavy assault rifle and taken to the air. The sole surviving warrior's widespread wings made a characteristic *whuf, whuf, whuf* as he fought for additional altitude.

Cato swung the rifle to the right, waited for the Lir to fill the scope, and applied the correct amount of pressure to the trigger. There was a loud *crack* as the butt thumped his shoulder, followed by an accusation from Phelonious. "You missed!" the robot complained loudly. "Don't let him escape. He'll bring the entire clan down on us!"

Phelonious was right. Should the warrior manage to get away and reach High Hold Meor, he *would* bring the clan down on them. And there was absolutely no doubt as to how that conflict would end. Still, Cato wasn't especially pleased with the robot's tone, which was clear when he spoke. "Shut the hell up, and stand in front of me," Cato ordered. "Or I'll shoot *you*! And believe me—I won't miss."

Phelonious did as he was told, which allowed Cato to rest the rifle on the android's left shoulder, and crouch behind him as the barrel tilted upward. The Lir had gained quite a bit of altitude by then, at least a hundred feet, but was still within range.

The light was fading, however, the warrior was hard to see against the gray sky, and there was no way to calculate wind speed. Still, Cato was pretty sure that the cold mountain breeze was blowing right to left. So, having made allowance for that, Cato aimed at a spot a few feet in front of the fugitive and fired.

The Lir seemed to pause, as if to take a rest, before spiraling down into the forest below. There was a momentary explosion of snow as the warrior hit a treetop, followed by what sounded like a pistol shot as a branch broke, and a soft *thump* when the limp body hit the ground. Three lives had been taken, and three lives had been spared, which, insofar as the majestic mountains were concerned, mattered not at all.

EIGHT

The city of Solace, on the planet Dantha

IT WAS NEARLY MIDNIGHT, SO THE SLAVES WHO worked the day shift were in bed, and that included Alamy. There were twenty beds in the long, narrow dormitory, each having a thin mattress, two sheets, and a single blanket. A wooden footlocker was located at the end of each bed and used to store personal belongings. Not that Alamy had any belongings other than the items issued to her in the palace.

What little light there was emanated from the shared bathrooms that bracketed the main entrance, but having lain awake for more than an hour, Alamy knew they were empty. And that was important if she was to slip out of bed and exit the dormitory undetected. That would result in twenty-five lashes if she was caught because Hingo didn't want to have off-duty slaves wandering around the palace at all hours of the day and night.

But dangerous though such an enterprise might be, Alamy couldn't resist the pull of the seldom-used library, and the vast amount of material that could be accessed from there. By sitting down at one of four terminals, she could call up millions of books, videos, and the latest news summaries from Corin. Though weeks old by the time they arrived on Dantha, they were a source of fascination to a young woman who knew there were hundreds of Uman-settled planets but had never been to one.

So rather than sleep, as she knew she should, Alamy had been sneaking out every third or fourth night to surreptitiously visit the library and plunder the treasures available there. The first step was to slip out of bed, push her pillow down under the covers, and grab the clothes that were waiting on top of her footlocker.

Then, with the clothing tucked under one arm, it was time to make her way down the center aisle to the bathroom on the right. That was where she slipped into both her uniform and a pair of sandals so that if one of the guards caught a glimpse of her on a security camera he would assume she was working nights. Unless he checked the duty roster—when he would discover otherwise.

But if everything went as it had on past occasions, Alamy wouldn't be spotted. The need to be stealthy was very much on Alamy's mind as she left the bathroom and paused to consider her route before entering the hallway. By taking the back stairs up to the first floor, and walking a short distance down the hall, it was possible to open a small, unobtrusive door and slip inside a service room.

Then, by entering instructions into a touch screen, she could summon a food cart, hop aboard, and ride it up to the fourth-floor library which didn't get much use. Confident that the route was clear in her mind, and not having heard anything unusual, Alamy slipped out into the hallway. But as Alamy hurried toward the back stairs, she heard a distant shout, followed by the quick *slap*, *slap*, *slap* that bare feet made as they hit the marble flooring. Someone was not only running Alamy's way but would spot her the moment they turned the corner unless she could find a place to hide!

So the young woman slipped into one of the alcoves that lined the hall. It was tight but there was just enough room for someone small to crouch behind a likeness of a five-foot-tall Esselon Dire Beast. The statue wasn't large enough to conceal all of her body, but the stylized animal threw a dark shadow against the back wall, and that would have to do.

As Alamy peered out from behind the Dire Beast, she was perfectly positioned to see a half-naked slave dash past, her features contorted with fear, as a couple of guards pounded after her. Then the woman vanished from sight, but Alamy heard a distant *thump* as the fugitive was thrown to the floor, followed by a harsh male voice. "Stupid bitch! Grab an arm, Darius. . . . She won't get away again."

"I'll put some stripes on *your* back if she does," Hingo said ominously, as he passed through Alamy's field of vision. "I don't have all night. . . . Let's get on with it."

The woman, whom Alamy had recognized as a slave named Lea, sobbed loudly as the men hauled her away. Shocked by what she'd seen, and no longer interested in visiting the library, Alamy waited to make sure the group was truly gone before returning to the dormitory. Once there, she removed her uniform and slipped into bed.

It took the better part of an hour to get to sleep, and once she did, the slave found herself trapped in a series of vivid nightmares. The worst of which found her staring into Hingo's soulless face as his eyes raped her, and his bare knuckles caressed her cheek.

Near High Hold Meor, on the planet Dantha

Big snowflakes were falling, and had been for hours, as a pair of hooded figures led a string of six shaggy angens around a blind curve, and onto the flawless carpet of white that marked the trail's end. It was as far as the party could go without venturing out onto the rope bridge beyond. And given the fact that the other end of the span was invisible, thanks to the swirling snow, Cato thought it was safe to pause for a few minutes before tackling what would almost certainly be the most dangerous phase of the trip. For even though visibility was poor, he could see the vague outlines of the jagged peak beyond, and the keep that crowned the top of it. That, according to information extracted from Issit, was where Cato would find the Lir Chieftain he was after.

Belok, who was riding in one of the large saddlebags that the lead angen carried, stood, thereby exposing his head and shoulders to the elements. "Brrr!" the Kelf said cheerfully. "It's cold out here!"

Even though Cato was wearing a mountain parka, matching pants, and heavy-duty boots with a Lir robe thrown on top of that, he was still cold. So the thickly furred Kelf wasn't going to get any sympathy from *him*. "It is a bit chilly," Cato admitted, "and the snow makes it difficult to see. Are you ready?"

Having killed three Lir warriors and appropriated their angens and weapons, Cato and his companions were well armed. Belok wasn't big enough to handle a Uman-made assault rifle, but the energy pistols that the Lir typically carried as sidearms were small enough to wrap his fingers around, and he had three of them. One for each hand plus a backup that protruded from the back of his leather britches.

Like Cato, Phelonious was at least partially disguised by a robe that hung to his mechanical knee joints, and was carrying an assault rifle plus ten clips of ammo. The problem was that Phelonious had only been able to fire a dozen practice rounds on the way up the trail and, outside of some barroom brawls, had never been in combat before. Phelonious was determined to help, however, and would be an asset, so long as he didn't fire on his friends.

Cato knew that the sniper rifle would be of limited use in

a close-quarters firefight and had chosen to carry an assault rifle instead. Would the additional firepower combined with the element of surprise be enough to carry the day? There was only one way to find out. "Okay," Cato said. "Let's get going. . . . And remember, it's very important to deal with the sentries quietly, because a single gunshot will bring the entire clan down upon our heads."

"Don't worry," Belok said stoutly, as he sat down. "We know what to do." Cato closed the pack but left the flap undone so Belok could push the top open when the need arose.

Cato and Phelonious positioned themselves at the front of the column of pack angens, knowing it would probably be necessary to tackle the sentries as a team. The rope-and-wood suspension bridge was a simple affair that consisted of wooden planks supported by two sturdy cables, with two more located at waist level, where they doubled as hand ropes. Woven side lashings served to bind all of the elements together and prevent people or things from spilling out over the sides into the river gorge below.

At first Cato was hesitant to put his full weight on the structure. But Phelonious seemed oblivious to the potential danger, and the angens were not only familiar with the span, but eager to reach the food that waited beyond it. So, with the animals pushing from behind, Cato had no choice but to accompany Phelonious onto the span.

The rope bridge began to sag once they were out on it, the cables creaked in response to the additional strain, and when the wind hit the pack train from the side, the entire assemblage began to sway. That, plus the fact that the wooden planks under Cato's feet were covered with a thick layer of ice, made it difficult to remain upright. Cato discovered it was all he could do to move himself ahead, never mind looking out for Belok, or the heavily burdened angens.

But the span held, and as they passed the halfway point

Cato saw the far end of the bridge and the stone hut positioned next to it. Judging from the wisp of smoke that issued from the chimney, it was heated by a dung-fed fire. Did that mean the sentries were lounging inside? Drinking whatever cold warriors drink? Or were they waiting at the bridgehead with weapons at the ready? Squint as he might, Cato's eyes couldn't penetrate the murk, but by swiveling the assault weapon around so that it hung across his chest, he was ready for anything. Cato knew the shit would truly hit the fan if he was forced to fire the weapon, because at that point he and his companions would be forced to retreat across the bridge while the Lir attacked from above. Not a pleasant prospect.

The question of how many sentries were posted at the bridgehead soon became clear. As Cato and Phelonious neared the north side of the span, a robe-clad warrior became visible. But only *one.* That suggested others were inside the hut taking a break. The sentry came forward as if to greet his returning clan brothers, and opened his beak to speak. Then he saw the Uman face, took a full step backward, and was about to fire his weapon when Cato threw the knife.

It wasn't a skill that Cato had mastered, partly because there had been no need to, and partly because of the considerable practice required. As a knife blade flies through the air it turns end over end making it necessary to be just the right distance from the target in order to score a clean strike. And that takes a good eye plus lots of experience.

That was why Cato's knife failed to hit the sentry point first in the middle of his scrawny chest, but *hilt first* between the eyes instead. Though not what Cato intended, it had the desired results. The blow knocked the Lir off his feet and onto his back. Phelonious was there to pounce, and a bone-crushing *thunk* was heard as the android's assault rifle came down on top of the Lir's crested skull.

*   *   *

Meanwhile, having opened the pack and jumped to the ground, Belok waddled over to the hut. The Lir were shorter than the average Uman, but taller than the average Kelf, so Belok had to tuck a pistol into his left armpit in order to reach up and pull the door lever. Then, with a fully charged weapon in each fist, Belok kicked the barrier open. As the door swung out of the way and the incoming air caused the fire to flicker, three Lir turned to complain. One of the warriors was standing, having just removed a kettle of hot water from the swing hook over the fire, so he took the first energy bolt. Because the Kelf was so short, it hit him in the crotch.

The warrior dropped the kettle as both of his clawlike hands went to cradle his badly damaged sex organs. He then uttered a birdlike scream as boiling-hot water splashed onto his right foot, and fell silent when Belok shot him in the head. Fortunately, energy weapons produce very little noise, the stone walls were enough to contain the scream, and no alarm was given.

The other two Lir were in motion by that time and going for their weapons, as Belok fired both pistols at once. The shots weren't aimed, but they didn't have to be, not in such a confined area. The stench of ozone filled the air as blue bolts flashed across the room. They hit one warrior, quickly followed by the other, who went down in a flurry of feathers as a pulse of coherent energy tunneled through his chest and scorched the rocks beyond. So, as Cato entered, assault rifle at the ready, there was nothing for him to do but stare. "Damn," Cato said in amazement. "Where did you learn to do *that*?"

"What?" Belok inquired dully, as his eyes panned the room. Then, as the reality of the carnage hit him, the Kelf ran outside to throw up.

Cato took note of the handheld com set that was sitting

at the center of a crudely made wooden table, gave thanks for the fact that none of the Lir had been given a chance to use it, and took a quick inventory of the room. There were more assault weapons, of course, but the *real* find was a box containing eight fragmentation grenades. Just the thing for defending a bridge against a determined enemy or evening the odds as the threesome pushed up to the fortress above.

Conscious of the fact that the dead warriors were no doubt expected to report in from time to time, Cato hurried to explain the way the miniature bombs worked to Phelonious and Belok before providing each of them with two grenades. Then, having appropriated the remaining bombs for himself, Cato went outside. The first part of the assault on High Hold Meor was a success. But the main part of the fortress loomed above, and there was no way to know how many warriors awaited him there, or how the invasion would go. But a promise had been made to those who had been slaughtered at Station 3, and having failed them before, Cato was determined to honor it.

The city of Solace, on the planet Dantha

Having witnessed a violent abduction the night before, Alamy rose, expecting to hear other slaves talking about it, except that, in marked contrast to what Alamy had seen with her own eyes, the word on the palace grapevine was that Lea had run away and was hiding deep inside The Warrens.

Alamy wanted to correct that version of things, but couldn't do so without admitting where she'd been, and why. A story one of her peers would no doubt sell to Hingo in return for a favor and thereby set Alamy up to receive twenty-five lashes.

So once the morning dishes were done, Alamy took advantage of a fifteen-minute biobreak to stop by the hallway table that she and Persus used as a message drop. But, as Alamy opened the drawer, she saw that a scrap of paper was already waiting inside. Persus had marked it with an "X," which meant that the need for a meeting was urgent. And that was curious indeed. Did Persus have information pertaining to Lea? And her disappearance? Or did the other slave have something else in mind? There was no way to know.

Having been granted the fifteen-minute break, Alamy dashed down a flight of concrete steps and opened a door marked MAINTENANCE PERSONNEL ONLY. She entered a space dominated by a maze of overhead ducts as well as the color-coded pipes that carried freshwater into, and wastewater out of, the palace.

After a quick check to make sure she was alone, Alamy slipped along the right-hand wall to the distal end of a huge pipe. It was no longer in use, not since the new pumping station had been brought online, which was why the terminating end had been severed. By climbing up into the pipe and walking bent over, Alamy was able to make her way to the old pumping station without being seen. Persus was waiting and offered a hand. Alamy took it and jumped down onto the floor, which was bare except for some metal brackets to which huge pumps had been bolted. What light there was slanted down through a skylight high above. Dust motes rode the air, shadows commanded the corners, and there were no sounds other than the ones the women made.

In marked contrast to her normally sunny disposition, Persus was clearly distraught, so Alamy put an arm around the other woman's shoulders, and gave her a hug. "What's wrong, Persus? What happened?"

Persus shook her head. "I'm scared that's all. Early this morning, one of the overseers rousted me out of bed and sent me down to clean up a mess in Storage Room 3B13. I assumed that the plumbing was leaking, or something of that sort, but the walls were splattered with blood! Even the ceiling had blood on it! And as I went in two of the grounds-keepers were carrying a garbage can out. I think there was a body inside. . . . Or parts of a body."

Persus was sobbing by then, and as Alamy sought to console her, something akin to ice water trickled into the slave's veins. Because even though people claimed that Lea had run, Alamy knew it wasn't true, and based on what Persus had seen, it seemed logical to believe that Lea had been murdered!

But why? Having witnessed the scene in the hallway, Alamy had assumed that Hingo was going to rape Lea, but that seemed trivial now. Alamy sensed that something even darker was afoot—something extremely dangerous.

High Hold Meor, on the planet Dantha

Cato and Phelonious followed a trail of snow-blurred foot-steps up a narrow passageway toward the fortress above. Six angens, all eager to return to their stable, followed along behind. Just as he had been earlier, Belok was hidden in a saddlebag, with a pistol clutched in each fist.

Having successfully crossed what amounted to an air moat, and dealt with the sentries posted at the end of the bridge, Cato knew the next task was to penetrate the keep's defenses and find the Lir named Hybor Iddyn.

His plans were somewhat vague after that, since prisoners would be hard to guard with such a small force, and the march out of the mountains would be difficult. Especially if vengeful warriors were attacking from above, but there was no point in dwelling on such issues until such time as they became real.

And right then, in that moment, Cato and his companions were walking through what felt like a slow-motion dream. There were no sounds to be heard other than the rhythmic *crunch, crunch, crunch* of the snow under his boots, the soft *whir* of the android's servos, and the occasional *creak* of a harness as the angens plodded upward.

Meanwhile, snow fell like a silent veil around them, hiding their true identities from High Hold Meor's citizenry, some of whom had emerged to watch the incoming caravan. One of them issued what might have been a greeting, and Cato waved, as if to acknowledge it. The warrior raised his arm as well, the magic held, and the intruders climbed higher.

The keep was built on a series of hand-excavated terraces. Each blocky warehouse, shop, or home stood wall to wall with the rest and was stacked vertically. The structures had slitlike windows plus plenty of balconies, terraces, and verandas from which the locals could launch themselves into the air without having to beat their way upward. All of it was now covered by a thick blanket of white, which acted to soften otherwise harsh lines and make High Hold Meor look picturesque.

All dreams must end, and the one Cato had been walking through was shattered not by a gunshot, but a ten-year-old Lir who ran out to greet her father. But he was dead, having been buried in a shallow grave many miles to the southwest, right next to his war brothers. So what she saw instead was a monster, just like the ones the elders told stories about, which elicited a high-pitched cry. That caused all of the adults to take another look, as Cato yelled, "Run!"

The plan was to take cover between *two* files of angens, with Phelonious bringing the last three up to parallel the lead animals. This strategy worked as warriors opened fire from all sides. Including from above, which was Belok's responsibility, as the Kelf directed his fire toward the lead gray sky. The effort produced immediate results, as one warrior took a bolt through his left wing and went spiraling down, while another was killed outright and fell like a stone.

Meanwhile, as the sturdy angens were struck by bolts of

energy *and* dozens of bullets, they squealed pitifully, and one of them fell. The body was like an anchor that brought the rest of the string to a halt, forcing Cato, Phelonious, and Belok to make a run for it.

The Kelf was up on the android's shoulders by then, firing his pistols at the Lir who circled above, as a force of six warriors rushed out to block further progress. Two of the defenders went down immediately when Phelonious fired short three-round bursts at them, and the rest were torn apart as one of Cato's grenades landed in the middle of the group, going off with a loud *bang*. The echoes of the explosion were still dying away as Cato pointed to the blocky building that sat atop the rest, and yelled, "That looks like the place we want. Get inside!"

Incoming energy beams stuttered past, and bullets pinged off stone pavers while the threesome dashed across an open area, making for what Cato believed to be the "roost" where Chieftain Hybor Iddyn and his family lived. The habitat wasn't undefended, however, and, when warriors spilled out through the front door, it was necessary to open up on them.

Lir bodies danced and jerked, and a steady stream of bright casings arced through the air, as Cato felt something hot nick his side. He'd been hit, he knew that, but there was no time in which to inspect the wound as one of the defenders fell back against the half-open door. That served to push the barrier open, which gave Cato an opportunity to throw a grenade into the space beyond. The otherwise-dark room was momentarily illuminated by a flash of light as the bomb went off, sending chunks of jagged metal in every direction.

The explosion had the desired effect, with Cato and Phelonious able to enter the structure and pull the door closed behind them. It was extremely thick and secured by a sturdy crossbar that was intended to keep attackers out.

There wasn't a lot of light, but what there was came from both narrow slitlike windows and chemical glow strips that dangled in among dried foodstuffs suspended from a smoke-stained ceiling. Once Cato turned his back to the door, he was confronted by a gruesome sight. Because in addition to the warriors who lay dead, four or five females had been slaughtered as well, along with half a dozen juveniles—all of whom lay in a pool of blood.

The scene was very reminiscent of what Cato had seen inside Station 3. But it wasn't what his dead team members would have wanted, or what *he* wanted, for that matter, with one of the older females cradling a warrior's head in her lap and making soft keening sounds in the back of her throat. A form of communication that required no translation.

Cato was not only sickened by what he'd done, but effectively frozen in place as a series of *thump*s were heard. "They have axes," Phelonious observed dispassionately. "And they are trying to hack their way in."

"Hybor Iddyn," Cato said desperately, as he looked from face to face. "I'm an Imperial police officer—and I'm looking for Hybor Iddyn."

The statement was met with silence except for the muffled chopping sounds, but all eyes shifted to the female at the center of the room, and the dead warrior who lay beside her. The misery in her big yellow eyes was clear to see, and Cato could not only "feel" what she felt, but the sorrow, anger, and rage that boiled around him. It was almost overwhelming, and while most variants could suppress it, Cato lacked that ability. Slowly, as if choosing each word with care, the female spoke. "Hybor Iddyn, *here*. He dead. You kill."

Cato looked at the body, wondered if the female was lying to him, and knew she wasn't. Because he could "feel" that she wasn't lying just as he could "feel" how much all the rest of the Lir in the room hated him. Iddyn was dead—and it was *his* fault. The irony of the situation wasn't lost on Cato as he swore under his breath and swiveled toward Phelonious. "Fire a couple of rounds through that gun port. That will force the warriors with the axes to back off and buy us more time."

The android obeyed, the chopping sounds stopped, and Cato turned his attention to Belok, who was standing on a tabletop with both pistols aimed at the group of survivors huddled at the center of the room. "Explore this place," Cato ordered. Look for another way out. And for any point where the Lir warriors could break in. *Hurry!*"

Belok's feet made a soft *thump* as they hit the floor, and he took off at a fast waddle. There were half a dozen weapons lying around, so Cato hurried to collect them, as survivors gave each other first aid. His side hurt, but there wasn't much blood; that was typical of wounds inflicted by energy weapons.

"We have a visitor," Phelonious said, from his post next to the door. "A single warrior with his hands on top of his head. Should I shoot him? Or let him in?"

"Ask him what he wants," Cato replied, as he put the last of the captured weapons down.

Some muffled conversation followed as Phelonious spoke to the Lir, turned his back to the door, and delivered his report. "His name is Issit. . . . And he wants to talk to you."

Cato went to the door, took a quick peek through the gun port, and stepped back. "Let him in. But then close the door quickly."

A blast of cold air pushed its way into the room as the robot opened the door and allowed Issit to enter. The warrior was clearly taken aback by what he saw as Cato patted him down. "This bad," Issit said. "*Very* bad."

Cato felt the same way but wasn't about to say that, so didn't. "Your people broke the law, Issit. They murdered nearly a dozen police officers for money. So, what did you expect? A pat on the back? I want Pak Nassali and Etir Lood.

Give them to me, and I'll leave." It was a bold request under the circumstances, but Cato had nothing to lose and everything to gain.

"They gone," Issit replied woodenly. "No give."

"So why are you here?" Cato demanded.

"Let females and juveniles go," Issit insisted levelly. "Then die like warrior."

"Thanks," Cato replied dryly. "I'll give your suggestion the consideration it deserves. You say that Nassali and Lood aren't here. Where are they? In Solace?"

"No," Issit answered staunchly. But the Lir was lying—and Cato could "feel" it. It was clear that the warriors *were* in Solace, and, assuming that Cato could find them, he might be able to pry additional information out of the pair. Such as who paid for the attack on Station 3 and why. This was a goal made even more urgent by the fact that Fiss Verafti was not only missing but very dangerous.

Cato's thoughts were interrupted as Belok returned, and judging from the Kelf's expression, he was excited. "I found an air car! It's one level down in a workshop!"

"Air car broken," Issit put in bleakly. "Need fix."

"I could take a look at it," Phelonious offered. "I'm pretty good with machinery."

"You do that," Cato agreed. "I'll guard the door."

As the robot departed for the other side of the room and the stairs, Cato turned to Belok. "Did you find a back door? Some way to get out of here without being seen?"

Belok shook his head. "Not unless we sprout wings and fly! There are two doors on the west face of the building, but both are located a good twenty feet off the ground, and warriors are all around. I think they're massing for an attack."

"You die like warrior," Issit insisted helpfully. "That best."

"You're starting to piss me off," Cato growled as he aimed

the assault weapon at the Lir. "Lie down on the floor and keep your beak shut! Belok, tie him up. We have enough people to keep track of as it is."

Then, as if to reinforce Cato's words, there was a resounding *BOOM*, something hit the front door, and a cloud of dust appeared. Cato went over to look through the gun port and swore. "They have a log, damn it! And they're using it as a battering ram."

And then, as the variant began to pull back, a bullet passed within an inch of his nose, smacking into the wall behind him. That was when Cato realized that besides the effort to break in, the blow to the door had been intended to bring someone to the gun port so a sharpshooter could put them down! The fact that he was still alive had been a matter of good luck rather than skill.

Now, if he went to the port to fire at the warriors with the battering ram, the sharp-eyed sniper would get *another* opportunity to blow his head off! But if he didn't chase the warriors away, the assault would continue. There was a second *BOOM*, the door shook, and wood splintered. Two additional hits, three at the most, and the Lir warriors would be inside.

Belok had immobilized Issit by then, and Cato motioned to the Kelf, as another rifle bullet entered through the port. It hit the far wall, bounced off stone, and made a high-pitched whine as it traversed the room again. "Come on, we aren't going to hold them here, we've got to fall back."

"What about the weapons?" Belok wanted to know.

"We'll take them with us," Cato replied grimly, as he gathered three rifles into his arms. "It looks like we're going to need them."

The Lir survivors, many of whom were clutching blood-stained bandages, eyed the twosome sullenly as Cato and Belok crossed the room. Cato knew they would open the front door the moment he was gone, but couldn't bring himself to shoot them, especially given the fact that it would have been pointless.

So the heavily encumbered invaders hurried past and made their way over to the flight of stairs located on the west side of the room. Meanwhile the front door shuddered as still another *BOOM* was heard.

Belok descended the stairs first, quickly followed by Cato, who lowered the weapons he was carrying to the Kelf. Once his hands were free, Cato secured a grip on the heavy trapdoor that was lying on the floor and pulled it down over his head. There were iron bolts to hold the thick slab of wood firmly in place, so Cato took a moment to push both into their respective fittings before completing the journey into the workshop below. "That will keep the bastards out for five minutes or so," Cato observed. "But that's all."

The last couple of words were almost inaudible as a loud chattering noise came from the back of the room. When Cato turned to look he saw that an air car was parked in the middle of the multipurpose workshop, and judging from the thick layer of dust on it, the ancient vehicle had been sitting there for quite some time. The rear engine compartment was propped open, and Phelonious was bent over it, as the air car's starter struggled to bring the dead power plant online.

Would the android succeed? Probably not, but with no other options remaining, Cato made his way over to a large set of double doors. They would need to be open if Phelonious was successful—even if that meant giving the Lir an opportunity to fire into the shop.

The warriors knew where the alien invaders were by then, and when Cato removed the bar that held the doors in place, energy bolts burned holes into them. "Get ready to fire!" Cato shouted, swinging the right-hand door open. "You'll have plenty of targets!"

The prediction proved to be true as light flooded into the otherwise-murky shop, and the cold wind blew a host of snowflakes into the room. Four winged warriors, all of whom were armed with energy pistols, hovered outside. Or attempted to, since the wind was pushing them toward the building, and a lot of work was required just to stay aloft.

Belok opened fire first, with Cato joining him moments later, in an effort to drive the Lir away. Energy bolts flashed, bullets flew, and one of the warriors went down. But the incoming fire forced both defenders to seek cover as a thrumming was heard, and the venerable air car lurched up off the floor. It wobbled from side to side as the breeze hit it, and coughed uncertainly before catching again. "The ignition system was miswired!" Phelonious proclaimed triumphantly. "Hop in!"

There was no need to issue a second invitation as Phelonious took the controls and the others scrambled into the backseat. The utilitarian vehicle was open to the weather *and* incoming fire. That meant Cato and Belok had plenty of targets to fire at while the air car surged out into the snowstorm.

There was one extremely vulnerable moment when a single grenade would have been sufficient to blow the vehicle out of the air. But none of the Lir was expecting such an escape, so the surrounding warriors were caught off guard as Phelonious pulled back on the control yoke, sending the air car slanting upward. The bottom fell out of Cato's stomach as the power cut out, and he was bracing himself for a crash when the engine came back on. The tubby vehicle had begun to trail black smoke by then, but wounded or not, it still had sufficient power to leave High Hold Meor behind.

Less than a minute later, Phelonious sent the air car down into the adjacent gorge, where it banked back and forth as it followed the twisting, turning canyon west toward the foothills and desert beyond. Cato was alive, and glad of it, but felt none of the joy he might have expected. Because while a victory had been won, the price had been steep, and only the passage of time would tell whether all of the dying had been worth it.

NINE

The city of Solace, on the planet Dantha

THOUGH NOT THE LARGEST CLASS OF WARSHIP THAT the Navy had, the destroyer *Imperialus* was still huge, and as the ship coasted in from the east, it blocked the morning sun, throwing a dark shadow over both the palace and the city of Solace. The thrumming produced by the vessel's main drives, combined with the roar of her mighty repellers, rattled windows throughout the city and brought thousands out to stare. The ship's repellers caused the waters of Lake Imperium to boil; clouds of steam rose, and the warship seemed to float on them. Having hovered in place for exactly three minutes, the vessel pivoted toward the spaceport and slowly moved away. The whole thing was calculated to impress both the plebeians *and* Procurator Nalomy.

Brightly colored flags were flying, hundreds of militia troops stood at attention, and a crowd of local dignitaries was assembled in front of the one-story passenger terminal as the massive destroyer slid in over the spaceport and came to a well-timed stop. But in spite of the attempt to dress the place up, there was no hiding how run-down the spaceport was as Legate Usurlus eyed it via the screens in the destroyer's U-shaped control room. Then the views of the surrounding landscape vanished as the ship's repellers stabbed the ground, and the ship was lost in a momentary dust storm.

Once the massive skids made contact with the sun-baked tarmac, and the main engines started to spool down, the Captain rose from his seat and turned to face Usurlus. The Legate had been easy to deal with as VIPs go, but the role of taxi driver was one that the officer despised, and would be glad to get rid of. Though small of stature, he seemed larger thanks to an expansive personality and the aura of relaxed competence that surrounded him. "Welcome to Dantha," the naval officer said cheerfully. "Your luggage will be on the ground in five minutes."

Usurlus smiled. He knew that the Vord raiders had been aggressive of late, the Navy was short of ships, and couldn't afford to leave the *Imperialus* sitting on Dantha. He also knew that the officer in front of him would be happy to lift off. "And you'll be airborne twenty minutes after that?"

The Captain grinned. "No, sir. . . . I'm aiming for ten!"

Both men laughed. But as Usurlus made his way down to the main entry port and from there to the ramp that led to the ground, he was conscious of how vulnerable he would be once the ship left. Not *entirely* vulnerable, however, since Vedius Albus was waiting for him on the tarmac, along with a force of twenty smartly uniformed bodyguards. Their function was to provide a show of force and divert attention away from forty men who had exited the ship earlier and were boarding unmarked vehicles. One section would be stationed along the route into town, where it would serve as a quick-reaction force, while the rest continued to the palace, where the quarters assigned to Usurlus would have to be secured, inspected, and electronically debugged before he could take up residence there.

Would a force of sixty men be sufficient? If he ordered

Nalomy to step down? And she refused to go? No, probably not, but that was the chance Usurlus had to take as Nalomy came forward to greet him. Usurlus had met her before, of course, but was still struck by how attractive she was, and made a note to steer well clear of her bed. "Welcome to Dantha!" Nalomy said brightly, as she came to a stop two feet away. "You look wonderful!"

Imperial etiquette was a bit vague where the relationship between Legates and Procurators was concerned. But technically, as the legal embodiment of the Emperor's authority, Usurlus was entitled to a curtsy, and the honorific "Excellency," upon an initial greeting. Especially if others were present. But in keeping with the size of her ego, Nalomy chose to greet Usurlus as an equal.

Though conscious of the slight, the Legate accepted the forearm-to-forearm grip, and the brief embrace that went with it. "You look wonderful as well," Usurlus replied, cautiously. "It appears that the local climate suits you."

Though seemingly innocuous, Nalomy knew the comment could be interpreted to mean that life on a rim world suited her, as opposed to higher office. That suggestion rankled, but Nalomy was far too practiced to let her unhappiness show, as she led Usurlus between two ranks of perfectly matched soldiers to the open ground car beyond. Such vehicles were vulnerable, especially to snipers and anyone who could fashion some sort of bomb. By riding in it, Nalomy hoped to demonstrate how peaceful Dantha was. Thanks to her.

Having spotted the open car, Vedius spoke to Usurlus via the plug in the Legate's right ear, and urged him to insist on safer transport. But the last thing Usurlus wanted to do was to appear fearful, so he chose to ignore the bodyguard's advice. *Besides,* Usurlus reasoned, *Nalomy isn't likely to ride in an open car unless she thinks it will be safe for her.*

The motorcade consisted of two cars packed with specially trained militia, followed by the open limo, and two hover trucks loaded with troops. Once under way, it traveled the empty road at a steady fifteen miles per hour. There weren't any homes in the vicinity of the noisy spaceport, but cheering people lined both sides of the road nevertheless, which suggested that they had been trucked out from the city and *paid* to cheer. Or forced to do so by the militiamen who were stationed along the way—a stratagem Usurlus had employed on behalf of the Emperor on Corin.

Even though Usurlus was aware of the extent to which the situation had been stage-managed, it suited his purposes to ignore it. So he smiled and waved at the onlookers as if entirely taken in. Eventually, as the motorcade entered Solace, the crowds grew larger. And, by all appearances, it looked as though they had turned out voluntarily. That suggested that the flyover, combined with curiosity regarding the Imperial visit, had brought a substantial number of unpaid citizens out to gawk.

In marked contrast to the bystanders on the outskirts of town, *these* onlookers were almost universally silent, the single exception being the occasional insult often accompanied by a piece of flying fruit. Most of the missiles fell woefully short, but one struck the passenger-side door with an audible *thump*, and was celebrated with a reedy cheer.

None of which seemed to trouble Nalomy, who shrugged philosophically, as members of the militia went after the perpetrators with riot clubs. "Every planet has a few troublemakers," Nalomy said dismissively. "And Dantha is no exception. A good thumping will put them right."

What Nalomy said was true, Usurlus knew that, but as the limo turned onto Imperial Boulevard, he sensed that the hostility emanating from the crowd ran a lot deeper than Nalomy had implied. But the final determination would come during the days ahead. For in keeping with Emperor Emor's wishes, Usurlus was going to need hard evidence of crimes committed by Nalomy herself, before removing her from power.

The latest bodies, both of which were quite ripe, had been taken down lest Usurlus see them and jump to the wrong conclusion. As the car passed below one of the gibbets, a long, thin shadow flickered across Nalomy's face, but she failed to notice. Her eyes were on the palace, the future that lay somewhere beyond, and the eternal glory that was rightfully hers.

As the motorcade neared its destination, Fiss Verafti stood atop the palace's flat roof and eyed the convoy through a pair of military-issue binos. He was still using the name Inhor Rypool, and still *looked* like Centurion Ben Sivio, since that cover was as good as any. His mind churned as the glasses found the man seated next to Nalomy and automatically held the image in focus while the convoy entered a U-shaped driveway. Killing Legate Usurlus would be easy—but what then? Nalomy had promised to free him, but she could go back on her word, which would leave the shape shifter right where he was: a prisoner with an explosive device attached to his right wrist.

Unless he could obtain a key . . . But *how*? Both Nalomy and Hingo wore pendants around their necks. But they were never alone, not around him, anyway, and what about the mysterious *third* person? Who was he or she? It was a puzzle, a very interesting puzzle, and one Verafti was determined to solve.

The balance of Usurlus's first day in Solace was a long, drawn-out affair that began with a reception for local movers and shakers, and ended with an interminable dinner, during which Usurlus was sandwiched between a corpulent mining magnate, and a woman so elderly that her frail body was cradled inside of a life-support exoskeleton that whirred when she moved.

But Usurlus had survived worse gatherings on Corin. So when the sun rose the following morning, he was rested and ready to meet with the dozen people who had been granted audiences for that day, eleven of whom were seeking a favor and were of little interest. However, it was necessary to spend time with them in order to provide cover for the individual with whom Usurlus *wanted* to meet. That man was ushered into the guest suite at exactly 3:00 PM, where he was subjected to a search, before being allowed to enter a large sitting room. Usurlus rose from a couch and came forward to greet the newly arrived visitor. "Hason!" Usurlus said heartily. "It's a pleasure to see you again!"

Meanwhile, comfortably ensconced in her lavish quarters only a few hundred feet away, Nalomy was receiving a pedicure while watching a feed that came straight from the guest suite. Her dog was sitting on her lap, and Centurion Pasayo was seated a few feet away. By leaving some nearly microscopic bugs where they would be found, the Legate's staff had been lulled into believing that the quarters were secure, which they certainly weren't.

Now, as the Legate's latest guest arrived, Nalomy found herself looking at a man with a receding hairline and large, expressive eyes. The meetings between Usurlus and his previous visitors had been rather boring to say the least, a fact which was reflected in Nalomy's listless manner, and her choice of words. "So, who is this? Someone interesting I hope. The earlier meetings were dull, dull, dull."

Pasayo consulted a printout. "His name is Hason Ovidius, Highness. He owns a small furniture factory located in The Warrens. His record is clean, but according to the information supplied by my agents, he's rather nosy. Citizen Ovidius has made a number of inquiries regarding government auctions, but has yet to purchase anything, which raises the question why? Because he lacks sufficient funds? Or for some other reason?"

Nalomy had pocketed millions of Imperials by declaring government property surplus, skimming money off each sale, and sending the rest to Corin for the Emperor and his toadies to waste. So the report was enough to make Nalomy sit up and take notice as the men on the screen embraced and took seats opposite each other. The dog produced a squeaking sound as it was unceremoniously dumped onto the marble floor. "A furniture maker . . ." Nalomy mused out loud. "I'll be interested to see why an Imperial Legate would meet with such a man."

"So," Usurlus said, as Ovidius took a seat. "What's it been? A year or so?"

The businessman nodded soberly. "Sixteen standard months. But it *feels* like two years."

Usurlus nodded. "Yes, I'm sure it's been difficult. So, has Procurator Nalomy been earning her pay? Or been paying herself?"

"The latter I'm afraid, sir," Ovidius replied earnestly. "It's just as you suspected. With the exception of the militia, which Nalomy needs to keep the population in line, she is systematically robbing Dantha's citizens of all the things they are entitled to. A lot of government property is surplused before it even sees service, and money is skimmed off each transaction. The strategy enables Nalomy to make money for herself, and curry favor with influential citizens who buy the goods at submarket prices, *and* refund significant sums to the Imperial government! Which, up to this point, seems happy to receive it."

"Yes," Usurlus agreed darkly. "The Senate is always happy to receive and spend money. But do you have hard evidence? Because if I charge Nalomy, and the charges fail to stick, it would be embarrassing for the Emperor. . . . Not to mention myself."

"That's a problem, sir," the spy admitted reluctantly. "Even though it's obvious that the Procurator is stealing from the government, no one wants to testify to that fact for fear of retribution, and written records, if any, are all under her control."

"I was afraid of that," Usurlus said bleakly. "But we can't afford to let the situation continue as is, so I may have to pull the plug on Nalomy, even though her father is bound to raise hell in the Senate."

"That's when the necessary witnesses will come forward," Ovidius predicted. "Once you remove her from power. Believe me, there are lots of people who will support your actions, and among them they have a great deal of information."

"I hope so," Usurlus said. "Please tell them to be ready on Founder's Day."

"I will," Ovidius promised.

"And one more thing," Usurlus added. "Don't give up on trying to find hard evidence. I'm sure it's out there. All we need to do is find it."

Ovidius swallowed. He'd been trying to do that for months without success. And to push harder could easily cost him his life. But Usurlus knew that, or should have known that, which left him with nothing to say. Ovidius bowed his head humbly. "Yes, sir. I'll do what I can."

The wall-mounted video screen shattered as Nalomy hurled a heavy vase at it. "I'm going to kill you!" she screamed, as the picture of Usurlus flew into hundreds of pieces. "I'll ship you to the Emperor in a box!" And with that, the Procurator stormed out of the room.

The slave who had been massaging the Procurator's feet only moments before had collected her tools and was backing away. Her eyes were on the floor, and she was striving to render herself invisible. Centurion Pasayo sighed, drew his sidearm, and shot her in the chest. The body hit the marble, and left a bloody mark on the otherwise-pristine floor, as it skidded to a stop. There were advantages to Pasayo's job, but cleaning up after Nalomy wasn't one of them, and there were times when he wondered if what he stood to gain was worth it.

Near the town of Donk's Well, on the planet Dantha

Cato had been hiking for three hours. Though well below the snow line, that particular portion of the trail was high enough to be cold at night, and as the sun began to sink in the west, Cato could feel a nip in the air. Having arrived at a point where a small pile of rocks marked his turnoff point, he paused to scan the darkening skies for Lir scouts.

Fifteen minutes after the escape from High Hold Meor, the air car's engine had given out for good, and since the tubby little aircraft had the glide characteristics of a rock, the fact that Phelonious had been able to drop it into a small clearing was nothing short of a miracle. Lir warriors were searching for the threesome by then, but by covering the vehicle with tree branches, the fugitives had been able to avoid notice.

After a cold night spent without a sleeping bag, Cato set out for Donk's Well, where he hoped to purchase a heat exchanger for the air car. A part that, if Phelonious was correct, would bring the vehicle back to life.

But Lir scouts had been circling high above, searching for

the aliens who had attacked their fortress, and Cato had been forced to hide for hours at a time waiting for the airborne warriors to go away. Finally, after a long, nerve-wracking hike, Cato made it to Donk's Well and the sprawling junk-yard located just north of town. Predictably enough, the proprietor didn't have a VH3BT47 heat exchanger. But he did have a VH3BT48 heat exchanger, which was identical to the part Cato was looking for, except that the mounting flange was set up to receive four bolts rather than *six*.

However, by drilling two additional holes, the junk mer-chant swore he could make it fit. Cato had very little choice but to go along with the plan because the alternative was to hike all the way to Solace while Lir warriors sought to track him down.

Now, having hauled the part plus some much-needed sup-plies back into the foothills, Cato wanted to make sure that no one was following him. So he spent a good five minutes examining both the sky *and* his back trail before stepping off the main track and scrambling up a steep embankment. A trail of half-broken branches led Cato through a stand of bristle trees to the clearing beyond.

The carefully camouflaged air car was right where he had left it, but his companions were nowhere to be seen until Phelonious stepped out from behind a tree and Belok popped up at the center of some rocks. The Kelf was clutch-ing two energy pistols, which he shoved into the waistband of his britches. "It's about time," the diminutive alien said disrespectfully. "Did you get it?"

"Yes, no thanks to you," Cato replied, as he shrugged the pack off. "It isn't the same part, but it should do the trick, assuming the guy who modified it knows what he's doing."

"We'll see," Phelonious intoned cynically. "The citizens of Donk's Well aren't the brightest bunch." The robot was eager to install the heat exchanger before the sun dropped below the western horizon, and immediately went to work.

Fortunately, the installation went smoothly, the engine caught right away, and the air car was ready for takeoff. However, that led to a *second* problem as Phelonious closed the engine compartment. It was dark by then, and they were still in the foothills. "Do you think you can fly us out of here?" Cato wanted to know.

"Sure," Phelonious answered confidently. "And this is the best time to do it. When the Lir can't see us."

That made sense, or seemed to, except that it was pitch-black and Cato was more concerned about what *Phelonious* could see. Still, it was a chance that they were going to have to take, so all Cato could do was strap himself in and hope for the best. The engine roared, the air car lurched into the air, and the only thing he could do was pray.

The city of Solace, on the planet Dantha

It was nearly noon by the time Usurlus awoke, which was typical for a man who normally either worked or played until 3:00 AM, although given his lifestyle it was often difficult to tell one activity from the other. Especially since sex was a good way to secure important relationships, parties were ideal situations in which to start rumors, and information obtained in the senatorial baths was frequently more reliable than the pap that was available from the news combines.

Having rolled out of the huge bed, Usurlus made his way into the palatial bath and spent the next hour showering, shaving, and otherwise grooming himself. It was an exacting process in which unwanted hairs were plucked, trimmed, and in some cases chemically removed. Then, after reviewing every inch of his body for potential flaws, it was time to apply a selection of lotions, creams, and gels—all of which were calculated to tone, tighten, and conceal tiny imperfections.

Finally, having prepared his body for the day ahead,

Usurlus ventured into the suite's huge walk-in closet, where all of his clothes had been hung on identical hangers. The fact that they were grouped by both function and color made it that much easier to assemble an outfit quickly. In the present circumstances, that meant a loose-fitting set of daytime pajamas made out of gray synsilk. They shimmered subtly as Usurlus made his way out into the formal sitting room.

It was a beautifully furnished space and well lit thanks to the sunshine that streamed in through a well-placed skylight. The resulting light reflected off a small fishpond and danced across the ceiling. A breakfast table had been set up in front of a bank of curved windows. And there, beyond the projectile-proof glass, the blue waters of Lake Imperium sparkled as if lit from below. It was a pleasant scene, and made even more so by the presence of a very comely slave girl, who introduced herself as Alamy. Not the sort of creature one could take to a party on one of the inner planets, Usurlus thought to himself, but well worth taking to bed, should the opportunity present itself. The chair sighed softly as the Legate put his weight on it and took his napkin off the table.

As Alamy opened the warming cart and began to serve breakfast, Usurlus noticed a box positioned on the chair next to his. "What have we here?" Usurlus wanted to know, reaching over to take possession of the neatly wrapped cube. His name had been hand-printed across the top in block letters. "A gift perhaps?"

"It arrived half an hour ago," Alamy replied, as she placed a basket of freshly baked pastries on the table. "One of the housekeepers brought it. She told me a man gave it to one of the soldiers at the main gate."

The contents of the box weren't very heavy. Usurlus shook the package experimentally, but wasn't able to hear any telltale noises, which deepened the mystery. What was in the box anyway? Usurlus took hold of a knife, and was about to sever the string that held the wrapping paper in place, when a well-honed sense of caution reasserted itself. Were Nalomy's people on the ball? Had the package been scanned? Assassins were theoretically everywhere. Even on Dantha. "Summon my chief bodyguard," Usurlus ordered, as he put the box back on the chair. "And pass that pot. . . . I could use some tea."

Alamy said, "Yes, Excellency," and having passed the teapot, pushed the cart across the room.

Vedius Albus was never far from his master's side and entered the room a few seconds later. He wore civilian clothing over light armor and was carrying a number of concealed weapons. "Yes, sire. You called?"

"Yes," Usurlus replied, as he made use of his napkin to dab at his lips. "I did. What, if anything, can you tell me about that box?"

Albus eyed the object in question. "An unidentified person left it for you, sire. . . . Procurator Nalomy's security people scanned the package before allowing it into the palace, and it was rescanned by my team when a slave brought it upstairs. No traces of explosives, toxins, or other threats were detected."

Usurlus nodded and put his cup down. "Thank you, Vedius. I assumed as much—but it never hurts to be careful. Place the box on the table please. Let's see what's inside."

Albus lifted the container, placed it on the table, and produced a wicked-looking flick knife. There was a decisive *click* as the weapon locked into the open position, and the string parted under the supersharp blade. The wrapping paper rattled as it was removed. That was when Usurlus noticed a peculiar odor and frowned. But the scent was so faint that he might have been mistaken. So Usurlus kept the observation to himself as he stood up and came around to peer over the other man's shoulder. He was the first to react once Albus removed the lid. "Oh, no," Usurlus said sadly. "It's Hason Ovidius."

Albus had to agree. It *was* Ovidius, or part of him anyway, since there was no mistaking the spy's face or the head that was wedged inside the box. The odor of rotting flesh was stronger now, and Albus wrinkled his nose as he replaced the lid.

Perhaps another man would have fainted, or become sick to his stomach, but—like most of his political peers—Usurlus was no stranger to bloodshed. Because the give-and-take of death was a constant within the upper reaches of Imperial Society, and anyone with a weak stomach wasn't likely to last long. And, even though he hadn't worn a uniform during the past few years, he was a military officer.

So rather than call for help, or waste his time bemoaning the spy's fate, Usurlus jerked his head toward the doors that led to the veranda. Being no fool, Albus knew what Usurlus was thinking. Given the reason for his employer's visit to Dantha, and the nature of the spy's activities, it seemed logical to suppose that Procurator Nalomy was responsible for Ovidius's death. But how could she know? The answer was obvious.

Warm air pushed its way into the air-conditioned room as Usurlus opened the twin doors and made his way out onto the tiled surface beyond. When he turned back toward the palace, Albus was waiting. "Please accept my profound apologies, sire," the bodyguard said miserably, as he looked down at his boots. "We thought we had located all of the bugs—but it appears we failed."

"So it would seem," Usurlus agreed indulgently, "because if Nalomy saw or heard Ovidius make his report, she would certainly want him dead. Both as a means to protect herself and as a way to intimidate me. So resweep the suite, destroy any bugs you find, and keep a sharp eye out for new ones."

"Yes, sire," Albus agreed humbly, his head still down.

"And one more thing," Usurlus added thoughtfully. "Once the suite is secure, take my brother out of storage— and energize my face mask. We're going out."

Albus brought his head up. His eyes were filled with concern. "Please, sire, I don't have enough men to fully protect you here, much less out on the streets,"

"No, you don't," Usurlus agreed. "Which is why you and I will go alone."

In addition to Legate Usurlus, the destroyer *Imperialus* had been carrying other cargo as well, including a great deal of correspondence for Nalomy. Much of it related to routine governmental matters, but the sealed container included personal messages as well, like the holo that Nalomy's father had sent her. So when Centurion Pasayo entered the Procurator's office, a full-sized likeness of Senator Tegor Nalomy was striding back and forth in front of his daughter's elaborate desk. His voice was raised far more than was necessary as he railed on about how incompetent Emperor Emor was and always had been. One of his favorite subjects. Nalomy cut her father off in midrant by touching a button as she turned toward Pasayo. "Yes?"

"The box was delivered, Highness," the soldier said expressionlessly.

Nalomy's carefully sculpted eyebrows rose incrementally. "And?"

"After opening it, Legate Usurlus went out onto the veranda with his chief bodyguard," the officer added. "He remained there while members of his staff searched the suite for bugs. Subsequent to that palace security officers were summoned and the box was given to them. When questioned regarding its contents, Legate Usurlus admitted that he knew Hason Ovidius and identified him as being little more than an acquaintance."

Nalomy smiled tightly. "And were they able to find the remaining bugs?"

Pasayo nodded. "Yes, Highness. All of them."

"See if you can get some more in there," Nalomy instructed. "But, even if you can't, the trade-off was worth it. Now he knows that I know. And that will slow the bastard down until we can get rid of him permanently."

Pasayo wasn't so sure about the benefits to be derived from the so-called trade-off, since he thought that killing Ovidius, and thereby revealing how much Nalomy knew, was a tactical error. But she rarely took his advice on such matters. The real truth was that the decision to eliminate Ovidius had been the result of Nalomy's unreasoning anger rather than the master stroke she claimed it to be. But the soldier couldn't say that, so he didn't. "Yes, Highness. . . . It shall be as you say."

"Of course it will," Nalomy replied smugly. She pressed a button, her father blossomed in front of her, and continued his rant.

It was a long walk up from the Bone Yard, where Hason Ovidius's remains were waiting to be cremated, to the terraced hillside where many middle-class homes looked out over The Warrens to the south and the lake to the east. But Lucia Ovidius welcomed both the hard exercise and the opportunity to be by herself after being required to deal with so many people. Her husband had lots of friends, business associates, and business contacts, many of whom had been part of the long, sad processional that had taken the body from the point where it was found to the Bone Yard below.

There had been tears, lots of them, and there would be more. But at the moment, Lucia was trying to think, trying to adjust to the very different life suddenly thrust upon her.

Lucia had been opposed to what she initially called "a dangerous waste of time." But as Nalomy's despotic rule gradually became even worse, and the resistance to it grew stronger, her cynicism had eventually been supplanted by a zeal that was just as strong as her husband's. The main difference between them was that Hason was an idealist, who enjoyed political discourse, while Lucia was a pragmatist who preferred action over words.

And now, having lost her husband to Nalomy's agents, Lucia was focused on revenge. As were many other members of the resistance—one of whom was crouched next to the long flight of stairs that led up to her whitewashed home. He was dressed as a beggar and pushed the usual bowl out in front of her. "Two men, mistress," the man said. "Both waiting at your house."

That was sufficient to bring Lucia to a halt and open her purse. Because even though Hason was dead, Nalomy's agents could have been sent after *her* as well, which was why the "beggar" had been assigned to keep an eye on her house. Of course the visitors could be well-wishers, come to convey their condolences, or business partners who wanted to follow up on some transaction. Two decims rattled as they hit the bottom of the otherwise-empty bowl. "Are they security agents?" Lucia inquired. "Or regular citizens?"

"There's no way to be sure," the man answered cautiously. "But they didn't look like agents. Their clothes were expensive, both of them had off-world accents, and one gave me an Imperial! How many security men would do that?"

"Not many," Lucia admitted with a wan smile. "Watch my veranda. . . . If I hang a rug over the rail, everything is okay."

The beggar eyed Lucia from under his hood. He had

brown eyes and three days' worth of carefully cultivated stubble. "And if you don't?"

"Then send help," Lucia answered grimly. "*Lots* of it." And with that she began to climb the stairs.

"Here she comes," Albus said evenly, as he peered through the window.

Usurlus was on the other side of the nicely decorated living room inspecting a photograph of Hason Ovidius and his wife Lucia. She had short brown hair, intelligent eyes, and a face that while attractive was too narrow to be called beautiful. Would she blame him for her husband's death? Yes, probably, and with good reason. Because immediately after meeting the businessman the year before, Usurlus had taken advantage of Hason's anger toward Nalomy to re-cruit him as a spy. Which led directly to his death. Usurlus turned toward the front of the house. "Did she talk with the beggar?"

Albus was still looking out between the white curtains. "Yes, sir. She did."

"So she knows we're here and still has the courage to climb the stairs," Usurlus mused out loud. "Something tells me that Hason was a lucky man."

Lucky men got to keep their heads on their shoulders, or so it seemed to Albus, but the bodyguard knew better than to voice his opinion. "If you say so, sire."

"I do," Usurlus replied. "Now come over here so she'll see both of us when she enters."

Albus obeyed, which meant that as Lucia pushed the front door open, the sun threw a carpet of gold over the floor. Usurlus watched Lucia Ovidius enter the room and pause. There was uncertainty in the woman's eyes, but de-termination as well, and her voice was steady. "You broke into my home."

"Albus picked the lock," Usurlus replied, with a nod toward the other man. "But the effect was the same. And for that we apologize. Please accept our deepest sympathies regarding the death of your husband. . . . He was a brave man and a patriot. I know it will be small recompense but I will do everything in my power to see that his service to the Empire is officially recognized, and that you as his widow receive the financial support that is due you."

Lucia's expression remained unchanged. Her eyes shifted from face to face. "And you are?"

"I am Legate Isulu Usurlus," the official said. "And this is Vedius Albus. My chief bodyguard."

"I've seen Legate Usurlus," Lucia said skeptically. "In fact I was in the crowd when his motorcade carried him down Imperial Boulevard. And he's better-looking than you are."

Usurlus brought a hand up, pressed the nodule located behind his right ear with his right index finger, and felt the face mask begin to squirm. Then, once the pseudoflesh had separated itself from his real skin, it fell free. Usurlus's hands were positioned to catch it. "There," he said. "How's that?"

"Better," Lucia said grudgingly. "Please wait here. . . . There's something I need to do."

Both men watched as Lucia went over to pick up a colorful throw rug, which she carried out onto the veranda that spanned the front of the house and threw over a railing. Once that was accomplished, she came back inside. The two men were right where she had left them. "Please," Lucia said politely, "have a seat. Can I get you something to drink?"

"No," Usurlus said, as he sat on what had been Hason's favorite chair. "Thank you."

Albus, who had taken up a position at the window, made no reply. He was scanning the surrounding buildings with a small but powerful pair of binoculars.

"All right then," Lucia said, as she took the chair next to the one Usurlus was seated on. "It was dangerous for you to come here. Dangerous for you—and dangerous for *me*. And while I appreciate all of the nice things that you said—every one of those sentiments could have been expressed in a letter or holo. What do you want?"

Usurlus took note of not only the direct manner in which Lucia spoke, but also the woman's failure to use any of the honorifics to which he was entitled, and felt a mix of emotions. Lucia Ovidius was strong, which was important given the task he wanted her to carry out, but she was either lacking in the social graces or simply disrespectful. Which made a marked contrast to her husband, who had been a good deal more deferential, and properly so.

But with only a limited number of tools at his disposal, Usurlus was in no position to be picky. So, as his eyes locked with hers, Usurlus was frank. "I know that you were aware of your husband's work on behalf of the Empire. . . . So you have an excellent understanding of what's at stake. Were it not for the steadily increasing conflict with the Vord, I would have arrived with a Legion of Imperial troops, and been able to carry out my investigation in a normal manner.

"But, because his resources are stretched rather thin at the moment, all the Emperor could send was me and my personal bodyguard. That means that when I make my move, which will occur in the coliseum on Founder's Day, popular support will be critical. And not just acquiescence, but active support by such a large majority of citizens that the people in command of the militia will realize that it would be foolhardy to continue their support for Nalomy. Then, and only then, will I be able to pull this tyrant down! So what I 'want,' as you put it, is for you to continue your husband's work. Which was to find hard proof of Nalomy's guilt, or failing that, to help build the support I need. If you refuse, his death will have been for nothing."

*   *   *

The last was a blatant attempt to manipulate Lucia's emotions and she knew it. But the tactic was effective nevertheless, because Hason *had* given his life to improve conditions on Dantha, and Usurlus was the only person who could deliver on that dream. Lucia was silent for a moment, but in the end she bowed her head as if in submission, and spoke the words Usurlus wanted to hear. "I will serve you as my husband did regardless of the cost."

TEN

THE ENGINE WAS RUNNING, AND THE AIR CAR WAS ready for takeoff, assuming that the repairs held. But it was pitch-black in the mountain clearing, and without even the stars to guide them, it would be easy to hit one of the trees that stood all around. Still, Phelonious claimed that he could manage it, and Cato *wanted* to believe him. Because if the threesome remained where they were, and waited for daybreak, there was a good chance that they would be discovered by High Hold Meor's warriors.

So as Cato and Belok checked their seat belts, Phelonious checked the air car's instrument panel, before applying power and lifting straight up. There was a limit to how high an air car could go without traveling horizontally. And, because some of the surrounding trees were a good twenty feet tall, it was necessary for Phelonious to push the tubby vehicle to the very edge of a stall before finally leveling out. The air car shuddered as the hull brushed a treetop before soaring out over the slope below. They were free! And, more importantly, alive.

Ten minutes later, when the lights of Donk's Well appeared in the distance, the air car turned toward the south. The little aircraft wasn't designed to fly higher than a thousand feet, which meant it couldn't cross the Sawtooth Mountains directly, and would have to negotiate the S-shaped east-west pass instead. A tricky business at night, but not impossible, thanks to the solar-powered nav beacons positioned along the way.

The heater was just one of the many things that didn't work on the vehicle, so Cato was sitting in the backseat cocooned inside a newly purchased sleeping bag as the air car banked to the left and entered Heartbreak Pass. He fell asleep eventually, and remained that way for more than an hour, as the air car continued to bore through the darkness.

Finally, having cleared the east end of the pass, Phelonious was able to turn north. City lights appeared fifteen minutes later, and Cato awoke as the engine sputtered and caught again. Belok, who had a thick layer of fur to protect him from the cold, was seated next to the police officer. It was necessary to yell in order to be heard over the combined roar of the engine and the slipstream. "Where are we going to land? Assuming we don't crash?"

"On the palace," Cato responded. "I'm going straight to the top! Once Procurator Nalomy learns about the murders at Station 3, and the fact that a homicidal shape shifter is on the loose, she'll have to respond."

"I think you're crazy!" the Kelf countered. His high-pitched voice was barely audible over all of the noise. "If your theory is correct, and government officials were somehow involved in the attack on Station 3, then Nalomy could be in on it. What then?"

"Then she's going down," Cato answered darkly. And because of the way the Uman said it, as well as the expression on his face, Belok was inclined to believe him. The engine roared, the lights grew brighter, and the decision was made.

The dining room had never looked better. Two dozen candles produced most of the ambient light. They flickered whenever a servant passed by before becoming steady again. The linen-covered table was set with Nalomy's personal china, delicate glassware, and gleaming silver that bore her family's crest. The Procurator's hair was piled high on her head, she was wearing a small fortune in jewelry, and her toga was cut to reveal a shapely breast. The rest of the guests were well dressed, too, though less interesting to look at, and working hard to impress both their hostess and the guest of honor with how witty they were.

The meal had been under way for an hour by then, and Fiss Verafti was seated only two people away from Legate Usurlus, the man he would eventually be called upon to kill. So even though the conversation was boring, the knowledge of what was to come made the situation more interesting, as did the opportunity to sift through the emotions that swirled around him. Being fully aware that Usurlus was determined to remove her from power, Nalomy hated him. And, knowing that Nalomy was aware of his plans, Usurlus hated *her*! Plus, thanks to the emotional content provided by various other guests, there was plenty of anger, envy, and jealously to provide additional flavor to the feast.

As Verafti had discovered in the past, many of the most unadulterated emotions originated from the servers, who were constantly at risk. The female named Alamy was an excellent example of that. Verafti watched the Uman female through half-slitted eyes as the man to his right babbled nonsense into his ear and sought to impress the person he believed the shape shifter to be.

Alamy was frightened, as prey should be, but she was hopeful, too. Even if there wasn't much reason to be. Verafti had requested permission to dine on Alamy's body as well as her emotions, but Hingo had insisted that he feed on a slave named Lea instead. Why? Because, based on the lust that surrounded Hingo when Alamy was around, the Uman was determined to have sex with her. A perfectly understandable motivation insofar as Verafti was concerned but one that put the two of them at odds, and would have to be resolved. In Verafti's favor, of course. And sooner rather than later. Because while Verafti's metabolism was slow, his hunger pangs were growing stronger, and would soon have to be dealt with.

Verafti's ruminations were interrupted by the sudden *bleat* of a Klaxon, a series of *thump*s as steel security doors dropped into place, and a computer-generated voice announcing that a "Class II security violation" had taken place. There were expressions of alarm, followed by the scrape of chairs, as some of the Procurator's guests pushed themselves back from the linen-covered table.

Nalomy, who was seated at the opposite end of the table from Usurlus, stood and forced a smile. "Please. . . . Remain calm. It's probably a false alarm, not that it matters. Even if the palace is under attack, my troops have the resources necessary to deal with any threat."

Usurlus didn't doubt that, since no expense had been spared in the effort to protect his hostess and, therefore, the palace from the local populace. But what about a Vord raid? Surface attacks had been rare so far but weren't unheard of, and he had serious doubts about whether Dantha's militia would be equal to a contingent of Vord Nightstalkers.

But Vedius was on duty, as were roughly half of the Legate's bodyguards, and it was only a matter of seconds before the ex-legionnaire was talking to Usurlus via the earplug. "An unauthorized air car landed on the roof, sir," Vedius said calmly. "I have no idea why the militia failed to shoot it down a mile out. But I will investigate and report back."

Nalomy must have had a similar link with *her* people, because as the security doors began to rise, she spoke to her guests. "The situation is under control," Nalomy said reassuringly. "It seems that an air car declared a mechanical emergency, requested permission to land on the roof, and was denied. But the pilot came in anyway, and that triggered the alarms, just as it should have. I'm sorry about the interruption," she continued sweetly, "but I believe dessert will more than make up for the delay! Please continue to eat while I check with the head of security."

Most of the guests were happy with that explanation, and the incident generated a buzz of conversation, as Alamy pushed the dessert cart into the room. But some of the guests, Usurlus and Verafti among them, were curious and took the opportunity to follow Nalomy out of the room. The Procurator resented it, but couldn't object, given the fact that Usurlus outranked her.

So as Nalomy entered the elevator that would carry her up to the roof, she was accompanied by four guests, half of whom had brought glasses of wine along with them. Cold air rushed in to fill the elevator as it opened onto the flat roof and a very remarkable scene. Because there, sitting at the center of Nalomy's pristine landing pad, was a very old air car. It was bathed in the glare produced by three powerful spotlights. Standing next to the disreputable machine were an unkempt Uman, an olive drab android, and a Kelf. All with both hands on tops of their heads.

A frantic Section Leader, who was clearly distraught by what had occurred, rushed over to greet Nalomy. "I'm sorry, Highness!" the man said. "They said it was an emergency! We told them to land elsewhere, but they kept coming! Then, when I ordered the missile batteries to fire, the air car was too close! An explosion might have done damage to the palace."

The air car should have been blown out of the sky the moment it entered the one-mile-deep security perimeter that surrounded the palace. So Nalomy was quietly furious, and might well have had the responsible parties executed on the spot, had it not been for the presence of so many witnesses. Especially one who reported directly to the Emperor. But the intruders were fair game. So soldiers stared as the partially nude Procurator made her way out into the glare that surrounded the unauthorized visitors and stood with hands on shapely hips. "Who are you people?" she demanded angrily. "And how dare you enter a restricted area!"

Cato squinted into the bright light. He wasn't sure who the partially clad woman was, but judging from the way everyone deferred to her, she held a position of authority. Nalomy herself? Yes, quite possibly, which was fine with him. "My name is Jak Cato," he said authoritatively. "And I'm an Imperial police officer. I'm here on official business, and I hereby call upon you, and your staff, to render the full measure of support required by the law."

The request was not only exceedingly bold, but completely unexpected, and Nalomy reacted accordingly. "An Imperial police officer?" she inquired skeptically. "That seems rather unlikely based on appearances."

There were expressions of surprise all around as Cato removed a hand from the top of his head and held it palm out. The glowing blue badge left no doubt as to the extent of his authority. "Well, I'll be damned!" Usurlus exclaimed. "He *is* a cop!"

But one of the onlookers *wasn't* surprised, because he knew Cato rather well, and knew what the Xeno cop was capable of. Which was why Fiss Verafti was already on the elevator, and on his way down, when Cato sensed the shape shifter's presence.

And there was no mistaking who the person was, because each individual's emotions were as unique as a fingerprint insofar as Cato was concerned, and Verafti had a very distinctive profile. It consisted of a brooding paranoia, overlaid by seething anger, and propelled by a deep hunger. The totality of which was unmistakable.

"Verafti!" the policeman exclaimed, as he drew his weapon and looked from face to face. I know you're here, you bastard! Everyone freeze!"

But the sight of the seemingly deranged policeman holding a weapon that was pointed in Nalomy's direction was too much for the already shamed Section Leader. He drew a stunner, aimed it at Cato, and fired.

Cato staggered, felt his muscles lock up as if seized by a gigantic cramp, and would have screamed had his body been functioning properly. But it wasn't, so he fell, and his pistol skittered away as he hit the roof.

There was a moment of silence after that—which Nalomy broke as she turned to her guests. The sudden appearance of a Xeno cop, plus the mention of Verafti's name, had been something of a shock. But the Procurator was a skilled actress, and none of that was visible in her expression. "Well," she said brightly. "That was unexpected! But it looks as though everything is under control—so let's return to the dining room. Our desserts are on the table by now—and we wouldn't want to keep the others waiting."

Cato wanted to warn Nalomy about Verafti, but discovered that his jaw wouldn't work, as his entire body began to spasm. The back of his head hit duracrete, the arms of darkness reached out to enfold him, and Cato was gone.

The city of Solace, on the planet Dantha

In keeping with the standard template that Emperor Deronious had laid down 252 years before, the coliseum was located a short walk from the palace. Like the militia, the arena was well maintained, and for much the same reason: to keep Dantha's population in line. Because to the extent that the plebeians could be bought off with bloody sporting contests, musical concerts, and 3-D holo dramas imported from Corin, Nalomy was not only happy to oblige but usually present when such events took place. That gave the citizens an opportunity to look up at her as she looked *down* on them from her thronelike seat in the Imperial Box. The suite of well-appointed rooms was located high above the seats on the south side of the coliseum, where Nalomy's guests could see the entire arena, and never be required to stare into direct sunlight.

But as Nalomy entered the Imperial suite and took her place on the thronelike chair that Emperor Emor would sit on should he ever get around to visiting Dantha, there was nothing to look at other than the rusty red awnings that hung over empty seats, and the carefully raked arena below. The awnings flapped gently as a breeze took a shortcut across the coliseum on its way to Lake Imperium, and Nalomy heard the steady *thump*, *thump*, *thump* of boots as Pasayo marched Verafti and a section of heavily armed militiamen up to the open door, where the formation came to a crashing halt.

Nalomy stood and waited for the man who looked exactly like one of the officers on the prison ship *Pax Umana* to enter. The form Verafti had chosen was tall, handsome, and easy on the eye. So much so that the official could easily imagine taking the man to bed. But the knowledge of what she was *truly* looking at was sufficient to keep Nalomy's libido in check and release something cold into her bloodstream. "So," Nalomy said evenly, "it didn't take Officer Cato long to notice your presence, did it?"

Verafti shrugged indifferently. "Cato is one of the less reliable members of the Xeno Corps, but he's an empath nevertheless, and very familiar with my emotional profile. So yes, he was able to recognize me right away, just as I was able to recognize *him*. And that raises a rather interesting question. . . . Why is Officer Cato still alive?"

Nalomy didn't like being challenged, especially by someone she saw as an inferior, so Verafti could "feel" the sudden flood of resentment produced by his question. Nalomy's bodyguards were present, but too far away to hear what was being said, which allowed her to answer the question honestly. "The Lir were supposed to arrange for Officer Cato's death, and make it look like an accident, but he's more resourceful than he appears. And, now that Usurlus is aware of his presence, a different strategy will be necessary."

The shape shifter's eyebrows rose incrementally. "But not for long. Or have you changed your mind regarding Usurlus?"

"Don't be silly," Nalomy replied dismissively. "That's why I invited you here. This is where I want you to kill him. Not in the Imperial Box, but down *there*, on the platform, where everyone can see it take place."

Verafti made his way over to the open window and looked down on the arena below. There were four platforms, one marking each point of the compass. They were rectangular in shape, and set eight feet off the floor of the arena, just beyond the walkway that circled the coliseum. Nalomy had joined Verafti by then but stood well out of arm's reach. It was a very prudent thing to do, all things considered. "The platforms serve a variety of purposes," she explained. "Officials use them during sporting events and Usurlus will speak from one of them on Founder's Day. But," Nalomy continued, "about halfway through his comments, one of the Legate's own bodyguards will draw a weapon and shoot him in the head."

At that point the Procurator turned to look Verafti in the eye. There was no denying the intensity of her gaze or the anger that flared around her. "And that's important," Nalomy emphasized. "Because he may be wearing body armor. So be sure to shoot him in the head. *Twice*."

"And then?" Verafti inquired dispassionately.

Nalomy looked away. "And then you will shift into whatever form you choose, blend in with the crowd, and make your escape."

Was the Uman lying? Verafti thought so because of a sudden spike in her emotions, but he couldn't be absolutely sure, since the additional stress could have been caused by other factors. Such as fear for herself should something go wrong. "And the explosive device?" Verafti wanted to know, as his fingers went to the bracelet that encircled his left wrist. "What about that?"

"Thirty minutes," Nalomy answered reassuringly. "I will make sure that it is deactivated within thirty minutes. Then it will be safe to cut it off."

Verafti's eyes were inexorably drawn to the pendant that hung around Nalomy's neck. She saw the look and smiled knowingly. "Six days. And then you will be free."

Verafti brought his eyes up to meet hers. It was like looking into two bottomless wells. His voice was soft and sibilant. "Yes, Highness, in six days I will be free."

Cato was at the bottom of a lake. That was the way it felt anyway, as he floated on his back, and stared up toward the surface. It was difficult to see through the blue-green water, but the distant glow hinted at sunlight, and a world beyond. Cato knew it was important to reach the surface, so he began to swim, and the light grew brighter as he rose. Then the water faded away and a face appeared to replace it. A *beautiful* face with big eyes, a straight nose, and full lips. Cato could *see* the concern in the girl's eyes, but more than that he could "feel" it, and was unexpectedly grateful. Her lips formed his name. "Officer Cato? Are you all right? I brought some breakfast. But your arms were moving, and you were making noises."

Cato's mouth was desert dry. He worked his tongue from

side to side in an attempt to summon some additional saliva. "I was swimming," Cato croaked. "Up to you . . . What happened?"

The girl's eyes widened slightly. "They fired a stun gun at you. It takes about eight hours to recover. That's what they told me anyway."

Cato made as if to sit up, felt how sore his muscles were, and wished he hadn't. He groaned, and when the girl leaned in to help, he noticed that she smelled like soap. Only better somehow, even though there wasn't a trace of perfume in the air, or anything else to explain the difference.

And there was something about the girl that "felt" good in a way he hadn't experienced in a long time. Not since the horrible night when an armor-piercing bullet had torn through Officer Bree Mora's body armor taking her life *and* his future. Cato felt his feet hit the cold marble, wondered where he was, and took a look around. The canopied bed was positioned on a raised platform with two steps leading down to a highly polished floor. Sunlight streamed in through a glass door off to the left, a combination dresser and makeup table took up most of the wall in front of him, with a door to the right of that. A cart sat between the bed and the door. The simple act of turning his head caused it to throb. "Where am I?"

"In the palace," the girl answered simply. "In one of the guest rooms."

Cato remembered landing on the roof, the subsequent confrontation, and the sudden burst of pain as all of his muscles locked up. "And my companions? Where are they?"

The girl looked away as if embarrassed. "They're under house arrest. Until you're up and around."

Cato grimaced. "Good idea . . . They've been helpful. But only because it suits their purposes. And you are?"

"My name is Alamy," the girl answered shyly, as her

eyes came back to make contact with his. "I work in the kitchen."

There was nothing seductive about the long tunic she wore or the way it hung on her, but Cato thought she was beautiful nevertheless. "In the kitchen? You're a slave?"

Blood rushed to color Alamy's cheeks. She felt ashamed. Especially in front of the man with three days' worth of stubble on his face, the serious mouth, and the bright green eyes. "Yes, master. The cook ordered me to bring your breakfast. The food is probably cold by now. Should I take it back?"

Much to his surprise Cato discovered he was hungry. "No," he answered. "Let me see what they sent."

Alamy left Cato's bedside to get the cart and bring it over. There were numerous hot dishes, all covered with metal lids, plus a large basket of freshly baked pastries. "Are you hungry?" Cato inquired. "If so, pull up a chair. . . . There's enough food for three people here."

"No, thank you," Alamy responded politely. "I ate earlier."

Cato could "feel" her fear and knew that the girl was lying. She was at least slightly hungry. But if she ate, or lingered, Alamy would get into trouble. Cato *wanted* the slave to stay, but couldn't ask her to do so, knowing what would happen if she did. "Well, thank you, Alamy. What should I do when I'm finished?"

"Press the kitchen button," the slave answered simply, as she pointed to a control panel. "They will send someone for the cart."

Cato smiled. "Will they send you?"

Alamy blushed. "No, master. . . . Probably not."

"That will be my loss," Cato replied soberly. "One last thing . . ."

Alamy curtsied. "Yes, master?"

"Don't call me 'master.'"

Alamy said, "Yes, master," and fled the room.

Having returned from the arena and her meeting with Ver-afti, Nalomy was seated on the veranda that fronted the lake. It was a pleasant afternoon. The sun was shining, a light breeze ruffled the surface of the water, and half a dozen triangular sails were visible in the distance. Fisherfolk probably, harvesting some of the two-hundred-pound genetically engineered "Good Fish" that had been brought to Dantha shortly after the first landing. And not just the fish, but the entire ecosystem required to support them, which was ruthlessly superimposed over the so-called incumbent system. It was a piece of scientific handiwork that the Procurator heartily approved of since catching a two-hundred-pound Good Fish was clearly superior to harvesting one of the five-pound eels that had occupied the lake previously.

Such were Nalomy's thoughts when Hingo escorted Xeno Corps Officer Jak Cato out onto the terrace. Cato had sandy-colored hair, light brown skin, bright green eyes, a firm chin, and judging from the way the militia-style kilt and armor fit him, a hard body. Thanks to a shave, and a hot bath, he was a very different man from the one Nalomy had first seen on the roof. Cato bowed formally, and the Procurator replied with a nod. She was stretched out on a chaise lounge with her long slim legs fully exposed. "This is Officer Cato," Hingo said formally, as he eyed Nalomy's body. "Will there be anything else?"

"*No,*" Nalomy replied emphatically, knowing full well what was going through her subordinate's mind. "You may withdraw."

Hingo was in no way nonplussed and backed away. Because Cato could "read" some of the emotional content that surrounded him, he could not only sense the sexual tension between the two of them, but see why. Nalomy was very attractive, well aware of that fact, and willing to use sex as a way to advance her interests. Not that Cato cared what the woman did so long as she provided him with the support he needed.

Nalomy said, "Please, have a seat," and pointed to a chair. It was only three feet away, and as Cato sat down, he battled the urge to stare at her legs. Nalomy could be charming when she chose to be, and such was the case at the moment. "Welcome to the palace," she said melodiously. "Can I offer some refreshments? A drink perhaps?"

Cato wanted to say, "Yes," but having already betrayed himself where alcohol was concerned, he was determined to refuse. Besides . . . Was Nalomy aware of his occasional weakness? And attempting to use it against him? There was no way to be sure, but he wasn't going to give her the chance. "No," Cato replied. "But thank you."

"I'm sorry about what happened to you last night," Nalomy said, "but security is important. As I'm sure you understand."

If Nalomy felt sorry, Cato couldn't detect any such emotion emanating from her, but nodded anyway. "Thank you, Excellency. . . . I *do* understand. But, by the same token, my job is to apprehend criminals. And, judging from what I sensed last night, a Sagathi shape shifter named Fiss Verafti was not only present in the palace but may have been on the roof."

There was no doubt about the look of concern on Nalomy's face, or the sudden spike of fear attendant on Cato's statement, but the question was why? Was the Procurator worried about the possibility that a dangerous criminal was on the loose? Or already aware of that fact—and concerned regarding her own outcomes? Those were the sorts of fine discriminations that even an empath couldn't make.

"A shape shifter?" Nalomy demanded incredulously. "I've heard of them—but they're rare aren't they?"

"Yes," Cato agreed soberly. "Very rare. But, after Lir bandits attacked our compound at Station 3, Verafti was either transported to Solace for purposes unknown, or escaped from captivity and came here on his own. Where, given his capacity to change shapes, he could impersonate just about anyone."

Nalomy had no reason to pursue the subject, and every reason to change it, so she smiled seductively. "How about me, Officer Cato? Could Fiss Verafti look like *me?*"

The correct answer was "Yes," but Cato knew what she wanted him to say, so he shook his head. "No, Excellency. . . . That would be impossible. There is no way Verafti could look like you do."

Nalomy laughed. "You're a liar, Officer Cato. But a charming one! And for that I give you credit. What kind of assistance will you require?"

"Full access to the palace," Cato replied. "In case Verafti is still here. And permission to question staff. *All* of them if necessary."

Verafti was in Storage Room 3B13 at the moment, where Cato was unlikely to come across him, but there were no guarantees. So Nalomy knew it would be necessary to keep a close eye on the variant. A chore she would delegate to Hingo. All of which was better than forcing Cato out of the palace, where it would be more difficult to keep track of him. "Of course," Nalomy said sweetly. "Although you will need to make some sort of arrangement with the Legate's staff should you desire to interview *his* people. Please keep me advised." The meeting was over.

Having been ordered to take a bowl of freshly picked fruit up to Nalomy's quarters, Alamy chose to climb the back stairs rather than make use of the service elevator. For even though the stairs required more effort, she was less likely to encounter Hingo if she used them, and the Majordomo had been more aggressive of late. After following the slave into a storage room the day before, Hingo had successfully maneuvered her into a corner, and was busy pawing at her when the head chef barged in. And, having correctly assessed the situation, the chef gave Alamy an errand to run.

That was why Alamy opened the door a tiny bit and paused to peer through the crack before pushing the barrier open and stepping out into the hallway. Then, walking briskly, she made for Nalomy's quarters. The young woman was only twenty feet from her destination when Hingo stepped out of an open linen closet to confront her. "Well," Hingo said ominously, as he moved out to block the way. "Look what we have here. . . . There's no point in playing hard to get, my dear! You have something I want. You can give it to me—or I'll take it. Which will it be?"

Alamy was backing away, with the bowl of fruit still in her hands, when Hingo came for her. He was quick for a man of his size and soon had Alamy by the arm. She said, "No!" and was trying to break free, when Hingo heard a male voice.

"You heard the lady. She said 'no.'"

Hingo turned his head to find that Officer Jak Cato had approached him from behind. It appeared that the meeting with Nalomy was over, and Cato had been on the way to his quarters, when he witnessed the confrontation and chose to intervene. "This is none of your business," Hingo said loftily, as he maintained the grip on Alamy's arm.

"*Everything* is my business if I choose to make it so," Cato replied coolly. "Release the girl."

"She's a slave," Hingo grated, as he stood his ground. "And as such is subject to my authority!"

There was a blur as Cato's hand dipped and came back up. Suddenly Hingo found himself looking down the barrel of the police officer's handgun. "She's a *person*," Cato replied gravely, "and you're going to lose an ear if you don't remove your hand from her arm. Unless I miss of course, in which case you could wind up dead, which would be unfortunate indeed."

Slowly, reluctantly, Hingo let go of Alamy's arm. Her skin was white where Hingo's steely fingers had left impressions on her flesh. The gun made a whispering sound as it went back into the holster. "Good," Cato said. "You made the right decision. Two ears *are* better than one. Now, make another good decision and leave."

Seconds passed as the two men stared at each other, but finally, after what seemed like an eternity to Alamy, it was Hingo who bowed stiffly. But, as Hingo turned to go, anger was visible in his eyes. A great deal of anger. And Alamy knew that if Hingo caught up with her, as he surely would, the subsequent rape would be as painful as he could make it. But even that wasn't enough to erase the gratitude Alamy felt as Cato came forward to take her free hand. "Are you all right?"

"Yes," Alamy answered shakily. "Thanks to you. But he's angry now—and next time will be worse. My friend Persus says that I should accept my fate and give in. Perhaps she's right."

Cato looked into Alamy's eyes. In spite of the fear she felt, it was peaceful there. So much so that he wished he could just stand and stare. The problem was that Hingo was correct. Alamy *was* a slave, and Hingo could treat her any way that he chose, so long as Nalomy allowed him to do so. And there was no evidence to suggest that the Procurator cared one way or the other. So the reality was that his intervention could and probably would cause trouble for the girl. Truth be told, it was possible that her friend Persus was correct. But Cato didn't want Alamy to give herself to Hingo even if he wasn't sure why. "I'm sorry if I made the situation worse," he said. "Stay away from him if you can. In the meantime,

I'll look for an opportunity to speak with him. Who knows? Maybe I can bring him around."

Alamy had little hope of that, but knew that the police officer meant well, and bowed her head respectfully. "I'll do my best. I must go now, or I'll be in trouble."

Cato released her hand and took a step backward. Alamy made as if to leave, seemed to think better of it, and turned his way. Cato felt her lips brush his cheek and barely had time to breathe in the soap-fresh smell of her before Alamy was gone.

ELEVEN

The city of Solace, on the planet Dantha

CENTURION PASAYO'S OFFICE WAS A NEAT, ORDERLY place where things always made sense, even if the outside world didn't. Rather than being in the palace where civilians held sway, Pasayo's headquarters were located in a separate building that looked out onto a small parade ground and the glaringly white barracks beyond.

This arrangement conferred numerous benefits on the officer, including the fact he had at least double the amount of space that would have been allotted him inside the palace. That was important, because the walls of Pasayo's office were hung with more than two dozen hunting trophies.

As a result, visitors were forced to walk the length of a long narrow room while being subjected to the glassy-eyed scrutiny of a coterie of snarling beasts, all of whom had fallen to Pasayo's rifle, compound bow, or in one case a fiber-composite spear. So, as Specialist Nalan completed that intimidating journey, and crashed to a halt in front of his commanding officer's fortresslike desk, he was extremely nervous. "Specialist Nalan, reporting as ordered, *sir*!"

Pasayo looked up from the latest intelligence summary and nodded. "At ease, soldier. . . . I was reading your report. It's interesting, not to mention a bit disturbing. If I understand the situation correctly, you were undercover in Solace for two weeks. During that time you took part in various clandestine meetings sponsored by the so-called resistance. And, based on what you both saw and heard, it's your belief that organized opposition to Procurator Nalomy's rule continues to increase. Is that correct?"

Nalan's eyes were focused on a point approximately six inches above his superior's head. "Sir, yes, sir," the intelligence specialist answered.

Pasayo eyed the soldier thoughtfully as he toyed with a silver stylus. It was tipped with a bullet that had been removed from one of his most memorable kills. "Furthermore, you indicate that while a significant portion of the population believes the Emperor ignorant of what they view as deplorable conditions on Dantha, others see the Legate's visit as a reason for hope and plan to stir up trouble while he's here. Would you agree with my characterization?"

"Sir! Yes, sir," the soldier responded stoutly.

"So," Pasayo continued thoughtfully, tapping his chin with the stylus. "Tell me what *isn't* in your report. Tell me what you think we should do to counter the resistance."

Most officers *never* sought opinions from their subordinates. But Pasayo was one of those rare individuals who had risen step by step up through the enlisted ranks to become not only an officer but commander of all the militia troops on Dantha. The rank of General was reserved for Imperial officers, but Pasayo had been loyal to Nalomy. And he had reason to believe that she would engineer a transfer for him once she was appointed to higher office.

Though unaware of all the politics involved, Nalan was both shocked and pleased to be asked for his opinion by such a high-ranking officer, and sought to frame his reply as succinctly as possible. "Sir," the soldier replied, "as you know, the simplest and most direct way to defeat any organization is to kill its leaders."

Pasayo was silent for a moment. Then, as he eyed the heads that lined the walls to both the right and left, he nodded. "Thank you, Specialist Nalan. I couldn't agree more."

The tour was to be an all-day affair, beginning at the palace, and taking Legate Usurlus to various points of interest in and around Solace. These included a school attended by children of wealthy families, a medical clinic established for the Procurator's supporters, and the new water-treatment plant which had been constructed by an off-planet firm working under a no-bid contract.

Each stop in the daylong series of visits was to be documented by Nalomy's Office of Public Information, then shipped to the news combines on Corin. There the narrative would become part of a carefully woven tapestry of self-serving stories calculated to position the Nalomy clan for the ultimate prize: the family patriarch Tegor Nalomy as successor to Emperor Emor.

So there was a good deal of hustle and bustle as staff members ran to and fro on various errands, a motorcade was assembled in front of the palace, and Legate Usurlus left the palace through the front door. He was impeccably dressed and appeared to be in good spirits as he paused to say a few words to Nalomy before entering an armor-plated limo. It was a closed vehicle that had been painstakingly swept for bugs and was equipped with running boards for use by his bodyguards.

Then, with a brace of powerful gyrostabilized unicycles leading the way, the motorcade left. And the *real* Usurlus watched it go. Because he was disguised as one of his own bodyguards, a fortunate fellow who, having been confined to the Legate's bedroom for the day, was presumably taking a nap.

As the motorcade disappeared in the distance, and Nalomy retreated into the palace, Usurlus and five bodyguards made their way to the front gate, where a guard scanned their passes and allowed the group to pass. "Lucky bastards," he said to a second guard, as the men in civilian garb ambled away. "They get to drink while *we* stand duty."

The other soldier shrugged. "True. But there are worse things. . . . We could be out on the frontier!"

There was truth in that, so the guard took comfort from knowledge that some people had it even worse than *he* did, and went back to work.

With Usurlus safely out of the way for the day, Nalomy was free to pursue her normal routines, one of which was a daily workout calculated to keep her near-perfect body in tiptop shape. So that was what she was doing when Pasayo knocked on the door to the private gymnasium located adjacent to her quarters, and heard Nalomy say, "Enter!" Being a heterosexual man, Pasayo couldn't help but notice Nalomy's scantily clad body. But he felt none of the lust that Hingo would have because he saw the Procurator for what she was. A very dangerous predator. And a person he could never fully trust.

For her part, Nalomy, who was walking on a treadmill as Pasayo entered, was in no way embarrassed by her lack of clothing. After all, she reasoned, the whole point of working out was to look good for other people. "Yes?" she inquired. "Is the Legate's tour running smoothly?"

"Yes, Highness," Pasayo replied. "But something strange occurred. You will recall that we were able to electronically tag the Legate's clothes when they were sent out for cleaning."

"Yes," Nalomy acknowledged, as the treadmill began to pick up speed. "So?"

"So, according to the signals we're receiving, Usurlus is traveling with the motorcade, *and* walking down Market Street at the same time!"

"The Legate is a very talented man," Nalomy observed sarcastically. "Odds are that the Usurlus in the motorcade is a fake. Such things are common on Corin. Follow the second Usurlus—but don't kill him. I want everyone to witness his death on Founder's Day. Is that understood?"

"Yes, Highness," Pasayo replied. "And the people he meets with? Assuming there are some?"

"Kill them," Nalomy said coldly, as the machine forced her to run.

It was the order Pasayo had been hoping for, because if Usurlus was headed for a meeting, it would be with the men and women who were running the resistance. He bowed formally. "Yes, Highness. We will do our best."

Usurlus had absolutely no idea where he and his bodyguards were going, which for reasons of security, was a very good idea. The only guidance he had was a cryptic note from Lucia Ovidius instructing him to, "Take a walk in The Warrens," along with a time and a date. The message incinerated itself ten seconds after the envelope had been opened, leaving him with nothing more than a scattering of ash.

The message had simply "appeared" while Usurlus was taking a shower, suggesting that at least one member of Nalomy's staff had links to the resistance, in spite of Hingo's efforts to vet everyone who worked in the palace.

So, as Usurlus and his bodyguards made their way down Market Street, he was waiting for some sort of contact while enjoying the sights and sounds around him. The air was thick with the combined scents of incense and spices overlaid by the persistent tang of charcoal smoke that issued from countless braziers. And, with both breakfast and lunch cooking at the same time, lots of mouthwatering smells wafted through the air.

The street was crowded with locals and people from out of town who were there to participate in the Founder's Day festivities. There were angen-borne desert dwellers, their skin dark from exposure to the sun, swaying rhythmically, as metal shod hooves clopped down the street. There were townspeople too, some of whom wore crisp white togas, and rode in sedan chairs with heavily burdened slaves trotting close behind. And there were less wealthy people as well, including metalsmiths, carpenters, and stonemasons, many of whom wore leather aprons and were trailed by pimply-faced apprentices, each burdened with his or her master's tools.

And while technically free, some of the city folk were not only destitute, but worse off than the slaves they looked down on. They sat with their begging bowls extended, telling stories of woe, or slouched against sun-splashed walls, watching while the rest of the world passed them by.

There were others, too, including the occasional robot, servos whining as it minced along next to a gaggle of spacers, just off a tramp freighter. And militiamen were everywhere, their hard eyes scanning the crowd for criminals and dissidents, as children chased balls, birds squawked from their cages, and a holy man turned endless circles on one of the street corners. The totality of it was an assault on the senses, and for a man who rarely got to walk the streets, a wonderful, horrible, and ultimately educational experience.

The better part of fifteen minutes had passed without being contacted, and Usurlus was beginning to wonder if something had gone wrong, when he felt a tug at his tunic. Looking down, he saw a little girl with scraggly hair, bright, sparkling eyes, and a dirt smudge on the bridge of her nose. "Hey, mister!" the street urchin said. "Follow me!"

Vedius Albus had been forced to accompany the fake Usurlus on the tour since everyone knew that the chief body-guard was never far from the Legate's side, so Usurlus turned to make eye contact with the Section Leader who had been assigned to protect him. His name was Dom Livius. He was a big man with craggy brows, a fist-flattened nose, and an underthrust jaw. He looked at the little girl and shrugged. "I don't know what to say, sire. This could be the contact that you've been waiting for—or a plan to suck you into a trap! What if the note was from someone *other* than this Ovidius person?"

Livius was correct regarding the potential danger, Usur-lus knew that, but couldn't see a way around it. The meet-ing was important, no *critical*, and he would have to take the chance. He held out his hand to the little girl. "You lead—we'll follow."

The little girl knew right where to go and towed Usurlus down the street to a side corridor where she took a right, fol-lowed by a left, then a series of rights that left Usurlus hope-lessly confused. Meanwhile, had the Imperials been able to go back and look, they would have seen a fistfight break out between two adjacent stall operators, even as an angen-drawn cart pulled out to block the passageway behind them. All of which had been arranged by members of the resistance in an effort to block, delay, and confuse anyone who might attempt to follow.

But Usurlus and his men weren't aware of the precautions taken on their behalf as they followed the little girl through a bakery and a busy back room. There, half a dozen men and women stood kneading bread, crafting it into various shapes that would soon go into the ovens.

It was beyond this workroom, in a storage nook added to the back of the building, that a six-foot square of what had once been public street could be seen. And right in the middle of the cobblestones was an open manhole! The hinged lid was open, the faint sound of running water could be heard from somewhere below, and the nature of the invitation was obvious. Usurlus was about to check that impression with the girl when she pulled free of his hand and scampered away. A bodyguard took a swipe at her but missed, as she ducked under his arm and disappeared.

Usurlus grinned and turned to Livius. "I'll go first."

"Like hell you will," Livius replied grimly. "No offense, sire, but Albus would shoot me! I'll go first, followed by Quatri, and yourself. Chesami, Himus, Belos, and Thoos will bring up the rear."

Usurlus understood the wisdom of the proposal, and having been heard to volunteer, was perfectly willing to let Livius have his way. "All right, if you insist," Usurlus said. "But don't get your feet wet!"

The comment was supposed to elicit a chuckle from the rest of the men and did, as Livius backed his way into the vertical shaft, and felt for the first rung of the rusty ladder with his right foot. Then, having tested the metal bar by putting his weight on it, Livius disappeared. Quatri went next, followed by Usurlus, who soon found himself standing on an elevated walkway above a fifteen-foot-wide channel through which noisy water was rushing downhill toward Lake Imperium. It was dirty stuff, runoff from the streets mostly and heavily polluted by every sort of contaminant imaginable.

Not sewage, however, not very much of it anyway, since Solace had a separate system for that. So while sour, the odor wasn't as bad as it might have been, so long as Usurlus remembered to breathe through his mouth. Livius and the other bodyguards pulled back against the wall as Lucia Ovidius arrived to greet him.

"Good morning, sire," Lucia said cheerfully. "That's the

Solace River running past us below. It carries the snowmelt down from the mountains and runs full during the spring. But, with winter coming on, the water level is relatively low right now. And since the river is paved over, most of the city's residents are only vaguely aware that it's here. All of which makes it a relatively safe place to meet. Please follow me."

It was dangerous to fly over The Warrens, especially during the day, and especially at low altitude. Because many of the citizens below were armed with government surplus weapons and rather liked taking potshots at government vehicles. One had been shot down two months earlier, a fact of which Pasayo was uncomfortably aware as the air car's boxy shadow rippled over roofs made of tile, metal, and sheets of blue plastic. There were elevated gardens, too, where people stood and shaded their eyes, the persistent thrumming noise alerting them to the presence of the air car above. As Pasayo looked down children waved, a bullet pinged off the underside of the hull, and the rifle's dull report echoed back and forth between the buildings below. That caused a flock of birds to burst out of a rooftop shack and explode into the air, where they wheeled as if all part of the same organism.

But dangerous as an airborne trip over The Warrens might be, it beat the hell out of trying to follow Usurlus and his bodyguards through the teeming streets below. And why should he? Given the fact that tiny bits of electronic "lint" had been attached to the Legate's clothes, including the tunic he'd chosen to wear that very morning. The bugs required no power source, and therefore didn't produce any heat or electronic signature, other than the so-called bounce-back that occurred whenever they were pinged. Which was how the technician riding in the back of the air car had been able to track Usurlus to a spot directly below the air car. But all good things must come to an end, just as Pasayo's mother had warned, and such was the case now as the technician spoke. "We lost him, sir! He was there—now he's gone."

Pasayo swore and looked back over his shoulder. "How? Why?"

"I don't know for sure," the tech replied honestly, "but there are two possibilities. Either he identified the reflector and destroyed it, or he went underground. Our signals can't penetrate more than six inches of solid duracrete."

"I'm betting on the second possibility," Pasayo replied thoughtfully. "Stay on it—maybe the bastard will surface."

It was dark and gloomy under the streets of Solace. What light there was came from the torch that Lucia held—and the coin-sized shafts of sunshine that slanted down through the drain holes in the metal covers above. They made bright circles on the walkway below.

As Lucia led the way, Usurlus noticed that they were walking slightly uphill, which suggested they were headed west, toward the foothills. It was too dark to make out the details, but old storefronts could be seen along the way, most of which had been boarded up. But a few doors hung open, inviting both the adventurous and foolhardy to enter, and explore the darkness within.

Judging from the fresh graffiti on the walls, the well-maintained fish traps that spanned the river, and the occasional remains of a campfire, there were people who frequented the underground cavern on a regular basis. But if any were present on that particular day, they saw the party of seven men and a woman as a threat, and quickly made themselves scarce.

After a brisk ten-minute walk, the tunnel widened and opened up into what had once been a small lake. A four-foot-high waterfall marked the outfall and made a continual roaring sound as they passed it. The ceiling arched high overhead, where a steady supply of water was leaking through cracks in the lid, thereby producing cascades of localized "rain." And, thanks to groupings of still-functional solar tubes, shafts of dusty sunlight slanted down to highlight some of the ever-expanding circles that the "raindrops" made as they hit the surface of the water.

Thick columns had been installed to support the weight of the city above, and judging from the cracks that were visible some were in need of maintenance. *Still another problem that I'll have to be deal with,* Usurlus thought to himself, as he eyed the storefronts around the lake. Their empty windows stared toward the artificial island at the center of the water as if waiting for something to happen. Twin bridges linked the island with the walkways to either side. They were supported by a series of graceful arches and hung with fanciful sculptures.

The group paused to look out over the lake. "That's where we're going," Lucia said, as she pointed at the island and the domed pavilion that sat atop it. "As you can see, all of this was at ground level back when Dantha was first settled. But, due to the scarcity of land between the mountains and Lake Imperium, Procurator Decius built a lid over this lake about 150 years ago. It was maintained as an underground shopping area for a while but, without the necessary maintenance, eventually became a center for crime and was sealed off from the streets above. Come on. The resistance leaders are waiting."

It was a short walk to the point where they could cross what Usurlus judged to be the southern bridge. From there they followed Lucia out onto the island, where five men and a woman were waiting to greet him. They looked uncertain at first, but that changed when Usurlus revealed his *true* face, and stuck the wad of pseudoflesh into one of his pockets. None of the resistance leaders had ever met a Procurator, much less a Legate, and hurried to execute awkward bows and one of the worst curtsies Usurlus had ever witnessed. But he was careful to keep a straight face as he acknowledged the honors, memorized each person's name, and turned on every bit of charm he had. Because if he was to carry out his mission successfully, *and* survive, it would take every bit of help they could give him.

In the meantime, Livius posted guards halfway along both of the bridges, ordered two of his men to patrol the perimeter of the island, paying special attention to what was going on in the water, and fervently wished that Vedius Albus was present to advise him. Because at the moment his charge was trapped on an island, with 360 degrees of exposure to worry about, and two very fragile lines of retreat! It was hard to imagine a worse situation—and Livius had no desire to do so.

The next hour was spent going over the many grievances the opposition leaders had, plans for a demonstration of how strong the resistance was, and the need to show a unified front on Founder's Day. For even though the various groups represented at the meeting were united in their hatred of Nalomy, plenty of issues divided them, and Usurlus had to make a number of extravagant promises to secure their support. And that was what he was doing when the militia arrived, a shot rang out, and the high-velocity slug blew the top of a resistance fighter's head off, thereby spraying Lucia with warm blood. The meeting was over.

Luck always plays an important role in any military endeavor, and Pasayo had been lucky. Having lost contact with the tiny reflector attached to the tunic that Usurlus was wearing, the Centurion ordered the air car's pilot to crisscross the city, in hopes of pinging the Legate again. The effort had been fruitless at first, but then, just as the officer was beginning to wonder if he should give up, the technician riding in the back of the air car issued a whoop of joy. "I have him, sir! He's right below us. The signal is intermittent but static."

Was Usurlus on the street? Or deeper underground? Pasayo had a hunch that it was the latter, and having made use of a handheld comp to access files stored in the palace, he knew he was right. Because the buildings directly below him were resting on a duracrete lid, a barrier thick enough to interfere with electronic signals. And below the lid was the cavernous space that he and his men had to clean out every few months lest criminals filter in to occupy it. The perfect place for a clandestine meeting.

The rest was a matter of good communications, speedy reaction times, and relentless efficiency—all things that Pasayo was good at. The result was that he and a team of specially trained commandos were able to find a convenient route down and into the underground world quite quickly. Lookouts and sentries were positioned to stop an incursion, but Pasayo and his team took them out with silent efficiency, and arrived on the west side of the lake only forty minutes after the operation had been launched.

Then, having called upon his snipers to "Kill everyone except Legate Usurlus," it was time to sit back and watch the show. The marksmen were in position and had permission to fire. There was a loud *crack*, followed by an echo, and the *tinkle* of an empty casing landing on duracrete. The first shot produced a clean kill. A good omen on any kind of hunt. It was exhilarating to be back in action.

Having been shot at before, Usurlus hit the floor within seconds of the first shot, and was immediately pinned in place by Livius. "Sorry, sire," the ex-legionnaire said apologetically, as he placed a bony knee on the Legate's left shoulder. "But we can't have you up and running around just yet!"

Then, to everyone else, the Section Leader yelled, "Keep your heads down! Bridge guards pull back!" And, having turned toward Quatri: "Assemble the rifle. I want some outgoing fire on those bastards!"

Usurlus had managed to roll out from under the knee by that time and held up a hand. "Don't worry. I'll stay down. Rifle? *What* rifle?"

Meanwhile there was a steady *crack, crack, crack* as at least two high-powered rifles blew divots out of the dome, the arches that supported it, and the rails on both bridges. Livius grinned wolfishly. "We couldn't carry a lot of heavy weapons without giving ourselves away—but we had one rifle in our pockets!"

While Livius and his men were armed with pistols, two each in some cases, Usurlus knew their handguns had been hidden. But now, in response to the order from Livius, his subordinates were pulling out all manner of parts from their pockets and passing them to Quatri, who was in charge of putting them together. Usurlus noticed that the rifle's long black barrel, possibly the most difficult component to conceal, had been hidden within a hollowed-out walking stick.

There was a series of *click*s as the pieces went together, followed by a distinctive clacking as Quatri pushed the first cartridge into the breech, at which point he was ready to fire. It took the better part of a minute to elbow his way forward, push the weapon's barrel out between a couple of balustrades, and make some final adjustments. At that point Quatri peered into the telescopic sight, took a deep breath, and let it out. The trigger gave slightly, the firing pin snapped forward, and there was a loud *bang* as the rifle fired.

The sniper to Pasayo's left had just cranked another round into the chamber of his weapon, and was about to fire again, when his head jerked backward. A fraction of a second later a mixture of blood and brains sprayed the wall behind him. He slumped sideways as the rifle clattered to the pavement.

Pasayo swore as the body half fell on him and he worked to push it away. The bastards weren't supposed to have any long guns god damn it! So where had the weapon come from? One of the resistance leaders most likely. . . . Not that it mattered, as the teams who were supposed to force their way across the bridges yelled bravely and ran into a hail of bullets. Small stuff mostly, fired by the pistols that Usurlus's bodyguards were carrying, but interspersed with the occasional rifle round, each of which flew true.

But even as two of his men were plucked off their feet, Pasayo was confident that his forces would win in the long run, because the resistance leaders were trapped, *and* they were outnumbered. Would he be able to protect Usurlus the way Nalomy wanted him to? Maybe, but if Usurlus went down, Pasayo would blame the Legate's death on the fog of war. And while disappointed, Nalomy would find a way to deal with it, because dead is dead. And ultimately that was the fate she had in mind for Usurlus. So Pasayo fumbled for the rifle that lay to his left, brought the weapon up, and began looking for someone to kill.

While both sides continued to exchange fire, Livius was holding an impromptu strategy session on the floor of the domed pavilion. "It's the only way," Livius insisted, as he examined each face. "And we need to do it *now*, before those bastards can bring reinforcements to bear, and really pound the hell out of us."

"Okay," Usurlus agreed reluctantly. "You're the expert. I'm game. How 'bout everyone else?"

Lucia and the other resistance leaders knew without being told that their lookouts and sentries were dead. That left them with no protection other than what Usurlus and his bodyguards could provide. So there was very little choice. One by one they nodded.

"All right," Livius said approvingly. "Slip into the lake one at a time. Stay underwater as long as you can and be sure to put the island between you and the people who are shooting at us. Then, once you go over the falls, let the current carry you out of sight. At that point it will be safe to climb out, make your way back to the surface, and regroup at a later date. Understood?"

All of them nodded. Livius told Usurlus to go first, and Usurlus *wanted* to go first but knew a political opportunity when he saw one. "Absolutely not," the Legate replied sternly. "Citizen Ovidius, let's start with you, followed by Citizen Rustus, and the rest of our brave resistance leaders. We must get them to safety for the sake of those who are oppressed."

Livius thought that the last sentence was especially nauseating, but knew what Usurlus was trying to accomplish, and gave the official credit for having a large set of balls. "You heard Legate Usurlus," Livius said urgently. "You first, Citizen Ovidius. . . . Let's get going."

There was a hole in the east side of the railing, where three balustrades had been kicked out by vandals many years before, and Lucia scuttled over to it. Her toga wasn't appropriate for swimming, so the others caught a glimpse of smooth mocha-colored flesh as the blood-splattered cloth fell away, and Lucia slid feet first into the water below. She was a good swimmer, and the better part of two minutes elapsed before she was forced to come up for air, prior to diving under the surface again. But she was a good fifty feet away from the island by that time—and hidden by the darkness that the shafts of light couldn't entirely dispel.

Meanwhile, the other female resistance leader had removed *her* toga, and was just about to follow Lucia into the lake, when she inadvertently raised her head too far. That was the sort of error that Pasayo had been hoping for. His right index finger tightened on the trigger, the rifle nudged his shoulder, and the bullet produced a loud cracking sound as it broke the sound barrier. It was a tiny bit high. Too high for a solid kill, but it did plow a furrow through the top of Citizen Hatha's skull and the shock of it triggered a heart attack. She collapsed as if poleaxed from above.

But the rest of the resistance fighters made it, followed by Usurlus, and two bodyguards. Both of them had orders to stick with him, or face Livius in the kickboxing ring, a fate they wanted to avoid.

After the people he regarded as civilians had been given a head start, it was time for Livius and his remaining men to withdraw, a process that began with throwing the rifle into the lake. They went one by one, while Livius fired two handguns for effect, dashing from one side of the pavilion to the other in order to keep the attackers at bay.

Usurlus liked to immerse himself in water, but only when it was *hot*, which the snow-fed lake wasn't, and *clear*, which wasn't the case either. So he was far from pleased as a steady current bore him along toward the roaring falls while bullets threw up geysers of water all around. Making matters worse were the two bodyguards who kept yelling for him to "dive," something Usurlus steadfastly declined to do, since his ability to swim was limited to a rough-and-ready crawl, sufficient for dips in a pool but not for feats of underwater athleticism. Especially in cold, filthy water.

Fortunately, all three men managed to reach the falls unscathed at a point where the greenish water rushed between large piles of debris built up over the years. The current carried the swimmers along, and Usurlus was airborne for one brief moment before splashing into the river below, where he sank until his feet touched bottom. He took the opportunity to push off, and shortly after his head broke the surface, was swimming again. "Keep your feet downstream, sire!" one of the bodyguards instructed from a few yards away. "In case you run into an obstruction!"

It was good advice, so Usurlus fought to bring his feet around, and eventually managed to do so. He was floating on his back by that time, staring upward while dimly lit drain holes flashed past, and an elevated walkway appeared off to his right. "That's where we need to go, sire," the second bodyguard shouted, battling to stay abreast of his charge. "Move right!"

It was easier said than done, but bit by bit Usurlus was able to steer himself toward the right side of the channel, even as the bottom came up to make the task a little bit easier. Then, as he neared the edge, a resistance leader was there to grab his right wrist, and haul him in. The bodyguards were carried downstream for ten more yards before they, too, were able to escape the underground river.

Less than two minutes later, Livius and the other members of the rear guard arrived and were quickly plucked from the water. Lucia, who stood half-naked with her arms wrapped around her chest, was happy to accept a tunic from one of the men. Then, still shivering from the cold, she hurried to wring the top out and pull it on.

"It's time to get out of here," one of the surviving resistance leaders said, once the last bodyguard was standing on the walkway. "But believe me, Excellency, we won't forget the risk you took in coming here, or your bravery! What you plan to do won't be easy. But you will have friends in the coliseum on Founder's Day."

There were murmurs of agreement all around. That was good, but as the two men embraced, Usurlus couldn't help but wonder how *many* friends he would have on that fateful day. And whether they would be enough.

TWELVE

The city of Solace, on the planet Dantha

FOR REASONS THAT HADN'T BEEN SHARED WITH FILE
Leader Korem, a man in a Navy uniform had been confined
in Storage Room 3B13 since the night before. If that was
strange, so were the orders that governed the way Korem
and his subordinates were supposed to interact with the
prisoner at mealtimes. But, having served in the militia for
more than ten years, Korem had an appreciation for written
protocols; he knew it was almost impossible to go wrong so
long as a person followed them.

The first step in the process required Korem to assemble
a two-man team. Both individuals were to be unarmed, but
equipped with com sets that would enable them to communicate with both Korem, and the heavily armed team
stationed immediately outside the room. Once everything
was ready, the soldiers were to enter the storage room, being
careful to keep each other under observation at all times,
and if they noticed anything unusual, to report it immediately. Then, having served Procurator Nalomy's "guest,"
they were to withdraw. Once they were outside, it would be

Korem's job to scan the troopers' tamperproof ID bracelets to ensure that they were the same people who had gone in. An unnecessary step in the NCO's judgment, but typical of the militia's officers, who seemed to delight in creating unnecessary things for their subordinates to do.

But if the need for that particular step was hard to understand, the *last* directive, the one labeled FOR NCO EYES ONLY, was not only impossible to fathom but difficult to accept, given Korem's affection for his men. And that was the order instructing him to kill everyone both outside and inside the storage room should he witness anything suspicious.

Fortunately, Centurion Pasayo had made it clear that such a situation was very unlikely. That made Korem feel better as he turned his attention to a monitor and watched the two-man team enter the storage room. Everything appeared normal at first, but the horror began five seconds later, when the prisoner morphed into a green-scaled reptile! The thing had extendable claws, and when it took a swipe at the first soldier's vulnerable throat, a sheet of blood flew sideways to splash a wall. The metal tray made a clanging sound as it hit duracrete, followed by the crash of broken crockery, and the rattle of a water carafe as it hit the floor and flipped over.

Then, even as the first body continued to fall, the monster attacked the *second* militiaman with a degree of ferocity that Korem had never seen. And even though the noncom knew he should do something, he stood momentarily transfixed, as the poor soul backpedaled, and held the metal tray up in an attempt to shield himself from the coming attack. But there was no stopping the creature that leapt at him! It sank curved claws into the militiaman's shoulders, wrapped heavily muscled thighs around the soldier's waist, and took a bloody bite out of his unprotected throat.

Finally, like a man coming out of a trance, Korem began to move. But the truth was that no more than ten seconds had passed since the beginning of the first attack. "Kill it!"

Korem screamed frantically, as he fumbled for the weapon slung across his back. "Kill it now!" But the lizard-thing was fast, very fast, and was already through the door and rushing at the guards. One of them opened fire, but his bullets went wide, and dug divots out of a duracrete wall as death hurtled his way.

Verafti's heart was filled with joy as the kinesthetic feedback from his extremely athletic body combined with a tidal wave of fear generated by his victims to provide the shape shifter with something akin to a physical orgasm. Except that the pleasure was more intense and could be extended, so long as there were sentient beings available to kill!

And, as the Sagathi launched himself out into the room, he saw six more victims all waiting to be slaughtered. Ideally, had such a thing been possible, Verafti would have toyed with the soldiers to prolong his pleasure. But they were armed, and even though the Umans were slow by his standards, one of them had been able to fire.

Verafti slapped the rifle aside as he closed with the nearest soldier, sank his claws into the Uman's shoulders, and swiveled the soldier's body to the left. There was a loud ripping sound as a second militiaman opened fire. Verafti's shield jerked spasmodically when half a dozen bullets slammed into his back.

Then, as the body fell, Verafti morphed into a likeness of Centurion Pasayo. Not a *perfect* likeness, since the officer was dressed in little more than blood-splashed rags, but close enough. "Cease fire!" the officer shouted, and in keeping with all of their training the soldiers obeyed. That gave Verafti the split second in which to scoop up a weapon and turn it on the soldiers arrayed around him. They weren't wearing body armor, so there was no need to aim. The submachine gun produced a sustained *buuurrurp* as empty casings arced away and bodies began to fall. Korem was the last person to be hit, and as the noncom went down, he spent the last half second of his life wondering what he was dying for.

Gun smoke drifted just below the ceiling, and an eerie silence settled over the room, as Verafti went to secure the outside door. The entire battle had consumed less than four minutes, and, based on Verafti's painstaking observations over the last sixteen hours, at least half an hour would elapse before anyone came by. Could he close with Nalomy, secure her pendant, and hunt Hingo down all within that amount of time? And what about the mysterious *third* pendant? There was only one way to find out.

But before Verafti could leave, it was first necessary to choose which Uman to impersonate. That task was made easier by the fact that one of the men had been killed by a neat and tidy bullet to the head. Removing the soldier's clothing was a difficult and time-consuming task, however—one which left Verafti feeling frustrated by the time he finally pulled the militiaman's tight-fitting leather cuirass down over his head. Having emptied the submachine gun, and having been unable to locate a backup magazine for it, Verafti armed himself with one of the assault rifles that was lying on the floor.

It would have been nice to drag all of the bodies into the storeroom in hopes of hiding the slaughter for a longer period of time, but Verafti was in a hurry, and there was way too much blood to make that strategy practical. So all he could do was step out into the hall and lock the door behind him.

At that point Verafti's knowledge of the palace came into play. And not just the physical layout of the building but the routines that staff followed each day and who was allowed to go where within the highly regulated environment.

And that was a problem with his current persona. Because common soldiers weren't allowed on the fifth floor, where Nalomy lived. That floor was the province of the Procurator's specially trained bodyguards, who would not only refuse to let him enter, but would report his presence to Pasayo, thereby triggering an investigation. So as Verafti arrived on the fourth floor, and exchanged greetings with a militiaman who was clearly friends with the man he was impersonating, the shape shifter knew it would be necessary to assume still another identity before invading Nalomy's private quarters. The only question was whom to kill?

Persus was in the fourth-floor utility room, pouring a mixture of water and detergent into a robotic floor scrubber, when the door opened behind her. Her supervisor, an older woman named Mitha, had been very controlling ever since the Legate's arrival. That was why Persus spoke without bothering to look over her shoulder. "I'm nearly done, Mitha. I'll be out in a moment."

Closing the door, Verafti stepped in behind the slave, and dropped a leather loop over the unsuspecting woman's head. Persus saw the belt and began to respond, but it was too late. The shape shifter was pulling both ends of the makeshift garrote in opposite directions by then! Persus let go of the jug in order to reach up and grab the loop that was choking off her air supply. But it was too tight, and her desperate fingers were unable to get a sufficient purchase.

Verafti sampled her fear, found it to his liking, and took in the emotion. His victim made unpleasant gasping noises, followed by a lot of pointless thrashing, but the episode eventually came to an abrupt end as she went limp. That was when Verafti took a moment to listen, and not having heard an alarm, immediately went to work removing the Uman's clothing. It was easier to take off than the soldier's had been, and thanks to the manner of the woman's death, was free of telltale stains.

After he had morphed into a likeness of Persus, it was a simple matter to change clothes and peek through the door. Then, assuring himself that the hallway was clear, Verafti slipped outside, carefully closing the door behind him. From there it was a short walk to the back stairs that would take him up to the fifth floor, where, if Nalomy was following her usual schedule, she would be about halfway through her daily beauty regimen, a process entirely lost on Verafti.

Two uniformed guards were posted outside the fifth-floor stairway entrance, and when the woman they knew as Persus emerged, they smiled and nodded. The housekeeper wasn't much to look at—but her sunny disposition was infectious, and all the soldiers liked her.

Successful though he had been up to that point, Verafti knew that the most difficult part of his mission lay ahead. And that was to kill Nalomy, take control of her key, and summon Hingo. Then, once Hingo revealed the identity of the mysterious third person, he, too, would die. Finally, having dealt with *that* individual, Verafti would be free to go wherever he chose! Would the plan work? The odds were against it, Verafti knew, but he preferred to take action than sit in a cell waiting to be used.

Such were the Sagathi's thoughts as he made his way down a broad corridor and paused to retrieve some cleaning supplies from the utility closet before entering Nalomy's quarters. That necessitated passing between two *more* guards, both of whom offered cheerful greetings to the person they knew as Persus, and she responded in kind.

Nalomy was seated next to the bottom-lit pool, reading a synopsis of Legate Usurlus's activities from the day before, as a slave braided her hair. Bells tinkled near the formal entryway, and Nalomy glanced up toward the door. She watched a slave enter the room, then turned her attention back to her reading as a page boy rolled a red rubber ball across the highly polished floor. Nalomy's much-pampered dog scampered after it. The animal's nails made clicking sounds as they fought for a purchase. The boy shouted words of encouragement when the dog lost traction and the ball came straight at Verafti. "Grab it!" the youngster instructed enthusiastically. "And roll it back!"

Verafti bent to obey, but the animal had arrived by then, and quickly took possession of the ball. "Roll it back!" the boy commanded for a second time. "He'll chase it."

So Verafti scooped the dog up, and was attempting to free the saliva-coated ball from the animal's mouth, when he saw something that literally took his breath away. Because there, dangling from the animal's collar, was a pendant identical to the ones that both Nalomy and Hingo wore around their necks! The mysterious "third person" was right there in his arms! And what had once been a virtually impossible mission suddenly stood a chance of success.

Nalomy felt the pendant vibrate against her skin, looked down, and knew that either Hingo was trying to remove his key, which was unlikely, or someone was in the process of taking the third device off her dog!

A single glance was sufficient to confirm that the slave named Persus was not only in possession of the animal but fiddling with its collar. A harmless activity unless . . . The very thought of what could potentially happen were Verafti to gain possession of all three keys sent a chill down the Procurator's spine. Should she call for help? That seemed like a good idea given the circumstances. But what if the dog's collar had come undone? And the slave was simply buckling it back in place? Nalomy would look like a fool. It was a chance the Procurator was willing to take as she came to her feet. "Guards! Surround that woman! But don't get too close. And be careful. She could be dangerous."

All of the men assigned to guard Nalomy had been chosen for their intelligence, as well as their physical attributes, and were quick to react. So quickly that Verafti was just starting to run with the collar in hand when the militiamen rushed in to surround him. But it was Nalomy, her eyes filled with anger, who prevented what could have been a horrific battle. "Stop where you are, Verafti! Or shall I blow your left hand off?"

As if to emphasize her words, Nalomy was holding on to her pendant. The device was open to reveal a red button within.

Verafti stopped, turned a full circle, and saw that there was no way to escape. None of the men was close enough to slash, all were aiming weapons at him, and the Sagathi knew Nalomy would trigger the explosive bracelet if he tried to change shapes. The situation was hopeless, so he extended the collar toward the Procurator and produced a wan smile. The voice that came out of the slave's mouth was unexpectedly male. "Sorry about that. I believe this belongs to you."

"Throw it," Nalomy ordered grimly, as she came forward to catch the object. "How many people did you kill?"

"Eight?" Verafti responded lightly. "Ten? I didn't keep track. I was pretty busy."

Nalomy allowed herself a grimace. Not only did she hate to lose valuable assets, but there was morale to consider, as well as the possibility that Cato or Usurlus would get wind of what had occurred. "Call Pasayo," she ordered. "And Hingo, too. Order them to get up here on the double. And tell them to bring the cage. They'll know what I mean."

As a noncom hurried off to execute the Procurator's orders, Nalomy turned to look at Verafti. Much to the amazement of the militiamen who were aiming their weapons at the Sagathi he morphed back into his actual form. Cloth ripped as the tunic he was wearing came apart. *"Why?"* Nalomy wanted to know, as she stood with hands on hips. "Why would you do something like that?"

"Because I'm *me*," Verafti answered simply. "What did you expect?"

THIRTEEN

The city of Solace, on the planet Dantha

IT WAS A BEAUTIFUL DAY. THE SKY WAS BLUE, HIGH-
flying puffy white clouds sailed toward the east, while the
snowcapped Sawtooth Mountains looked on from the west.
Light glittered like gold on the surface of the lake, the air
was cool and sweet, and everyone knew that a holiday lay
ahead. All of which explained why so many people were out
and about.

Belok was riding on Cato's shoulders as the police officer
and Phelonious left the palace and made their way along
Imperial Boulevard toward Market Street and The Warrens
beyond. And that, to Cato's mind, was where Pak Nassali
and Etir Lood were probably hiding. Because it seemed logical to believe that the Lir warriors had been informed of the
attack on High Hold Meor and were either lying low, or
had already returned home, which was a definite possibility
given their capacity to fly. If that was the case, Cato would
have to return to the mountains or give up. The latter was
something he stubbornly refused to do. Not yet anyway.
Not until every possibility of finding the killers had been

exhausted. Especially now that he knew Verafti was present in the city. *Knew* but couldn't prove. For Cato had explored all five floors of the palace and the basements below without having "felt" the shape shifter's presence. That wasn't absolutely definitive, of course, since Verafti could at least partially block his emotional emanations if he chose to and might be hidden away somewhere.

But that would require Procurator Nalomy's active cooperation, and why would she provide it? How would she benefit? No, minus a clear motive for Nalomy to harbor a fugitive, it made more sense to assume that Verafti had taken on the identity of a dinner guest, or some member of the palace's staff, and subsequently been forced to flee when Cato arrived. Hingo had promised to provide him with a head count but hadn't done so yet. That wasn't too surprising, given the confrontation over Alamy. Cato's thoughts were interrupted as Belok spoke into his right ear. "We're being followed."

Cato wanted to look but knew better than to do so. "How many?"

"Four," the Kelf answered matter-of-factly. "All in plain clothes."

"That figures," Cato replied. "The Procurator wants to keep an eye on me."

"We could kill them," Phelonious suggested pragmatically.

"Are you crazy?" Cato demanded incredulously, as he turned to look at the robot. "Okay, stupid question," Cato allowed. "Of course you're crazy. . . . Most robots are busy doing something useful! No, we're not going to kill Nalomy's spies. Once we arrive in The Warrens, we'll split up. That will force the people who are following us to do likewise. And after we shake the bastards, we'll meet at Hason Ovidius's furniture factory. He helped me the last time I was in Solace—and I'm hoping he'll do so again."

"But what if they don't? Split up that is," Belok inquired. "What if all of them follow *you*?"

"Then I'll have to deal with that," Cato responded. "Just meet me at the factory."

The threesome had turned onto Market Street by that time. There was lots of foot traffic thanks to the good weather, the time of day, and the fact that thousands of people were flooding into the city to take part in the upcoming Founder's Day festivities. Some of the pedestrians stared at the strange threesome, but most had other things on their minds.

"And if we don't meet you there?" Phelonious inquired pointedly. The question had a contentious quality, but when Cato turned to look at the android's features, they were blank. That, plus the fact that robots don't produce emotions the way flesh-and-blood beings do, left the police officer with no choice but to take what the robot said at face value. If Belok and Phelonious were something less than thrilled by the manner in which they had been co-opted, it was perfectly understandable. But Cato was in need of some additional arms and legs, even if four of them were extremely short, and he wasn't above stretching the extent of his authority when necessary to carry out his self-assigned mission. The answer he offered to Phelonious reflected that fact. "If you don't show up at the factory, I'll track you down, saw your legs off, and hand you over to the city for use down in the sewers!"

"There's no need to be hostile," Phelonious replied. "I was curious, that's all."

"Think of the next few days as an opportunity to perform a public service and thereby make up for your various crimes," Cato retorted, as he and his companions entered the maze of streets, alleys, and passageways that constituted The Warrens. "Okay," Cato said. "This is where we split up. One hour. . . . That's how much time I'm allowing you. Don't let me down," he added sternly.

So saying, Cato lifted Belok down off his shoulders and turned to say good-bye to Phelonious, only to discover the robot gone. That brought a grin to the policeman's face as Belok scuttled away, and a river of flesh carried Cato forward.

"Damn it to hell!" Agent Thona exclaimed, as the three beings split up. He was a balding man, with flinty eyes and a weak jaw. His clothes consisted of a sweat-stained tunic, a broad leather belt, and a pair of baggy pants. It was just the sort of everyday working uniform that many of the craftsmen who swirled around him wore. Except for the fact that their hands were callused and his weren't, they were semi-illiterate while he had been schooled on one of the Empire's inner worlds, and they were struggling to make a living while his paychecks were piling up in a bank account on Corin. "Intalo! Follow the robot! Brum! Go after the Kelf! Narris and I will follow Cato. And keep those com units on! You'll be sorry if I call and you fail to answer."

The men nodded, slipped into the crowd, and disappeared. The chase was on.

Because Cato was a cop, he was used to following people rather than being followed. Still, having been dumped by some very talented criminals in his time, Cato knew that one of the most important factors to consider was speed. People who were being followed, or believed that they were, had a natural tendency to move quickly in hopes of shaking their pursuers. But, by pushing, shoving, and otherwise forcing their way through a crowd, criminals were frequently the cause of the very disturbance that gave them away.

So as Cato sought to evade the two men who were following him, he was careful to maintain the same pace as those around him, both as a means to convey the impression that he was ignorant of the tail and to reduce his overall visibility.

In the meantime the empath sifted through the kaleidoscope of emotions that ebbed and flowed around him, searching for those that might be directed his way. Because while some emotions were passive, as was the case with the woman in front of him, others had "direction," meaning that some thought forms shot away from their creators like multicolored arrows, often striking the person or thing to which they were connected, such as the momentary anger that one member of the crowd "sent" toward the pedicab operator who was in the way.

It was a very inexact science, and one that was frequently fruitless, given the emotional stew generated by all of the minds in range. But when successful, the strategy could provide Cato with what amounted to a sixth sense, a way to keep track of the people who were following him and, more than that, gauge what they might do next.

So as Cato took an impulsive right-hand turn into a narrow passageway, he was able to "identify" one of his pursuers. The emotion came in via a sudden and heartfelt spike of annoyance that momentarily overrode all other emotional input. Cato responded by readying some money. Then, as he passed between a series of clothing stalls, he was quickly able to acquire a disguise of robe and cap by paying twice what they were worth, rather than haggling over the price as was the usual custom.

Finally, it was a simple matter to don the cap, belt the generously proportioned robe around his middle, and wait for his tail to pass him by.

Agent Thona couldn't get too close to his subject without giving himself away, which meant there were moments when

Cato was lost from sight. Such interludes were brief, how-ever, and to be expected, so when Cato went around a bend, Thona wasn't especially worried. Not until he and Narris rounded the same curve to discover that Cato had disap-peared! The question, and one they had no way to answer, was whether the off-worlder had *intentionally* given them the slip or unknowingly done so by turning into a dimly lit passageway.

Thona swore under his breath and began to run. Narris was right on his heels. A woman fell as Thona shouldered her aside. Fruit spilled into the passageway as Narris knocked a basket over, and neither one of the government agents took notice of the man in the white skullcap and gray robe when they raced past him, their eyes searching for someone who looked entirely different.

Cato didn't know the agents by sight, but he recognized their emotional signatures as they hurried by, and knew it was safe to turn and walk in the other direction. It took about three minutes to reach Market Street, merge with the fleshy flow, and resume his journey. Contact had been broken.

Lucia Ovidius was seated at what had been her husband's desk, sipping a tiny cup of very strong caf, when a man wearing a skullcap and a voluminous robe entered through the front door. He nodded politely. "My name is Cato, and I'm looking for Citizen Ovidius. Is he here?"

It wasn't the first time that someone had come through the door looking for Hason since his death, there had been dozens of them, but Lucia still had difficulty dealing with it. There was something familiar about the name Cato, but she couldn't place it. "No," Lucia answered, as she battled to keep her voice steady. "My name is Lucia Ovidius. . . . And I'm sorry to inform you that my husband was murdered four days ago."

The surprise was clear to see on the man's face. "Murdered?" he exclaimed. "That's terrible! Please accept my deepest condolences. Your husband was a fine man. And the only one who was willing to help me when I was in trouble."

There was something different about the man and the way he spoke. An off-planet accent? Yes, Lucia thought so. Was he a customer? Come to talk about a furniture order? Or one of Hason's political contacts? Either was of interest to her. "Please," Lucia said, "have a seat. Perhaps *I* can help you."

The man looked doubtful, but accepted both her invitation, and a cup of caf from the thermos on the desk. "So," Lucia said, once the man named Cato had been served, "what can I do for you?"

Cato had an instinctive liking for the woman with the intelligent eyes, just as he'd had for her husband, but could she offer the type of help he was looking for? And, even if she could, would it be wise to trust her? Cato resolved to go slowly and break the conversation off if she said anything that made him uncomfortable. "I am a member of the Xeno Corps," Cato said levelly, "and I need some help."

Lucia's eyes widened slightly. "Now I remember. . . . Hason told me about you. There was an attack on Station 3, the rest of your team was killed, and you went back to bury them."

"That's correct," Cato agreed. "And now, having obtained additional information, I have two suspects. Both of whom may be hiding in Solace."

"And you were going to ask my husband to help find them?"

"Yes," Cato answered, as he drained the tiny cup dry and put it down on the table beside him.

Lucia had enough problems already now that she had a

business to run while simultaneously providing support to Legate Usurlus and those who wanted to remove Nalomy from power. So the last thing Lucia needed was another issue to deal with. But, before she said "No," it seemed prudent to gather whatever information she could. "It's true that Hason knew all sorts of people," Lucia said cautiously. "But Solace is the largest city on Dantha. So the chances of locating the people you seek are rather slim."

"Granted," Cato conceded. "It would be difficult to find two Umans if that was the only thing I had to go on. However, the individuals I'm looking for are Lir bandits! And it's my guess there aren't that many Lir living in Solace."

"It's hard to say for sure," Lucia replied carefully. "But you're probably correct."

"Which means the fugitives I'm after will be all the more visible," Cato pointed out. "And that's all I need from you—a sighting that will put me on the right trail. I can handle the rest. I can pay if that will help. . . . And Procurator Nalomy will provide support if I request it."

The mention of Nalomy's name brought a frown to Lucia's face. If the Procurator was involved, Usurlus would want to know about it. "Perhaps I could be of at least limited assistance," the businesswoman allowed. "Please tell me everything that occurred, starting with your trip to Station 3."

Police work was all about details, so Cato knew how important they could be, and having put his trust in the woman's husband, he was inclined to trust her as well. It took the better part of fifteen minutes, and once he was done, Lucia nodded sagely. "You're correct. The warriors you seek could be back in the mountains by now. But, if they're in Solace, the first place to look is the Xeno Quarter. That's where most of the non-Umans live—and where the Lir would naturally hide."

That made perfect sense to Cato and was the sort of information he'd been looking for. "Good!" Cato said enthusiastically. "But if my friends and I barge in there, everyone will take notice, and the people I'm after might hear about it. . . . Do you have contacts in the Xeno Quarter? People who could help us zero in on the bandits?"

Lucia was about to answer when the front door opened and a Kelf waddled in. A six-foot-tall android was right behind him. "Don't tell me, let me guess," the businesswoman said dryly. "These are your friends."

"That's right," Cato confirmed. "Belok, Phelonious, meet Citizen Ovidius. She's going to help us."

Lucia hadn't agreed to that, not really, but couldn't see a way to steer clear of it. Not if she wanted to know what was going on. "That's right," the spy lied smoothly. "It would be my pleasure to help."

Rather than return to the palace for the night, and be forced to shake Nalomy's surveillance team the following day, Cato decided to find a hotel where he and his companions could stay. The problem was that not only had prices soared over the last few days, but most of the better hotels were filled with people in town for Founder's Day. This forced latecomers such as himself to book rooms in the flophouses down by the docks.

It was early afternoon by then, and secure in the knowledge that Ovidius was hard at work searching for the Lir bandits, Cato took the opportunity to look for Verafti. Because so long as the Sagathi was on the loose, no one was safe. But how to find the shape shifter among hundreds of sentient beings?

Having given the matter some thought, Cato came up with the only possibility that stood any chance of success short of getting Nalomy's people involved. That was something he was hesitant to do, fearing that the militiamen would unintentionally spook the Lir bandits and cause them to flee if they hadn't done so already.

The solution, or so it seemed to Cato, was to look for Verafti's victims rather than the shape shifter himself. Because there were bound to be some, given the passage of time plus the Sagathi's irrepressible hunger. And if Cato could identify the killer's victims, and group them in a meaningful way, that could provide valuable information regarding Verafti's whereabouts.

So with Belok and Phelonious in tow, Cato left the hotel and made his way toward the aptly named Bone Yard. It was easy to find thanks to the streams of white smoke issuing from the facility's brick chimneys. Because of religious tradition, the scarcity of land in and around Solace, and the so-called Death Tax levied on entombments, the vast majority of the city's dead were cremated in one of the Bone Yard's glowing furnaces.

Some of the bodies were a bit ripe by the time they arrived at the Bone Yard, which accounted for the nauseating odor that Cato and Belok detected while still a block away. Phelonious, who lacked a sense of smell but could "see" the heat coming off the smoke stacks, was completely unaffected. Fortunately, the predominant winds blew west to east, thereby pushing the worst of the stomach-churning odor out over Lake Imperium. But every now and then the breezes blew the *other* way, adding to the misery of those who lived in The Warrens.

The area immediately around the Bone Yard was dominated by the commercial enterprises that depended on a constant flow of dead people to make their various livings. Because once the bodies were incinerated, the resulting ash was bagged and delivered to the next of kin, who were expected to buy a respectable urn from one of the local potters. However, that was just the beginning. Once a container for the departed's remains was secured, it was time to sign up for a Farewell Cruise aboard a dreary-looking death barge, and purchase flowers to scatter on the lake once the urn had been committed to the deep.

Now, as the threesome neared the front gate, it was necessary to force their way through a mini–traffic jam comprised
of sobbing relatives, some of whom were following behind
a professional body collector. Others, lacking the money to
hire such a person, were bringing a body to the Bone Yard
on their own. Often in carts or wheelbarrows, but sometimes on homemade stretchers, carried by grieving family
members.

And, making the situation that much worse, was the
presence of often raucous hucksters. They were selling everything from incense intended to neutralize the surrounding stench to religious medals guaranteed to open the gates
of heaven to even the worst of sinners.

Being unencumbered by a body, Cato and his companions were able to bypass the check-in stations and enter the
Bone Yard without delay. But they hadn't gone far when a
burly man attired in a black rubber apron and matching
boots came forward to challenge them. "No relatives or body
collectors beyond this point," he said officiously. "If you're
here to collect cremated remains, you should report to the
south gate."

"I'm an Imperial law officer," Cato announced, and flashed
his badge. "These individuals are with me. Please take me to
the person in charge."

The Bone Yard worker took a second look at the glowing
badge, concluded that it was real, and waved the threesome
forward. "Follow me. . . . I'll take you to the Director."

In order to cross the yard, it was first necessary to wait for
a break in the steady flow of carts that were being trundled
back toward the furnaces beyond. Most of the bodies were
covered, but Cato could see that many were those of children, which said a great deal about life in The Warrens.

Once the carts had passed, the man in the black apron
led the visitors up a flight of wooden stairs to a second-floor
reception area. There, Cato and his friends were invited to

wait under a secretary's watchful gaze while their guide disappeared into the office beyond. Then, after a minute or two, he was back. "Citizen Breus will see you now," the man announced formally, as his dust-reddened eyes met Cato's. "But only *you*. Your associates must remain here until you return."

Cato nodded, and directed stern looks to both Belok and Phelonious, before allowing himself to be ushered into the office. It was pleasant, or would have been, had it not been for the slight odor of corruption that continually seeped into the space from the Bone Yard below. Beams of diluted sunlight streamed in via a row of dirty windows, all of which were securely closed, and nicely framed photos of previous Bone Yard managers hung in orderly rows on the walls. The furniture matched, and though a bit worn, was still in good shape. The woman who rose to greet Cato had black hair streaked with white, a kindly face, and was dressed in a loose-fitting toga. It was yellow. As if to brighten the otherwise-dreary atmosphere with a bright splash of color. "Hello!" the woman said cheerfully. "I'm Olivia Breus. And you are?"

"Xeno Corps Officer Jak Cato," the variant replied, as he offered a formal bow.

"My goodness!" Breus exclaimed. "I hope we aren't in any trouble. Please take a seat."

"No, ma'am, you aren't in any trouble," Cato assured her as he sat down. "I'm looking for a killer. A serial killer. . . . Who likes to *eat* his victims. So, if you and your staff have taken delivery on partially eaten or dismembered bodies, I'd like to know about it."

Breus was clearly shocked, and after asking all of the predictable questions, sent for her foreman, who turned out to be the same man who'd brought Cato up to the office in the first place. He listened to what Cato had to say and shook his head. "No, we haven't taken delivery on any dismembered bodies. Not since the air-car crash a month ago."

Cato felt his spirits plummet. The inquiry had been a long shot, he knew that, but the results were disappointing nevertheless. So, after another five minutes of fruitless questioning, Cato left, taking Belok and Phelonious with him. The sun had dropped behind the mountains by that time, but the dead continued to arrive, and the furnaces were ready to receive them. It was the one service that the citizens of Solace could really count on.

FOURTEEN

The city of Solace, on the planet Dantha

THE SKY WAS GRAY, AND IT WAS RAINING, WHICH WAS
sure to put a damper on the series of lesser events that tra-
ditionally led up to Founder's Day. And Cato, who had been
forced to share a hotel room with his companions due to the
shortage thereof, was in a foul mood as Lucia Ovidius led
the three of them through the rain-slicked early-morning
streets. Very few people were up and around, but some of the
more-enterprising vendors were open for business, and Cato
insisted that the group stop at one of them.

Ten minutes later, having filled his belly with a hearty
breakfast wrap and two cups of hot caf, the policeman was
in much better spirits as Lucia led the threesome into the
Xeno Quarter. In spite of the early hour, a few non-Umans
were out on the street, and Cato noticed that while many
of the signs were in standard, many bore other forms of
writing including Kelf swift script, Tekan dot text, and Lir
pictographs. This seemed to suggest that while the majority of Dantha's winged humanoids lived in mountain aeries
like High Hold Meor, some, perhaps a couple of hundred,

were permanent residents of Solace. That meant Nassali and Lood could move around the Xeno Quarter without exciting comment.

They would need a place to stay, however, and by putting out the word to her contacts, Lucia had been able to identify what could be a Lir safe house, meaning an informal hostelry mountain bandits could stay in while buying supplies with their loot. And when the group rounded a corner and Lucia said, "There it is," Cato had to agree that the strange-looking tower certainly *looked* the part.

The structure at the far end of the block stood head and shoulders above the two- and three-level buildings crammed in around it and was festooned with semicircular platforms which, had they been equipped with railings, might have been called balconies. But, having been to High Hold Meor, Cato recognized the extensions for what they *really* were, landing platforms. And he saw something else as well. Something that *shouldn't* have been there but was. "Soldiers!" he said urgently. "Quick! Off the street!"

Cato's companions followed him into a side passageway, but Lucia was far from convinced. Her face was half-hidden by a hooded raincoat as she peered around the corner. "I don't see any soldiers," she said skeptically.

"But you *do* see five Umans," Cato countered, as he came to stand next to her. "Two lounging in front of the safe house, two seated in the food stall across the street, and one standing on the roof of the building just west of the tower. All of whom look as if they're on sentry duty. Why *is* that do you suppose?"

Lucia was embarrassed to see that Cato was correct. The presence of so many Umans around a building in Xeno Quarter *was* suspicious. "So, what does it mean?" Lucia inquired as she pulled back into the passageway.

"It means the bastards are *here*!" Cato said emphatically. "And either the government is protecting them, or has taken them into custody; although that seems unlikely since why keep them here? No," Cato continued grimly, "I'm guessing that Nalomy knows all about the Lir, and Verafti, too, which would explain how he's been able to hide so successfully!"

Suddenly Lucia knew she was onto something important, something Usurlus should know about, but kept her thoughts to herself. "Okay," Phelonious said pragmatically, "what should we do?"

"Get inside," Cato answered simply. "And ask those flying bastards some very pointed questions."

Lood was still asleep, but Nassali was awake, and had been for hours. The window on the west side of the tower was barred, but it still offered a view of the Sawtooth Mountains, and as the warrior stared at the jagged peaks, that was where he longed to be. In High Hold Meor, with his mate, and their extended family. Especially now that Hybor Iddyn was dead. Because he, more than Lood or the idiot Issit, was the chieftain's logical successor. But rather than make his case to the elders as was his right, Nassali and his companion had been held hostage ever since the night when the creature in the cage had been delivered to the Imperial Palace.

Not for ransom, as was the Lir way, but as what Centurion Pasayo referred to as a "security deposit." It would be a guarantee that Iddyn and his clan would remain silent about the attack on Station 3 and the creature they had abducted from the Plain of Pain until Founder's Day had come and gone. *And that,* Nassali told himself, *will happen soon.* Which was the one thing he had to look forward to.

The guards posted in front of the Lir safe house were tired, and had every right to be, since they had been on duty for nearly eight hours by then. And would remain so for another half hour until their reliefs were scheduled to arrive. So the soldiers weren't as sharp as they might have been when a raggedly dressed android strolled down the street, paused directly in front of them, and began to rummage around in the bag that hung over his right shoulder. "Hey, you!" one of the two men growled. "Keep moving!"

At that point, Phelonious produced two pieces of half-rotten fruit and threw one of them. His aim was good, and the first guard took a direct hit, which splattered the second man with gooey pulp as well. That produced a roar of mutual outrage along with a concerted charge. Rather than throw the second piece of fruit, Phelonious was forced to turn and run instead. His robe swirled around skinny legs, and his servos whined urgently, as the soldiers pounded along behind him. Fortunately for Phelonious, the body armor and concealed weapons they wore under their civilian clothes had the effect of slowing them down. The race was on.

The noncom who was stationed on a nearby roof sought to prevent his men from giving chase by yelling at them via a handheld com set, but they weren't listening, and took off anyway. That left the front door unguarded. The NCO swore, and was about to turn toward the stairway behind him, when Lucia shot him from behind.

It had been relatively easy to sneak up on him because the possibility that someone might stalk him had never even occurred to the soldier, who screamed shrilly as the bolt of energy hit him, and his muscles locked up. And there he was, lying on the roof with raindrops hitting his face, when Lucia arrived to look down at him. Lucia wondered if the noncom had been one of the men who had murdered her husband.

There was no way to know, but it felt good to kick him just in case, before she left the roof.

The soldiers seated in the food stall came to their feet as Phelonious threw the fruit at their buddies, then charged out onto the street, where they would have been positioned to block him, had it not been for Belok, who scuttled out of his hiding place to throw rotten fruit at *them*. That drew the guards away as the Kelf disappeared into a narrow passageway, and they ran after him. The soldiers hadn't traveled more than ten feet when they heard a loud *clang*, and turned to see a Uman place a brand-new padlock on the gate behind them! The militiamen were still considering the implications of that development when another piece of fruit came sailing out of the darkness. It hit one of them in the head. That produced a cry of outrage as both soldiers turned to chase Belok.

Having cleared the way, Cato crossed the street, climbed a flight of three stairs, and tried the door. It opened smoothly, allowing him to enter. Conscious of the fact that he wouldn't have the place to himself for very long Cato locked the door, drew his pistol, and conducted a quick search of the first floor. There was a filthy bathroom, a kitchen that wasn't much better, and what was supposed to be a sitting room but had been co-opted for use as a guardroom. It was dirty, too.

Pistol at the ready, Cato went over to the spiral staircase located at the center of the tower and began to climb the metal treads. The second floor had been subdivided into pie-shaped cubicles, but all of them proved to be empty, as were those located on the level above. But as Cato neared the fourth floor, he could tell that it was occupied because of the emotions that swirled there. And sure enough, as he came up through the hole in the floor, the policeman found himself at the center of a circular room. Two Lir were present, and both turned to look at the Uman, who they assumed to be a guard. Except that *this* Uman was pointing a gun at them, and that was reason for concern.

Cato felt the fear in the room spike as both of the Lir backed away and began to separate as if hoping to divide his fire. "Oh, no you don't," Cato said, as he waved the handgun at them. "Move back together. . . . Or I'll shoot one of you and resolve the problem that way!"

The threat had the desired effect, and as the wary Lir stood side by side, Cato looked from one bandit to the other. "Okay, which one of you is Lood? And which one is Nassali?"

"I Nassali," the Lir on the right side said. He was the taller of the two, part of his crest was missing where someone or something had taken a chunk out of it, and his saucerlike yellow eyes never seemed to blink.

"And that makes you Lood," Cato said, as his gaze shifted to the second warrior, a rail-thin specimen, who clearly didn't have an extra ounce of flesh on his body. His wings were half-deployed in spite of the bars on the windows. He offered no response, but was clearly ready for action, a notion supported by the emotions that swirled around him.

"My name is Cato," the police officer informed them, as he raised a hand palm forward. The badge that was part of his right hand glowed, and while both of the Lir stared at it, neither appeared to recognize the symbol.

"I'm a Xeno Corps officer," Cato told them. "And I have reason to believe that both of you were involved in the attack on Station 3, the murder of half a dozen law officers, and the unlawful release of an Imperial prisoner. You are now under arrest. I am about to read you your rights and take you into custody. Once an Imperial Prosecutor has had a chance to review the relevant evidence, you will be formally charged. Do you have any questions?"

Nassali thought about the process the Uman had laid out, the likelihood of months if not years spent in prison, and made his decision. The only decision that made sense for him.

Cato "felt" the sudden surge of emotion, and shouted, "No!" But it was too late. As with all of his kind, Nassali's bony fingers were equipped with talons, which—thanks to weeks of surreptitious sharpening—were like razors. So when the bandit brought his right hand up, and slashed his throat, four scarlet wounds appeared. As the air rushed out of Nassali's partially severed windpipe, it pushed a thick blood mist out into the air. The pinkish cloud continued to hang suspended in space even as his body toppled over backward.

Then, while Cato was still in the process of trying to absorb what he'd seen, Lood dove headfirst down the circular stairway! The policeman fired and missed. The bullet hit something, bounced off, and whined as it passed within a foot of Cato's head. Desperate to catch up with Lood, the police officer plunged down the circular stairway, only to see that the birdlike sentient had not only been able to right himself but was already halfway to the ground floor! By the time Cato arrived on the main level, Lood was in the process of unlocking the front door and pushing it open. Lucia was there, waiting to enter, but fell over backward as the Lir gave her a shove.

Cato swore a blue streak as he jumped over the businesswoman's body and ran out into the middle of the narrow street. Lood was airborne by that time, his wings beating mightily, as he fought to clear the maze of crisscrossing clotheslines that blocked the way. Cato raised his gun, took careful aim, and fired.

It was a long pistol shot, but Cato saw the fugitive jerk

as the bullet struck. Then, no longer able to gain altitude, Lood was forced to glide. And such was his height by that time that the Lir was able to clear the surrounding structures and disappear from sight, thereby evading justice and taking everything Cato needed to know with him. The rain stopped right about then, the sun broke through the clouds, and the pavement began to steam. Cato had failed.

As CeCe Alamy stood in the hall, waiting for the line that led into Imood Hingo's office to advance, she was frightened. And for good reason. Because her friend Persus had been missing for an entire day by then, and none of the people in charge seemed to be very concerned about it. That was strange because a missing slave would generally be cause for a huge uproar.

There were rumors, of course, one of which was that Persus was ill and had been taken to the hospital in Solace. But Alamy didn't believe that, because she and Persus met every afternoon, and her friend had been in good health the day prior to her disappearance. So where was she? That was the question Alamy was determined to ask Hingo even though it meant confronting a man who was still angry about the confrontation with Cato and might assault her.

But if Hingo was angry, Alamy believed that he was at least slightly scared of Cato as well, which might be enough to protect her for the moment at least. There was no guarantee of that, however, and as the line jerked forward, Alamy knew she was taking a chance. Because once inside Hingo's office, the Majordomo could close the door and assault her if he chose to. Still, it was a risk the young woman was willing to take in order to find out what had become of her friend.

The next fifteen minutes passed slowly as various members of the household staff filed into the basement office. There were two groups. Those who had been ordered to report because they were in trouble, and could expect to receive one of Hingo's famous tongue lashings, and those who were seeking some sort of favor. Both of which took time. And as it passed, the chasm at the bottom of Alamy's stomach grew ever deeper. So that by the time Alamy arrived at Hingo's door she was ready to flee, and would have, if the man in front of her hadn't been released at that moment. Her name was called as he hurried away. "CeCe Alamy!" Alamy knew who the voice belonged to, and being right outside Hingo's door, had no choice but to enter.

Once inside, Alamy took her place on the black "X" set into the floor opposite Hingo's raised desk. He was busy entering data into a keyboard, or that was the way it appeared, although it was common knowledge that Hingo often forced subordinates to wait. It was a tactic calculated to make them even more frightened and nervous, although Alamy wasn't sure that such a thing was possible.

Finally, after what seemed like an eternity, Hingo rose from his chair and circled the huge desk. Then, having stepped down onto the marble floor, he took up a position directly in front of the slave. His dark obsidian eyes searched Alamy's face as if looking for minute flaws or a way to get into her head. "So," he said gravely. "Why did you come? To apologize?"

Not only was Hingo standing only inches away, and staring into her eyes, Alamy could feel the warmth of his breath on her face. The effect was *very* intimidating, and Alamy felt her chin start to tremble. "No, master," she managed to blurt out. "I came about Persus. She's missing."

Hingo put his right index finger on Alamy's bare arm and drew a line along it. The slave shuddered and battled the impulse to take a step back as the Majordomo spoke. "Of course she's missing," Hingo said dismissively. "She ran. The militia is looking for her now, and when they find the bitch, she's going to pay!"

That was what everyone had said about Lea, the girl Alamy had seen Hingo chase down a hallway, and she had never been seen again. Although Persus had found what might have been Lea's blood in one of the storage rooms. But Alamy couldn't mention that, not without giving herself away, so the young woman chose a different approach. "Are you sure?" Alamy inquired meekly, careful to keep her eyes down. "Persus told me that it's stupid to run—that runners always get caught."

"It seems that Persus should have listened to her own advice," Hingo replied dismissively, as he leaned in to brush his lips across a partially bared shoulder. "Because she's gone. Which, I might add, is no business of yours."

"Some of the soldiers are gone, too," Alamy observed tightly, as she stared over her superior's left shoulder. Her entire body was rigid, and her fingers were balled into fists, which were held at her sides. "So I thought there might be a connection."

Hingo's head came up as if jerked by a rope. For one brief moment, Alamy saw a flash of fear in his eyes before it was replaced by anger. "Your job is to work in the kitchen, *not* to track the comings and goings of your betters," Hingo growled angrily. "The militiamen you mentioned were sent to the Imang Province as part of a regular troop rotation. There. Are you satisfied?"

It was a rhetorical question, and knowing that she had already pushed her luck to the limit, Alamy remained silent. But Hingo was scared of something—and that alone constituted a discovery. Why would a man in his position be frightened of anything other than Nalomy? Fortunately, for reasons the slave could only guess at, Hingo returned to his desk. "Get out," the Majordomo said with a wave of his hand. "And mind your business from now on. . . . Or I'll put a set of stripes on your back as a way to remind you!"

Alamy was only too happy to curtsy, turn to her left,

and leave Hingo's office as quickly as she could. It wasn't until she was outside and twenty feet down the corridor that Alamy discovered that she was holding her breath and allowed herself to exhale. The session was over, and she had survived, but without learning anything really significant. Except that Hingo was not only lying but afraid of someone or something. But who? Or what? The answer, or so it seemed to Alamy, was to keep an eye peeled for anything unusual and follow up on it.

The rest of the day was largely uneventful. But that evening, Chef Undara summoned Alamy into his tiny office just off the kitchen. He'd been nice to Alamy, so she had positive feelings for the head cook, and wanted to please him. But now, as Alamy looked at Undara, she wondered why he was so pale. Tiny beads of perspiration could be seen on the chef's broad forehead, and as he made use of a dishcloth to wipe them away, two of his four hands shook as if palsied. Alamy frowned. "Are you all right, sir? Should I call for a doctor?"

Undara swallowed, as if worried that the contents of his stomach might come up, and forced a hesitant smile. "No, child," he answered kindly. "But thank you for asking. It's just a bug. I'll be fine in the morning. But there is something you could do for me. Go find Ooly. She'll give you a cart. Do you know where the old pumping station is?"

Having been replaced by a new facility, the old pumping station was empty, and Alamy was well aware of this fact, since she had met Persus there on a regular basis. "Yes, sir," she answered honestly. "I do."

"Good," Undara replied. "Deliver the cart to the old pumping station. Then you can take the rest of the evening off. Okay?"

Alamy was a slave, so there was only one thing to say, and that was "Yes, master."

"And one more thing," Undara added as she started to

turn away. "You're smarter than most, Alamy, so when I tell you to keep this errand to yourself, I trust you'll do so. Correct?"

Alamy nodded solemnly. "Yes, sir."

"Good," Undara said, as he dabbed at his forehead. "Run along now. . . . And deliver that cart."

Never having seen the normally relaxed chef so upset, Alamy was extremely curious as she reported to a tight-lipped Ooly. The other slave provided instructions nearly identical to the ones Alamy already had, and opened the back door, so she could push the cart outside.

It was nearly dark by then, but conscious of the fact that she was passing beneath a series of pole-mounted lights, Alamy waited until the path took a tight right-hand turn before pushing the cart into a shadow where she could carry out a quick inspection of the wheeled conveyance. That was when Alamy discovered a strange fact—unlike every other cart she had been required to handle—this one was locked!

Unable to open the cart and see what was inside, Alamy had little choice but to continue her journey. And it was then, as she rounded the side of the maintenance shop, that Alamy was confronted by a *second* mystery. It seemed that the person the cart was intended for was dangerous, or in need of protection, because a dozen heavily armed soldiers had been posted outside the pumping station! An alert non-com spotted Alamy and came forward to meet her. "I'll take charge of that," he said officiously. "You can go."

Ordered to leave, there was nothing Alamy could do but curtsy and withdraw. But she wanted to know what was in the cart, who was being held within the pumping station, and why he or she was important. So, excused from further work by Chef Undara, Alamy passed through the kitchen and entered the maintenance room beyond.

As usual, the dimly lit space was empty of people, making it easy to slip along the right-hand wall to the open end of the big blue pipe. Seconds later, Alamy was inside the pipe, walking bent over just as she had on many previous occasions. Except she had been on her way to meet with Persus back then, and now she was trying to find her friend, or failing that, to determine the other woman's fate.

It was pitch-black inside the metal tube, but Alamy could see a small circle of light up ahead, and hear the faint rumble of muted conversation. As Alamy drew closer she saw that steel mesh had been welded over the other end of the pipe. There was no way to know if the barrier was intended to prevent intruders from entering or to keep a prisoner in. But that didn't matter to her so long as she could see through the mesh and hear what was being said on the far side of it.

Alamy removed her sandals so as to move quietly and felt the cold metal under her feet as she crept forward. At that point she went to her knees, knowing that the slime on the inside of pipe would stain her clothes, but working herself forward anyway. Finally, when her nose was only inches from the wire mesh, Alamy could peer down into the room beyond. And it was something to see.

A large cage occupied the end of the room off to her right, and crouched within, a green reptile could be seen. It was roughly the size of an adult Uman, and judging from the muscles that rippled just below the creature's slightly iridescent skin, its body was quite strong. The lizardlike thing's triangular head narrowed into a short snout, which was covered with scales and pierced by two vertical nostrils.

That was strange enough, since the presence of what appeared to be an animal made little sense, but there was more. The table that had been placed adjacent to the cage was set for a formal dinner, complete with a crisp white tablecloth, and gleaming silverware! The beautifully dressed Procurator was seated at the end of the table opposite from the cage with Hingo on her right and Pasayo on her left. Both men wore formal attire.

"A toast is in order," Nalomy said cheerfully, as she raised a glittering glass. "To our actor, the role he's about to play, and the most memorable Founder's Day the citizens of Dantha have ever witnessed!"

Then, much to Alamy's astonishment, the creature in the cage morphed into an exact likeness of Vedius Albus, the man she knew as the Legate's chief bodyguard! The Umans laughed as Verafti lifted a glass of his own. "Thank you," he said smoothly. "I, too, look forward to the day after tomorrow, both as an opportunity to repay Procurator Nalomy's hospitality, *and* earn my freedom. Please accept my heartfelt apologies for past indiscretions as well as my assurances that nothing of that sort will happen again."

That statement elicited a pro forma, "Hear, hear," from Pasayo, and a "Well said," from Nalomy, who didn't believe a word of it. Of course she didn't care *what* Verafti said, so long as he killed Usurlus as planned.

For his part Verafti was under no illusions regarding his own fate, especially after the failed escape attempt, but was perfectly willing to take part in the charade in order to obtain a few moments of precious freedom. What happened subsequent to that would depend on him and dumb luck. In the meantime, he could sense the presence of a *fifth* person in the immediate area. A female persona, if he wasn't mistaken, who was radiating a combination of curiosity, excitement, and fear. *Should I tell the others?* Verafti wondered. *Or keep it to myself?* Knowledge is power, and Verafti wanted power, so he chose to remain silent. For the moment at least.

Alamy struggled to take it all in as the imposter sipped his wine, and Nalomy signaled for the food to be served. That was when Ooly pushed a cart out of the shadows. Quickly, and with an efficiency that bespoke long practice, the senior slave served Nalomy and her Uman guests first.

Once that was accomplished, Ooly brought a *second* cart out into the light and positioned it next to the cage. Alamy recognized the cart as being the same one that she'd been ordered to deliver earlier. She watched with considerable interest as Ooly pressed a button and the top of the stainless-steel cart parted to reveal a large silver platter. And there, lying on a bed of greens was the unmistakable form of a pale Uman leg! Which, given all of the finely wrought tattoos that decorated it, clearly belonged to Persus! Alamy gave an involuntary gasp.

Nalomy heard something but wasn't sure what it was until Verafti pointed at the screen. "She's up there," he said calmly. "Hiding in that pipe."

Nalomy came to her feet, Pasayo spoke into a handheld com set, and Alamy had no choice but to run for her life!

It was dark in the Xeno Quarter except for the lights that glowed behind closely drawn shades, the occasional sweep of headlights as an armored ground car passed, and the harsh blue, red, and yellow glare produced by the signs that were hung along both sides of Orby Avenue. According to Lucia Ovidius, it was where all of the most important businesses in the so-called X-Quarter were located, including the medical center located directly across the street from the flophouse in which Cato and his two companions were staying.

The room had been darkened so that no one could see in, and Cato was positioned in front of one of three tall windows that looked down into the street below. Cato had a pair of binos Lucia had loaned him and was busy scanning the surrounding buildings when Phelonious came over to stand next to him. "So," Phelonious said, as he stared through the dirty glass, "do you think this will work?"

"How the hell would I know?" Cato answered irritably. "It *might* work. And that's all we have right now." This was true, since even though the Lir bandit had been wounded while fleeing the safe house a half mile away, the bastard was still on the loose. And, assuming he needed medical attention, could be expected to show up at the clinic.

But more than twelve hours had passed since Lood's escape, which seemed to suggest that the Lir didn't need medical attention, had been able to get help elsewhere, or was lying dead in an alley somewhere—the worst of all the various possibilities insofar as Cato was concerned. But with no other leads to follow, all Cato could do was stake out the medical facility and hope for a lucky break. That explained why he was so irritable.

Having seen nothing of interest, Cato placed the glasses on a rickety table right next to a half-eaten take-out dinner and crossed the room to a sagging bed. It creaked loudly when he put his weight on it, but it felt good to close his eyes, and sleep came quickly.

Belok was already asleep, having prepared a nest for himself in a dresser drawer and conked out minutes earlier. Each one of his snores ended in gentle wheezing sounds, which were as regular as a metronome and familiar to Phelonious, who continued to scan the street below. And that was the scene some twenty minutes later when Phelonious heard three knocks and went over to open the door. Lucia's eyes were bright with excitement, and she was carrying a canvas shopping bag. "Wake up, everyone!" she ordered loudly. "I know where Lood is!"

"Where?" Cato demanded, as he swung his feet off the bed.

"West of Solace," Lucia answered smugly as she opened the bag. "He's waiting for a caravan to depart! It leaves at daybreak. Isn't it wonderful what money can buy?"

"It certainly is," Cato agreed gratefully, as he accepted a roll and a cup of hot caf. Though not an expert on Dantha, Cato knew that caravans left for the west every couple of weeks or so, carrying supplies to communities like Donk's Well. It was a slow way to reach High Hold Meor, but quite possibly the *only* way, if the Lir couldn't fly.

So he gobbled the roll, made use of the caf to wash it down, and was soon ready to go. Five minutes later, Cato, Lucia, Phelonious, and Belok were outside jogging through the mostly empty streets. Being too short to keep up on his own, the Kelf was perched on top of his friend's shoulders, where he felt free to offer a steady stream of instructions, a habit Phelonious had learned to ignore.

Thanks to Lucia's intimate knowledge of the city, the group was able to pursue the shortest possible route through the shadowy streets. There were dangers, of course, including the militia patrols intended to keep dissidents under control, and criminals who made a living by preying on the quarter's largely unprotected citizens.

So as the party followed a twisting path between gated courtyards, looming tenements, and shadowy alleys, dozens of eyes tracked their progress. Most of the local predators preferred to prey on citizens who were either too old or too weak to defend themselves rather than people so confident they were willing to jog down the center of a nighttime street. They let the foursome pass.

But one group of predators wasn't so easily intimidated. Like Cato, they were variants who had been bioengineered to fulfill a specific need. In their case it was to perform physical labor on heavy-gravity planets, where most Umans could barely move, much less work.

The Crushers as they referred to themselves, were big, hulking brutes who were best known for running citywide protection rackets, but weren't above strong-arm robberies when the opportunity presented itself. So, having received word that a group of "norms" were headed their way, three heavies emerged from the shadows and were waiting when the marks rounded a corner and came straight toward them.

The X-Quarter wasn't well lit, but the Crushers had chosen to stand in the pool of light shed by one of the few streetlights, so their victims could appreciate how big they were and see the cudgels they carried. The sight brought most norms to their knees.

And consistent with the group's expectations the marks *did* slow, then came to a stop. That was when three additional Crushers appeared *behind* the norms, thereby locking them in place. A heavy named Thok led the group by virtue of both his size and intelligence. He smiled evilly, and when he spoke, the words sounded as if they had been produced by a rock crusher. "You can pay," Thok said menacingly, "or you can play! Which will it be?"

Cato swore under his breath. The caravan that would carry Lood away was scheduled to depart at daybreak, so time was of the essence. He brought his hand up and held it palm out. The badge glowed brightly. "I am an Imperial police officer. Let us pass."

"And I am Thok," the biggest brute answered evenly. "Empty your pockets."

Cato sighed wearily. "Okay, Citizen Thok," he replied. "Have it your way." Then, having turned to Lucia, he said, "Shoot the bastard."

The stun gun was already in Lucia's hand. She brought it up, pressed the firing stud, and saw Thok jerk as the invisible bolt hit him. But, rather than collapse the way he was supposed to, the Crusher shook the pain off, and took a step forward!

Cato swore, pulled the pistol out of a voluminous sleeve, and brought it up. There were three loud reports, and three grunts of pain, as each heavy took a bullet in a knee! The Crushers fell like trees, all wrapping their arms around what hurt, their plans to commit robbery momentarily forgotten.

Had that constituted the entire gang, Cato and his companions would have been free to advance. But that wasn't the case as Lucia shouted a warning. "Cato! Behind us!"

Cato turned, gun at the ready, only to have it knocked out of his hand by a blow from a well-swung cudgel. The pistol went skittering away as a 275-pound heavy hit him with a massive shoulder and bowled him over. The air had been knocked out of Cato's lungs, and he was lying on his back fighting to breathe, when the Crusher appeared above him. He had close-set eyes, a pug nose, and thick rubbery lips. They were pulled back into a snarl as he spoke. "Say good-bye, Xeno cop. Because *this* life is over."

The cudgel had already been raised, and was just about to fall, when Lucia drew the baton she always carried and pressed a button. There was an audible *click* as three feet of tempered steel shot out of the handle and locked into place. That was followed by a whirring sound as she brought the weapon around and struck the heavy across his kidneys. He uttered a scream of pain, and was trying to turn toward his attacker, when the baton hit him behind the left knee.

Cato barely managed to roll out of the way in time as the brute smacked face-first into the pavement. Then, having scrambled to his feet, Cato took up the fallen cudgel. It was too heavy for him, but the only weapon available. Two Crushers had Phelonious by the arms at that time, and were clearly intending to pull them off, as Belok wrapped his arms around a leg and sank his teeth into a meaty calf. That forced one of the would-be robbers to release Phelonious in order to hop around while trying to dislodge the Kelf.

Cato was in position by then, and the cudgel produced a satisfying *thump* as it made contact with the heavy's head and knocked him unconscious. Belok, his sharp teeth still firmly locked in place, rode the giant down.

Phelonious was lying on the street by that time and being stomped by the sole surviving Crusher as Cato spotted his pistol and hurried to scoop it up. Then, with the weapon in hand, he shouted, "Hold it right there!" But the heavy wasn't listening. There was a horrible screeching sound as a gigantic boot crushed the android's alloy skull. Sparks shot out of the robot's eye sockets, and his heels drummed against the ground, as all of his systems shut down.

Cato fired as the monster turned his way, fired *again*, and was forced to empty the magazine into the Crusher's enormous chest as the variant staggered forward. Finally, unable to proceed any farther, the giant collapsed.

With acrid odors of gun smoke and ozone floating in the air, Belok ran to his best friend's side and cradled what remained of the robot's badly mangled head in his little arms. "Phelonious!" the Kelf said miserably. "Say something! Talk to me!" But there was no response.

Cato's hands were shaking as he ejected the spent magazine and inserted a fresh one into the pistol's grip. "Cato," Lucia said urgently, "look left!"

Cato turned, and saw that two of the kneecapped variants were dragging themselves forward, in an apparent attempt to rejoin the battle. Cato raised the pistol, but realized that there was no need to shoot them, not so long as he and his companions left. So he backed away.

Belok was kneeling next to Phelonious, moaning softly, when Lucia went to pick him up. He struggled, but she was too strong for him, so it was to no avail. "I'll give you a ride," she said gently, and boosted Belok up onto her shoulders. Still sobbing as he looked back over his shoulder, Belok was borne away. Meanwhile, the first blush of dawn had appeared in the east, and a new day had begun.

FIFTEEN

The city of Solace, on the planet Dantha

THE SUN WASN'T VISIBLE YET, BUT A LONG PINK SLASH marked the horizon, and hinted at a warm day ahead. The sprawling maze of holding pens, watering tanks, and shacks that constituted the caravan park were located at the foot of the steep slopes that marked the point where the Sawtooth Mountains began. That meant the mountain peaks were *close*. About ten to fifteen thousand feet straight up. But to reach them, Etir Lood would have to fly, which he was no longer capable of doing. The Uman bullet had torn through the muscle controlling his right wing, thereby rendering it useless. That meant Lood would have to endure a long, tiresome trip south and west, before he would arrive in the area that he and his clan considered to be their territory. The vast stretch of land included the foothills below High Hold Meor, the area around Donk's Well, and a large portion of the Plain of Pain. Upon arrival on the other side of the mountains, Lood would signal one of the flock's high-flying scouts, and his fellow warriors would come to take him home, even if it meant strapping him to an angen.

In the meantime, Lood felt very nervous as he sat on a crudely constructed bench in front of a smoldering fire and waited for the mostly Uman caravan to depart. The complex business involved loading three dozen angens with packs they didn't want to carry, pushing and shoving the recalcitrant animals into a single column, and breaking up frequent fights as the more aggressive angens nipped their peers.

It was an ugly and undignified business, which was not only beneath Lood but made even more disgusting by the presence of half a dozen flightless Umans, two Kelfs, and a snooty cyborg.

Still, thanks to Nassali's decision to commit suicide, Lood was free! And that, Golor be praised, was something to be thankful for even if he was a captive of both the ground and the Godless creatures who were eternally confined to it. Such were the bandit's thoughts when he heard the crunch of gravel behind him and began to turn. But it was too late as something hard pressed against the back of his skull. The voice was Uman. "Well, well," Cato said sarcastically. "Look what we have here! A weary traveler on his way home."

Lood felt something heavy fall into the pit of his stomach as the pressure was removed, and Cato came around to stand between him and the fire. The Caravan Master stepped in to join him. He was a tall man, who wore a long scarf wrapped around his head and favored the sort of loose robe that many desert travelers wore. His eyes were hard and regarded Lood without the least sign of pity. "So, this is the one you were looking for?" he inquired.

"Yes," a female Uman said, as she joined the two men. "Thank you."

Lood saw a leather purse change hands and knew he'd been sold out. A clawlike hand went to the place where the ceramic dagger should have been but wasn't. Every Imperial that the bandit possessed had been spent to purchase a place in the caravan, with not so much as a decim left over for a weapon. "It is I who should thank *you*," the Caravan Master replied gravely, as the leather pouch disappeared. "Who knows what this one had in mind? The last thing I need is a run-in with Lir bandits."

"We'll take it from here," Cato said grimly. "You might hear some strange sounds. If so, don't let it bother you."

The Caravan Master smiled grimly. His teeth were very white. "Don't worry, I won't," he assured them and bowed as if to seal the transaction. Moments later, he was gone, having been absorbed into the dusty chaos as angens bawled, orders were shouted, and the lead animals began the long journey from which some of them would never return.

Mindful of Nassali's suicide, Cato ordered Belok to tie Lood's hands behind him. But, judging from the emotions that swirled around the Lir, he was anything but suicidal. Lood was frightened, *very* frightened, and Cato planned to take full advantage of that. Even if it meant bending a few laws in order to do so. "Good," Cato said, once Lood's hands were properly secured. "Now, let's haul him over to that fence, where we can fasten his wings to a crosspiece. I wish I had some nails—but a couple of belts should do the job."

The mention of his wings, which meant everything to the Lir warrior, filled Lood with a sense of dread. As the Umans hauled him over to the fence, Lood broke his silence. "No hurt! Me obey," he said pitifully. The wound had broken open by that time and began to ooze blood as the Umans pulled his wings back.

"I don't believe you," Cato said coldly as he pushed the bandit up against a crosspiece. "Buckle his left wing to the fence, Lucia. I'll take care of the right. Once we cut them off, Citizen Lood will be grounded for life." The flick knife produced a loud *click* as a four-inch-long blade appeared.

"What want?" Lood inquired desperately. "Don't cut! Don't cut! Me tell."

"Really?" Cato inquired skeptically, as if pausing to reconsider. "Because if you say you're going to answer my questions, then you don't, I'll become very angry."

"I tell! I tell!" Lood said eagerly. "You ask."

"Okay," Cato said reasonably, as he removed a camcorder from one of his pockets. "Let's see if you're going to keep those wings—or spend the rest of your miserable life as a pedestrian."

By the time the caravan was gone, and the sun was a quarter of the way up into the sky, Cato had conducted an interrogation unlike any he'd ever been part of before. The questions were the ones he'd been asking himself for weeks by that time. Who hired the Lir bandits? Who planned the raid on Station 3? And who took part?

Lood's answers came in short, inarticulate bursts. The story the bandit told started with a visit to the Imperial Palace, a meeting with Procurator Nalomy herself, and a payment so large that the Lir warriors had been forced to bury half of the coins and come back for them later.

Then, on the agreed-upon night, Chieftain Hybor Iddyn and a large contingent of his warriors had taken the law officers by surprise. Some of the Imperials were killed instantly; others fought back but were quickly overwhelmed. "They brave," Lood admitted reluctantly, "like *real* warriors. We respect."

Cato felt a large lump rise to block the back of his throat. "Yes," he said hoarsely, remembering what he'd found in and around Station 3. "They *were* brave. What happened then?"

Lucia, who had been silent throughout, listened with a rising sense of excitement as Lood told Cato about the Imperial transport, the troops led by Centurion Pasayo, and the manner in which the strange shape-shifting prisoner had been spirited away. There, right in front of her, was the sort of proof that Usurlus had been hoping to get his hands on! It was evidence Usurlus could use to not only justify his actions but bring formal charges against Nalomy and have her tried on Corin!

Then something extremely important occurred to Lucia, and she felt something akin to ice water trickle into her veins. "Cato!" she said urgently. "Nalomy plans to use the shape shifter to assassinate Legate Usurlus!"

Cato frowned. "Why would Nalomy want to do that?"

"Usurlus plans to remove her from power," Lucia answered. "There's a good chance that she either knows or suspects that. If so, it would make sense to kill him *before* he delivers the bad news. I know all of this because my husband was working for Usurlus prior to his death—and I've been working for the Legate since!"

It took Cato a moment to process Lucia's words, but once he had, the whole thing made a horrible kind of sense. Usurlus was the missing piece! The reason behind everything that had occurred thus far. And, based on what Cato knew about Nalomy, the only hope for the citizens of Dantha. *If* he could warn Usurlus in time. "We have what we came for," Cato said soberly. "After we stash Citizen Lood in a safe place, I'll return to the palace. Usurlus has a sizeable number of bodyguards. They can help me find Verafti and put him under lock and key. Or maybe, if I'm lucky, it will be necessary to shoot the bastard! Nothing would please me more."

Lucia agreed and, knowing how important Lood would be as a witness, knew it was time to call on the resistance for support. Belok was dispatched to find some transportation, and having been unable to locate anything better, returned with an angen-drawn cart. But while slow, the back of the cart was enclosed, which meant no one could see the strange menagerie of passengers hidden inside.

It took the better part of two hours to transport Lood to

a gloomy warehouse, which was owned by an anti-Nalomy businessman. Once the prisoner had been secured in a storeroom, Lucia requested enough resistance fighters to hold off a company of militiamen if necessary. Belok was put in charge of the makeshift prison facility, while Lucia left to consult with her fellow resistance leaders, and Cato set off for the palace. For that was where Usurlus was, and given the plan to assassinate the Legate, that was where he would find Verafti as well.

Having made her way through the old water pipe to the point where it opened into the pumping station, Alamy had seen Nalomy, Hingo, and Pasayo preparing to have dinner with an alien. Not a Lir, or a Kelf, or a member of some other species who could be seen walking the streets of the X-Quarter, but a reptilian shape shifter who was about to dine on a Uman leg! Persus's leg! That was when Alamy had been forced to flee.

The horror of what she'd seen combined with raw gut-wrenching fear drove all thoughts from Alamy's mind as she scuttled through the pipe in a desperate attempt to reach the other end of it before Pasayo's security troops did. And, thanks to the speed with which she made her way through the pipe, the maintenance room was still empty when Alamy arrived inside the palace. But what to do next?

The rational part of Alamy's mind had begun to reassert itself by then, and as her bare feet hit the concrete floor, she realized her sandals were back in the pipe! Worse yet, her clothing was stained as a result of kneeling inside the pipe, which would make it impossible to reintegrate herself into the kitchen's workforce without being noticed.

No sooner had that thought occurred to Alamy than she heard the sound of muffled voices and knew Nalomy's security men were in the kitchen and about to enter the maintenance room. There weren't any other doors, so Alamy did the only thing she *could* do, which was to climb upward.

The big intake pipe was only a few feet off the floor. Above that a maze of electrical conduits, insulation-wrapped pipes, and air ducts could be seen, all of which crisscrossed each other, thereby creating spaces in which a relatively small person could hide. So Alamy went straight up by climbing onto the big water pipe, then pulling herself up onto a large air duct. And that's where she was when two militiamen entered the room.

By peering over the side of the duct, Alamy could see the tops of their heads as the men searched the room, assault rifles at the ready. The red dots from their targeting lasers floated over the big water pipe, the walls, and eventually the area over their heads as the soldiers prowled the room. At one point a ruby red dot came within inches of Alamy's face as it probed the maze around her. But, not having seen anything out of the ordinary, the security man moved on.

Finally, having satisfied themselves that the fugitive wasn't in the room, the soldiers were about to tackle the pipe when Pasayo and one of his Section Leaders entered from the kitchen. "Did you find her?" Pasayo demanded harshly.

"No, sir," one of the militiamen answered. "I was just about to enter the pipe."

"Well, get on with it," Pasayo responded impatiently. "She has to be somewhere. Hingo is in the process of assembling the entire staff for a head count. So we'll know who's missing within the next fifteen minutes."

Alamy wanted to whimper but bit her bottom lip instead. Because once they knew who was missing, it would no longer be possible to rejoin the staff, even if she managed to find some clean clothes to wear.

"What about the space above us?" Pasayo wanted to

know, as the first soldier entered the pipe. "Have you been up there?"

"No, sir," the remaining soldier answered. "But we took a look from down here."

That wasn't good enough, and Pasayo was about to say as much, when a voice came over his com set. "This is Assistant Section Leader Frolis, sir. I'm on duty at the front gate and what looks like a pretty good-sized crowd is marching down Imperial Boulevard in the direction of the palace. They have torches, sir. And they're shouting antigovernment slogans."

Pasayo swore. "Damn it! The rabble are trying to stir up trouble in hopes that Usurlus will see it and sympathize with them! I'll be right there."

The door slammed closed as Pasayo left. The first soldier emerged from the pipe a few moments later. "It's empty," the militiaman reported, as his boots smacked the floor. "But I found her sandals!" he added triumphantly, and held the sandals up like trophies.

"Well done," the NCO said sarcastically. "I'll put you in for a frigging medal the moment this evolution is over. In the meantime, I have a feeling that Centurion Pasayo could use a hero like you out front. Let's go."

Alamy heaved a sigh of relief as the troops left, and the minute the door was completely closed, she hurried to climb down off her perch. Thanks to the demonstration in front of the palace, all of Pasayo's people were going to be distracted for the next few minutes. So the time to make her move was *now*. But to where? Not the dormitory . . . That was the first place they would look for her. And with all of the sentries on high-alert, she would never make it off the palace grounds.

But as Alamy's bare feet hit cold concrete, an idea occurred to her. A wild, somewhat improbable idea, but one with at least some chance of success. Alamy padded across the room, climbed the short flight of stairs to the kitchen, and opened the door an inch or so. The hiding place she had in mind wasn't more than a thousand feet away, but given the degree of difficulty involved, it might as well have been a thousand miles.

It was early afternoon, as Cato's pedicab took a left onto Imperial Boulevard, and began to weave back and forth as the sixty-three-year-old driver sought to avoid the debris that lay on the road. As he was thrown from side to side, Cato saw hundreds of half-burned torches, dozens of crudely made signs, pieces of clothing, stray shoes, an artificial leg, and bits of paper that fluttered along the ground as a light breeze chased them toward the palace. There were also pools of what might have been dried blood.

A new roadblock had been established half a mile from the palace, where Cato was forced to identify himself. "What the hell happened here?" Cato inquired, as he waited for a tired-looking noncom to run his pass through a scanner.

"Nothing much," the soldier replied cautiously. "You know how it is. All sorts of rabble come into the city for Founder's Day. Some of them get liquored up and want to make trouble. But we whupped 'em good! They won't try that again!"

"No," Cato said soberly as he looked up to where three bodies dangled from a gibbet. "I guess they won't."

Having been cleared through the checkpoint, the pedicab continued to swerve left and right as the driver maneuvered his three-wheeled vehicle between the work parties that had been dispatched to clean up the sprawling mess. Then, once the rickety conveyance arrived at the front gate, Cato was required to identify himself for a second time before being allowed to enter the palace.

After paying the driver twice the normal fare, Cato entered the building through the formal lobby, and made his way to the elevators. Two formally dressed functionaries were on duty behind the reception desk, and having spotted Cato, one of them was busy talking into a handset. It appeared that his arrival was of interest to someone in a position of authority. That was fine with Cato as he rode the elevator up, exited on the fourth floor, and made his way down the hall.

A red LED turned green the moment he palmed the lock outside his room, the door popped open, and he pushed it out of the way. The room was immaculate and had clearly been cleaned during his absence. Cato hadn't had a shower in two days, was badly in need of a shave, and figured he should take care of both items before paying a visit to Legate Usurlus. Especially if he wanted the official to take him seriously.

So Cato took off his waist-length jacket, and was in the process of removing his pullover shirt, when he heard movement behind him. The shirt was still fluttering toward the floor as Cato pulled his weapon and turned ready to fire.

As Alamy pushed the door open, and stepped out of the closet, she saw Cato react. But before she could say her name, Alamy found herself staring down the business end of a pistol that was aimed at her head. She froze, held her hands away from her body, and closed her eyes. But the shot didn't come, and when she opened them again, the gun had disappeared, and Cato was only inches away. "Alamy! That was a dangerous thing to do. I nearly shot you."

Alamy had been holding her breath. She let some of it out. "I'm sorry, master, but when I heard someone at the door, I had no way to know if it was one of the security people."

Cato frowned. "Security people? Why? What's wrong?"

Alamy stared up into his face. She took note of the tan, the look of concern in his bright green eyes, and the serious set of his mouth. What would Cato think when she told him about what she'd seen? Would he believe her? Or call security? Because if he did that, she was as good as dead. But there was no real alternative so she told the truth. "I'm in trouble," Alamy confessed, as her eyes fell.

Cato put his hands on her shoulders. They felt warm and strong. "Trouble? What kind of trouble? Is Hingo after you again?"

"Yes," Alamy answered, "but not in the way you mean. *Everyone* is after me because of what I saw last night."

Cato listened with a growing sense of concern as Alamy described her journey through the pipe, the horror of what she'd seen in the pump house, and her harrowing escape. "There's a dumbwaiter," she said finally. "Located next to the kitchen. We use it to send trays of food up to the fourth and fifth floors. It was tight," she added. "But I managed to squeeze inside—and send myself upstairs! That allowed me to evade the security cameras, and because I was authorized to enter your room, the door opened right away. I know my story is hard to believe, but I swear that it's true, and even though I'm a slave, I thought that you would listen to me."

There were tears running down Alamy's cheeks by that time, and Cato made use of a thumb to wipe some of them away. Then he took Alamy into his arms. The kiss was aimed at her cheek, but somehow landed on her lips, which were salty with tears. They were also very soft and seemed to melt beneath his as her hands came up to caress the back of his neck.

Cato could "feel" her passion as well as his own, and therefore knew that it was not only genuine but very precious. It was an exhilarating discovery, which would have been well worth celebrating under normal circumstances, but nothing had been normal since the *Umana* had put down on Dantha, thereby triggering all of the events that followed. The latest being the discovery that Nalomy was responsible for the massacre at Station 3 and, judging from Alamy's story, had been hiding Verafti in or near the palace!

As the kiss ended, Alamy looked up into Cato's eyes. "So you believe me?"

"Yes," Cato answered grimly. "I not only believe you, I know who the lizardlike bastard is, and I'm going to arrest the scumbag! But first I need to see Legate Usurlus and warn him. Because there's a very good chance that Verafti will attempt to kill him."

Alamy's eyebrows rose. "Verafti?"

"That's the lizard's name," Cato explained. "He's a Sagathi shape shifter. He escaped from prison, and my team and I were taking him back, when we were forced to land on Dantha. Nalomy had my team slaughtered in order to gain control of him. I have reason to believe that she's going to use Verafti to kill Legate Usurlus. Probably at the Founder's Day ceremony tomorrow."

Alamy didn't really know Usurlus, but he'd been nice to her, even though she was a slave. "You must warn him!" she said urgently.

"We'll do it together," Cato replied confidently. "But there are a couple of things I need to take care of first."

But that wasn't to be, because as Cato turned to head for the bathroom, the door opened and Alamy screamed as two soldiers burst into the room. What happened next was entirely reflexive as Cato drew his weapon and fired low. The bullets hit the militiamen in the legs, well below their body armor, and sent them sprawling. More troops were lined up to enter, but stopped where they were, as Cato triggered two additional rounds. He pointed at Alamy, then at the door to the veranda, before yelling, "Hold your fire! I don't know what this is all about, but I'm an Imperial police officer, so back off!"

"I know who you are," Pasayo said contemptuously.

"And I know *what* you are. Which is a worthless piece of shit who was busy getting drunk while his teammates were dying out in the desert! I also know that you led an attack on a government-run facility in the Xeno Quarter, assaulted my troops, and freed two prisoners. You may be a police officer—but even police officers are subject to the law! Surrender now or face the consequences!"

But the words were wasted because both Cato and Alamy were outside by then, having left through the door that provided access to a shared balcony, and were already two doors down. The glass door opened to Alamy's touch, they ran through the empty guest suite, and from there into the hall. Pasayo and most of his troops had entered Cato's room by then, but a couple of soldiers were still out in the passageway, and saw the fugitives appear. They shouted a warning, and one of them fired a submachine gun. His bullets dug divots out of the wall as Cato and Alamy turned a corner and started down a stairwell.

But more troops were on the way up, and having seen them, Cato was forced to turn, and pull Alamy upward. More bullets riddled the walls as the twosome pounded their way up to the fifth floor, only to discover that it was sealed off behind a locked door, forcing them up onto the roof. A guard was coming down, probably in response to all of the shooting, and Cato was forced to shoot him. The bullet hit the center of soldier's chest, and even though the projectile didn't penetrate his armor, the force of the impact was sufficient to put the man on his ass. That was fine with Cato, who pistol-whipped the guard as he ran up the last flight of stairs.

There hadn't been any plan up until that point, just an overriding desire to escape the palace, because Cato knew that surrender wasn't an option. Not to people who had already killed a dozen police officers and planned to assassinate an Imperial Legate! But as he surfaced on the roof only fifty feet from the spot where Phelonious had put the old air car down, Cato saw his chance. And that was Nalomy's immaculate air limo, which was sitting on the far side of the pad, door wide open! Was Nalomy about to go somewhere? Yes, that was the way it appeared, so Cato waved Alamy forward. "Come on! There's our transportation!"

But either the pilot saw them coming, or received a radio message warning him that a madman was on the loose, because the hatch started to whir closed. So Cato ran even faster and managed to dive through the dwindling opening just before it closed. But that left Alamy on the outside! Cato fumbled with the hatch controls in a vain attempt to open the door but stopped as the air car wobbled and took to the air. That sent him forward to the cockpit where he jammed the barrel of his pistol into the base of the pilot's skull. Cato "felt" the extent of his surprise and realized that the pilot had been unaware of the battle inside the palace and was on an errand of some sort. "Turn back!" Cato ordered. "Turn back, or I'll blow your frigging head off!"

Having found himself at the mercy of a half-naked lunatic with a gun, the pilot hurried to obey. The air limo was at least a hundred feet off the ground by that time, and as it banked toward the west, Cato caught a glimpse of the roof. Pasayo and at least a dozen troops were out on the landing pad by then; two of them had Alamy by her arms and were in the process of dragging her away! The rest had weapons raised as Pasayo shaded his eyes. "Damn it!" Cato exclaimed angrily. "I changed my mind. Get us out of here. . . . *Now!*"

Alamy felt the bottom drop out of her stomach as Cato disappeared into the air car, and the hatch closed in front of her. She shouted, "No!" and beat on the door with her fists, but was forced to back away as the air limo's retros fired, and a wall of heat threatened to blister her skin. Then the soldiers were there, grabbing her arms, and dragging her backward as the aircraft took off. Had Cato abandoned her? In order to save himself? Or been trapped in the cabin? There was no way to be sure, but as the air car banked away, it appeared that Cato was in control.

Having been betrayed only months earlier, Alamy was already familiar with the horrible sick feeling that filled the pit of her stomach, and the overwhelming despair that followed her spirits down. So that by the time the soldiers brought Alamy in front of Pasayo, she no longer cared what happened to her. Because the worst was already over as far as she was concerned.

Pasayo slapped Alamy twice across the face. Her head jerked from side to side and a trickle of blood ran down from a cut on the right side of her mouth. But rather than the terror Pasayo expected to see in Alamy's eyes, there was nothing but dull acceptance. That infuriated him even more. "You know what I'm going to do to you?" Pasayo demanded loudly. "I'm going to give you to Hingo! And then, once he's done with you, I'll send whatever's left to our green friend. You saw what he likes to eat! Now it's *your* turn." The soldiers took her away after that, to a place of darkness, where there was nothing for Alamy to do but cry.

Out beyond the windows of the guest suite, sunlight lay like gold foil on the waters of Lake Imperium as Usurlus sat at a table that still bore the remains of his lunch. He was working on his speech, the one he was scheduled to deliver the following day. When, instead of the political pap that citizens expected to hear, he was going to drop a bombshell on them by detailing three examples of government corruption.

Having laid the appropriate groundwork, Usurlus was going to announce that by order of Emperor Emor, Procurator Nalomy had been removed from power and would subsequently be sent to Corin, where she would face criminal charges! Usurlus knew that by doing so he was going to risk not only his own position, but to a lesser extent the Emperor's as well, because if the corruption charges failed to stick, the Nalomy clan would be out for blood!

But lacking the sort of hard evidence that he'd been hoping for, Usurlus was faced with a horrible choice. To either give up and allow Nalomy to rape Dantha unimpeded, or to press charges in hopes that once she was removed from power, heretofore terrified witnesses would come forward with additional evidence.

It was a big gamble, especially since the strategy ran counter to the instructions cousin Emor had given Usurlus, which meant that the Emperor could hang him out to dry. Assuming he survived what could be a rather violent confrontation in the coliseum since Nalomy was unlikely to receive the news with good grace.

Still, Usurlus took comfort from the knowledge that his entire force of bodyguards would be present, under the command of Vedius Albus. Not to mention the fact that Lucia Ovidius and her fellow opposition leaders had promised to pack the stands with anti-Nalomy citizens, who could be counted upon to rise up against the militia should that become necessary. The demonstration on Imperial Boulevard was a good indication of how dedicated they were.

Usurlus looked up from the screen in front of him as the sound of muffled gunfire was heard. Not the distant stuff, which could sometimes be heard at night, but close by. As if within the palace itself!

Usurlus stood, and was about to go in search of Albus, when the chief bodyguard appeared. He looked concerned. "I heard it, too, sire. We're trying to reach Centurion Pasayo to find out what's going on but no luck so far. In the meantime, I authorized heavy weapons, doubled your guards, and put the rest of the men on active standby."

"Thank you, Vedius," Usurlus said gratefully, as he turned back toward the table. "Please let me know what's going on when you hear back from Pasayo."

The *real* Vedius Albus was dead, and had been for more than an hour by that time, but Fiss Verafti was very much on duty. The shape shifter said, "Yes, sire," delivered a bow, and withdrew. It felt good to be free. . . . Even if Nalomy's electronic leash was very, very short.

S!XTEEN

The city of Solace, on the planet Dantha

HAVING ESCAPED THE PALACE, BUT WITHOUT HAVING had an opportunity to warn Usurlus about the assassination plot, Cato ordered Nalomy's pilot to land the air car in the open area that fronted the slave market. There wasn't any auction scheduled for that day, but the sudden arrival of the air car sent street vendors, homeless people, and a flock of birds scattering in every direction. Cato forced the other man to surrender his shirt, pulled the garment over his head, and exited the car. Retros fired, and it took off moments later.

The highly polished limo with the government seal on both front doors was starting to attract attention by then, and the pilot heard the occasional *thud*, *clang*, and *ping*, as rocks, bottles, and the other missiles hit the armored hull. Having rid himself of the madman with the gun, the pilot began to climb, banked toward the east, and circled back toward the safety of the palace.

Cato thought about Alamy and felt a mixture of anger, fear, and self-recrimination sweep over him as the air car sped away. Because he knew that if Alamy was still alive, she was going through hell.

But there was nothing he could do about that, not at the present time anyway, so Cato made his way through the now-familiar streets to the warehouse where Lood was being held. New guards were on duty by then and refused to let Cato enter the building until he demanded to see Belok. Then, having been cleared by the Kelf, Cato was allowed to enter a large, gloomy room.

Hundreds of bales of dried lake weed were stacked to either side of the corridor that ran down the center of a room that was at least a hundred feet long. The spicy weed was the main ingredient for a seasoning that was popular throughout the Empire, making it one of Dantha's most important exports.

There wasn't any place to shower in the warehouse, but there was a restroom, complete with a dirty sink that Cato used to take a sponge bath. He couldn't shave, though, not without a razor, which left him with nothing to do until Lucia returned.

So Cato made a place for himself on a couple of weed bales and was soon sound asleep although a series of bad dreams caused him to toss and turn. All of them had one thing in common, and that was Alamy, who kept asking him, "Why?"

Cato was trying to answer that question, trying to explain his actions, when someone touched his arm. "Cato? It's me. . . . Lucia."

Cato opened his eyes and saw that Lucia was looking down at him. He glanced at his watch, realized that more than four hours had passed, and knew it must be dark outside. Lucia looked concerned. "Belok told me what happened. . . . I guess we should have known that they would be waiting for you after we stole Lood right out from under their noses."

Cato rolled off the makeshift bed and stood. "I need to get into the coliseum. Can you help me?"

"I don't think that's a very good idea," Lucia cautioned. "Take a look at this." The piece of paper that Lucia handed Cato was rolled up, so he had to smooth it out before being able to see the picture which occupied most of the poster. It was a photo of his face and identical to the one on the pass that Nalomy's security people had issued to him earlier. The words printed below the photo read, "Wanted Dead or Alive! One thousand Imperials will be paid to any citizen or slave who provides information that leads to the arrest of renegade Xeno Corps Officer Jak Cato or to anyone who kills Cato and can produce at least some of his body for DNA analysis and confirmation."

Smaller print at the bottom of the poster included information on how to make contact with the correct person within Nalomy's Department of Public Security. It was the same organization charged with keeping the population under control. "They're fast," Cato said darkly. "You have to grant them that."

"Yes, they are," Lucia agreed. "So it would be foolish to go out."

"And Legate Usurlus is going to be assassinated if I stay here," Cato countered. "I wasn't able to reach him. . . . So tomorrow, when he enters the coliseum, he won't know how vulnerable he is. That's why I have to find a way into the coliseum tonight. Security will be twice as tight in the morning."

Lucia looked skeptical. "There's no need for you to go. The resistance can take care of it for you."

"*No,*" Cato replied emphatically. "Verafti can look like Nalomy herself if he wants to. I'm the only one who can spot him regardless of what shape he takes."

There was a moment of silence while Lucia thought it over. "Okay," she said reluctantly, "I guess you're correct.

But you're going to need a disguise. And it needs to be a good one."

It was dark, and at a time when the streets of Solace would normally be empty of everything except thieves, militia patrols, and feral dogs, tens of thousands of noisy, often drunk celebrants were out strolling around. Some wore fanciful masks and in some cases complete costumes, as they formed long, sinuous lines and followed energetic drummers through the city's streets. The spectators who lined roofs, balconies, and sidewalks shouted greetings, and pelted the dancers with pieces of candy as they passed by. It was a loud, raucous scene, and one of the few times each year when the city's more prosperous citizens *wanted* to visit The Warrens.

But if most of the people were enjoying the revelry, the same couldn't be said of the grim-faced militia, who were visible on almost every street corner and ready to come down on anyone or anything that bore the least resemblance to a political gathering. Their brooding presence, plus the ominous thrumming sound produced by the military patrol cars as they passed overhead, combined to leach some of the joy from the celebration.

Nor were *all* of the residents of Solace free to participate in the festivities, as was evident when a column of manacled slaves shuffled through The Warrens, chains rattling as they were led toward the coliseum. In spite of the cheerful crowds that surrounded them on all sides, they walked with heads down, eyes on the cobblestones in front of them, seemingly unaware of their surroundings. All of their heads had been shaved in order to prevent the spread of lice, all of them wore nearly identical gray cloaks over tunics and kilts, and all were shod with sturdy sandals. In fact the only thing that served to distinguish one slave from the next were the tools that some carried, the packs that others wore on their backs, and the lucky few who carried no burden at all.

But as harmless as the column of slaves appeared, Nalomy's militiamen were under strict orders not only to maintain order, but to find the renegade Xeno-freak named Jak Cato. So as the work party neared one of the many checkpoints established during the last twelve hours, they were ordered to stop, and a stern-faced Section Leader walked the line, checking to make sure that Cato wasn't hidden among them.

The slave master in charge of the work party objected, insisting that the slaves be allowed to continue on their way unimpeded, but to no avail. The SL was determined to examine the slaves individually, a process that involved lifting each chin up with his swagger stick, while shining a bright light into the subjects' blank faces.

Cato was about fifteen people back from the head of the column and felt his heart start to beat faster as the noncom drew closer. The concept of sending Cato into the coliseum along with a group of real slaves had been Lucia's idea and a brilliant one. Or that's how it seemed until she cut Cato's hair off, provided filthy clothes for him to wear, and turned him over to the tender mercies of a very real slave master. A man who was part of the resistance and therefore willing to help.

Cato was wearing body armor that had been taken from a dead militiaman, and he was armed with a variety of weapons, but the whole idea was to get inside the coliseum, not start a war! So when the Section Leader arrived next to him, and slid the swagger stick in under his chin, Cato affected an empty-eyed stare. In addition to his smooth-shaven skull and the tattoolike serial number that had been inked onto his forehead, dirt had been rubbed into Cato's face to make it that much harder to recognize.

Still, even with all of that, Cato held his breath as a blinding light stabbed his eyes and the SL consulted a photo of the man he was supposed to look for. If Cato "felt" a flash of recognition, he was ready to drop the unlocked manacles, and go for one of his weapons.

After what seemed like an eternity, Cato heard the Section Leader grunt, and was left with a constellation of floating afterimages when the light was removed. "Too ugly," the SL commented as he passed Cato by, and turned his attention to the next slave.

Cato released his breath slowly after that and stood head down until the column was allowed to pass through the checkpoint. Thanks to the disk-shaped pass that had been given to him at the roadblock, the slave master was able to lead the column to the coliseum without further delay. Then, when they arrived on the north side of the huge structure, a noncom waved the work party through the arched gate that provided access to the arena beyond.

Work was under way, and had been for quite some time, so that as Cato took a look around, the first thing he saw was the six-foot-high wall that circled the arena. It was pierced at regular intervals by stairs that provided access to the tiers of seats above. The Imperial Box could be seen on the south side of the coliseum. Colorful awnings were positioned to protect the upper seats from both the sun and the possibility of rain. They flapped as a light breeze swept in from the west and circled the arena as if to examine it. It was an impressive sight, and would be even more so the following day, when thousands of people filled the now-empty seats.

When the slave master came to a halt, the column was forced to do likewise. A guard made his way down the line and chains rattled as each set of manacles was unlocked and fell free. If the guard thought it was strange that one man's wrist bracelets were already unlocked he gave no sign of it as he passed Cato by. "All right!" the slave master said, as Cato took a moment to rub his sore wrists. "You can pile your stuff next to the gate. Our first task is to rake the arena so it will look pretty in the morning. So start in the middle and move outward. I don't want to see any footprints when you're done. Those who don't have rakes will report to me for other tasks. Got it?"

Cato heard mumbling sounds that might have constituted assent although it didn't really matter since the slaves were slaves. Once the other men and women had begun to amble toward the center of the arena, he walked away. And if the guards saw him depart, they gave no sign of it as they spread out in order to supervise the work.

Having successfully infiltrated the coliseum, Cato sought out a heavily shadowed spot where he could rid himself of both the backpack and the tattered robe. Then, having removed the components for his second disguise from the pack, Cato transformed himself from a slave into a Section Leader. And not just any Section Leader, but one who wore the insignia of a unit assigned to the frontier, which would help to explain why the local militiamen hadn't encountered him before.

That was Lucia's plan anyway. And only time would tell if it would work. One thing was for sure, however, and that was Cato's need for a disguise that would allow him to move freely. Because even though he knew *what* was supposed to happen the following day, Cato didn't know *how*, and that would be important if he was going to stop it.

Having removed the fake tattoo from his forehead, and completed the change from one identity to the other, Cato dumped both the robe and the empty pack into a garbage can, and began a tour of the coliseum. And that meant not just looking like a noncom but acting like one while strutting about and sticking his nose into everybody's business. A role that *he*, as a Section Leader himself, knew how to play.

So Cato climbed all the way up to the top of the brightly

lit coliseum, where he followed the gently curving wall from north to east. One of the first things Cato noticed was the platform on the south side of the arena, which was located immediately below the Imperial Box. Workers were busy putting the finishing touches on the elaborate framework that rested on the ledgelike platform. And it didn't take a genius *or* an official program to know that was the spot where Usurlus would be standing when the assassination attempt took place.

The immediate area would be heavily guarded, of course, but with any luck at all, Cato would be able to use his disguise to penetrate the outermost ring of security and warn one of the Legate's bodyguards if not Usurlus himself.

Then Cato would implement the *second* part of his plan, which was to identify Fiss Verafti, and take him into custody. Or, failing that, to put a dozen bullets into the bastard! It would be a lot less expensive than another trial!

Such were Cato's thoughts as the walkway carried him around the edge of the coliseum to the point where one of the facility's blocky projection booths stood. Cato knew that at least four holoprojectors were required to show a 3-D movie, and some arenas were equipped with as many as eight of the devices, so as to provide high-quality images. Especially during the early-evening hours, when it was still light out.

But as Cato approached the booth, it appeared as though civilian workers were removing the projection equipment from the walled-in booth. The question was, why? The holo equipment couldn't be used during the day; Cato knew that, so maybe the projector was going in for maintenance. Still, nosy Section Leaders should be nosy, so Cato paused next to the doorway. "What's going on here?" he demanded officiously, as the civilians loaded the projector onto a dolly.

"That's a very good question," one of the two men said sarcastically, as he straightened up. He had a long lugubrious face, and a pair of droopy eyelids made him look sleepy. "We were told to take this unit out, even though it works fine, and install a table. But you should know, because the work order came from what's his name, Centurion Piss-ayo."

"That's P*a*sayo," the other technician corrected him, "and you talk too much. Come on, let's get this thing out of here. We'll come back for the mount."

The civilians left at that point, and the door to the projection booth stood open, so Cato stepped inside. Though not necessarily important, the mere mention of Pasayo's name had been sufficient to pique his interest. There wasn't a whole lot to see other than the mount for the missing projector, which was still bolted to the floor, and a roughly one-foot-by-one-foot aperture through which a holobeam could be projected.

But as Cato bent over to look through the hole, he found himself staring directly across the arena to the platform on which Usurlus was going to speak. Was that a matter of coincidence? Or something more? Especially if there was nothing wrong with the holoprojector.

Then there was the matter of a table. . . . Why would Pasayo give orders for a table to be placed inside the booth? It didn't make any sense unless . . . Suddenly Cato had it! Like all police officers, he was required to qualify with certain weapons each year. Typically that meant a nerve-wracking stroll through a virtual reality (VR) scenario in which good guys and bad guys appeared at regular intervals, requiring the person who was running the course to make a series of split-second decisions regarding whom to shoot. And more than that, once shots were fired, how effective they were.

But certain weapons, sniper rifles being a good example, were frequently fired on an actual range in addition to VR scenarios. Often from a bench, where the marksman was allowed to sit, while experimenting with various loads. Was that what Pasayo had in mind here? A table that he or another marksman could use to support a large-caliber sniper's rifle? The aperture, the containment, and the angle would be perfect for that. The only problem was that it didn't make sense. Not given the fact that Verafti would be able to kill Usurlus from close range.

Then Cato had it. Verafti! That was the answer. The sniper's job was to kill Verafti once Usurlus had been murdered. Not only to silence a potential witness—but to get rid of a very dangerous serial killer. One who, if allowed to go free, could threaten Nalomy herself. And, should anything go wrong with the primary plan, the sniper would be in the perfect position to shoot Usurlus as well!

All of the pieces fit, and as Cato left the booth, he felt that he had a good understanding of the way the assassination plot was supposed to unfold. But could he put a stop to it? That remained to be seen.

There were still a good four hours to go before the sun rose. So with nothing better to do, and concerned lest someone challenge his right to be there, Cato chose to climb up to the highest seats. Once there, he found a spot where he could wrap himself up in the red militia cape around his body, sit down, and get some shut-eye. But it was difficult to put Alamy out of his mind, so it was quite a while before sleep finally came, and eventually carried him away.

As Pasayo left his quarters, gun case in hand, he felt better than he had in weeks. Because here, after months of stultifying staff work, was the sort of day any hunter would welcome! The sky was clear, the air was cool, and the newly risen sun had just begun to push long thin shadows west toward the Sawtooth Mountains, all made memorable by the nature of the challenge before him—to lie in wait for one of the most dangerous killers in the Empire, drop Verafti with one shot, and hang his head on the wall with all the rest! In the process, he would secure a trophy that no other hunter could equal!

The possibility of that put a spring in Pasayo's step as two bodyguards fell in behind him and the three men made their way along a series of well-manicured pathways to the looming coliseum beyond. Sentries crashed to attention as Pasayo arrived, but he was only marginally aware of the soldiers as he marched past, his mind focused on what lay ahead.

It took the better part of ten minutes for Pasayo to climb all the steps and follow the outer wall to the west until he arrived at the projection booth that would serve as his hide. Originally, back when Nalomy first identified the need to eliminate Verafti, their discussions centered around something close-up, an approach that would make Verafti's death look like a natural reaction to the assassination. But, given the empath's ability to sense what people were going to do, that approach was abandoned in favor of the long-distance solution that Pasayo assigned to himself.

The door to the projection booth was unlocked. A light came on as Pasayo entered and paused to look around. A table had been placed in front of the aperture. A tripod-style bench rest was bolted to the flat surface, and an unpadded chair was positioned in front of it. A thermos of hot caf sat at one end of the table, an empty bucket had been placed in one of the corners, and a com set was sitting on a shelf. All the preparations were consistent with the orders Pasayo had given.

Satisfied that his requirements had been met, Pasayo lowered the gun case onto the table before turning to the door and ordering both bodyguards to leave. Even though it didn't matter at the moment, guards could draw attention to the booth, and that was the sort of thing that someone like Verafti might very well notice. Nor did Pasayo want two people looking over his shoulder as he made the most important shot of his life.

Once the soldiers were gone, Pasayo closed the door, went over to the table, and opened the case. All of the components for the FARO 3025 sniper's rifle lay nestled within. Once it was fully assembled, the forty-two-pound weapon would be nearly six feet long. And with a muzzle velocity of 4,750 fps, the tungsten darts were capable of penetrating two-inch-thick armor from a distance of three thousand feet.

That made the FARO an excellent weapon for attacking light-armored vehicles, airborne troop transports, and homicidal lizards! Even ones who were wearing body armor. The only problem was that, once the fléchette hit Verafti, the resulting devastation would be so complete that there wouldn't be much of him left to scrape up. But, by aiming for Verafti's chest rather than his head, Pasayo hoped to preserve a trophy.

Pasayo smiled grimly as he pulled on a pair of white gloves, removed the black matte receiver from the case, and went to work. Not only did Nalomy want Verafti dead, the slimeball was responsible for killing nearly a dozen members of Pasayo's militia, and now he was going to pay.

In spite of the early-morning sun that poured in through the windows, and the soothing music that was playing from the overhead speakers, Usurlus was nervous. And for good reason since he was about to walk into the coliseum and bring charges of corruption against a woman who had thousands of troops under her command. So, being out of sorts, little things took on exaggerated importance. Like the fact that a slave named Ooly had been sent to serve his breakfast instead of Alamy, who not only knew all of his preferences, but was more enjoyable to look at.

Adding to the dissatisfaction that Usurlus felt was the fact that Vedius Albus, the man he sometimes referred to as "my rock," had been making a lot of mistakes lately. Nothing major, just little things like his failure to lay out Usurlus's body armor without first being prompted to do so, and the way he kept calling Usurlus "Excellency," rather than "sire." They were small things, and of no great consequence, but annoying on a day when so much was at stake.

But, even though Usurlus *wanted* to lash out at Albus, he managed not to do so and was eventually able to calm himself by retreating to the bathroom, where he spent a full hour examining his face inch by inch while delivering the carefully memorized speech for the umpteenth time.

Finally, as ready as he could be, and surrounded by heavily armed bodyguards, Usurlus departed his quarters. Fiss Verafti, in his role as Vedius Albus, led the way.

The sun was halfway to its zenith, thousands of people were seated in the coliseum, and hundreds more arrived every minute. At exactly 10:30, Nalomy was scheduled to introduce Usurlus who, assuming that Lucia was correct, would publicly bring charges of corruption against the Procurator. Unless Verafti shot Usurlus first . . . which would almost certainly take place unless Cato found a way to prevent it.

The crowd roared as Nalomy, Usurlus, and various bodyguards stepped out onto the gaily decorated platform. But the roar had an ominous quality, and judging from the tenor of it, the crowd noise was born of anger rather than joy, as many of Dantha's citizens took the opportunity to make their feelings known. But thanks to both the volume of the response, and the fact that everyone was staring at the VIP platform, Cato had the opportunity he'd been waiting for.

The projection booth was closed and had been ever since Pasayo had entered the enclosure an hour earlier. And it seemed safe to assume that the door was locked from within. Fortunately, Cato had a key in the form of his right foot! It hit the thin sheet metal right below the handle, the door flew open, and there was a loud *bang* as it struck a wall. No sound was audible over the crowd noise.

Pasayo was seated at the table, peering into the FARO's 10X scope, when Cato exploded into the booth. The sudden movement caught Pasayo by surprise, and he had just started to turn around, when the door slammed shut, thereby cutting off any hope of reinforcements. "Hold it right there," Cato said grimly, as he aimed his pistol at Pasayo's head. "Or would you like me to splatter your brains all over the wall?"

It took a moment to see past the uniform, but the voice was familiar, and Pasayo made the connection. "Cato! Well I'll be damned. . . . You *can* accomplish something when you put your mind to it!"

Nalomy was speaking by then, and while Cato couldn't make out the exact words, he knew that precious seconds were ticking away. "Tell me what Verafti looks like," he grated, "and tell me *now*."

Pasayo's eyes narrowed. Somehow, by means unknown, Cato knew about the assassination. And if Cato was allowed to interfere, Usurlus might survive, thereby ending Nalomy's political career, and Pasayo's plan to become a general. All of that flashed through Pasayo's mind in less than a second and resulted in a fierce determination to kill Cato quickly so there would still be enough time to fire the critical shot.

Cato "sensed" what was about to happen a moment before Pasayo rolled sideways. So Cato was already readjusting his aim, and could have killed Pasayo, but he chose not to. He needed to keep Pasayo alive long enough to find out what Verafti looked like. But there was no reason not to kick the sonofabitch, which Cato attempted to do, only to have Pasayo grab his foot and twist it.

Then it was Cato's turn to fall. His arm hit the floor, the gun skittered away, and as Pasayo lurched to his feet, he fumbled for his handgun. But it was held in place by a retaining strap, and by the time Pasayo thumbed it off, Cato had drawn the ceremonial dagger that all Section Leaders carry as part of their dress uniforms. Having rolled to his knees, he brought the double-edged weapon up under his opponent's unprotected rib cage, and felt the eight-inch blade go deep. The sliver of steel missed Pasayo's heart but found a lung, and cut an artery. The dagger remained there for a full second—until Cato jerked it out.

Pasayo's face registered an expression of profound surprise, his hand fell away from the gun, and he toppled over backward. Cato scrambled forward to kneel next to the wounded officer. Pasayo's eyes were still open; he was gasping for breath, and jerking spasmodically. "Tell me," Cato demanded harshly. "Tell me what Verafti looks like."

Pink bubbles appeared on Pasayo's lips. He was dying and knew it. A sly smile appeared on his face. There was even more blood by then, and the officer was gargling as he spoke. "Alamy," Pasayo said, as Cato's face floated above him. "I gave her to Hingo!"

The knife flashed downward, penetrated Pasayo's right eye, and entered his brain. The force of the blow caused Pasayo's skull to bounce off the duracrete floor, and that produced an audible *thud*. Cato attempted to pull the blade free, discovered that it was stuck, and left the dagger where it was. His pistol was two feet away, which made it necessary to crawl over and retrieve it.

Because Cato was an empath he could "taste" the bitter residue of his own hatred as he lurched to his feet. Then, feeling slightly sick to his stomach, he stumbled to the table and bent over to peer through the hole. Nalomy was speaking, and thanks to the PA system, her words could be heard throughout the coliseum. "And now," she said, "in memory of those who have given their lives for the Empire, please welcome the cavalcade of flags!"

There was a momentary blare of trumpets, followed by an

upwelling of martial music as two columns of mounted militiamen cantered into the arena on nearly identical angens, each carrying a rectangle of brightly colored cloth representing one of the Empire's Legions, a planetary militia, or one of the many auxiliary units. There was scattered applause, but not much, since Dantha's militiamen were generally viewed as oppressors rather than defenders.

But since Cato needed every second he could get, he welcomed the ceremony as an opportunity to scan the VIP platform and try to figure out which of the dozen or so people standing around Usurlus was really an alien shape shifter. Then he realized that he could look *through* the 10X scope instead and sat down in an empty chair. The moment that Cato put his eye to the scope he discovered something interesting. The crosshairs were centered on one of the Legate's bodyguards! A well-turned-out individual who was located immediately to the official's left, where he was in an excellent position to either protect Usurlus or shoot him!

But was that who Pasayo had been planning to kill? Yes, based on the way the FARO was locked down, which meant that Cato knew whom to go after! More than that, he had a rifle that was clearly capable of putting Verafti down for good. So it was tempting to release the FARO's safety, snuggle up to the skeletal stock, and take the shot Pasayo had set up for him.

The problem was that Cato couldn't be absolutely sure that the man standing at the center of the crosshairs was Verafti without getting close enough to verify the shape shifter's emotional "fingerprint." So Cato rose, made his way over to the door, and slipped outside. The latch was broken, so all he could do was pull the door closed, and hope for the best.

Cato was faced with a choice. He could run down, jump off the wall, and make a mad dash for the other side of the arena. Or he could follow the edge of the coliseum around to a point above the VIP platform.

After looking at the angens continuing to circle the arena

below, and the militiamen who were riding them, Cato turned and began to run. Three walkways circled the coliseum, and Cato was on the second level, which was crowded with late arrivals, people purchasing food from vendors, and those lined up to use the restrooms.

As he ran along Cato yelled things like, "Coming through! Stand aside!" and "Get out of the way!" Most people scuttled out of the way, but one man was too slow, and went sprawling as Cato shouldered him aside. There were guards of course, *lots* of them, but because the man causing the disturbance was in uniform, they made no effort to intervene.

While Cato ran, he took occasional glances to the right, where the last of the mounted militia could be seen leaving the arena, their gaily colored flags snapping in the breeze. That was Nalomy's cue to introduce her guest. "Now, on behalf of the citizens of Dantha, it is my privilege and honor to introduce His Excellency, Legate Isulu Usurlus!"

There was enthusiastic applause this time, both because Emperor Emor remained popular in spite of Nalomy's failings, and because Usurlus was the only person that the planet's dissatisfied citizens could look to for relief.

Adding to the strength of the applause was the fact that resistance leaders like Lucia Ovidius had gone to great lengths to pack the coliseum with their followers. All of them were eager to embarrass Nalomy by giving the Legate the sort of reception denied her.

All of that was lost on Cato as he bellowed, "Clear the way!" and sent a flock of schoolchildren scattering in every direction as he arrived on the south side of the coliseum and ran toward a point directly above the VIP platform. Meanwhile, with the applause fading, Usurlus began his speech.

Usurlus had given lots of speeches, hundreds, maybe even a thousand of them. But never had he delivered one that was so important, incendiary, and dangerous. As he stood on the platform, and looked out at thousands of faces, everything was crystal clear. The warmth of the sun on his face, the rich smell of fried food that hung in the air, and the sound of blood pounding in his ears. Usurlus was afraid that he would fail, afraid that he would succeed, and afraid of being afraid. Fortunately, the much-practiced words were ready and waiting. "Thank you," Usurlus said, "both on behalf of myself and Emperor Emor. . . ."

Nalomy began to edge her way to the right-hand side of the platform. Verafti was standing to Usurlus's left, which meant he would fire to the right, and what if he missed? Nalomy had no desire to be killed by a stray bullet or have all of her clothes ruined if the projectile flew true and sent a bloody spray in her direction.

Then there was the matter of what was going to happen to Verafti in the wake of Usurlus's death. When Pasayo fired, the tungsten dart would probably blow the shape shifter into a thousand pieces. That gave Nalomy even more reason to move sideways. Fortunately, the whole thing would be over soon. Should she accompany the Legate's body to Corin? Yes, Nalomy decided. That would not only be a nice touch—but provide her with an opportunity to put herself forward as the dead man's logical successor! A smile touched Nalomy's lips as she waited for the people around her to die.

Cato! Verafti could "feel" the Xeno cop's presence. But where was he? Verafti felt a sudden surge of fear. He was supposed to fire *now*, before Usurlus had time to say anything of consequence, but was reluctant to do so unless he knew where Cato was. And there were other dangers to consider, too,

including the possibility that Nalomy had assigned someone to shoot him as Usurlus fell, thereby ridding herself of a
witness. Slowly, so as not to draw attention to what he was
doing, Verafti freed the strap that held his pistol in place
and began to turn. Cato was behind him. . . . But where?

Usurlus had completed the formalities by then and was
ready to deliver the most important part of his speech. "As
we come together today," he said soberly, "it is on a planet
where the rights of individual citizens have been systematically trampled, and where the institutions normally charged
with protecting those rights are riddled with corruption.
Unfortunately, the rot I speak of begins at the very topmost
level of the planetary government and extends downward
through the bureaucracy and into the militia."

There was a moment in which reality seemed to slow, as
the citizens of Dantha sat in stunned silence and struggled
to assimilate what they had heard. Then, as the full import
of the words came clear to them, there was a sudden roar
of approval as thousands of people surged to their feet and
began to chant. *"Usurlus! Usurlus! Usurlus!"*

Nalomy's normally beautiful face was contorted by anger as
she turned to look at Verafti. But, rather than shoot Usurlus
the way he was supposed to, Verafti stood weapon in hand,
staring up into the stands. Having seen the man they knew
as Albus draw his pistol, the rest of the bodyguards had
turned, and were looking in that direction as well. Usurlus, who was oblivious to the byplay, was waiting for the
applause to die down so he could continue his speech. But
another voice was heard instead.

Cato was standing in a position ten rows above the platform.
That was as close as the off-world bodyguards would let him

get without a special pass. "Legate Usurlus!" he shouted. "The man to your left is an assassin!"

The applause had started to fade by then, so Usurlus heard the shout and turned toward Albus. That was when he saw his chief bodyguard fire into the stands. But Cato was a good fifty feet away, Verafti had very little experience with firearms, and missed. A merchant seated next to Cato uttered a grunt of pain as the bullet hit him in the shoulder, and his neatly draped toga began to turn red.

Having missed Cato, Verafti turned to his left, hoping to kill Usurlus. And, thanks to the fact that the surrounding bodyguards were confused, there was a reasonable chance of success.

Cato raised his weapon and fired. The projectile hit Verafti's body armor but didn't penetrate. Still, it was sufficient to ruin Verafti's aim, so that when he fired, the bullet missed Usurlus by a full inch.

That was enough for Livius, who threw himself on top of Usurlus, as Verafti took on the appearance of Centurion Pasayo and began to shout nonsensical orders. A few moments later Verafti assumed another form, and *another*, until the crowd closed around him.

Meanwhile, on orders from resistance leaders salted throughout the coliseum, thousands of people left their seats and began to surge through the aisles. Shots were fired as frightened guards attempted to hold the crowd back, but the militiamen were overwhelmed, and it wasn't long before resistance fighters were carrying their rifles.

Nalomy felt a sudden spike of fear as she waited for Pasayo to kill both Livius *and* Usurlus. Then, when it became obvious that the backup plan wasn't going to work, and people started to chant her name, she jumped into the arena and began to run. But that was a mistake, as Nalomy learned when she tripped, fell, and got up again. The citizens of Dantha were pouring into the arena from every possible direction. And they were angry, *very* angry, as a hungry howl went up, and hundreds of people converged on the spot where Nalomy stood frozen. "No!" she said, as the first hand reached out to touch her smooth skin. "How dare you?"

But the protests were for naught as more steely fingers sank into her flesh, the crowd growled, and Nalomy was torn apart. There were screams, but not very many, and by the time the killing frenzy was over, Nalomy's remains were spread far and wide.

As the mob began to disperse, a sixteen-year-old girl named Celia spotted something shiny lying on the ground, and bent to pick it up. The object consisted of a red gemstone and a gold necklace that was attached to it. Eventually Celia would discover that a button was concealed behind the stone, but that wouldn't occur for many days yet, and her immediate instinct was to hide the wonderful find as quickly as possible. It was a day that Celia would never forget.

SEVENTEEN

The city of Solace, on the planet Dantha

CATO WAS HALF WALKING, HALF RUNNING, AS HE pursued Verafti through the streets of Solace. The majority of the city's citizens, visitors, and food vendors were inside the coliseum, which left The Warrens' normally bustling streets nearly empty of foot traffic. That should have made the task of finding Verafti easier, but due to the shape shifter's ability to continually change his appearance, there was no way to know *who* to look for other than a man wearing a military uniform. And there were plenty of those given all of the militiamen in town. The longer the chase went on, the more likely it became that Verafti would find an opportunity to change clothes. So rather than simply look for the fugitive with his eyes, Cato was also scanning the area for Verafti's emotions, which were as unique as his fingerprints. And, depending on how strong the emanations were, he would be able to gauge how close the shape shifter was. It was a nerve-wracking process that was anything but exact.

Fortunately, Cato had help in the form of an Assistant Section Leader Jaith and five members of the Legate's bodyguard, whom Livius had detailed to assist him. Not only had Livius seen Cato's badge and been impressed by it, he knew Albus had been murdered and was eager for revenge. Since the fast-moving group was clearly military, and the militiamen who patrolled the streets were unaware of what had taken place within the coliseum, Cato and his escorts were allowed to proceed unimpeded.

Suddenly, as Cato rounded a corner with the bodyguards right behind him, the strength of Verafti's emotions soared by tenfold! Because, unlike Cato, who couldn't conceal his emotions from other empaths, Verafti could mask his to a large extent. But not at extremely close range. So as the two of them came together—Cato could sense the other empath's presence. But the trap had been sprung, and when Cato turned onto a side street, a sudden volley of shots rang out.

One of the bodyguards swore as a bullet smacked into his right thigh, and he made an instinctive grab for the wound as he fell. Assistant Section Leader Jaith raised his rifle, peered through its scope, and fired. "He looks like a woman!" Jaith shouted. "The one in the blue toga! Shoot her!"

A number of people tried, and bullets dug divots out of a graffiti-covered wall, but Verafti had disappeared. The wounded bodyguard was a loss, as was the man left to care for him, but all Cato could do was carry on. And he was closer, *much* closer, as Verafti entered the maze of wooden stalls inside the animal market. The pungent odor of animal feces hung in the air as the angens bawled, snorted, and squealed. "Split up!" Cato ordered, pointing to the right and left. "I'll go down the middle."

The bodyguards obeyed, and, as they spread out to either side, Cato began to advance down the main corridor. His weapon was ready, and all of the empath's senses were on high alert, as he sought to detect where Verafti was hiding.

Cato could "feel" what the animals felt, including sensations of hunger, fear, and in some cases mindless contentment. Then, seeing a group of people ahead, he "felt" their curiosity, fear, and hatred. The men and women who owned the animals believed they were looking at a group of Nalomy's militia and had every reason to be suspicious of their motives.

Such were Cato's thoughts when the stocky meatimal in the stall immediately to his right suddenly morphed into a green lizard! That was when Verafti took hold of the shovel leaning against a wooden partition and swung the tool through the air. There was barely enough time for Cato to make note of the blue toga that lay in a corner—and realize the extent of his mistake—before the flat part of the shovel made contact with the side of his head. There was a *clang*, followed by an explosion of pain, and a fast fall into darkness.

Verafti felt a profound sense of satisfaction as the blow connected with Cato's head. He would have struck again, and finished the job, but Jaith spotted him and fired a short burst. Two of the bullets went wide, but the third passed between Verafti's left arm and his side, as he morphed into a replica of Cato and bent to retrieve his pistol.

Then, with weapon in hand, Verafti bolted from the pen while a hail of bullets punched holes in the wooden stalls, ripped splinters out of support beams, and slammed into some of the animals. The noises they made were so pitiful that Jaith and his men stopped firing to give chase on foot as Verafti zigzagged his way to the far side of the market.

With no empaths on his trail, Verafti stood a better chance of escaping. The problem was that the wound in his side hurt like hell and was bleeding copiously. Verafti started to limp, and that slowed him down, as he made a dash for the other side of the narrow street.

There weren't many people about, but those there turned to stare, as a man without any clothes on dashed out of the animal market, ran across the street, and hurried into a bazaar crammed with secondhand goods.

Verafti was in need of clothes, so as he hobbled down a crowded aisle, he took whatever was handy. He paused occasionally to fire a shot back toward his pursuers and to pull items on. Then, having morphed into a likeness of Albus, he left the bazaar for a cobblestone street and tucked the gun away. The thoroughfare sloped downhill toward the industrial area that bordered the lake, and that was fine with Verafti so long as there was a place to hide.

Jaith was down to three men, counting himself, having been forced to leave one of the bodyguards to look after Cato. The good news, such as it was, lay in the fact that Verafti was bleeding. And even though Jaith wasn't an empath, he could sure as hell follow a blood spoor, which led straight across the street and through a bazaar hung with pots, pans, ladles, tools, clothing, and other items. Some of them were still swaying in the wake of the shape shifter's recent passage. Then, having kept his eyes down, Jaith was rewarded with a tight grouping of three red droplets. He waved his men forward. "Come on! Stay sharp! This is one tricky bastard."

The Imperial Coliseum, the city of Solace, on the planet Dantha

By the time Usurlus rolled out from under Livius and stood, the angry crowd had already surrounded Nalomy, and was tearing the Procurator apart. Her piteous screams were audible over the angry roar. It was *not* the sort of process that Usurlus had envisioned, but having no way to put a stop to it, all he could do was try to restore order.

Half of the seats were empty, the arena was filled with angry citizens, and it wouldn't be long before they began to stream out of the coliseum into the streets of Solace, where Usurlus feared that *more* violence would occur. "Livius!" Usurlus said urgently. "Where's Centurion Pasayo? Never mind. Take some men, find a senior officer, and take command of the militia. Then seal all of the gates. Don't let anyone out until I say it's okay. Got it?"

Livius nodded obediently. "Yes, sir. And if they refuse?"

"Place them under arrest and find someone else," Usurlus replied. "Shoot them if you have to. Now hurry! We don't have much time."

As Livius departed, Usurlus went out onto the platform, bent to retrieve one of the fallen microphones, and straightened up again. His voice boomed through the coliseum's speakers. "My fellow citizens!" Usurlus said. "There has been enough violence on Dantha. . . . Enough corruption . . . And enough suffering. Return to your seats and listen to what I have to say! Because while the wrongs of the past cannot be righted, a new day is about to dawn. Emperor Emor is aware of all that you've been through. . . . That's why I was sent to Dantha, why I made the announcement that I did, and why I stand before you now!"

The words were enough to cause most people to stop what they were doing and listen. There was even a reedy cheer. So while a few people made for the exits, most of the crowd remained in the arena, curious as to what the Legate would say. And Usurlus, who was anxious to prevent rioting, went on to deliver the speech begun earlier. He told the mob that a commission would be established to review governmental procedures on Dantha and bring them into compliance with Imperial standards. He told them about plans to rotate the militia off-planet for retraining, and to try corrupt officials, and to create jobs by replacing crumbling infrastructure. And while there were some boos, most of the audience cheered, as slaves scuttled out to throw buckets of sand onto the bloodied ground.

Usurlus felt someone at his side and turned to find that Livius had returned. "Pasayo is dead," the Section Leader informed him, "and most of the militia officers are cooperating. All of the gates have been sealed."

"And Albus?"

"We assume the shape shifter killed him, sire. . . . And took his place. The bastard escaped, but a Xeno Corps officer is on his trail, with help from six of my men."

"Let's hope they catch him," Usurlus said grimly. "Now . . . Let's get that circus troupe in here. . . . The crowd has had their blood. It's time to entertain them."

The city of Solace, on the planet Dantha

Verafti followed the gradient down toward the industrial area below. Not because he had a plan, but because his side hurt, and the downward slope made it easier to jog. What he needed was a place to hide, a den where he could stop the bleeding, and wait for the excitement to die down. Then, once Verafti had room to breathe, he would formulate a plan.

So when Verafti saw the foundry and the sprawl of sheds, outbuildings, and ore containments that surrounded it, he paused to check his back trail, and with no pursuers in sight, entered the complex through an unguarded gate. From there it was a short walk over to a set of double doors that had been left open to let out some of the heat. A glowing furnace was visible against the far wall where a group of heavily swathed workers were preparing to pour molten metal into a form. That gave Verafti an idea.

He entered the foundry room, turned to pull the doors closed, and felt for the gun. Then, with the weapon held down along his right leg, Verafti made his way toward the furnace. It was *hot*, extremely hot, which made it difficult to breathe. The workers were aware of him by then, curious as to why he had closed the doors, and annoyed as well. There were five in all, and as the foreman opened his mouth to speak, Verafti shot him in the face. There was a sudden explosion of both blood and fear as the others tried to run. They didn't get far. Verafti killed them one after the other. He wasn't a very good shot, but his victims were only a few feet away, and that made the process easy.

Once all of the Umans were dead, Verafti took the moment necessary to throw the pistol into the furnace. The remaining rounds cooked off almost immediately, but the *pop*, *pop*, *pop* could barely be heard over the persistent roar of hot air and the blood pounding in his ears.

Having rid himself of incriminating evidence, Verafti selected the smallest Uman, pulled the long scarf away from the man's face, and took a good look. Then, after memorizing the worker's features, he managed to heave the body up off the floor and stagger over to the furnace. The last few feet were extremely difficult, both because of the persistent pain in his side, and the skin-blistering heat. But thanks to his indomitable will, Verafti was able to get close enough to throw the dead worker into the glowing maw, before backing off, to watch the body melt away.

The next part was going to be hard, *very* hard, but there was no getting around it. Not if he wanted to get off Dantha and find the person he'd been searching for when the Xeno cops captured him. So Verafti morphed into his true form, went over to a workbench, and chose a hatchet from the hodgepodge of implements lying scattered on the surface of it. With the tool in hand, he went back to where the bodies lay sprawled on the floor.

The tourniquet was already in place, and had been since early that morning, just in case Nalomy decided to trigger the explosive device attached to Verafti's wrist in spite of her promises to let him go. It would have been able to stop the bleeding quickly. So all he had to do was to tighten the elastic band and tie it off. Then, while he still had the courage to do so, Verafti knelt in front of the anvil, and placed his wrist on top of it. He lifted the hatchet high, brought it down until sharp steel made contact with his scaly skin, then raised it again. At that point he brought the hatchet down with all of the strength he could muster!

There was a loud *clink* as steel met steel, followed by a sudden lightness, and a feeling of unexpected warmth. Blood spurted, stopped just as quickly, and began to congeal in response to the heat. Then, before the pain could begin, Verafti morphed into Uman form. That was when Verafti allowed himself to clutch a seemingly uninjured left hand to his abdomen and howl. It was a primal sound that had been born in the hot primordial jungles of Sagatha, where pain was a constant.

Even as he battled the dizziness that threatened to pull him down, Verafti managed to summon up enough strength to pick up the severed hand and throw it toward the furnace before collapsing onto the pool of half-coagulated blood that lapped around the dead workers.

Meanwhile, out in front of the doors, Jaith eyed a small pool of blood. "Okay, men," he said tightly, as he raised his rifle. "We've got the bastard now. . . . Remember, we don't know what he looks like, so arrest everyone you see, and we'll find a way to sort them out later."

So saying, Jaith pulled a door open and led the way into a large room. It took a moment for his eyes to adjust to the relative darkness, but once they did, he saw the bodies sprawled in front of the open furnace and felt a sudden stab of fear. The shape shifter was there all right—probably in the shadows. "Ignore the bodies," Jaith ordered tersely, "and watch the perimeter! There are a lot of places to hide in here. . . . . I'll go right, you go left, and we'll meet in front of the furnace."

The other two men nodded and the search got under way. But the room was empty except for the bodies, so that when the threesome came together, none of them had anything to report. Jaith was about to turn his attention to the murder victims when one of his men said, "Hey! Section . . . Look at this!"

Jaith went over to where the man was standing and saw that a severed hand was lying on the floor. And not just *any* hand, but what Jaith judged to be a *left* hand, which was covered with green scales! A tight-fitting bracelet was attached to the six-inch length of wrist from which two shattered bones were protruding. "Don't touch it," Jaith ordered. "Check the bodies. Maybe one of them is minus a hand."

But after circling the murder victims, it quickly became clear that all of the dead men had both hands. That was when one of the bodies groaned—and attempted to sit up! A bodyguard gave a reflexive jerk, fired a shot into the floor, and looked embarrassed. Jaith gave the miscreant a dirty look and went over to kneel next to the ragged slave. Having slipped an arm under the man's shoulders, he held his head up off the floor. "Are you wounded?"

"No," Verafti lied. "He shot the others one by one—so I took a run at him with a hatchet. We fought; I took a whack at him, and slipped. I think my head hit the floor when I fell. Where is he?"

"I don't know," Jaith replied. "We found a hand—but no body."

"The furnace!" Verafti said emphatically. "He was holding his wrist, and backing toward the furnace, so maybe he fell in."

Jaith made eye contact with the man who had fired his

rifle into the floor. "Stand guard over the hand and bodies." Then, to the second man, "Go find some ice. . . . Buy it from a street vendor. I want that hand preserved!"

Verafti sampled the noncom's emotions, was unable to find any signs of distrust, and felt a growing sense of confidence. The hardest part was over! Now all he had to do was play his part, wait for an opening, and slip away. "Please," he said imploringly. "Help me to stand."

Jaith obliged, helping Verafti over to the door, where the air was at least twenty degrees cooler, and lowering him onto a wooden bench. With that accomplished, Jaith walked twenty feet away, selected the priority push on his com set, and was forced to wait as Livius delivered a string of orders to various subordinates. From the sound of it, Livius had taken command of the planetary militia, and mere noncoms were being put in charge of entire battalions, even as the citizens of Solace began to stream out onto the streets. There was a lot of work to do and very few people to do it.

Finally, after waiting for a good five minutes for a chance to speak, Jaith was able to make his report. And, just as that task was completed, Cato arrived with bodyguard in tow. "I'm glad to see you!" Jaith said enthusiastically. "How's the head?"

"It hurts like hell," Cato replied bitterly, as he reached up to touch a very tender bump. "But it beats being dead. . . . Thank you."

"My pleasure," Jaith said sincerely. "And you'll be happy to hear that the shape shifter is dead!"

"He is?" Cato inquired skeptically. "That's great news if it's true." In an effort to confirm the truth of the other man's statement, Cato sought to find Verafti's telltale emotional "signature" in the area and was unable to do so. That wasn't conclusive, however, because Verafti could block his emotional emanations at anything other than close range.

"It *is* true," Jaith insisted, "or that's the way it looks.

Come on. . . . There's someone I want you to meet. Then I'll show you the hard evidence."

But when Jaith turned toward the building, the bench the foundry worker had been sitting on was empty! That caused a sudden spike of fear as Jaith rushed inside to make sure that the hand was still lying on the floor. It was, and that resulted in a heartfelt sigh of relief as Cato arrived at his side. "Look at that!" Jaith said triumphantly. "You're the expert. Is that what a Sagathi hand looks like?"

Cato felt a growing sense of hope as he knelt next to the hand. "Yes," Cato admitted, "it is. Where's the rest of the body?"

"In there," Jaith answered, as he jabbed a finger toward the furnace. "There was a man. . . . One of the workers. He attacked the shape shifter with a hatchet, missed his head, and lopped a hand off. He slipped at that point, but the lizard was backing toward the furnace, and probably fell in."

Cato looked up. "He saw that?"

"No," Jaith admitted. "The worker hit his head, and that knocked him unconscious."

"Where is he?" Cato inquired, as he stood. "I'd like to talk to him."

Jaith was embarrassed as was clear from both his emotions and the look on his face. "He was here a moment ago, over by the door, but he can't be very far away. We'll find him."

"You do that," Cato said, as a bodyguard with a box of ice arrived. "Good job."

And it *was* a good job, or so it seemed to Cato as Jaith hurried off, especially with a severed hand as proof of what had occurred. Yet Jaith's story was almost too good to be true. But without any other way to explain the evidence, Cato was forced to accept the possibility that Verafti's luck had finally run out. That felt good, *really* good, even if his head didn't. Finally, the promise that had been made to Sivio and the rest of the team had been kept.

Sun streamed in through the palace windows, the lake sparkled beyond, but Usurlus was unaware of the beauty that lay beyond the glass. He was focused on the transcript in front of him, one of many reports, requests, and other documents stacked beside his right elbow. Rather than moving into the Imperial suite, as was his right as both Procurator *and* Legate, Usurlus had chosen to remain in the guest suite both because it was easier to do so, and because he preferred to receive visitors in an unpretentious atmosphere. Especially in the wake of Nalomy's many excesses.

A row of worktables had been set up in front of the windows, where Usurlus and two recently hired administrative assistants could sit side by side at data screens and talk freely. Now that Nalomy was dead, and Dantha's militia was under Imperial control, all sorts of evidence was flowing in. And that, combined with the truly startling report that Officer Cato had submitted, was going to be loaded onto an Imperial courier ship that very afternoon. Because it was crucial to get all of the relevant information to Emperor Emor quickly so that he could release it to the news combines *his* way rather than allow the Nalomy clan to put their self-serving spin on it.

Usurlus's thoughts were interrupted as an assistant appeared at his side. He was a plain young man. That was just as well, however, given all the work Usurlus needed to do. "Officer Cato is here to see you, sire," the assistant said gravely.

"Excellent," Usurlus said, as he rose to greet his visitor. "Please send him in."

Cato had gone to considerable lengths in order to look

the way an Imperial police officer *should* look—and was wearing his full uniform plus sidearm as he entered. A rare privilege indeed given all of the security precautions Livius had in place. Cato bowed.

"Officer Cato!" Usurlus said enthusiastically as he came forward to embrace his visitor. "I owe you a huge debt of gratitude! Had it not been for your timely warning, Nalomy and her henchmen would be preparing to send me home in a box right now! Please, have a seat. . . . Can we offer you some refreshments?"

What had once been the breakfast table was now used for informal meetings, and as Cato took a seat he shook his head. "No, sire, thank you."

"I was reading the Lood transcript when you arrived," Usurlus said, reclaiming the seat on the other side of the circular table. "I knew Nalomy was a very skilled thief. That's why I came here. . . . But even I was surprised to learn how ruthless she was! Please accept my condolences regarding the loss of Centurion Sivio and the rest of your team."

Cato could "feel" what Usurlus felt and knew the comment was genuine. "Thank you, sire. . . . They were fine people—and they deserved better."

"Yes," Usurlus agreed soberly, "they did. I want you to know that a permanent memorial will be built next to Station 3—and that your comrades will be reburied with full military honors."

"Thank you, sire," Cato said sincerely. "All the members of the Xeno Corps will appreciate that."

"Which reminds me," Usurlus put in. "I have something for you. . . . Normally it would be presented with a speech, a brass band, and your fellow police officers in attendance. But the sad truth is that I don't have time for a speech, Nalomy's band can't be trusted, and you're the only Imperial police officer on the planet! So, please accept my apologies, along with the Imperial Legion of Valor and a promotion to Centurion. You deserve both." And with that Usurlus gave Cato a box containing the Empire's third-highest decoration for bravery and a nearly indestructible document naming him as a Centurion. Both honors left Cato shocked and at a momentary loss for words. But then, as Usurlus eyed him curiously, Cato attempted to return the document. "I can't accept this, sire. . . . I was the least worthy member of my team—and by all rights should have been buried with them."

Usurlus smiled grimly. "We all have regrets, Centurion Cato. . . . Things we wish we had done differently. But, like it or not, you will accept this promotion! Partly because you deserve it—and partly because I need a senior police officer on Dantha. Someone who can help me enforce the law and rebuild trust. That's an order. One which I will copy and send to your superiors later today."

There was only one thing that Cato could say. "Yes, sire."

"And there's something else," Usurlus added thoughtfully. "Verafti is dead, but I think you'll agree that it was a close call, and who knows what might have occurred had he been able to escape! When I return to Corin, I want you to accompany me. Assuming that Emperor Emor is willing to go along with it, we'll take a request for additional Xeno Corps funding to the Senate, and see if we can expand the Xeno Corps. I'm just guessing, but I'll bet the people you report to will favor that, and offer plenty of help!"

Cato knew that was true and nodded obediently. "Yes, sire."

A new "feeling" was in the air, and Cato knew his time was up, but wasn't willing to leave without asking for the one thing that he wanted more than a medal or a promotion. "Sire . . . Could I ask a favor?"

Usurlus raised a skeptical eyebrow. "That depends. . . . What did you have in mind?"

"Majordomo Hingo, sire. Shortly after Procurator Nalomy's death Hingo returned to the palace, where he and four guards took twelve slaves and left. Neither he nor the slaves have been seen since. I want to find him."

Usurlus eyed the police officer skeptically. "Because he's a criminal? Or for personal reasons?"

"Both, sire. . . . One of the slaves who was removed, a young woman named Alamy, is a friend of mine."

Usurlus remembered Alamy, how attractive she was, and instinctively knew that Cato saw the young woman as something more than a "friend." "There is a lot of work to do," Usurlus responded carefully, "and I'm going to need your help. But I'll give you three days. . . . Not a minute more."

Cato rose. "Thank you, sire." His eyes were bright—and filled with intensity.

"You're welcome," Usurlus replied. "And, Cato . . ."

"Yes, sire?"

"Remember. . . . You are the senior law enforcement officer on Dantha. So you will enforce the law—and never break it. Not for me, not for the people who report to me, and not for your own benefit. Am I clear?"

Cato came to rigid attention. His fist hit the center of his sculpted body armor. "Yes, sire!"

Usurlus nodded. "I hope you find her. Dismissed."

Narbu Province, on the planet Dantha

The assault boat's slightly distorted black shadow caressed the land, as the boxy ship carrying Cato and a section of handpicked militiamen droned toward Imood Hingo's country retreat, a large land grant, that was located 125 miles southeast of Solace. The complex was intentionally remote, both for the sake of privacy, and to serve as a place to which Hingo could retreat should the need arise. Plus, Hingo had always been aware that Nalomy would leave Dantha one day, and unlike Centurion Pasayo, he had no desire to follow her. And why should he? Given all he had accumulated on Dantha.

So when the unimaginable happened, and Nalomy was torn apart by the crowd in the coliseum, Hingo's instinct was to run. And, as the pilot followed the gently flowing Na-Na River through a narrow pass and into the valley beyond, Cato could see why Hingo would want to live there. Hundreds of slaves could be seen working in the neatly-laid-out fields, angens grazed on rich green grass, and silos marked where grain was stored.

"The retreat," as Hingo referred to it, occupied the top of a low hill. It consisted of a main building that looked more like a fortress than a house, a swimming pool, and a landing pad, where two air cars were parked. There were weapons emplacements, too, one at each corner of the roughly rect-angular house, all presumably for the purpose of keeping bandits at bay. "Get them on the com," Cato ordered, as he looked over the pilot's left shoulder. "Tell them we're going to land."

But before the pilot could obey, all four of the guns opened fire, and the ship's computer spoke over the inter-com. "The ship is taking ground fire, a surface-to-air mis-sile has been launched, and electronic countermeasures have been activated."

The pilot jinked right, left, and right again as half a dozen flares shot away from the assault boat. Cato felt his stomach muscles tighten then relax when the missile went for one of the flares and exploded. "Okay," he said grimly, "Citizen Hingo wants to play. . . . Take out the machine guns and put a missile into the house."

The pilot grinned wolfishly as he put the assault boat into a tight turn. "Roger that, sir. Your wish is my command."

It took less than five minutes to destroy the machine guns with the assault boat's twin energy cannons—and fire a high-explosive missile at the house. The result was a very satisfying explosion. The house was extremely well built, however—so most of it still stood. "I can take the whole place down if you want me to," the pilot offered eagerly, as the boat circled the compound.

"That won't be necessary," Cato replied dryly. "Put this thing down. I want to have a chat with Citizen Hingo. Not just look at his body."

The assault boat's skids touched down two minutes later, the rear ramp made a loud clanging sound as it hit pavement, and Jaith led twelve militiamen out onto the hilltop with their weapons at the ready. Cato had been impressed by Jaith's competency during the search for Verafti, and, after buying Livius six beers, finally convinced the reluctant chief bodyguard to release the Assistant Section Leader to the newly formed Civilian Constabulary. And now, having been promoted to Section Leader, Jaith was in charge of the assault team.

Mercenaries fired automatic weapons, and the militiamen fired back by sending smoke grenades and tear-gas canisters in through the narrow window slits. That brought most of the defenders out into the open. Some continued to fire and were immediately cut down while most hurried to surrender. Having put them under guard, Jaith ordered a demolitions expert to blow the front door. The charge generated a resonant *boom*, the barrier sagged on its hinges, and Cato followed Jaith inside.

Smoke swirled as they made their way through a large foyer and into a beautifully furnished living room, where Hingo sat waiting for him. A huge thronelike chair provided a frame for his body, his white tunic and trousers were immaculate, and his feet were bare. The impression was that of someone who was about to receive guests. "Cato. . . . I should have known," Hingo said contemptuously. "Don't tell me—let me guess. . . . You're here to collect Alamy."

"I'm here to collect Alamy *and* eleven other slaves that you stole as you left the palace," Cato replied.

"They hadn't been registered as belonging to Nalomy yet, so I didn't steal them, not that it matters," Hingo replied dismissively.

"You can discuss that with the Imperial Prosecutor," Cato said unsympathetically. "Along with your decision to open fire on an Imperial police officer and the military team assigned to assist him. My job is to recover the slaves. . . . Where are they?"

"Don't play high-and-mighty with me," Hingo responded contemptuously. "I know what you *really* want—and I've already been there! And legally too, because Alamy is a slave, and it's impossible to rape a slave."

Cato battled to control his steadily growing rage. "Where are they?" he grated.

"I have no idea," Hingo replied serenely. "Conditions being what they were, I was in something of a hurry, so I sold the entire group to Citizen Mortha in Solace, and I suspect he will resell them to the highest bidder. Think about it, Cato! One of Mortha's slave handlers could be humping your precious Alamy right now!"

It was a stupid thing to say given the circumstances, but such was Hingo's resentment regarding the possibility that he would lose everything he'd worked so hard to build, that he chose to lash out. Cato's handgun was already out of its holster, and hanging at his side so all he had to do was bring up the weapon and fire. Three shots rang out, three bullets passed within a fraction of an inch of Hingo's smoothly shaved skull, and three holes appeared in the wood next to his left ear.

It took Hingo a moment to figure out that he was still alive. Then the militiamen began to laugh, and as Hingo looked down, he saw the yellow stain on the front of his white trousers. "Put leg shackles on him," Cato said grimly, as the weapon went into its holster. "And chain the bastard to the flight deck. He's going on trial."

The city of Solace, on the planet Dantha

Raindrops rattled on the sheet-metal roof, and water ran off the lower edges to splash into puddles all around. The hodgepodge of slave pens were exactly as Alamy remembered them, but she had changed. She was older for one thing. *Much* older in terms of her understanding of both the world and the cruelty of which people were capable. All she had left was an existence of sorts, which could get worse, but wasn't likely to get better. Because as Citizen Mortha sold her for the second time, it could be to someone even more abusive than Hingo had been. That possibility lay like a lump of lead in the pit of her stomach.

Alamy's thoughts were interrupted as metal rattled on metal and the door to her pen squeaked open. "All right, sweet buns," the slave handler said wearily, "come on out. And don't give me no trouble. I ain't in the mood."

Alamy recognized the guard as the man that she and Persus called Skanker, but if he recognized her, there was no sign of it on his face. Alamy stood. Bruises covered her body from the beating Hingo had administered, so everything hurt. The rape had been a perfunctory affair, as if Hingo had been going through the motions, rather than savoring it. She was strangely grateful for that.

The tunic Alamy wore was damp, ripped in places, and smeared with dirt. It fell to midthigh and her feet were bare. She stepped out of the doorway, fell in behind five other women, and followed them through a maze of passageways to the switchbacking ramps that led up to the platform above. The slaves knew each other from the palace, but none were in the mood to talk, and kept whatever thoughts they had to themselves as they shuffled along.

The group paused in the holding area that was located immediately behind the mural, which served as a backdrop for the stage as well. Alamy could hear Mortha's voice coming from the area beyond but couldn't make out individual words as the slave master addressed the crowd. Her hair hung in strands around her face, her wet tunic clung to the lines of her body, and it was necessary to hug herself to keep from shivering. None of this was likely to help Mortha fetch the highest possible price, but the slave dealer was clearly intent on selling off Nalomy's slaves, before Usurlus could learn about it.

The change in government reminded Alamy of Cato and the moment when they had been separated. Was he still alive? And, if so, did he ever think of her? There had been something special about the kiss, for her at least, but Alamy knew it would be silly to assume that Cato felt the same way. He was an Imperial police officer, and she was a slave, so a romantic relationship was impossible. Especially now, as the people in front of Alamy began to shuffle forward, and she followed them around the corner and out onto the rain-slicked platform.

"And here they are!" Mortha announced enthusiastically, from under the protection of a well-rigged plastic tarp. The crowd was about half the size of the one Alamy had been forced to confront a couple of months before, and the applause was tepid, as if the people who were standing in the plaza weren't all that happy to be there.

"Look at them!" Mortha said admiringly, as he gestured to the slaves. "Fine young women who can cook your food, clean your home, and provide a host of other important services if you know what I mean."

The crowd knew what Mortha meant—and applauded more loudly this time. As Alamy scanned their faces, she remembered what the eternally optimistic Persus had told her. "Send yourself somewhere else. Go to a pretty place. . . . And stay there until it's over."

It was good advice, but Alamy knew that wasn't going to work for her, as Mortha ordered the group to remove their clothes, and a reedy cheer went up from some of the men in the crowd. Alamy was the first one up this time and could feel hungry eyes boring into her flesh. Though she was still embarrassed, she knew it was pointless to resist, and pulled the tunic up over her head and let it drop. Then, having removed her panties, she stared straight ahead. Not down at her feet, as she had before, but over the crowd instead.

There were at least a dozen bids to begin with, but it wasn't long before the price began to rise, and potential buyers began to drop out. Eventually there were only *two* bidders. The first was a steely-eyed young woman who was accompanied by two robed bodyguards. One of whom held a black umbrella over his employer's well-coiffed head while the other stood with arms crossed.

The other bidder was a potbellied man with a coarse-looking female on one side of him and an enormous Crusher on the other. Given the whip thrust through the Crusher's belt, he was clearly the couple's slave master. Neither party looked all that inviting, but Alamy felt a definite preference for the younger woman, mainly because the Crusher looked so scary.

Finally, after the dreary back-and-forth battle came to its conclusion, Alamy was relieved to see the steely-eyed woman emerge victorious and hoped that her new owner was nicer than she looked. The final price was twelve hundred Imperials, which was considerably less than Hingo had paid on Nalomy's behalf, and probably had something to do with both Alamy's disheveled appearance and the rainy weather.

The next half hour was one of the worst that Alamy had ever endured. She didn't know what to feel. Relief? Because the process was over? Dread? Because there was no way to know what lay ahead? Happiness? Because almost anything would be better than the horrors of the palace? There was no way to know.

So when her name was called, and Alamy was escorted up to the plaza, all sorts of emotions came and went. Most of the crowd had disappeared by then, the rain continued to fall, and she could see her new owner standing under the protection of the black umbrella. But rather than coming forward the way Alamy had assumed that she would, the woman remained where she was, thereby allowing the second man to handle the chore for her. He was wearing a robe, so it wasn't until Cato threw the hood back that she saw his face. Her heart seemed to jump out of her chest, and tears began to stream down her cheeks, as Alamy stared at him in disbelief. "Master? Is it truly *you*?"

"Yes," Cato said kindly, as he swept Alamy into his arms. "It's me. But how many times do I have to tell you? My name is Jak! I'm sorry CeCe, *very* sorry, but I came as quickly as I could."

Alamy looked up into Cato's face. Raindrops hit her eyes and she blinked them away. It was like a wonderful dream from which she never wanted to awake. "So I belong to you? You bought me?"

"Yes," Cato said gently, just before his lips met hers. "You belong to me."

Lucia Ovidius and Binn Jaith watched approvingly, and thunder rolled across the city as a ship fought its way up off the spaceport's blast-scarred duracrete. Moments later, the freighter was lost in the clouds as it battled gravity and struggled to escape Dantha's grip.

Aboard the freighter Hercules, off the planet Dantha

Safe within one of the freighter's tiny cabins, a merchant named Oxo Trevio lay back on the acceleration couch in his stateroom and wondered when the stump would stop aching. It was healing well, as he had known that it would, but the constant pain was annoying. Not that the missing hand mattered so long as he chose to look like a human. But what would Affa Denemi think when he found her? Would she still find him attractive? There was only one way to find out.

The pressure eased as the ship battled its way free of Dantha's gravitational pull, and, having eaten a *huge* meal just prior to liftoff, Fiss Verafti soon fell asleep.